ALPHA'S BURDEN

REJECTING FATES
BOOK 1

VERONICA EDEN WRITING AS
LUNA LARK

ALPHA'S BURDEN

PACK TERRITORIES
HILLFORD
SILVER FALLS PACK
CRESCENT VALLEY PACK
ASHBURY
DAVENPORT
TIMBER HOLLOW PACK
SOUTHBERG
WANDERER'S CANYON
THE DEADLANDS

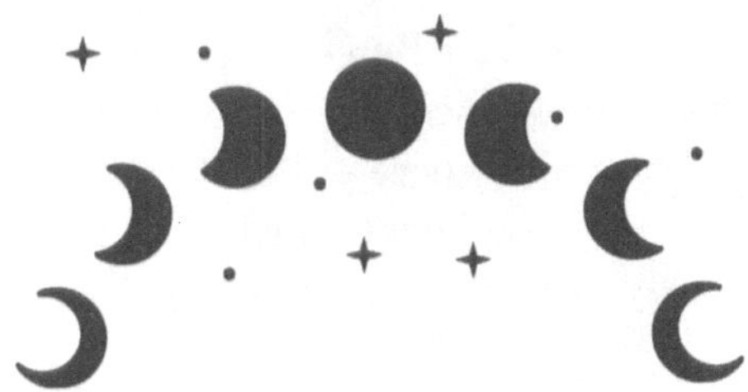

PLAYLIST

Forest Dream — Sacred Bansuri
Love and War — Fleurie
Burned — Grace VanderWaal
You Put A Spell On Me — Austin Giorgio
Achilles Heel — J. Maya
Who's Afraid of Little Old Me? — Taylor Swift
The Moon Will Sing — The Crane Wives
Nobody — Faith Marie
Fate — H.E.R.
Daylight — David Kushner
Moonrise — Anne Buckle
Runaway — AURORA
The Wolf — PHILDEL
Astronomical — SVRCINA
Power — Isak Danielson
Skin and Bones — David Kushner
Two Roads — J. Maya
Dandelion — Gabbie Hanna
The Killing Kind — Marianas Trench
Artemis — Stephen Rezza

Playlist

Run Baby Run — The Rigs
Messed Up — Once Monsters, Chloe Adams
Make Me Believe — The EverLove
Empires — Ruelle
My Love Mine All Mine — Mitski

Every heart sings a song, incomplete, until another heart whispers back.

— PLATO

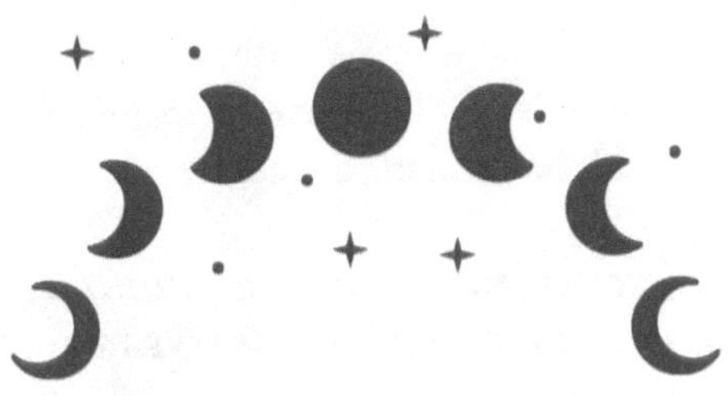

ABOUT THE BOOK

FATE CHOSE THE WORST POSSIBLE MATE
FOR ME...MY ENEMY.

Being bonded to Caden Blackburn used to be all I dreamed of. Those dreams were crushed the moment this pack branded my entire bloodline traitors for challenging his father.

Life in Silver Falls isn't easy. As the only packmate unable to shift, I'm considered broken. No one wants a useless mate. Especially not Caden. Imperfections don't fit within the rigid way he rules our pack as alpha.

I never thought he'd look at me with anything other than fury until our bond awakens. Instead of disgust, his gaze burns with desire, reviving feelings I buried once I'm in his powerful arms. We almost succumb to the pull to claim each other as fated mates.

But enemies don't belong together. He reminds me by rejecting me in front of everyone.

I've learned to overcome whatever tries to break me, but in my shattered heart I wonder if I'll survive the pain of Caden turning his back on me a second time.

YET IF HE REJECTED ME...WHY IS HE GOING FERAL IF ANY OTHER MALE TRIES TO GET NEAR ME?

AUTHOR'S NOTE

DEAR READER,

Welcome to the Rejecting Fates series!

This shifter romance series features rejected mates who still feel the pull of their fated love rather than in someone new. These pairs will find their guaranteed HEAs with each other after much groveling to earn a second chance with their fated mate.

The fated mate pairs will always end up together in these books.

PACKS & LOCATIONS

SILVER FALLS PACK
Alpha: Caden Blackburn
Previous Alpha: Dempsey Blackburn
Beta: Liam Jennings
Location: Silver Mountain

TIMBER HOLLOW PACK
Alpha: Alistair Ryan
Alpha Heir Apparent: Atlas Ryan
Location: Timber Hollow Forest

CRESCENT VALLEY PACK
Alpha: Rooke Bell
Location: Crescent Valley

WANDERER'S CANYON
Location: Canyonlands in the southern region
Where traitor, feral, and rogue lone wolves who are exiled or separate from the pack are sent. The unforgiving area is every wolf for themselves.

THE DEADLANDS

Location: Ruins beyond Wanderer's Canyon

The territory of the Original Pack that fractured into factions that formed the present day packs. Believed to be infertile and inhospitable land worse than Wanderer's Canyon.

ASHBURY

Location: In the foothills of Silver Mountain

Human town near Silver Falls Pack.

DAVENPORT

Location: West of Timber Hollow Forest

Human town near Timber Hollow Pack.

HILLFORD

Location: North of Crescent Valley

Human town near Crescent Valley Pack.

1

AVERY

THIS IS PUSHING IT. I know it, yet I couldn't pass up this golden opportunity.

Sneaking off packlands is enough of a risk without notifying anyone. Doing it to go to the human town nestled in the foothills at the base of Silver Mountain alone is worse.

Leaving the territory this close to a pack run?

I'm basically asking for our strict alpha to serve me with months of punishment for defying his rules—rules that hardly apply to me. As someone considered Wolfless, I can't shift and never will. I'm a shifter who has no wolf. My wild instincts are more muted, far easier to control with tonight's impending full moon.

Compared to the rest of my pack, I'm practically human. My strength, stamina, and senses are hardly better than a strong human male.

It's not like Alpha Blackburn keeps us from leaving the mountain at all. Anyone from Silver Falls Pack is allowed to visit Ashbury on designated days with supervision. Except those only come once every few months and I'm not likely to have his permission, so that doesn't work for me.

This is how I've adapted to survive.

As long as I'm not caught, it's fine. I've done this hundreds of times before. I have no regrets because sneaking in and out is part of how I make it in a pack of shifters that hate my entire family.

My routine is ironclad—wait for the gap in the scout patrols, leave from the old sloping trail that's overlooked because of overgrowth, and always stop at the first stream in the foothills to wash off any lingering scent of being around humans before I even step foot on Silver Mountain to return home.

No one ever notices when I'm gone, anyway.

Pausing to lean between the roots of a moss-covered tree, I check the worn leather pack slung across my body for the third time. The corner of my mouth lifts with pride.

Though I lack the blessing of a wolf from the moon goddess, putting me at a huge disadvantage when it comes to things like hunting, I'm still able to provide for my sisters and myself through trading with the people in Ashbury.

The town is small and every year it seems there are less humans around or something new is in disrepair. The younger ones are always talking about getting out, moving to cities.

The residents gladly part with their goods whenever I bring my collection of flora that are difficult for them to obtain from the unforgiving terrain. I don't have money to pay them otherwise. They've grown to rely on me as much as I have in return because the mountain range and river blocks Ashbury off from the accessibility granted to larger, more progressive towns like Davenport or Hillford.

The baker gives enough bread to last us two months for the assortment of mushrooms and wild nuts I find for her. The butcher inside the tiny grocery store has a long-standing arrangement with me. I bring him the rudimentary oils I make from mountain ginger and willow bark to help with the ache in his hands throughout winter better than the medicines his doctors prescribe. In exchange, I get my pick of seconds cuts, hard cheeses, and the candies he always throws in for my sisters.

I scored big for today's bounty. It isn't like those usual

exchanges. When I snuck into town last week, I heard there'd be a market passing through. I had to make a second trip today for the chance to get rarer things I don't usually have access to in Ashbury.

I rely on the supplies I'm able to barter from anyone outside, because if I counted on my own pack, we'd be dead by now. The measly allotment of meat distributed weekly by the kitchens is hardly enough to sustain the three of us. I learned that within days of being forced out of our family home at the heart of the pack. After our father's transgression led to his death by the alpha's hand, we had to move to the crumbling cottage we live in.

With the coil of wire I secured today, I should be able to finally splice the feeble electricity from an outbuilding near the cottage to run a line to the ice box in the back that's been dead for years. If I can get it running, it will make our stored food last so much longer. Most of the other cabins and buildings in the pack have electricity. The fanciest, like the Alpha's lodge and other high-ranking families in good standing, have even more amenities.

I check the contents of my satchel are secure before spotting a lucky find this late in the season twining along a vine climbing the thick tree root. I slip a pair of garden shears I stole from the deep pockets of my green, knee-length coverall dress and brush back strands of light brown hair dangling over my shoulder.

Despite the chill in the air, a shifter's body temperature always runs warmer. I'm comfortable enough in the dress and short-sleeved shirt beneath.

Crouching down, I admire the tall, bristly appearance of the purple flower shoots blooming on the liatris plant. I have some left from the ones I've picked throughout the summer, but I can always use more to help with my youngest sister Lena's sore throats in the colder months. Once it's cut, I tie it so it dangles upside-down from the side of my bag as I continue picking my way through the woods.

It's not much further to the border designating pack territory. There was a time when I could come and go as I pleased rather than sneaking around like this, same as anyone else in the pack. I'd leave the mountain to visit other packs, like my aunt in Timber Hollow Pack, especially after she became the only other family I have besides my sisters. The freedom only lasted through the last couple of years of the previous alpha's reign, before his son took over as the current alpha. Since then, rules in the pack have grown stricter.

I'm nearly back, undetected as always. It's lucky the usual patrol schedule isn't something I have to worry about today, so it's easy to cross the pack border without worrying about evading someone like Liam Jennings, head of pack security. He's a stickler for obeying the rules. I've learned it's best to remain unnoticed by anyone in this pack.

A twig snaps. I stifle a gasp, ducking into a circle of bushes to blend in with my surroundings. Straining my ears, I sag in relief when it's not anyone from Silver Falls, only a deer. I watch it nose at the ground. It lifts its head, ears perked, swiveling in my direction, then behind it. Once it moves on, I linger for another moment, enjoying the sound of the trees rustling.

This is my happy place. Well, this has become my happy place that I've discovered for myself. Being in nature, not living in this pack.

That happiness was shredded beyond recognition seven years ago when I was sixteen. The day my life changed forever, going from a prominent and respected family in the pack to the scorned outcast at the bottom of the ranks overnight. My sisters and I are the only ones left bearing the disgraced Morgan name.

I clear the heavy memory of that dark day with a shake of my head and step over the boundary. It's strange how old magic works. The wards for the pack's border were set long ago, when shifters and witches weren't at odds. The invisible threads of magic woven to protect us recognize my blood as a shifter, welcoming me home. If humans hike this far up the mountain—an uncommon feat, but one that's happened a time or two—the magic deters them, sending them in another direction.

It was designed for a time in the distant past when humans had no idea they weren't alone in this world amongst countless beings, each with our own unique set of powers and abilities. Shifters, witches, vampires, and the like have all left the shadows to mingle openly with humans. It's no longer necessary to hide after humans discovered supernaturals weren't figments of their imaginations from storybooks around forty years ago.

I huff at the irony that we still use the wards so we always have the safety of our dens to return to, as if we're still hiding our bones away like the beasts we descend from.

An inviting scent of spicy cedar tickles my nose as I reach the narrow path that connects the lower, well-traveled trails to the one that leads home. The loggers must have been through this section to cut trees to replenish the winter firewood store and building material. They often dip into the day's quota when it's a full moon to feed the massive bonfire for the pre-run festivities.

I halt, realizing the mistake too late. It's not the freshly chopped wood for tonight's bonfire. There's a male with a massive muscular build ahead. The smell of the forest is coming from him.

It's all too familiar, tugging harshly on my heartstrings.

Every part of me seizes, my breath catching in my throat and my body rigid. I duck my head, gripping the leather strap so tight the aged leather might disintegrate.

I know the imposing, powerful shifter striding towards me, blocking my path back to the dilapidated remains of a cabin I call home.

Caden Blackburn. He's *Alpha* Blackburn to me now.

2

AVERY

"WHAT ARE YOU DOING OUT HERE?" Caden demands.

His sharp order is bolstered by his mighty presence. His voice is domineering, expecting compliance, and his broad stature towers over me, jaw set. He's every bit the alpha I'm meant to bow for.

I swallow, slowly lifting my face to meet his stormy blue glare. Tousled dark brown hair falls across his forehead. This close, his masculine woodsy musk that used to be a comfort to me is overwhelming, even to my muted senses.

This is the first time he's been near enough to look at me in ages. It still hurts the softest parts of my heart and my pride to see his ire directed at me when he used to look at me so differently.

Back when we were friends. Before he was the one to argue with his father exile was too harsh for three young girls, only to convince him we deserved to be sent to live in the old cottage at the far edges to the north of the packlands, high up the mountain surrounded by hard soil inhospitable to any food I might grow.

My throat stings with the memory of him dragging our things from the nice cabin we lived in after the judgment, burning the broken pile of furniture outside. My childhood home's been given to someone else now.

Caden must believe he spared us certain death. He only made my life hell after his father killed mine.

His piercing gaze narrows when I remain stubbornly silent. He searches our surroundings as if the trees will whisper my transgressions.

They won't—or rather, can't turn their backs on me the way he did. They remain as silent as me, branches creaking and swaying with the breeze. According to the legends shifters pass on to their pups of this land's history, dryads, the trees' spirits that once nurtured and protected the natural land from those who would bring harm, fell into deep slumber, long before the maiden of the moon descended from the Heavens and granted the first wolves our ability to shift forms between animal and man.

When I was a girl, I used to murmur to the trees hoping a dryad would talk back to me. It was one of my favorite stories my mother told us when we were small. The idea of ancient magic fascinated me for the vastness of its possibilities.

There was a time it was richly infused all around us. Only witches and other supernatural beings remain to keep it alive.

Caden cocks his head, waiting. His impatience is palpable, an invisible force pulling taut between us to make me answer.

His jaw works, cheek spasming. He folds his arms, the thin material of his shirt stretching over his sculpted biceps and shoulders. His muscles bunch and bulge larger with the low warning rumble vibrating from him. I snap my gaze up to meet his surly expression.

"I don't have time for this. What," he repeats, slow and firm, "are you doing all the way out here, Avery?"

The roughness of my name leaving his lips makes my breath hitch. I haven't heard him say my name since we were teenagers. It's tinged with his Alpha command, compelling me to obey his wishes.

"Nothing, Alpha Blackburn," I finally answer after the longest stretch I can get away with, offering the barest dip of my chin.

The title leaves my tongue thick and heavy. It's difficult to say anything else as bitter memories stir a pang in my heart, flitting through my mind. Running through the forest with Caden when we were young. Splashing each other at the big natural spring everyone swims at and him pushing me in the deep end near the waterfall.

My father clashing with his. Claws slicing through skin. My attention cut to his shoulder, pulse going jagged as our past haunts me.

He's dissatisfied with the answer. "That doesn't tell me why you're out here. Explain yourself."

I almost choke the liatris clipping when I yank it free of my bag, tucking the satchel behind me. If I keep him distracted, he won't ask to search it.

"Just on a walk to gather herbs and medicinal plants. *Sir*," I tack on after a beat.

My throat stings, clogging with my buried emotions. I deaden my heart to every member of the pack...except when it comes to him.

He glances from the flowering purple stalk in my clutches to my patched up hiking boots, giving me a slow once over, frowning.

"Alone?"

I blink. "Of course."

It's not like anyone in the pack other than my sisters would be caught dead hanging out with me. Except Taryn, but she's a wild she-wolf who just likes the thrill of anything illicit and off-limits.

Another disgruntled rumble leaves him. He opens his mouth as if he's going to question me further, then tears his attention from me, swiping a hand over his stubbled jaw. I'm reluctant to admit he looks ruggedly handsome when he does that, and my bitter hatred for him grows a new thorn.

"Don't cause me any more problems than you already have," he says.

I bite back the caustic reply I want to sling at him, though I can't quite keep my face clear of my outrage. He gets in my face to intimidate me into submission. I hold my ground, daring to maintain eye contact instead of lowering my gaze.

I shouldn't even try him like this. He's the pack alpha. Has been for four years since his father passed.

Giving Caden Blackburn an ounce of attitude, or anything less than my absolute loyalty, is a terrible idea.

At my insolent display, he huffs, carved body seeming to grow larger—the universal sign amongst shifters that they're feeling their wolf because of high emotions. Still, I don't give him an inch of ground, instinct pushing me to get closer. My chest rises and falls faster and I slip a hand into my pocket to wrap around my shears. Without the true increased power a wolf would grant me, they're all I have to defend myself with.

As Alpha, he could decide to make my situation worse whenever he wants for any reason, I remind myself.

Scream it at myself, really, because for some insane reason, I find myself succumbing to instinct by leaning in another inch, daring him to close the scarce gap of space left between us rather than trying to end this so I can get as far from him as possible.

His pupils dilate, blue swirling with the gold of his wolf. I lick my lips, lost to the thrall of the strange moment we're locked in. We breathe the same air, an invisible tether drawing us together.

My heart pounds, stomach tightening as he begins to dip his nose.

Is he going to scent me?

He lingers at my jaw, chest rising and falling. Awareness of him tingles through me, warmth pooling in my core.

The broad expanse of his rugged body.

The heat of him bleeding through my clothes.

The taste of his spicy musk on my tongue.

Caden jerks back with a grunt before reaching my neck, coming to his senses. I release a shaking breath, unsure what just transpired between us.

Or why part of me...wanted him to graze his nose along my

neck to mix our pheromones together so I'd smell like him. I blink rapidly, ignoring the flush spreading through my body.

He stares at me, eyes narrowing at my hand still in my pocket. I step back too slowly for his full shifter speed. His grip yanks my arm free, growling when he sees the shears.

"You've always been your father's daughter, haven't you?" he accuses.

"No," I grit out.

"No?" His handsome features contort with anger. "You weren't trying to get close enough to stab me with these? That's not how challenging the alpha works."

He wrenches them from me with little effort and brandishes them in my face. I foolishly try to snatch them back. He blocks me with his arm. I retreat, blowing out a frazzled exhale.

"It's not—I wasn't." I rub my forehead and screw my eyes shut as I push out the words. "I wasn't going to use them. You know I'd never be a match for your strength if you... They were only meant for protection."

He goes rigid, scrutinizing me in stony silence for several harrowing heartbeats. I can't read his expression.

"Go home, Avery," he bites out at last as he tosses the shears to the ground.

He storms past me, running his fingers through his hair. I watch him until he's out of sight, then hiss tightly, throat burning as I sink to my knees beside the discarded shears. I bury my face in my hands until my body stops trembling from the flood of adrenaline and tears stop pricking my eyes.

I scrub at them and push to my feet with a huff. That was reckless, but I survived it. At least he didn't find out about the actual rules I broke by going to town.

Seizing my abandoned shears, I spot the trampled cutting I dropped when Caden grabbed me. One of us stepped on it from the looks of how crushed it is.

Sighing, I brush it off as best I can. Hopefully I can salvage something useful out of it.

3

CADEN

AVERY'S SCENT follows me long after I let her go. I do my best to finish checking the borders with it tickling my nose. It's distracting. Far sweeter than I remember when I last caught it on the wind.

I shouldn't be able to pick up her scent still. Not at this distance, diluted by the smells of nature and other packmates as I venture closer to more populated areas.

Even as an alpha shifter, my heightened senses have a limit. So how the hell am I aware of exactly which direction she's in on this mountain right now?

Scrubbing my face, I dismiss it as my damn imagination conspiring with my lack of sleep to toy with me.

I know this land like the back of my hand. I've committed every mossy patch, every trickling stream, every tree hollow to memory since I was a pup knowing it would become mine to guard and protect when it was my time to take over the responsibility for my father as his successor.

Of course I know where Avery Morgan is. It's the alpha's duty to always be aware of his enemies.

Tonight is the full moon. As shifters, our connection to it and the moon goddess is strongest on these nights. We run as a pack to honor the gift she bestowed on the first wolf to walk amongst man and nature. It's a time of celebration every month, to guide the younger members of the pack coming of age for their first shift, but I'm not in the mood.

Coming off yet another territory squabble between elders doesn't help. They're debating over a stretch of land connecting their homes. I've been mediating it for them since I became Alpha. I swear, those crabby old bastards have been arguing over who the patch of sparse bushes and rocks belongs to for decades.

It's not just the trivialities I often have to deal with on top of my day to day agenda. Something's different today. It's in the brisk autumn mountain air that's made me off kilter, acting on odd impulses that I can't justify—like that inexplicable incident with Avery. It's growing more noticeable as the afternoon goes on.

Worse, since the moment I sent Avery away, my wolf has been acting strangely restless. He's more interested in turning around and tracking her over the gnarled roots of the trail she took rather than finish the task at hand. I pointedly ignore the yank on my instincts, continuing my descent along the edge of my territory.

I squeeze my nape to alleviate the tight bunch of muscles, finding no relief. Hopefully when I go to fur later tonight, this agitation will cure itself.

Another waft of fresh honey and summer rain teases my nostrils. I cast a glare over my shoulder.

"You've got me nearly believing the pack's whispers about you becoming a witch up here with this trickery," I mutter.

The only response is the sway of the branches overhead and the screech of a hawk soaring through the clouds. It's my memory that supplies the way Avery used to laugh when I told her something outlandish and how brightly her amber eyes would light up with amusement.

Gritting my teeth, I don't hesitate before swinging my fist against a thick trunk with a growl. The bark splinters, fragments exploding everywhere. A deep crack travels up the wood in staggered breaks. It ends at the base of a large branch that creaks ominously before snapping free, crashing to the ground.

Those memories are off-fucking-limits.

Any happy memories of Avery were locked away the day her family betrayed us, going from our most trusted allies as my father's beta to a threat when he challenged his alpha for the right to claim the pack.

I stare at the damage I've done to the tree and my knuckles. Black fur has sprouted on the back of my cut up hand and my nails have extended into claws. I heave a sigh as the angry gashes in my skin begin to mend thanks to the accelerated healing shifters are blessed with. They're gone by the time I've made short work of breaking the fallen limb into smaller pieces to use for firewood at tonight's bonfire.

A soft giggle alerts me to an audience peeking at me from behind a holly bush. Two children, a boy and a girl around age ten, step out when I wave them over. The girl bravely comes right up to me while the boy hovers behind her, glancing at me for permission.

I grimace. Kids were never wary of me when I was younger.

"Are you out here playing?" I ask.

The girl nods. They peer up at the abused tree with curious gazes.

Damn it. I hate anyone seeing me lose control. It's bad enough I have to work daily to make this pack respect my leadership, even four years after I became Alpha at twenty. It was necessary to be firm to ensure they'd follow me when others thought there were other choices better suited to lead the pack than one as young as me.

The girl turns to me. "Are you sad?"

I frown. "No."

"Mad?" She tilts her head. "Our Da goes into the trees behind our cabin to do that. Our Ma says he's working on his frustrations."

"No." The furrow in my brow deepens with a new worry to add to my endless list. I'm not sure their family name—possibly Merryweather's pups, but they could pass for the Farrows line with their eyes. "It'll be dinnertime soon. About time you ran back to your dam, isn't it?"

"Yes, Alpha," they answer in unison.

"Go on now."

I watch them scamper away, chasing each other in a zigzag along the trail until they reach the fork that leads towards the central part of the packlands. Once I no longer hear them, I work my jaw, scanning the wooded path along the borders the Blackburns have been guardians of for generations with a narrowed gaze.

My wolf chuffs in my head, tongue lolling from the side of his grinning maw. The bastard's amusement is another unwanted irritation. His eagerness for tonight's run has been impossible to ignore all day. While I've been taking care of preparations, he's frequently pressed close against the thin veil that separates a shifter's skin and beast forms. He's ready to be in control as usual.

It's not as though I don't shift every chance I get outside of the full moon. Some packs only let their wolf out once or twice a month. I get too restless to go more than a few days. It's a waste of a shifter's power to stay in one form all the time.

I take his taunting as his desire for me to hurry up so we can run and hunt with our pack, gathering the broken up pieces of branch and tucking the bundle beneath my arm.

No, his voice echoes through my psyche, thunderous and commanding. *Go back. Find the female.*

Some days he deigns to communicate with me with words rather than simply influence my instincts. Usually when he's being stubborn and wants something I'm not concerned with. Not all shifters can hear their wolf's internal manifestation when they're not in their fur, let alone converse with them.

The she-wolf smells good. We should hunt with her. She will be fast.

My brow furrows and I shake my head. He's wrong. She doesn't shift. There's no wolf for us to run with. Even if I wanted to, which I don't.

He's barking up the wrong tree. Or maybe he's gone insane with moon sickness if he thinks I'd want that with Avery. When I take a step, he stops me in my tracks, pulling hard with the need to turn around. I ball my free hand into a fist with the effort to remain planted in place.

This needs to stop. It's pissing me off now.

He has nothing else to say, growling as he turns around and flops down, tail thumping in agitation. Great, now he's fucking pouting.

Being at odds with my wolf is a first for me. Typically we're in harmony, agreeing on when to eat, when to assert our dominance, and when to mark what's ours. As long as I give him enough time in fur, he lets me do what I need to when it comes to everything else. He doesn't even have interest in chasing tail the way other males young and old always do, which works fine for me because I have enough on my hands managing pack matters to add juggling the attention of females who only want to fuck the alpha to lord the status over the others for a better cut of meat at dinner. It's better if I don't show anyone my favor to keep the rank-chasers from thinking I'll choose them as a mate.

I don't have time for any of this. Not with the impending summit.

This year it's being hosted by Timber Hollow Pack's alpha, Alistair Ryan. Packs from all over the region gather once a year as part of the accords between the groups of shifters that broke free from the Original Pack hundreds of years ago.

The pack was made up of direct descendants of the first shifters, and it died out thanks to the tyrannical rule of the successive line of power-hungry alphas driving its people away. Those that made their new settlements in the surrounding areas banded together in a treaty for alliance and prosperity while other groups went out into the world until the shifter population grew, rivaling today's human population globally.

Beyond the harsh terrain of Wanderer's Canyon to the far south, where feral and rogue shifters roam in their wolf forms, the wasteland known as the Deadlands serves as a warning to all shifters in the region of our history before we worked together peacefully.

If all goes well, I'll be able to improve trade between Silver Falls, Timber Hollow, and our other nearest neighbor, Crescent Valley Pack. It'll be my first time pushing for anything in this year's accords. The last few winters have been harsh. Alistair's pack and Crescent Valley both have better resources than we do on the mountain to sustain them throughout the year, which has only grown more challenging since I made the decision to cut back on unsanctioned travel off packlands.

I spent the most time in Timber Hollow's territory when other packs hosted me as heir apparent to Silver Falls as part of the peace agreement. It's a way for those who are next in line can build relationships between nearby packs for trade and learn different methods to lead. It's Silver Falls' turn to host Alistair's heir. I'm hoping that will make Alistair want to support my bid for an updated trade agreement between our packs.

I peer through the trees as the path curves around the south face of the mountain. The forest where Timber Hollow Pack lives is just visible in the distance past the foothills and woods surrounding Ashbury between our territories.

Visiting other packs opened my eyes to many things that make an alpha worthy of leading their pack, but those weeks down in that forest only made me want to come back here. They interact the most with humans and their technology out of all of us, and it was exhausting to regulate control over my more wild behaviors for their sake. Besides, the lake in Timber Hollow doesn't compare to the natural springs dotting the mountain. I missed hiking to the highest point for the best view in the region and the falls...and—

I cut myself off from reminiscing about what it is that makes this mountain home, tearing my gaze from a fallen leaf that's the right shade of amber to match—

Fuck. No. I blow out a terse breath and roll my neck, stretching a tense knot from my shoulders.

The interaction with Avery refuses to leave my head, poisoning every thought and bringing my awareness back to her no matter how much I steer myself away. If I don't address it head on, she'll own my mind the rest of the night.

A snort jerks my head. This shouldn't surprise me by now. After all, none of the Morgan clan turned out to be who my family thought they were.

Yet I'm stuck on her. More than I should be, noticing more than I allow myself to.

Like the dark circles smudged beneath her eyes. How lean she's grown ahead of the winter season.

The way the afternoon light catches on her golden light brown hair. The shape of her expressive mouth. The challenge in her eyes that always makes the blood in my veins pump faster. I bring my thoughts to a halt once more.

Noticing anything about Avery is a dangerous path. One I don't grant myself permission to venture. Not anymore.

Not since her father challenged mine a mere week after I returned home from Timber Hollow Pack.

I swipe a hand over my mouth, turning the encounter earlier over in my head. There's something I want to pin down about it that bothers me more than usual—other than the obvious way my wolf reacted to her rebellious attitude with interest—yet it evades me. What was she doing all the way at the edge of that border when she lives by the northernmost part of the territory?

I write the fixation off as part of my dedication to ensuring my pack is safe and cared for. Even traitors like her who live one step above banishment. Every shifter within this territory is my responsibility.

"I don't need this right now," I grumble.

Frowning at the picturesque view below the mountainside speckled in an array of oranges, reds, and yellows, I scratch my chest to rid myself of the phantom sensation of a spark attempting to flicker to life.

"What are you doing?"

I still at the voice, shocked I was so lost in thought that I didn't sense my second in command approaching. "Liam."

He dips his head in greeting, attention pausing on my shirt with a raised brow. I stop scratching and drop my hand, along with the bundle of wood.

"Itching to go to fur? Me too." He ruffles his dark brown hair with a lopsided grin. "Wolf's been acting up even though I went for a long hunt last night. You'd think he'd found his mate."

My lips quirk. I appreciate that he's never one to pry. He's been with me through everything. We've grown up together from pups. Once I was officially named heir at fifteen, I knew I'd appoint my best friend as my top lieutenant. There was no other choice I'd trust more than him for the role of my beta.

For the briefest second, I consider the possibility that an impending mate bond is my wolf's problem, quickly dismissing it. He's never taken much interest in any female in the pack before. I've also never heard of a fated pairing with a Wolfless shifter. An arranged mating, sure. As far as I know, no Wolfless has ever awoken a mating bond with someone.

Avery's the only Wolfless currently in our pack. Any we had in the past were blotted out when a wolf didn't emerge at coming of age ceremonies, driven from the territory or put down for tainting bloodlines with weakness. My jaw clenches. It's not how things are done around here anymore.

"Always is when there's a full moon."

"I don't know how some of the other packs out there handle not running whenever they want." He shudders. "It doesn't seem right."

I shrug. "They're traditionalists. They go by the oldest of ways, respecting the moon goddess' cycle. I couldn't live like that permanently, but it wasn't so bad when I spent time with the nomadic Tullut in the remote northern tundra during my time traveling to different packs. It makes you appreciate the shift more." My mouth stretches with a taunting smirk. "Teaches you how to maintain a harmonious balance with your wolf so you learn not to give in every time they want you to do stupid shit."

His expression mirrors mine. "Yeah, yeah. You've got us all

beat there. Are you done up here? The border line is good. I checked it myself this morning."

There's still one stretch left, but I let it go with a nod. "I got some extra wood for the bonfire."

Liam eyes the pile at my feet skeptically. "Wood? Those are twigs at best."

I exhale in amusement. "Shut up."

Gathering wood with him is the most normal I've felt all day. But as we follow the trail back to the center of the packlands, the odd sensation of flickering dances through my chest again.

4
AVERY

THE REST of the walk back to the cottage I share with Beatrix and Lena only takes minutes, except every step feels wrong somehow. Maybe I'm still coming down from the adrenaline of crossing paths with Caden.

When I reach the crooked gate Bea helped me build as a project to distract ourselves the first year we moved up here, I breathe easier. The wood's seen better days. We did what we could with the pieces we salvaged from the group assigned to manage the carpentry supply for the pack. Even though the scrap wood cost us twice the trade value than it should've because we're Morgans, it makes the place feel slightly homier.

The dilapidated tiny house is one of the original ones built on the mountain, dating back to the shifters that settled here to start Silver Falls Pack once they broke away from the first pack to exist. And it shows its age after being uninhabited for decades. The roof is in disrepair, there are cracks in the pockmarked stone steps, the door is hanging on for dear life to its creaky hinges. One of the narrow arched lattice windows has a chip from a hailstorm that's splintered outward with a fracture line.

We do everything we can to keep the place standing, though the cobbled stone foundation is deteriorating faster than I know how to patch with mud and whatever stones I'm able to collect. Last year I picked the sloping field behind the cottage clean to repair a corner.

It's not much, but it's ours now. Our love for each other fills the small space to make it a home.

I check my garden before heading in. It was hell to get this land to cooperate with me, but I won out as the more stubborn one in the end.

There was some help I received to get my garden to take. She caught me by chance in the woods, desperation driving me to search for food when we didn't receive enough the first week here.

"I wouldn't do that if I were you."

My head snapped up, searching my surroundings until I spotted the source of the voice. A woman. I should be alone out here, but there she was walking through the woods. I didn't hear her at all.

The stranger had braided dark hair threaded through with strands of silver. I couldn't tell her age, she could be near mine, or maybe older. Her face held an ethereal quality to match the clothes she wore—a colorful mix of shawls lined with tassels and trinkets over a layered skirt that resembled the vines of a willow tree.

No one was with her, and she definitely didn't belong on pack-lands. I'd never seen the woman before. Yet the woods seemed to welcome her, straining towards the path she walked as if she were their sun.

She surveyed me with a playful smirk. My hackles rose, already at my breaking point after the week I've had. After having every-thing taken from me, and learning none of the people I thought I could rely on were really my friends.

I sat on my haunches, not caring about the mud caked on my shoes and ankles. I would go to my favorite swimming hole later to wash before I dared bathe in my new prison.

She snorted when I lifted my nose to scent the air. My shoulders hunched. There was no way she could tell I didn't even feel a hint of my wolf yet, right?

"I mean, if you're doing it because you like the thrill of danger,

by all means." She waved her hand. "I'm not one for the nausea that will cause if you eat it, no matter how pretty and tasty it appears."

I narrowed my eyes, refusing to drop the mushroom I found. She was tricking me. She wanted my food for herself.

"Who are you? How are you here?" I asked, though I already had an idea of what she could be after she appeared here out of nowhere.

Her laughter sounded like bells, tinkling and bright. "I go where I please, as do my sisters and brothers." She strolled closer, perching on a nearby slab of rock. "I'm beholden to no borders. No wards, either."

"So you are a witch?" I choked out, suspicion confirmed.

She spread her arms wide, showing off the crystals dangling from her colorful shawls. "What of it, little wolf girl? What will you do to me?"

A witch shouldn't be here. Every shifter knew not to trust witches. They were our allies at one time, then they wanted to control us as their attack dogs, to use our power and numbers to boost their own.

"Get out of here!" I bared my teeth. "These are packlands. You can't be here. The alpha will—he'll..."

I slumped back, breathing hard to erase the moment of my father's death that looped in my head nonstop. Tears flowed freely. I didn't think I had any left to spill.

A gentle touch to my shoulder startled me. She drew me into her arms for a hug, hushing me when I broke down. I clung to her, letting everything out, and she held me through it.

When I calmed down, she took the mushroom and pointed out how poisonous it was, explaining the signs to look for. Nature had all sorts of signals. Patterns of certain leaf numbers, common looka-likes, and colorings to tip off if it's safe or not.

I stared in awe as she transfigured the mushroom into a small pile of blackberries on the altar she made on the rock out of a velvet bag of shells she had tied to her hip. She explained something about *equal value exchange, but I wasn't listening, too busy eating the berries.*

"Plants are my specialty," she said. "I'm only passing through, but I found a nice field over this ridge, just past your wards. Come see me. I'll show you how to avoid death by poison."

"Why would you help me?" I mumbled.

She smiled. "Give and take. All things work on balance. I help you when you need it, and someday you'll return it."

Throughout that summer I couldn't get her to tell me what she meant by that. She did give me her name, Jade. Her coven is nomadic, following the ley lines, pools of natural magic, around the world. She's since moved on, but the months she spent beyond the border, I snuck out to meet with her.

She taught me about foraging and what other ways to use what I find or grow. Her guidance, like the advice she gave me to plant sunflowers first to revitalize the soil, was invaluable to our survival up here the first year when the kitchens wouldn't give us a full ration depending on who had distribution duty.

A smile tugs at my mouth as I stroll past the potatoes and the herbs I've cultivated from foraging, and from seeds I traded for to the quarantined plants at the far end, their pots clearly marked with poison labels.

In the seven years since I met the witch, I've learned so much, finding a new passion for studying every plant and experimenting to figure out its uses. The pack's designated head healer doesn't recognize half of the ailments easily soothed by what the land provides all around us. The lazy old male's too reliant on our natural recovery abilities as shifters when he could be helping more.

"Stop obsessing over your babies, they've been fine and haven't grown an inch without your supervision while you've been gone," Beatrix calls from one of the open windows.

"How would you know? You never come out to tend to them for me," I tease.

She rolls her eyes. "I saw what happened when you got that nasty rash. No freaking thank you."

My heart warms as I make my way inside. At seventeen now, she's growing to look like the spitting image of our mother, her and Lena both getting Mom's lighter blonde hair while I have more of Dad's caramel tones streaking mine. I miss both of them so much, but at least I have my sisters.

Losing Mom is what drove our father to do what he did, I think. I remember overhearing him arguing with the alpha about looking for her when she went missing after a run. Shifters sometimes get lost if they're pulled too far tracking an interesting scent, or if they spend too much time in their fur the wolf can lose the human side, returning to our original nature.

I don't know what to believe happened to our mother. There weren't any signs of her turning feral. She was happily mated to Dad in a True Mate bond and loved to take us out on girls-only exploration trips. Was that a hint that she wanted to leave us? I don't like to dwell on it, because I can't change it now. I don't have the luxury of time to sit around dissecting the past when there's always so much to be done.

"Did you bring us anything?" Bea asks when I come through the door.

I pause from unloading my satchel on the table, setting aside the wire and some extra secondhand tools the man from the market threw in simply because he was eager to boast to his stall neighbors he'd traded with a shifter.

The main area of the house is one room we divide into our eating area by the sink and ancient wood burning stove, the bed Lena and Beatrix share shoved into the alcove in the corner, and the rest is nearly overtaken by my herb workbench by the windows. I've grown from having one bench to a whole corner overflowing with hanging plants and drying cuttings, potted propagations and seeds I'm coaxing to grow on the windowsill, and my tools.

Bea blinks her big brown eyes at me hopefully. "Say yes. For Lena, I mean. You know she loves a sweet treat."

The corner of my mouth lifts. "I got these in exchange for a vial of dried hyssop and lavender. One for each of you."

She squeals in delight at the matching pink sticks of rock candy I pull from one of the pockets. I grunt when she barrels into my side for a fierce hug. Her wolf is making her stronger every day. I have no doubt when she comes of age in another year, she'll be celebrating her first shift during a full moon run like tonight.

Lena's the one that worries me. I fear she'll be Wolfless like me.

I wish there were others in the pack to ask about the signs, but I'm the only one. A crabby Merryweather elder told me when my coming of age ceremony didn't result in a shift that I should consider myself lucky the pack won't allow Wolfless to be killed to keep bloodlines strong anymore before he spat at my feet.

Crossing the cramped space to my workbench, I pluck the liatris petals and leaves, depositing them in a bowl to grind later once they've dried out. Then I take one of the small knives from the leather roll sitting to the side, slicing the stem to small pieces. Next I add them to another bowl with a pinch of calendula flowers and a scoop of orange powder beneficial for inflammations from the row of vials on a spice shelf above the workbench.

I mash it together with a pestle and pour in a dollop of honey as Beatrix brings me a cup of hot water without being asked. She's watched me make poultices daily in the last week for Lena's cold.

"Thanks," I murmur before adding just enough water to moisten the ingredients to hold them together in a paste.

When it's ready, I nudge the frail lump bundled beneath the covers, perching on the bed. Lena stretches with a yawn from her nap.

"Hey, buttercup."

"You're back." She's groggy, her voice crackling.

"I'm back. Don't let Bea tell you I didn't bring anything." I help her lean up against the headboard and carefully prod her throat. "Good, the swelling's a little better today. How do you feel?"

"Just sleepy."

"Your throat doesn't hurt?"

She lowers her lashes. It's not her fault her health is fragile. It's mine.

In the winter during our first year living here, she caught a terrible pneumonia. She almost died and I didn't know what the fuck I was doing. It was bad enough I went down to the healer to beg him to help her because she was only seven, no one had a right to hate her for her name. He refused, slamming the door in my face.

I'll never fail her like that again.

I reach for the bowl. "Here. Let me put this on you anyway. Then you can have the rock candy I got you."

She tips her chin up obediently, used to the unpleasant feeling of her throat smeared with the mashed herbal treatment. I hum while I apply it, then clean my hands and bring her the candy and a cup of ginger tea Beatrix made. Smiling, I comb her hair with my fingers.

A timid knock sounds at the back door. I stop what I'm doing and glance at Beatrix.

"It's for you," she says without looking up from the potato she's returned to skinning for dinner.

I kiss Lena's head before getting up. "I know. I'm expecting this one."

The knock comes again, with a tad more force when I collect the sachet waiting on my workbench. I lift my brows when I open the back door.

"Sorry." The girl waiting is a couple years younger than me with unkempt hair and a fading bruise on her cheek, a shocking contrast to how put together she was when we were in school together. She bounces a chubby baby on her hip, glancing at the woods every few seconds. "I don't have much time before he'll be back."

My lips press into a thin line. If it were up to me, I'd love to give her something stronger than the monthly dose of valerian root to knock her horrible mate out early for the night so he'll leave her the hell alone. I'd even give it to her for the same price as the sedative, because like anyone from old Cormac's brood, he's a close-minded, short-tempered thug.

"Do you want a salve for your cheek? It'll help with the swelling," I offer.

She gives a feeble shake of her head. "Can't. Don't want him noticing me doing anything different. It's healing fast enough on its own."

I grimace, imagining how bad it must've been for it to still be puffy. When I offer the sachet, she takes it quickly, slipping it into the pocket of her loose smock dress. She turns to leave with a muttered thanks.

"Wait, Nina. Your payment." As sympathetic as I am to what she endures with her unfortunate arranged mating, I need whatever she's bartering with more.

She freezes on the stoop, lip quivering. "I—I forgot, I'm sorry. We've got a lot of meat this week. Can I give you some of that?"

I nod. "Food will always be accepted as a fair exchange."

"Okay. I don't have it with me. It's hard enough coming up the mountain discreetly. People will talk if they see me on the same path today," she mumbles, hushing her fussy baby. "Come down to the back of my cabin just after sundown? Trent will be at the gathering early with the security team. I can sneak it to you better that way instead of trying to come all the way up here."

The security team Trent's part of is bullshit. It's part of Cormac Blackburn's—Caden's uncle—not the official pack guards.

I chew the inside of my cheek in consideration. It would be wiser to refuse her so word doesn't get around that I'm going soft on my payment terms with the females in the pack. They visit me in secret despite my family's disgraced reputation. It's my new one they care about when they come for the herbal remedies and concoctions I provide that they can't get from the regular healer.

Normally, I avoid a full moon bonfire night whenever I can. When I attend, I'm at a disadvantage. But she's right, it's the only way people won't be suspicious if they see someone with a large pack of food heading away from the dining pavilion outside of a distribution day.

"Fine. I'll be down there in an hour."

That should give me just enough time to get in and out before the moon rising. Everyone else will be busy with the revelry to notice me.

Nina gives me a wobbling smile. "Thank you."

She leaves in a hurry, not lingering for friendly chatter. I don't bother with it, either. After the first few surprise visits by other female packmates in need of my help, I learned they were only after my resources. Some still whisper nasty things about me even as I hand over whatever quick fix cure they've come for.

"Don't make a portion for me," I tell Beatrix. "Make sure you and Lena both have second helpings."

Beatrix raises her brow, holding her tongue for once as she works on the stew she's preparing. I go through the narrow hall that leads to the bathroom and my shoebox of a bedroom. In the bathroom, I lean against the sink, sighing before I splash cool water on my face.

My stomach cramps when I straighten. I frown, laying a hand over my middle. It passes quickly, though I'm left with a tightness in my skin that doesn't ease when I roll my neck and shoulders.

I put off leaving as long as I can, not looking forward to being around so many packmates. Our stores need any food we can scrounge before winter, though.

"Avery." Bea grabs my hand on the way out, her nonchalance evaporating as her forehead creases. "Are you sure about this?"

"It'll be fine." I offer a relaxed smile and squeeze her hand. "Don't wait up for me. I'll be back when I can."

MOST OF THE cabins are quiet by the time I'm on the main road running through the middle of the packlands. Everyone's made their way to the bonfire by now. I can hear the lively notes of people playing fiddles and the occasional mirthful shout through the trees.

It's held at the fire pit on the commons, the central lawn in front of a semicircle made up of the alpha's massive lodge and offices, the log-style community building where shifters gather for meetings or stay in the dormitories, the patrol cabin where all pack security matters are handled, and the dining hall and pavilion. Anyone assigned to a kitchen duty rotation is likely bustling tonight for the party.

I make my way to Nina's cabin, grateful that she doesn't live on the Blackburn compound. Caden's uncle keeps his entire brood within the walled-off section of homes as if they're their own pack within the main pack. He usually has his many sons, nephews, and grandsons posted at the entrances like his own private security.

My guess is, her mate has either disappointed Cormac or isn't useful, so he's cast out from living amongst the rest of his extended family despite being a member of Cormac's shady guards. Caden mostly ignores his many cousins, though whenever you cross a Blackburn that isn't Caden or his sister, Callie, they act as though they're above everyone else for being related to the alpha, no matter how much space is spread between them on their family tree.

When I rap my knuckles lightly against Nina's back screened door, she answers out of breath, glancing behind me when she yanks me inside.

"Did anyone see you?"

I tug free. "No. It's deserted on your street. Everyone's already out."

She sags in relief. "Good."

I follow her through the dimly lit house. My cottage might be smaller, yet her place is depressingly oppressive, the walls stinking of her mate's aggression. I shudder, folding my arms. In the kitchen, her pup blows spit bubbles around a teething ring in his crib. She takes me through the pantry to her basement steps.

"No pack run for you tonight?"

Her head ducks. "No. Trent doesn't like letting anyone else but his own family watch the baby, even my mother. He says it's how his family has always done things. So I stay home instead of using the nursery for bonfire nights."

My nose wrinkles. I doubt he's hanging around to help her out with their pup himself.

It's not that this pack is one of those backwards ones I've heard of in the remote parts of the world that believe their females only serve one purpose, either. Our she-wolves work all the same job classes as the men, and some choose not to have pups at all. Yet injustices like this still exist here.

"Here." Nina closes her huge freezer, shoving a chilled hunk of meat wrapped in paper and twine into my chest. "Your payment. Now you should go. I can't have Trent smelling that anyone was here he didn't approve of inviting in."

She lifts her brows impatiently when I don't immediately

move. I want to tell her again that I have several poisons, most undetectable. No one would suspect a thing. There's no risk she'd be detained in the holding cells in the security crew's cabin.

Or I could convince her to take this to Caden's offices and plead her case for his mediation in the matter. He might be a bastard, but as strict as he is, he wouldn't overlook this if he knew how she's being treated. The last time he found out about a male smacking around his mate, he gave him a beating on the central lawn and made the entire pack watch.

Nina gives me a shove with a warning rumble. "Go. I don't want my baby around a Wolfless for too long. He needs to grow up big and strong like his father."

She acts as though I'm diseased and contagious. If I had a wolf, I'd love to snap at her to put her in her place. She sounds like the narrow-minded elders who are traditionalists, believing the lack of a wolf is a sign of weakness.

I show my teeth and push into her space. Annoyance flares fast, fading when she shuffles back. She's the weak one here. Fear's made her that way.

I offer her a wan smile. "Until next time."

Without waiting for her, I climb the stairs and head through the back door. I fantasize about all the ways to get retribution on Nina's behalf against her terrible chosen mate.

I don't realize I've walked to the bonfire on autopilot until I'm skirting the edge of the log benches circling the fire pit. A group of children race by shrieking with laughter. A pang echoes in my chest, filling me with the longing to be part of the pack the way I used to. It's not right to feel so isolated.

The strange urge to join them tugs at me. I glance down the empty road while trying to talk myself out of it, then inch closer to the festivities.

They're deep into the celebration now, the grills going with the savory aroma of succulent meat and fresh bread being passed around the long tables packed with food. Some are playing music on fiddles and singing folk songs for the moon goddess about her descent from the Heavens to be with the wolf she fell in love with. The elders sit around with cigars, some with wayward pups bouncing on their knees. I don't spot anyone in the white linens we wear for a coming of age ceremony, so no one will be shifting for the first time.

I tip my face up to the moon. Even without a wolf, there are times I'm able to sense a distant connection to it, stronger when it's in the full phase. It peeks behind the treetops as it rises.

Shift.

Something inside my chest flutters. I feel it sometimes. It's merely a phantom sensation after a lifetime of living amongst shifters who talk nonstop about what their wolf feels like.

I gave up hoping I would join them in that experience when mine never came by the time I turned eighteen, leaving me standing alone at the ceremony that month bearing the hard stares of everyone who didn't want a Morgan there anyway while the others chased each other in their new forms. There are late bloomers who grow up with minimal signs of their beast, but by twenty I knew the silence within me would never be filled.

I don't draw attention to myself as I weave around groups of people, giving a wide enough berth to not be noticed as someone not welcome for the bonfire.

Sticking to the shadows where the firelight doesn't reach, I amuse myself watching Callie Blackburn get into trouble at the drinks table with her feisty best friend, Taryn Barnes.

"I'm not supposed to serve more than three drinks," the bartender says.

"Who said that? My brother? I'm bringing this drink to him. You're not going to refuse our alpha another whiskey, are you?" Callie prompts. "He specifically asked me to get it for him."

She plays up the pack princess attitude people usually give her crap for behind her back, leaning across the bar to keep the attention on her as Taryn moves to the other end of it, eyeing the selection. I smirk, catching on to what they're doing. I'm not the only one, either. Liam's narrowed gaze is on Taryn from several feet away, already moving to push past the group of women deep in their wine glasses.

Callie keeps the guys manning the bar occupied while Taryn slips an entire bottle of liquor down her pants, flipping her shirt over it. She grins and shoots Callie a thumbs up. The triumphant expression falls off her face when Liam grabs her arm from behind.

"Can't go one night without trouble, can you, Miss Barnes?" He pulls her into his chest and frisks her.

"Jeez, buy a girl a drink first before you try to take her out to the woods to rut her," Taryn sasses with a laugh. "Didn't your dam teach you any manners?"

"Didn't yours teach you right from wrong?" he counters as he pulls the contraband free. "Yeah, guess you ditched that day of lessons. What a surprise."

"Live a little. It's good for you. Break one rule. Go on, I dare you."

Liam growls, leaning over her shoulder. She snaps her teeth at him playfully, completely unthreatened and unrepentant.

Callie laughs and knocks back the drink she convinced the barkeep was for her brother. "Goddess save us all. You two should just mate already for how often you bicker. You're worse than True Mates, always in each other's business."

Taryn pretends to retch. "If the Goddess did me like that, I'd question why she turned her back on me."

Liam clenches his jaw, tearing his scowl from Taryn. "Let's go. Both of you."

"Me?" Callie protests.

"Both of you," Liam reiterates through his teeth, snagging her elbow while yanking Taryn close enough that her red hair snags on the dark brown scruff shadowing his jaw.

"Both at once?" Taryn fakes a gasp. "Liam, you dirty dog. I can't wait to hear these rumors spread at breakfast tomorrow.

Think it'll reach the commissary by lunch? What will Alpha Caden say about his star lieutenant slipping off with his sister and her friend?"

The firelight is just bright enough to spot the vein throbbing above his brow. I roll my lips between my teeth and silently cheer Taryn on.

"That's enough. You're spending the night in the pen for stealing," Liam says resolutely.

Callie digs her feet in and argues, "What about—?"

"You can shift in the cells and sleep in a huddle to keep each other warm for all I care," he snaps.

I turn around when the three of them head my way, not wanting Liam to decide I'm doing something wrong, too. My chin dips to my chest and I weather the old ache of missing their friendship. When Caden went from my friend to my enemy, I also lost my relationship with all three of them. Only Taryn will speak to me these days if our paths cross.

A deep, unpleasant laugh draws my attention. Nina's mate cozies up with two females by the other end of the drinks table, standing far too close and admiring the view their low-cut tops grant him. He's shameless, sniffing after them when he's forced Nina to stay home.

My lip curls. I'm definitely adding something that causes hair loss to Nina's next sedative order. It's the least he deserves. I hope his wolf's fur turns out patchy, too.

It's not uncommon to find mates messing around with others. Some chosen matings turn out to be good matches that last the test of time. Others who aren't happy to be mated will settle their bond just to avoid the heat sickness that comes from resisting a mating frenzy, then avoid each other as long as possible.

Only those with a True Mate bond granted by fate are unable to stray because their mate is their world.

My parents had a bond like that. Their love was clear for anyone to see, always pulled to each other anywhere they went, eyes lighting up whenever they saw each other even if they'd only gone to the other room. It's impossible to say why Mom was able to walk away from it because it drove Dad crazy after she went missing, to the point he betrayed his closest friend when he wouldn't listen by challenging him for the alpha title.

There are only two ways to become a pack alpha—inherit it from the existing bloodline, or to take it by issuing a challenge to fight for the right to rule.

Shifters honor strength above all. The strongest survive. The strongest maintain the highest rank in the hierarchy.

I snag a roll from a table when I pass by, pleased it's still warm. It's a shame I didn't bring my satchel. I could've stocked up more for the girls. Maybe someone has an unattended bag they won't notice by the time they shift.

My lips twitch while nibbling on the roll, a plan forming to stick around longer than I intended. The elders always run for the shortest amount of time, just long enough to stretch their old bones before they return to hang around the fire to continue gossiping. I'll have enough time to raid the feast and be out of here before they're back.

The roll tastes great, though my stomach clenches. I'm usually hungrier in the colder months because I make sure my sisters are fed first, but this is more difficult to ignore. I finish it and sneak another from a different table. By the time I've grabbed a third one, I'm restless with a craving I can't sate.

I want more, but the drumstick I find abandoned on a plate doesn't appeal. Making a discontented noise, I change directions to see what's cooking on the grills.

The sight of Caden across the fire pit stops me in my tracks.

He's with a few of his guys from the patrol crew, drinking a beer and actually smiling for once, though it's not his full smile. I don't know if he smiles like he used to anymore.

He hasn't noticed me tonight. I should move on to keep it that way. Instead, I'm rooted in place, admiring the way the firelight dances off his muscled arms.

"You shouldn't be here," a smooth voice taunts beside my ear.

I whip around to find Lorne Blackburn. Shit. The only person worse than Caden to gain the attention of leers at me like a predator sizing up his prey. Cormac's eldest son is three years older than Caden and he's inherited everything from his father, including his shrewd mind.

"I was just leaving," I say.

"I didn't give you permission to leave yet."

He circles me, assessing me from head to toe while I remain frozen in place. His lips curve at the pack tucked beneath my arm.

"Oh good, you brought more meat. Nice to see you're finally settled into your place here after so many years skulking around when your father was put down," he croons.

My grip tightens when he tries to take it. I hold on a moment longer because it's mine. He uses his height and broad stature to intimidate me, flashing his fangs lengthening in his mouth. His posturing doesn't scare me, but it will draw everyone else's attention if he makes a big scene.

I release it, holding my hands up. My chin juts out and my gaze cuts to the side.

"There's a good little bitch," Lorne says with a satisfied snicker. Asshole.

He takes my chin, wrenching my head to the side to sniff at my throat. Bile rises from my stomach in a rush. I shove against his chest to break free. His cruel blue eyes glint. They're like Caden's, but dark and shadowy.

"Just making sure you know to respect your superiors. One day things will change around here and you'd better fall in line. Disobedient females will learn the hard way that it's better to bend the neck."

He's always spouting the same opinions as his father about how this pack should be run. About how we'd be better off living in the old ways—females silent, pushing out pups, and at the beck and call of the males.

No matter how much I want to shout and scream in his face for his vile opinions, I don't respond. It's the best way I've learned to get out of interacting with him as quickly as possible. I hate myself for it, but I bow my head the barest amount to show my submission. Best I get out of this now rather than have him drag me to Caden and claim I'm a problem for taking a hunk of flesh from his hide with my bare nails.

Lorne frowns, sloshing the rest of his drink into his mouth and sauntering off. I guess he's grown bored of me without any reaction on my part. If my situation was different, if I wasn't a pack outcast, then I'd feel safe enough to challenge him.

Because men like him don't want the demure women they go on about. He wants to goad me into exploding before he puts me in my place.

My chest expands with a pissed off rumble stronger than anything I should be able to produce with my vocal chords. I blink, touching my throat.

Lorne turns back. I hurry away and write off the growl as a figment of my imagination.

My plan to steal what I could of the leftover food goes up in flames before my eyes. With Lorne tracking every move I make, I won't be able to go unnoticed. He'll make sure of it.

The weird hunger pangs return. I eye the tables of food and none of it appeals to me.

I'm ready to leave. There's no reason to stick around to watch them all shift. It's foolish of me to spend more time than I have to amongst a pack that looks down on—

A scent hits me, strong and intense and *delicious*. I whip my head around, lifting my nose to catch it again, greedily inhaling more. I immediately want to be enveloped in it.

The earthy musk of cedar and oakmoss is so comforting, so right. It's the feeling of walking barefoot in my favorite meadow. The taste of the mists coming off the falls.

What is this? Who smells this amazing?

The scent leads me closer. At first I have no idea what's come over me, or why I'm being pulled hard by this instinctive need to track the scent.

Mate.

Oh. That makes sense.

Wait—no it doesn't. How can I have a mate?

It doesn't matter. My thoughts slip away. I'm driving purely on instinct.

I need to get over there, need to claim him—my mate.

6

AVERY

AFTER A FEW STEPS under the hypnotic lure tugging me forward, I falter to a stop, trying to make sense of what's happening. The pause doesn't last long as every fiber of my being begs for him to feel complete.

I pant, rushing through the grass towards the bonfire.

Someone's in my way. I elbow them aside with a grunt. Another person yells something at me. I growl in their direction, stalking across the lawn, jumping over an empty bench. I search the crowd, baring my teeth at their open disdain.

My hearing stretches farther than I'm used to. I hear *him*. Deep tones making a dulcet melody. Then another voice—female, too inviting.

Another wild noise tears from my chest. No! He's mine. No one else can claim him but me. I'll attack anyone who tries.

There's a crash across the fire pit, followed by a growled, "Get out of my way."

My knees threaten to buckle at his voice. I shove past the group in my way, then freeze at the male several feet from me.

Caden stares back at me, equally shocked.

My heart rises in my throat as I watch his scorn towards me

melt away. I gasp as his features soften and his gaze flares with reverence.

How can I have a mate? How can it be Caden after everything that's come between us?

I hate him, yet...I don't.

Not right now. I can't hate him now. He's my mate. He's made for me. To love me. To protect me. He's perfect, as he should be.

He's so handsome. Strong. It'll feel good to be wrapped in those huge arms at last. Tuck my nose in the crook of his neck to inhale more of his divine woodsy scent. Lick—yes, licking every carved muscle when I tear off his shirt and mark him all over.

Reason flits in and out of my head, fighting with another presence unfurling there.

Mate. Go now.

The inner force drives me forward, pacing behind my ribcage until I give in. I feel drunk out of my mind, releasing a delirious laugh.

The pull drawing me to Caden is so strong I stagger, eyes wide and locked on him. He's my mate. My heart's True match.

I mouth his name and a breath punches from his lungs. He holds an arm outstretched to me, striding for me at the same time I start running.

We don't stop until we collide. His arms circle my body and I press my face into his firm chest, dragging in deep lungfuls. He grips the back of my coverall dress, tugging me closer to press against the rapid thud of his heart.

It's still not enough to burn away the throbbing sensation in me that I mistook for hunger. Now I understand it was the mate bond forming to tie our souls together. The magic fills me, twining around my heart, reaching out to connect me to his. If I focus on the intangible threads of the bond, I recognize him at the other end.

I meet his fixed stare in wonder, lips parted. His blue eyes swallow me in their stormy depths ringed with gold.

Yes, mate. Handsome, perfect mate. Yes, yes, yes, yesyesyes—

Everything in me chants a celebration in a curious voice that isn't quite my own, matching the speed of my racing pulse as our bond lights me up from within. It drowns out my stunned surprise that I've found my fated match and the old, trampled wish I used to cling to, secretly hoping Caden Blackburn would be my mate.

Caden's fingertips graze the edge of my cheek, sending a tremor through my body that leaves me shivering. He emits a low rumble tinged with pride in response. My heart drums faster, warmth spreading outward from the glow emanating around it until my entire being is enveloped in it.

His chest rises and falls with ragged breaths as he tilts my face up, gaze roving greedily over every inch like this is the first time he's seen me, truly seen me, in years and he's making up for lost time.

Every inhale tinged with his delicious scent is so intense, I'm swooning, intoxicated by the sensation of the newly formed mate bond threading us together.

I want to say so much—his name, a plea, *mate*—yet all of it sticks in my throat. With a thick swallow, I rest my hand on his chest, hoping the bond will convey the rushing swell of emotions overwhelming me. His large, rough hand covers my wrist. His touch is gentle at first, as if he's worried I'll break.

Just before our lips brush he goes rigid, grip tightening until I wince. His gaze hardens when he pulls back, the bond turning hot, too hot, jolting my heart with a vicious lightning strike.

For a moment, the pain in my heart reflects in his expression before he shakes his head. His features contort to the hatred I forgot when our bond connected us as True Mates.

"No," Caden snarls through clenched teeth. "I reject you."

It's difficult to breathe as I'm lanced through at those words. Shocked murmurs break out around us.

He shoves me away when I cling to him in confusion. The whiplash from new bond-high to the first tear in the connection between us leaves me dizzy and unable to process what's happening.

"W-what?" I choke out as I reach for him. "Caden—"

He bats my hand aside. "Fate is wrong. I could never have a mate like *you*."

Something inside me shatters.

Oh.

My heart, I realize amidst the soul-deep pain of his rejection.

Distantly, I'm aware of more intense murmuring from the crowd surrounding us. Fate-blessed bonds are a gift from the moon goddess. It's taboo to refuse them, almost unheard of.

The fledgling mate bond frays, unable to complete fate's design. The incandescent glow that filled me with warmth and love dims to nothing but the shredded remains of what could've been. I clutch at my chest, a wounded sound escaping me.

Caden does nothing to help me, leaving me to fend for myself. I'm sure I'm dying. Does he not feel the same? I can't tell because his face is set in a stony mask.

My body aches with the throb of the mangled bond. My legs threaten to give out. Breathing is painful. Thinking hurts.

Through it all, one thing rings clear in my mind.

Fate chose the worst possible mate for me. My enemy.

Finding Caden Blackburn is my mate after everything I've been through has to be some cruel joke. The moon goddess must be laughing at me.

I shake my head, but the grating sound of snickering doesn't clear. It surrounds me, raking across my frayed nerves. I swing my blurred gaze around the circle of packmates that look on with open hunger and derision for this spectacle. Their wolves are close to the surface, poised to jump on my weakness and tear me apart.

My lip curls and I bare my teeth at them. I might not have the ability to shift into a wolf, but I'm still as fierce and will fight to survive anything. Even rejection from my fated mate.

Lorne smirks at the display and sweeps his gaze over me. He prowls into the circle, attention sliding to Caden over my head.

"Look at the little witchling playing at being a wolf. She's hardly worthy of a True Mate bond with you, is she, Alpha Blackburn?" he drawls the title with an open hint of mockery. "You're right to refuse her, cousin. The pack wouldn't follow you if you mated her. A Morgan in the Alpha lodge again?"

Lorne clicks his tongue in dismay. Caden's shoulders tense. He swipes a hand over his mouth, avoiding looking at me.

I want to get away from here, but I also want to crawl on my hands and knees to him. I fucking hate myself for it, battling the urge until it's suppressed.

Lorne blocks my view of Caden. My teeth ache as I sidestep him. He delights in my misery, toying with me by getting in my way repeatedly. I shove at him, too wound up to remember that I shouldn't.

He grins, leaning into me while speaking to Caden. "It's best not to leave a female like her unmated. Not to bear my pups, of course. To keep her under control. She might be Wolfless, but she's still pretty. I'm sure the bitch still knows how to present to be mounted all the same. I'd bet she'll look even prettier when I have her on all fours."

Lorne's disgusting remark is met with more laughter. He reaches for me. I veer away, his scent growing so offensive I nearly gag. His touch is wrong, too.

"No!" Caden roars.

The wild growl that tears from him is forbidding and possessive. It sends half of the pack crashing to their knees.

Lorne remains on his feet with some effort, fingers digging into my arm. "What's wrong, cousin? You rejected her. I'm glad to have your scraps, as always."

I whimper.

And Caden's composure *snaps*.

7

CADEN

The sight of another male touching Avery drives my wolf wild. Lorne's boasting of taking her for himself because I don't want her breaks the fragile restraint I managed to gain to refuse this bond.

My vision goes red.

I act without thinking. One minute I'm putting some needed distance between us, the next I'm wrenching Lorne away from her.

He grunts, struggling with me. My muscles bulge with the power of my wolf. He's pressed close, moments from taking my skin.

Threat. That's what's driven me to the breaking point. I sense that this male is a threat. He's trying to take from me.

Bloodlust pumps through my veins. It's not enough to get Lorne off her. The things he said loop through my mind and my fangs descend so fast they cut my lip. He fucking laughs.

"What are you losing control over?" he taunts. "Over that pathetic Wolfless who's nothing more than a cunt to use? The one you refused?"

I want to rip his tongue out and chew it up.

Then the sinews of his vocal chords.

I want his blood soaking the lawn for days so everyone knows not to go near her.

My body isn't my own. Reason has left me, along with my carefully maintained control.

Lorne's arrogant grin, his suggestion to use Avery, his hands all over her—I growl fiercely, my wolf making himself known. His shoulder pops from its socket when I twist his arm behind his back. He grits his teeth, aiming an elbow at my gut. I crush his arm in my powerful grip and the bones snap beneath the full strength I put into it.

He screams in fury, shoving at me. "You attack your packmate —your own blood? Over her? She's not one of us. Probably lying about being your fated, too. Your father should've killed every Morgan left after he won that challenge. Wipe out the whole rotten bloodline."

"Shut *up*," I snarl, my voice all wolf.

I lose him for a second when he breaks away, then I'm back on him immediately, harshly grabbing him by the injured part above his elbow to keep his accelerated healing from knitting the broken bones together. I'm not finished yet.

It's not enough. I could tear his damn arm off and burn it in front of her, and it would never be enough to erase his touch on what's *mine*.

My attention moves to Avery. She's breathing heavily, arms wrapped around herself. Her focus is locked on me. Tears fill her eyes, but there's an intent gleam to them when I drive my fist into Lorne's gut.

She likes this. My chest puffs out and fur sprouts down my arms. The material of my shirt strains over my body as it expands to contain the beast within. It tears at the seams, hanging from me in scraps of fabric when I punch him again and again until he doubles over.

Yes. See how strong we are? How we protect you?

I shake my head, ripping my gaze from her. Gripping Lorne's throat and a fistful of his shirt, I take him to the ground, pinning him on his back.

He's not laughing now, staring up at me with outrage. With

challenge. Still meeting my fucking eyes when he should be submitting to his alpha.

Lips peeled back, I squeeze his throat, watching his face turn purple. He jerks, holding my gaze with open defiance. My fingers curl tighter, feeling his rapid pulse hammering.

"Submit," I roar in his face.

A choked-off wail from the nearby crowd filters through the red haze consuming me. Sylvie, Lorne's mother. I spare her a glance, finding my uncle's fist clamped on her nape to keep her quiet.

"Don't interfere. You'll make him look weak," Cormac corrects angrily.

My uncle was never much of a problem when my father was alpha, but once his older brother passed, Cormac has never missed an opportunity to make it known what he thinks of my choices in leading the pack. Everyone measures me against Dempsey Blackburn's great reign, but he actively works to see his sons undermine me without any of them facing me in a challenge.

I fight with my wolf for control. I never let myself break like this. Cormac's going to use this against me. He'll probably whisper with the elders who waver between begrudging me their respect and griping about how things were in their day. I'm losing ground.

My wolf isn't listening. His hackles are raised, growling nonstop. He won't be satisfied, not by submission alone.

I'm on the verge of doing much worse to Lorne than breaking his arm and choking him out. My wolf wants to tear him limb from limb, death the only acceptable outcome to the challenge.

"That's enough," I seethe. "It's over. I have you pinned. Drop your fucking eyes and submit."

Lorne's eye twitches. Movement in the grass drags my focus from him.

Sweet notes of honey wash over me. Warm sunshine breaking through after a summer rain. I whip my head in Avery's direction.

She's edging closer. I lose what little thread of my control I've regained all over again with her near.

This is why I know fate is wrong. Look how quickly I almost destroyed the fragile balance of order I maintain over the pack because of her.

Pain flares in my sternum, jarring me with a sharp lance before fading. My wolf fights me for our skin, scratching at my restraint. He barrels against the barrier keeping him at bay. If she comes over to me, if she touches me again, I know he'll break through.

I snarl at her, battling between reason and my crazed wolf wanting the taste of Lorne's blood on my tongue when I rip his throat out. Everything I've worked to build in this pack is seconds from slipping through my fingers if I give in to what the beast within me wants, no, *demands*—to tear my packmate to shreds for daring to go near his mate.

The very mate I just rejected because this bond is wrong. She can't be mine. Fate is fucked up for thinking she's my destined match.

Avery is a Morgan. My enemy. I'll never trust her.

"Go!" I shout. "Get the hell away from here!"

She flinches, stumbling back another step with hunched shoulders. I grit my teeth, ceasing Lorne's struggle against my grip pinning him to the ground. My claws dig into his jugular, ready to pierce his skin and soak the ground with his blood.

"*Now*, Avery!" I order fiercely.

The powerful Alpha command infused in my words booms through the clearing, bringing anyone left standing to their knees in submission. Everyone except Avery.

She remains defiant on her feet, somehow unaffected by the strength of my dominant rule.

Impossible. No one should be able to ignore an order of a pack alpha with that much force behind the shifter magic.

A rumbling growl vibrates in my chest. My wolf is pleased with her. *Proud.*

8

AVERY

MY EARS POP and my gut twists when Caden issues his order for me to leave, but it doesn't feel the way it should. Not even the way the Alpha's command tried to influence me earlier when we crossed paths.

It's painful, but it's more from him doubling down on rejecting me as his mate. There's no spark running through my soul to demand my loyalty to his word.

A few packmates' whimpers and distressed whining reaches me through the blood rushing in my ears. Some have pissed themselves, faces pressed into the dirt, quivering in fear. Focusing on them becomes difficult, my attention returning inward to the storm battering my psyche.

Maybe this mangled bond that's burning a hole through the space in my chest where my heart should be has some way of sparing me from an alpha's power. I don't have time to examine it, fighting the cascading rush of everything crashing over me.

When he attacked Lorne for being near me, touching me, I thought—the bond made me believe he was changing his mind. Why else would my fated mate go so wild defending me if he didn't want me?

Well, I don't want him either.

I hate him.

It hurts to hate him.

I close my eyes in frustration. My soul feels like it's splitting in two. This is too much. All of it. Panic rises, threatening to suffocate me.

Should it hurt this badly?

I gasp for air, tripping backwards through small divots in the grass. Putting more and more distance between myself and Caden. Away from my mate.

Every wobbling step is agonizing. I'm pretty sure I've twisted an ankle, or worse, I fear when a sickening crack jolts me, fire shooting up my leg.

I cry out, nearly losing my balance. Tears stream freely down my face. Every heaving breath I draw burns my lungs and throat.

Goddess help me, I need to get out of here now or I might very well die. For my sisters' sake, I won't let that happen.

It's insane that a delusional part of me still wants to go back to his side. As if he'll somehow decide it was a mistake, take back the harshest words a shifter fears hearing, and engulf me in his strong embrace again. My aching heart breaks all over again because that will *never* happen.

Caden Blackburn rejected me.

He doesn't want a mate like me. A broken shifter who can't shift. The daughter of the man who turned on his father.

Enemies don't belong together.

I swallow, picking up the pace of my retreat. No matter how much I'm ready to turn and run until my legs fail me, something still tries to stop me from leaving as I stagger as fast as possible. I swing my wild gaze between the tree line and the scene behind me.

No one's on their feet yet, awaiting permission. Lorne is still pinned to the ground, Caden's hand around his throat.

I can't decide which slices me to the bone more—knowing I'll never have another chance at happiness again because the mate the moon goddess wrote in the stars cast me aside, or facing Caden's scowl as he tracks me across the clearing.

He already broke my heart once. The carefully hardened pieces I spent years mending with my own resolve to survive have shattered to thousands of shards, wrecked beyond any hope of repair.

I refuse to let him break my heart a second time.

Go. The venom in his tone echoes in my head.

My teeth chatter and needles prick my skin, spreading tiny fires down my arms. Something unfamiliar fights its way out of me. A growl rends the night air. It takes me a second to realize it came from me, my vocal chords still vibrating strangely with another wounded call.

Something's happening to my vision. It sharpens, focusing on details at a much greater distance than I should be able to make out, leaving me disoriented. My gaze locks with Caden's once more. His blue eyes flash gold, his wolf shining through, softening the force of his ire.

Get out of here. Go. We need to go. To run. Let's run.

I freeze in a patch of moonlight spilling through the trees, gasping for an entirely different reason than being a jilted mate. This voice—it's different. It's not Caden's, nor mine.

Then I sense her. A blurred figure emerges within my mind's eye in an unhurried four-legged trot. A wolf.

This has to be a hallucination. The rejected bond has to be triggering this. My chest heaves as I wait for the mirage to clear. But—no. She's really there, truly part of me.

I can't believe it. I actually have a wolf?

This means I'm not Wolfless. But why couldn't I sense her within me before?

My throat tightens, picturing the horrible sight of Dad when he died. Maybe the emotional stress kept her locked inside me, blocked from emerging.

All this time I've believed I was broken as much as my packmates did, but I feel her now.

With a hitched breath, I take in the deep red fur sprouting on my arms, my nails darkening as they lengthen into sharp points, the seams of my clothing tearing as my human form becomes something I've never experienced before.

Something I never believed I would ever experience.

I'm not dying from Caden's rejection...I'm shifting for the first time.

Yes. Shift, my wolf urges with an insistent yip, pawing at our mental connection. *Need to run. Time to run, race, leap.*

For a beat, I'm frozen. I'm mid-shift without any idea of how I've accomplished it while my emotions were overloading. With the awareness of my new ability, the discomfort hits me in full force, knocking the wind from me with a fresh wave of tears.

I don't know what to do. I'm stuck.

She pads in a circle, then I feel a strange invisible nudge that inspires my instincts. I stop fighting and let go of logical thought, focusing on the pull of the moon.

My lips part in awe as I go through the rest of the transformation.

It hurts like hell, but my nerve endings are so battered that the discomfort becomes a dull throbbing that's easily ignored once it's over. My perspective changes as I rise on four shaky legs.

Everything hits my senses at once with more intensity—so much to smell and hear and see. A whole new view of the world to explore.

It all blurs together, the scents of the earth and grass beneath my large paws, the bitterness of the smoke coiling from the bonfire and the warmth of the burning logs, the savory roasting meat that makes my mouth water. Packmates, so many pack scents it's difficult to pick them apart until I hone in on the one I've always been able to recognize.

I shy away from the inviting notes of smoky forest, fresh springs, and the overpowering sharpness of smoldering cedar that's so strong it makes me sneeze. The tail takes me by surprise when a tickle at the base of my spine results in it swishing.

My attention catches on Caden one last time. His hard expression is unreadable. The bond gives a feeble pulse in my chest, pulling a soft whine from me.

Mate, my wolf senses.

I toss my head in refusal. Again, the tattered bond tries to connect with him. *No. He hurt us.*

I never believed this moment would come, peering at him through my wolf's gaze. He holds it until I lift my head and let loose a somber howl to the moon.

Every shifter I know has some sense of their connection to their wolf before their first shift. The fact I'm meeting mine at last thanks to him causing us this heart-wrenching sadness sours my first time with her.

Turning my back on the clearing, I leap over a downed log and run into the trees. My control slips away, the wolf taking over for me. My steps lose their uncertainty, becoming a confident stride.

As much as I want to shut everything out to enjoy my first run with her, I'm still aware of every inch of growing distance between me and the male I don't want to think about anymore.

A distant howl sounds from the commons once I'm further away.

He might have ruined what fate wanted to gift us, but he's not overshadowing this.

The woods smell richer. Alive and thriving, teeming with so much I take for granted every day. The soft dirt gives way to my bounding paws. Bushes caress my flank when I wriggle between them. I splash through a pond, pausing when I feel the scales of a fish glide past me. My ears prick and I still, caught in a long stare into the water.

I snap my teeth, but the fish escapes the clutches of my jaw. A lively bark escapes me, sending a vibration of energy through my body. I shake it off and jump out of the water, moving to the edge of the pond.

The reflection of my wolf is beautiful. She's a sight to behold in her roan coat and large clever gold irises. She's so much bigger than

I ever expected or hoped for. No one will cross a wolf this size and hope to get away unscathed.

The prospect of fighting something excites her. I trot away from the pond, picking up speed into a loping run. This is amazing. I'm flying through the trees, covering so much ground in a short period of time.

Every sensation is a new revelation. I love this. It brings a renewed appreciation for the mountain to experience its beauty like this.

The thunder of others makes me hover between the trunks of two large trees. The pack is running together. The urge to join them tugs at me. I lick my lips with a whine.

My wolf wants to be with them, as she should because they're pack, they're hers. I stop her from following them. No, it's safer here. We're better off on our own.

I lower my nose to the ground, snuffling through dead leaves and underbrush to follow a tangy trail that snags my attention. I lick up a crunchy bug on the way and pause to paw at a worm before continuing. The trail leads to a scat pile.

Internally, I grimace while my wolf does her thing. When I listened to people talk of hunting, the details of the mechanics didn't occur to me.

Circling the area, the same sharp tang wafts through the trees in another direction. I pause, ears swiveling to take in the rustle of branches in the wind, the trickle of a nearby stream, and—there. Prey dashing through the woods.

I crouch low and stalk. When I cross an old fallen tree from the high vantage point to lower ground, I smell a rabbit. It's digging nearby. Though I'm careful to approach, it freezes, thumping the ground with its back foot to warn off others.

Impatience gets the best of me. I dart for it, lengthening my strides when it gives chase. Just as I think I have it, the rabbit swerves to escape my jaws. I jump into the air to pounce on it, sliding down a slope when I hit a pile of decaying leaves.

My wolf chuffs at my clumsiness, tugging control back from

me. My laughter becomes a series of yips from our upturned snout. Our tongue lolls from the side of our mouth.

Then I scent oakmoss, and a cooling breeze through the midday sun in the high field, and fresh cut cedar sticky with sap. Caden.

Once I hone in on his scent, the whole forest smells of him. He's in the trees and the dirt, at the water's edge where he's stopped to drink before, the traces of him fading. He's everywhere around me.

Mate.

No. He's not ours. We don't want him because he doesn't want us.

My wolf doesn't understand. If he doesn't want her, why did he attack the offensive male? She liked that. He is strong, a good fighter. She scents the air to find which direction he's in. To see his wolf and run with him.

No, I growl.

She flicks her tail at me, pacing through a patch of ferns. There's something she's focused on, but I can't figure it out.

With the reminder that Caden's out there somewhere, the aching throb of the incomplete bond returns. I stagger, flopping to my side, panting deeply. My wolf doesn't like this feeling. Her annoyed rumble becomes a drawn out somber howl.

I lay prone for a long time. Too long. Something could get us like this. A bear, another pack member. I'm just laying here feeling sorry for myself.

No. A broken bond won't be my end.

I'm stronger than this. So is my wolf.

With effort, I make it to my feet. We wobble a moment, enduring another wave of pain. Stupid mate. He did this to us. He doesn't get to hurt us anymore.

Bit by bit, the aching cavernous emptiness in my chest becomes bearable. Not gone, but a dulled throb of a freshly healing wound scabbing over. Bearable if I grit my teeth. Ignorable if I pretend it doesn't exist.

I haven't survived this long after everything changed to allow something like this to break me now.

As awful as being rejected is, I'm stronger than my despair. Being at odds with this pack has never been easy. I'll survive being rejected by my mate because I'm good at picking up the pieces.

I don't need Caden.

9

———

CADEN

Avery has a wolf. I hardly believe my eyes when she shifts before me, my wolf divided between the strong desire to go to her and biting my cousin's face off. Once she scampers off, the lashing heartbeat in my ears subsides. My chest heaves with my labored breathing and my hold on Lorne's throat flexes. I don't release him, keeping him pinned because I'm not satisfied yet.

"Let me up," Lorne says through his teeth.

"No."

He jerks, meeting my eyes again in another unspoken challenge. "Caden—"

I flash my teeth to shut him up. "You defy your alpha when he demands your submission? Show me your neck before I force you to shift and tear your pelt from your hide to teach you a lesson. *Submit.*"

Despite the roughness of my wolf bleeding into my voice with Alpha command, he holds out another second, five, ten. With each one I squeeze his throat a little tighter, grinding my knee into his abdomen. At last, his gaze drops away. With a rough grunt, I wrench his head to the side. He lies prone, hands out to expose his stomach when I rise to my feet.

Good. I can't deal with rebellions like his. It'll disrupt the pack, divide them into factions more than they already are. He could issue a challenge for the right to my title, the right to take the pack from me.

I won't let that happen. My attention drifts to the tree line, finding the spot Avery disappeared. My jaw clenches. She unbalances me. I need to be steadfast to lead.

Avery's wolf is surprisingly large, her coat a warm roan that gleamed beneath the moonlight. I push the thought of her beautiful wolf aside, wrestling myself under ironclad control as I address the crowd.

"I apologize for this interruption to our night of celebration. The matter's been dealt with," I announce. "Let's put this behind us and show the moon goddess our thanks for her gifts to us in tonight's run."

Cormac scoffs, dragging his timid mate with him when he's the first to stride past me for the trees. I work my jaw. One by one, the pack follows suit, stripping their clothes so they'll have something to wear when they're ready to return to the commons.

It's a damn good thing we don't have any first time shifters tonight, or their green energy could've tipped everything into more chaos. There are two coming of age at the next full moon. I'll need to keep a vigilant watch to ensure it goes smoothly. There will be no repeats of tonight's disastrous turn of events.

Energetic wolves chase each other around the commons while older ones sit off to the side, uninterested in the antics of the young. Once everyone's shifted, they begin heading into the woods in family groups and mated pairs.

Once I'm satisfied things are back to normal, I shred what's left of my shirt and join them. Before I get it off, my wolf makes himself known again with a fierce rumble.

I search the mostly emptied out clearing for what's got him riled up now. Then I catch the barest hint of summer honeysuckle on the breeze coming from the north of pack territory.

My wolf rides me hard, catching me off guard with the force of how fiercely he fights me to let us shift, to track our mate's scent, to provide and protect. I grit my teeth with the effort to maintain control once again.

Because if I don't go after Avery right now, he will.

And moon goddess be damned, he's winning.

He won't be swayed or listen to the logic of man. This time there's no stopping him. Teeth clenched to hang on to my eroding composure before he takes over, I signal for Liam. He's at my side in an instant.

"Lead the pack run," I push out, my voice already rougher with the wolf bleeding through. "Make sure there's no more trouble."

"Got it." Liam eyes me as I hold off the shift as long as I can. "You good?"

"No," I admit in a low huff, only because we're the last two standing on the commons. "I—need to run. Now."

"Do whatever you have to. I'll find you later to check in."

I nod, grateful to have his friendship and his loyalty as my beta. The shift happens faster than I've ever been through it, my body practically melting from two legs to four in a split second. The minute I'm my wolf, I'm on the move, snout low to the ground to catch the scent I'm after.

Loam. Pine and oak and birch. Prey. More prey, a stag I've been hunting for the last week. The stench of old man Elton Farrows seeping alcohol through his pores.

There—sweet, succulent mate.

I let loose a throaty howl before taking off. My claws dig into the ground to propel me faster. She hasn't gotten more than a couple of miles from the clearing. I slow my gait when I reach her, stopping several feet off, behind a thick patch of tall ferns. She's peering into the pond where Liam and I fish in our downtime.

He wants to go up to her. Sniff her, find all her parts that smell this good. Then lick them. His throat vibrates in pleasure and it takes way too much of my effort to cut it off before she hears us. He wrestles the little ground I gained from me, taking charge once more.

It's not difficult to tell he's unimpressed with me not wanting to close the distance and claim the beautiful, perfect mate fate chose for him.

I strain against the veil of our connection. She's not our fucking fated mate. There's no way fate would be that twisted to pair me with her.

He shakes his head, ignoring me once more. Stubborn bastard. But instead of making his presence known, he keeps his distance, observing her from afar.

When she takes off, we go with her, remaining just close enough to ensure she's safe. At first she maps territory that's familiar to her, finding her way to the trail head that leads north to her cottage. She marks it and my wolf does the same once she moves on to explore more.

The longer I follow her, the more satisfied my wolf is. He gradually eases back, granting me more than simple consciousness along for the ride. My thoughts become my own again now that he's checked on her.

Yet I keep trailing her throughout her run instead of turning around to join the others. Why? Fuck if I know.

Maybe it's still the wolf. Maybe I'm interested to see how she fares after watching her hide her crushing disappointment that she was supposedly Wolfless at her coming of age ceremony at eighteen the year before my father succumbed to the lasting injury he sustained. Her pride pissed me off then. I wanted to see her cry, but she didn't shed a single tear when people told her she was a broken shifter.

My teeth gnash at the memory, a low chord of anger reverberating from deep in my chest.

There's no telling when a fated bond will snap into place. When it does, it's lucky for those that feel some draw to each other.

But I question why a mate bond awoke between us now. Did the bond bring her wolf out at last, or is it her late bloom that's triggered it?

Some invisible pull keeps me on Avery's tail. Unable to stop watching her.

She's green, darting after every rustle through the bushes and getting distracted by every scent to blow this way. Yet I can't tear my gaze away.

Her reddish brown coat gleams every time the moonlight breaks through the treetops. She's built well, but spry enough to put power behind her jumps. Her large paws are well-balanced.

If I was into this, I see how she'd make a fine mate. My wolf chuffs in agreement, admiring how quickly she picks up on tracking.

Her hunting could do with practice. Twice she scares off two deer grazing not far off. She doesn't realize they're there, intent on a rabbit.

Several times, I back off when she seems to sense me there. I lay low on my haunches, belly to the ground, snout resting between my front paws. When I'm sure she's forgotten about me, I continue tracking her at a distance.

After her failed attempt at catching the rabbit, I nearly bound down the slope she disappeared over with a miscalculated jump. Her broken howl yanks at something in my chest. I hold my ground, barely.

Just when I'm about to give in, she climbs over the drop off, shaking off. I remain hidden beneath a large bush. She glances around—right at me, I swear—then as if she's seen right through me, judged me as unworthy of her attention, she dashes off once more.

I linger, planning to rejoin my packmates. Instead, I follow her paw prints.

When I catch up to her, she's finally noticed one of the deer. It's near a calm spring downstream from Silver Falls where most of the pack swims. She's fixated on the animal as it dips its head for a drink, pawing the ground in anticipation.

Not yet, I think. This opening isn't a good strategy. The deer has the advantage of more room to run than the more overgrown side of the stream we're on.

Avery shoots from behind the rock she hid behind. When she

hits the water, the deer takes off. Avery barks, probably swept up in the thrill of her hunt.

She's shit at it. Amusement filters through me, coming out in a toss of my head. I jump the stream in one clean leaping bound after she disappears, tearing after her prey.

The initial humor fades when she fails to catch it a second and third time. Then a fourth when I herd the doe back in her direction and give her the perfect opening. Her tail twitches with her agitation and impatience.

She gives up on it. I stifle a growl, pouncing on it before it gets away. It goes down easily under the weight of my huge black wolf. I could eat it. My wolf doesn't want the meat.

I drag it along once I pick up Avery's trail heading back in the direction of her cottage. By the time I reach it, she's inside.

10

CADEN

My wolf doesn't give up his fur right away, plopping down like an oversized guard dog twenty paces from her front door.

He watches for any threats for a while, then marks a perimeter around the place. He's claiming this as his territory, warning other predators and prey to keep away. I'm rolling my eyes by the time he finishes going over every inch.

At last, I feel the reins fully back in my hands. I remain in my wolf form a short while longer before shifting. I should leave, but I make no move to.

My wolf clearly hasn't realized I don't want Avery to be my mate, fated or chosen.

I don't know what it means for us to be so divided. There are shifters who go rogue, giving over to their wolves fully by staying in fur for too long. Their wolves are wild. Untamable. Then there are those susceptible to moon madness, driven feral, a danger to their pack. Others who are rumored to have lost their connection to their wolf by staying the other way, integrating completely with humans.

I shudder, not enjoying the thought of any of those outcomes. Not when I give every part of myself to upholding my father's legacy, and his father's before him. The good parts of that legacy, not my grandfather's backwards views when it came to females at the time. Blackburn alphas have led this pack since its formation.

Rejecting the gift of a bond is spitting in the moon goddess' face. It's taboo, but I had to make the choice. Fate can't be right all the time. This bond...it's an insult to think Avery is my destiny after her family's betrayal.

My chest reverberates with a dissenting growl.

I blow out a breath, raking my hands through my hair. I have no doubt I look insane right now, posted up outside her ramshackle cottage in the middle of the night, cock swinging in the breeze. Nudity is a fact of life for shifters, but this is a step beyond the norm. I'd leave to get clothes, yet I can't convince my legs to obey my wishes.

I've done my duty as her alpha. Checked on her and made sure she returned home safe. No one else in the pack is coming after her.

So why can't I walk away?

I nudge the deer carcass I took down. She doesn't even know how to hunt. Maybe that's why I'm still rooted to the spot because it's not clear how she'll fare with her wolf. It took everything in me while watching her pitiful failed attempts to hunt the deer to restrain myself from interrupting to show her how it's done. I don't want to examine why else I was inclined to take it down for her too closely.

Everyone believed she didn't have a wolf. So did I. There's never been any sign before. She couldn't shift before tonight. As the alpha, my wolf had to provide for his packmate.

I open and close my hand, scowling at it. The memory of holding her in my embrace is fresh in my mind. Her body is so much frailer compared to seven years ago. How have I not noticed something like that before today?

Because I haven't wanted to notice anything to do with her.

I shut down the line of thought with a terse sigh. This is ridiculous. What am I doing out here? What are my instincts driving me to defend her from?

Avery Morgan doesn't need protection—mine...or anyone else's. My teeth grind so hard at the idea of *anyone else* my jaw aches.

I distract myself from picturing other males in the pack sniffing around up here by glaring at the squat cabin on the hill ahead of me with the lopsided patched roof and crumbling stone foundation.

Her cottage can barely be called that. My brows pinch and my lip curls at myself for standing guard at such a pitiful excuse for a home.

This is the first I've been up here in years. Me and Liam used to come on dares with the other boys to see if the old settler's cabin was haunted or under a witch's curse. I've had the maintenance and carpentry teams repair and rebuild houses in far less dire condition than this to keep my pack members happy.

The door is barely attached to its hinges.

A chunk of the small porch has deteriorated, leaving a gaping crevice that's liable to break an ankle if it's not repaired.

The stones stacked at the foundation are making the house lean, meaning the cabin will eventually collapse when the old support beams give out from instability or age, whichever comes faster.

Two windowpanes in the narrow arched windows at the front spider with cracks in the glass, likely allowing the chilly mountain air to seep in. They'll need twice as much wood to keep warm throughout the winter.

My heartbeat kicks up and my stomach roils the longer I examine the state of the place.

I did this. I put her here.

Trapped her in this abandoned prison at the edges of pack territory rather than allow my father to send her away.

Breathing becomes difficult for a moment. I scrub at my face, fighting the angry throb in my chest.

What is that? It grows more insistent, jerking me forward a

step, then another. Balling my fists, I dig my heels in until they upturn the patchy grass.

The bond. It's hanging on by a thread, compelling me to complete it. To fix what I've broken by severing it with my rejection.

My hand goes to the juncture of my neck and shoulder, tracing the scars. Most shifters don't scar thanks to our healing abilities. They don't mature until we do. It's why we don't have our first shift until we're of age. Anything that happens to us growing up can leave its mark if the injury is severe enough.

It was Avery's idea to sneak out of lessons for the day. I hated to admit it when any elder packmates made the assumption it was the Fates at work drawing me to her, but I liked the funny feeling in my chest when she laughed, so I'd go along with most of her ideas. She had a way of getting everyone to go along with her.

Her giggle lit up something inside me when she peered down from the high branch she climbed. "Aren't you coming up any higher? You can see for miles up here."

"I'm three times your size. It takes me longer to climb than you." I jumped to reach the thick limb above me and hoisted myself up.

"Hurry up," she teased with another cute chuckle.

"If my dad finds out we skipped lessons, he'll make an example of me." I mimicked his tone whenever he was instilling his wisdom to me as his heir. "No one is above the rules. Not even the alpha."

These games were fine when me and Avery were feisty little pups. We're getting too old to get away with it. She was sixteen now, and I'd turn eighteen next year. My coming of age ceremony was already planned out. I couldn't wait to meet my wolf at last.

"He'll never find out," she swore.

She was right. The view when I reached the spot she perched was worth the climb. My attention slid from the majestic mountain and the sweeping shape of Crescent Valley to her.

Avery's focus swung to me and she beamed. "Pretty, isn't it? Dad said I had to see it from this vantage point to believe it."

A tingle spread throughout my chest. I licked my lips and nodded.

"Yeah. Beautiful."

She released another enchanting laugh. I wanted to take the end of her golden brown braid between my fingers. I wanted a lot of things with her that were becoming hard to ignore.

Succumbing to the urge, I played with the end of her braid, curling the soft tendrils around my knuckle. She blushed, peeking at me through her lashes. A strange tingle danced around in my chest, faintly tugging my stuttering heart.

When we made it back to the commons an hour later, something was wrong. A massive crowd was gathered on the lawn, nearly the entire pack. My wolf I had yet to meet was restless behind the veil that separated us, pacing in agitation. I exchanged a confused glance with Avery and pushed through the shouting people to find out what was going on.

When we broke through to the front, I froze. Avery bumped into me, then gasped at the sight of her father clashing with mine.

"Caden!" Liam found us and made his way over.

"What's happening?" I demanded.

He shook his head. "I don't know, but Clark challenged Alpha Blackburn."

"What?" I balked.

Clark Morgan was my father's beta. His most trusted member of his inner circle. There was no way.

My gut twisted watching Clark's punch snap Dad's head to the side. Blood dripped from his swollen mouth. He shifted, teeth sinking into the meat of his challenger's calf. With a vicious tug, he ripped flesh and tendons free. Clark grunted in pain, but instead of going down, he morphed into his wolf form.

They clashed again and again, man against man, beast against beast, taking pieces of each other without either gaining the upper hand. The lawn was spattered in their blood.

Avery grabbed my hand when my father's wolf pinned her dad mid-shift, releasing a brutal growl that carried his Alpha power, keeping him down. It worked for a moment, seeming like the challenge would end with my father victorious.

Then Clark broke through, managing to get his paws under Dad's stomach to kick him off. He took advantage of my father's momentary distraction to launch himself at him, swiping at his stomach with his claws when he knocked him to his side.

The attack slowed Dad down, giving Clark more opportunity to turn the tables on him. He took too long to get up after Clark charged him.

My heart rose into my throat. I'd already lost my mother when I was a pup. I couldn't lose my father, too.

No one was to interfere with an official challenge against the alpha. I knew that, even as I bolted into the circle on instinct, realizing the next blow would be the last.

"No! Caden!" Avery shouted, trying to hold me back.

I shook her off, pushing my legs to be faster. I skidded across the slippery grass, coming between them. Clark hesitated, but he didn't stop. His claws sliced through my shirt at my shoulder, ripping through my skin. My collarbone broke beneath the force and I tumbled back into my father's wolf.

His bark was full of fury. I scrambled to my feet to face Clark, knowing I was breaking every rule of a challenge. I couldn't just fucking stand there and watch it play out.

Clark's wolf knocked me out of the way. I gritted my teeth and pressed a hand to my bleeding shoulder. The claw marks left deep gashes and I didn't have the full strength of my wolf yet to speed up my healing. I spun around, intent on doing something to stop this.

It was over. By the time I was knocked aside and turned back to the fight, my father found the opening he needed and finished Clark. His wolf stood over Clark's, muzzle coated in the blood of his torn out throat.

Avery's scream shook me from my stupor. Why would her dad challenge mine? Anger swirled in my gut and the pain in my shoulder made my heart race.

I stalked to the edge of the circle while my father shifted back, dragging her away from hugging Liam.

"You—you're in on it. You fucking knew," I seethed. "You lured me out of here so I wouldn't be around."

Her amber eyes shone with her welling tears. "I, Caden, I didn't! I—my father—"

At her hitched breath, I grabbed her by her upper arms and shook her, ignoring the searing pain in my injured shoulder. "What? Tell me right now."

I might only be the Alpha heir, but I don't need the power of an Alpha command to make her confess to me.

"I didn't know," she swore between hiccuped gasps. "He said, he... All he said to me was that he had to convince Dempsey to listen about my mom."

My eyes narrowed dangerously. "He made you an enemy of the alpha clan, Avery."

My jaw clenches as I bury the memory in my mind. I was right to reject Avery.

I have to be. Because if I'm wrong about any of this...I'm no better than a monster for condemning her to the fate of living with a broken mate bond.

She'll never feel complete with anyone else, enduring a lifetime of longing never fulfilled.

An uncomfortable burning sensation grows in my chest. I ignore it.

It's near dawn when measured footfalls approach. I angle my head to the side just enough to see Liam without taking my attention completely off the cottage. His hands are in his pockets, pace slow and unthreatening.

"You stayed out here all night?" he observes in an overly neutral tone.

I grunt. He offers me the pair of pants folded over his arm. I accept them and yank them on.

"I tried to come over a few times to report on the run, but you were growling loud enough I couldn't get close," he says.

I pass a hand over my mouth, grounding myself with the scrape of stubble. Was I? Shit.

Clearing my throat, I turn my back on the cabin. It takes far more effort than it should. I blink at the blinding rays of sunlight rising above the treetops.

"The run?" I prompt.

"All good. A few curious about following you, but they were easily steered away." He rubs at his nape. "By the way, I put Taryn Barnes in the hold last night for stealing."

I huff. "What else is new? Put her on the usual punishment duty."

"Your sister, too. Callie was the distraction."

"Of course she was."

I press my thumb and finger into my eyelids to alleviate the dull throb building there, an echo of my father's admonition surfacing from my memories. I did the best I could raising Callie once he passed, yet still I feel like I'm failing him.

"Anything else to report?"

"The liaison from Timber Hollow Pack arrived this morning. I put them in one of the guest rooms in your lodge. You have a meeting scheduled with her at eleven."

Right. She's going pack to pack to review preliminary planning for the upcoming summit.

I glance at the dilapidated cabin. "I'll be down in an hour. My wolf's still a bit, ah..."

"Out of sorts?" Liam suggests with a hint of amusement.

He can laugh all he wants. I don't have time for this shit.

"Sure. Let's go with that."

He claps me on the shoulder. "So if you're not around in an hour, I should come up to drag you down to the commons for work?"

I rumble in response. He takes it as a yes before leaving me to wrestle with my wolf to let me walk the fuck away.

11

AVERY

As IF LAST night wasn't bad enough, Caden's standing proud in front of my house for some unknown reason, every inch of his carved body giving off an undeniable vibe of raw Alpha power. *Every* inch, because he's stark naked.

A noise sticks in my throat when I catch myself staring at his huge—I snap my gaze away with a huff. He has every she-wolf in the pack panting after him whether he notices their rapt attention on him whenever he's around or not. I won't be lusting after him, too.

He's fixated on the cottage. I watch him until the sky begins to lighten with the impending sunrise, frowning when he remains a still, muscled sentry.

The broken bond is less raw this morning. I'll live with it. It just means ignoring the twinge of what I imagine a hot poker to the chest would be like every time I look at him.

This is fine. Totally fine.

An absolutely manageable pain screaming in every movement.

I've survived the worst things imaginable, what's one more gash to my heart at his hand?

I first spotted him through the window when I got up with the sun to check on Lena, not liking the hacking sound of her cough.

His surly growling must be what made the windows rattle in the early hours before dawn. I'm so used to the wind knocking the loose panes around in the rotting frames, I wrote it off, too drained from my first shift to bother stuffing rags against them to muffle the noise.

My wolf seems pleased by his presence, though she's content as she is, stretched out and licking her paws. The only indication she gives that she's aware of him are her pricked ears poised to listen for him.

Rolling my eyes, I pretend he's not there. He's ridiculous, probably suspicious enough of me suddenly finding out I have a wolf and the ability to shift, that he's come up here himself.

A thrill swoops through me. I have a wolf. I bite my lip around a smile, marveling at the new sensation of my connection with her. She preens, tail wagging.

I'm so lost in thought over it, I drop the pot of honey I want to add to Lena's tea on my foot. Cursing, I bang my fist on the counter.

An answering growl sounds from outside, loud enough to wake my sisters when it grows closer, as if Caden took several strides towards the cottage. I glare at the wall as if I'll be able to burn a hole straight through it.

"Go bark up some other tree," I mutter while picking up the sticky, broken pieces.

This was my last jar. I got a whole crate of it in town from a beekeeper the baker knows because the price is too high at the commissary on the ground floor of the bunkhouse. For the likes of me, anyway. It was a big enough pot to last us through winter.

Lena's scratchy cough draws my attention. She rolls over with a feeble murmur and Beatrix automatically rubs her back in sleep.

The kitchens have honey in their stores. If I butter old Alma up with an anti-inflammatory paste for the arthritis she's developed in her hands, she might look the other way. I'll have to hope the head cook is feeling as doting as she used to when I was a pup, or that her hands are beginning to ache more with the cooler weather.

I salvage what I can of the spilled honey to add to the rusted tin kettle, then clean away the rest. By the time I'm finished preparing the girls oatmeal with dried wild raspberries I foraged over summer, the sun has risen above the trees, shining through the narrow windowpanes. Dust motes dance in the spotlight.

With my enhanced senses, my vision is sharper, allowing me to see much more detail than I previously could. I thought it was only last night while I was running in fur for the first time, everything appearing so new and vivid. If I concentrate, I can hear a bird making a nest beneath the eaves of our roof, a family of mice chittering in my herb garden, and the rasp of mucus in Lena's chest. I swallow, hoping it's not turning into pneumonia again.

This is the full strength I was born to have as a shifter, and it means I'll be able to use my heightened senses to forage better for plants that can be difficult to find.

A thump at the door startles me out of my thoughts. My wolf lifts her nose with an interested sniff. I smell it, too. Cedar, though the warm comforting scent is more like it's been heating for too long over a fire. Caden, and he's not happy.

"Let's get this over with," I say with a resigned sigh.

I open the door, steeled to face the alpha along with the pain of rejection all over again. The overpowering scent of Caden all around the cottage weakens my knees. My wolf rolls on her back, mewling.

Except he's not there. I blink, searching the sloping meadow.

He's left a deer on the stoop. My mouth hangs open when I realize it's the same one I tracked and failed to take down on my own last night.

I scan the area again, wondering why he'd bother bringing me meat. Especially after he made it clear last night by rejecting me in front of the entire pack that he wanted nothing to do with me.

Hesitation stops me from kicking it off the porch to the ground. Meat's hard enough for us to come by. I can't afford to be picky about where it comes from just because I would rather ingest poison foxglove and chew on the rusty nails holding this place together before eating anything Caden provided me.

Good mate, my wolf pipes up. *Provider.*

I bare my teeth at nothing since she's inside me. She's wrong. I'm the one that provides for my sisters. I don't need his charity handouts.

I don't know what she's in such a great mood over. By rejecting me, it means he rejects her, too. She gives a nasty yip, snapping her teeth. Whatever, she's on her own to figure it out.

Still, I'm not turning down the offering. Meat is meat, and to get it I didn't have to listen to vulgar suggestions about how I could earn an extra helping of food from pack males like Lorne and his brothers, Dane and Weston, trying to show off their superior rank to the cohorts that hang around them.

I just needed my fated mate to reject me, and then, I don't know, feel guilty enough about it to leave me with this consolation prize. *Sorry I don't want you, the least I can do is offer you a meal.* Asshole.

My lips thin into a line before I haul the carcass into my arms, mildly appeased by the fact I'm strong enough to do it now.

Once I take care of the deer, I grab my clipping shears and a basket before strolling the rows of my herb garden. I reach the candleflower, glad it's still in bloom thanks to the tricks Jade the traveling witch taught me to make my herbs last past their blooming seasons in the high altitude of Silver Mountain. This will help soothe Lena's coughing and hopefully open her lungs.

Beatrix is up when I come back inside. She prods at the oatmeal with a wooden spoon.

"Do you ever get tired of oatmeal? I'd much rather have bacon."

"It's good for you." I pull her hair from her sleep-mussed braid and redo it for her. She allows it, swatting me off only when I fuss with the ends. "They don't serve anything this packed with nutri-ents down in the dining hall. Only greasy bacon, eggs, and sugared cornbread."

She mumbles a complaint, rubbing her stomach. "But it's bacon."

My lips twitch. "Fine. I'll snag you some if Alma has any left. I have to go down there to talk to her. Make sure Lena finishes the whole teapot, okay?"

"Okay."

"Thanks."

She snatches my hand before I move away, pulling me back in with a curious sniff. "You smell different. Wait, no, not different. More you, but also something else."

My stomach clenches, worried her stronger nose can pick up remnants of Caden from when he had me in his arms before he shoved me away.

"I shifted," I explain. "I'm not sure how it happened so late, but I have a wolf. Is that what you smell?"

"Avery!" Her eyes widen and she throws her arms around me. "This is amazing. What was it like? Is she beautiful? Tell me everything."

"Later," I say with a laugh.

I lay out the candleflower on my workbench and make quick work of stripping the yellow blooms to brew in tea, the leaves that are still perky with life to make a syrup with, and save the stalks to dry out by hanging them from the rafters overhead with the rest of my dried herbal collection. When I'm finished, I set it aside and mix up a paste for Alma's arthritis.

The routine brings a moment of normalcy to ground me. Lena and Beatrix chat softly while I work, sharing a bowl of oatmeal. It allows me to push down the ever-present ache in my chest until it's bearable. I don't know how long it takes for a rejected bond to fade since there's no one in recent memory in our pack to compare this experience with, but I hope it's soon.

I give both of my sisters a kiss on the head before leaving for the commons. The dining pavilion is packed outside the hall. Small pups chase each other between the outdoor seating and two stone fireplaces with excited squeals, much to their tired dams' annoyance as they call after them to come eat. Fresh brewed coffee and the delectable scent of bacon makes my mouth water.

For a moment, I'm struck by a pang of longing to be part of the laughter over shared baskets of steaming cornbread and platters of fried eggs.

Shaking it off, I bypass the doors between the fireplaces that lead inside to head around back. The kitchen is bustling with the morning rush for breakfast by the time I poke my head in.

Alma's barking orders while mixing the next batch of cornbread batter. I hurry over with a full pitch prepared, only to be cut off by her before I open my mouth.

"Oh! Good, you're here," she says.

"Uh, yes?"

Is she psychic in her old age, too? She'd better watch it, or the pack will start calling her the next witchling. I fight to keep a smirk off my face.

She waves me off. "Well, don't just stand there, pup. I need someone on bacon at the far burner. Don't gape at me, go before it burns."

I open and close my mouth, brows pinched. I want to point out to her that I haven't been a kid in a long time, but she's dismissed me, groaning when she bends to load a pan of batter into the oven.

"Welcome to kitchen duty," Taryn says as I pass her.

"What?"

"I know. It sucks the most, definitely more than maintenance or laundry. At least on those rotations you get breaks. The kitchens are grueling work." She frowns, waving a spatula. "Liam knows I hate cooking because it's so much standing around waiting, so naturally I get assigned here every time I'm caught. That uptight bastard thinks it's funny."

I shake my head. "I'm still not following. Why does Alma think I'm also here to work?"

"You didn't see the new rotations posted this morning at Alpha Blackburn's lodge? You're on it."

"Great." Air gusts from my lungs.

Caden can take that deer and shove it up his perfectly toned ass. This is yet another way for him to punish me for things that aren't my fault. I didn't pick for us to be fated anymore than he did.

I'm usually left off the shared job duties. In the first few months of Caden's reign after Alpha Dempsey passed away, every job I was put on ended up causing a disruption because people either didn't want to be around me or they got aggressive to assert their dominant rank over me so I'd known my place was at the bottom of the hierarchy. I didn't dare go to Caden to tell him how the workloads were dumped on me or that I never received my cut of payment. Eventually, my name stopped appearing on the roster.

"Enough yapping, get to work or you'll be explaining to Alpha Blackburn why breakfast is delayed," Alma grouses.

I sigh, taking over the abandoned pan of sizzling bacon. When the rush slows down, I'll talk to Alma about the honey I want. Taryn chats my ear off. Despite being one of the few packmates to remain friendly, it's more than she's spoken to me in seven years. I don't hate it.

"You're burning that," I point out.

She spares the charring eggs an uninterested glance. "Feed them to Tobin. He'll eat anything."

"Can I just—?" I take her spatula and scrape the well-done eggs into a serving dish.

Unlike times in the past where it was clear all the work was being forced on me, this isn't so bad. She's still helping, I just take over when she loses track of the task.

"Avery!" Alma calls after I've cooked two platters and saved Taryn's batches of eggs from getting too crispy.

I turn off the burner and jog the last few steps when Alma beckons me impatiently. She shoves a large serving tray packed with food into my hands.

"Take the cornbread to the head table for a refill, then these other dishes go to the elders' tables and this one can go to the unmated males and females at the back."

Despite my best efforts to keep my face neutral, my expression gives me away.

"No pouting, now. Serving's part of duties here. Get used to it."

She nudges me and returns her attention to a male leaning against the counter talking to Emily, a she-wolf who usually comes to see me after she's fooled around with whoever's caught her fancy. She hasn't acknowledged me once since I've been here.

"How many times do I have to remind you not to stand around? If you've got time to stand, you're not working hard enough," Alma blusters.

If either of them had time to idle, they could've served this food instead of me. I glance at Taryn and she gives me a thumbs up. She's not the one who has to go serve her jerk of an alpha fresh off a mate bond rejection.

Rolling my shoulders back, I brave the swinging double doors with my chin held high. The din of chatter pauses. Caden's blue eyes snap to me for a beat, then slide past me as if I don't exist. Callie and Liam glance from me to Caden between them, then to each other. Everyone else resumes eating, but I feel the weight of their gazes following me as I make my way to his table first.

The closer I get, the more the bond acts up to remind me it's there, throbbing in my chest. As though proximity will somehow magically knit the spurned connection back together.

He's deep in conversation with Liam while I plop the corn-bread baskets in front of him. He doesn't pause, though the corners of his mouth turn down. A sharp pain twinges in my nerve endings and I stifle a gasp, refusing to allow him to see me hurting.

My wolf's not impressed with the ignoring act. She also wants to steal the bacon off his plate, and I need to focus on standing still instead of darting my hand out. My mind stutters over the division of my own complex emotions and her baser impulses.

Liam clears his throat when I linger. I jolt, ignoring the snickers from Lorne and his brothers at the other table full of Cormac's side of Blackburns nearby.

Lorne's grating laugh cuts off when I move to the other table of elders before serving Cormac's. He strides over, leaning over me to grab the platter of bacon I set down.

"That goes to my father's table," Lorne corrects.

A cup slams down on the head table hard enough to break something, possibly the table going by the violent crack of wood echoing through the room. It's followed by a harsh snarl from Caden that makes Lorne stiffen. He steps out of my space, but still blocks my way once I've given the table the other plate.

An irritated rumble sounds in my chest. I should shift. Charge Lorne and knock him down. Make him submit to me with my teeth around his neck. I pinch my thigh to anchor myself before my wolf makes this situation worse by challenging him.

"There's an order to these things, little witchling. Get it right."

Rather than take the food he wanted first so badly, he dumps it on the floor. The room is silent except for Cormac's husky chuckle.

Lorne lifts a brow. "Well? Clean it up."

His brothers can't contain their laughter any longer. I don't dare look to Caden, though his presence suffocates me from several feet away, eyes boring into my back.

"Enough. Sit down, Lorne," Caden bites out.

He ignores the order for a few seconds, holding my gaze. Then he backs away, tracking me as I finish handing out the remaining dishes on my way back to the kitchen to look for a broom and dustpan.

The whispering's worse when I return. I set my jaw and silently clean up Lorne's mess as my stomach burns. Part of me wants to dump it in his lap. It's what he deserves, but I'd rather not paint a bigger target on my back than there already is.

Without a word, I leave the hall and almost collide with Taryn. She eyes the dustpan in my hand curiously.

"What happened out there? The alpha sounded pissed. We heard it over Alma's barking."

"It's nothing."

"Yeah, okay. That's why your face looks like that and your eye is twitching."

"Nothing," I repeat. "It's fine. Just male posturing. Lorne always making sure I don't forget my place."

She tosses an unimpressed look through the small window in the door. "I hope a witch curses his dick. That'd take him down at least twenty pegs."

"I'd pay to see that." I stifle a surprised smile, not used to having anyone take my side other than my sisters.

"He deserves it." She flips off the door with a gesture I've seen the humans in Ashbury use when they're angry with each other.

A snort escapes me. It helps chase away the indignation upsetting my stomach.

I keep busy enough that Alma doesn't make me go back out there again, sending Emily when she catches her flirting instead of cooking. It works great to keep me off serving responsibilities, but by the time the breakfast shift ends Alma's nowhere in sight.

"Where did Alma go?" I ask Taryn.

"Home for a nap. Martine manages the kitchen for lunch," she answers.

"Oh, I wanted to talk to her." I thumb the tin of paste shoved into my pocket.

"Good luck. She's grouchy with anyone who tries to wake her up before she's snoozed for at least three hours."

There goes my plan. I'll have to try to catch her later to bribe her for letting me access the honey stores.

Taryn balances two plates of food and nudges me through the back door. The others on kitchen duty are eating together. She leads us to a shady patch of grass and plops down.

"I put some extra on yours. I didn't see your sisters and thought you'd want to take some back for them," she says.

I chew my lip, peeking at her. "What's up with that?"

"With what?" She's tearing into her food, stacking her eggs and bacon on her cornbread to make a sandwich.

"Talking to me. Being...nice."

She shrugs. "You're pack. Why wouldn't I talk to you?"

A lump forms in my throat. I pick at the food on my plate.

"You haven't talked to me in a long time. I mean, not like this. Like it matters."

Taryn stops eating to level me with a look. "Part of that is because you stay pretty secluded. Since—you know."

"Yeah."

"I don't have any problem with you, Avery. You're the girl who would braid my hair so that I didn't get it all tangled while I played with Callie because I told you it hurt when my mom brushed it. You taught me how to swim. And the time I ate those wild berries I shouldn't have, you were the one to run all the way back to the commons to get the healer."

I nibble on a piece of bacon, closing my eyes to keep the emotion clogging my throat at bay. If I hadn't made a point of making myself scarce, would I have kept some of the friendships I believed were lost?

She bumps her shoulder against mine, and I don't move away.

12

CADEN

THE SCENE at breakfast has me wrestling my wolf into submission before he takes my skin and fucks everything up by attacking Lorne again without an official challenge. It was hard enough to keep my attention from drifting to Avery the moment she stepped through the doors to the kitchen. Next to impossible to ignore her when she came near, tantalizing me with that divine scent I need to wipe from my memory.

Watching him get that close to her—again—as if he has a right to, mere fucking hours after I came close to tearing his throat out for it?

It's a miracle I managed to restrain myself, only going as far as breaking the table instead of every damned bone in my cousin's body.

Putting Avery on kitchen rotation was a mistake. I thought it would be best to show the pack nothing's changed after last night.

I'm fooling myself because everything feels so different.

Everything about her entices me. Tempts me to take her as mine.

To learn if her caramel hair is as soft as I've wondered when I wind it around my fist and use it as leverage to make her bare the delicate column of her throat for me. To see if it'll make her amber eyes flash in the audacious way that lights my veins on fire. To knead the dip of her waist and map her slight curves as I take my time scenting her, scraping my stubbled jaw over her skin until she smells so much like me no other male will come near her.

My wolf is amped up, prodding me to go find my female. Now, right *now*. I jerk with the force of his pull on my will, exhaling forcefully.

If I don't find a way to keep him in check, this mate bond will continue upturning the careful order I've strived for to run this pack smoothly. I rejected her, so my life should return to normal. A sharp buzz pings around inside my chest. I rub at it with an annoyed grimace.

Callie leans against the wall behind the broken head table, arms folded. Her sour assessment of me prods at what's left of my patience.

"What?" I ask through my teeth. "Are you pissed off because Liam made you face the consequences of your actions with Taryn last night? Tough."

She scoffs, shaking her head. "You're an idiot."

My head jerks. "Your undermining isn't funny. It's time you grow up, isn't it? Think of what Dad would say. I've told you a hundred times, everything reflects back on me. So when you follow Taryn's wild impulses—"

"Yeah, yeah. Follow your rules, set good examples, blah fucking blah," she snaps with an eyeroll. "I didn't mean that. It wasn't a big deal, anyway."

"I beg to differ," Liam interjects behind me. "How do you think it looks to have the alpha's own family doing as she pleases?"

She serves him a withering stare before turning it on me. "If you can't figure out why you're an idiot, goddess help us all."

My jaw sets when she stomps off. I scrub my face, adding one of her tantrums to my list of shit I don't need right now.

"Let's go."

Liam falls into step with me when we exit the building. "I take it your wolf's still attached to Av—"

"Yes." I whirl on him with a growl, fur sprouting across my forearms.

He freezes, lifting his brows. The outburst attracts attention from people milling around the commons. I grunt, shaking off the sense I need to fight my loyal beta and best friend. What's wrong with me? He's my trusted right hand man, not my enemy because he said her name.

"Sorry. I'm just—fuck. I don't know."

"Don't look at me." Liam smirks. "It's not like I know what happens when you reject the Fates' plan. This is why I'm more inclined to keep things strictly casual between me and any female interested in a night together. Maybe that's what you need to sort this out."

"*No.*"

This time the wolf rides me so hard I nearly choke on the thundering growl. It startles several birds from the trees. Liam bends his neck, as do the people dotted around the central lawn when my glare shifts around. I blow out a breath and shake off the intense power of my wolf.

"It must be an aftereffect," I mutter. "I'm handling it. We just need to go about our usual business, and in a few days it'll fade away."

It has to.

He stares at me. I can tell he wants to say something else, but he keeps his mouth shut as we head for my office in the lodge.

I barely manage to focus on a review of various trade teams. One's asking for personnel reassignments and another's put in a request for a new auger for drilling fence holes because they insist the one we have is busted and they're fed up with repairing it. I'll have Neil go over. If the mechanic can figure out how to keep the engines running on every vehicle we have, hopefully he'll be able to troubleshoot an alternative to get the thing running until after the summit.

Every few minutes, the words blur together. My mind strays to rain drenched meadows, and bright amber irises that dare me to chase, to hunt my prize and claim what's mine.

Adam bursts in. The youngest enforcer added to the patrol roster last year is a welcome interruption from my wayward thoughts. Liam stops him with a hand to the chest before he rushes my desk.

"What's the problem?" Liam urges.

"It's—Alpha, you need to come," Adam blurts.

I exchange a tense look with Liam and rise. "What's happened?"

"It's maintenance group C. They're on my patrol route. They wouldn't stop."

The three of us are on the move, Liam signaling for Ford to leave his post in the hall. Adam explains on the way that the group was causing a scene and turning on itself.

The raucous fighting echoes through the trees before we round a bend in the road, finding maintenance group C brawling. Two have shifted while the rest throw punches. It's unclear who the instigators are at first glance. Their truck is in a ditch at the side of the road and their tools are strewn everywhere.

Liam and Ford enter the fray, shouting orders to stop. One stocky female holds off one guy while elbowing another who charges her. An older male spots me and snarls.

"*Enough,*" I boom.

The fighting ceases, even Ford and Liam jerking to a stop midmovement from my Alpha command. I ease back to free them and they round up the three Adam points out as the cause of the scene.

I pace before the lineup, arms crossed. "What the fuck is going on here? Why are you turning on your packmates?"

"They didn't think they needed to work anymore," says a male who has shifted back and prods at his swollen eye. "When we tried to stop them, they did that to the truck."

"This is unacceptable. You've destroyed pack property and attacked the members of your group without cause."

"We got cause," the youngest male jeers.

He can't be more than eighteen. I stop in front of him, staring him down until he falters and lowers his gaze to glare at my shoes.

"And how long have you been assigned to team C?"

"Six months too fucking long," the older one beside him complains. "I'm sick of it. I ain't doin' no more."

The other two pipe up with similar sentiments.

"It doesn't give you a right to do this. The job rotations mean everyone pulls their weight and puts in their fair share," I say. "If you want to remain part of this pack, you contribute no matter what the pack requires of you. It's so we're all working together."

"I didn't sign up for it," he objects.

I shake my head. "And what do you expect instead?"

"What I been promised!"

My eyes narrow. "What promise?"

"Promise of somethin' better. Not working to the bone doing grunt work day in and day out. Not this bullshit life you're forcing on me with a rule and schedule for every little thing, down to when I shit."

Liam jerks him with a warning snarl for his outright disrespect, forcing his head to bow. "Watch how you talk to our alpha. Where did you hear that?"

"Jana's tavern," he spits.

I go rigid. The seedy tavern is where I've heard my uncle is known to harp about how good he had it coming up under my grandfather until he wasn't named heir. There's no doubt in my mind this traces back to him influencing drunken packmates who feel overworked and overlooked. If he sways enough of them to splinter the pack into factions, I'll lose the footing I've busted my ass to stabilize in the wake of the trouble with the Morgans turning on my father.

The pack won't survive a second revolt.

"Liam, Ford, take them to the patrol cabin," I order.

"Don't worry, we'll deal with them," Liam says.

"Alpha Dempsey never shoulda named you his heir," the older male gripes as he's dragged off.

I pinch the bridge of my nose and turn to the rest of the workers. "Let's get this cleaned up. I'll have the other teams from maintenance send over replacements until this is all resolved so your group won't be shorthanded."

The she-wolf that held her own against two of the workers in the fight gives me an approving smile. "You heard the alpha."

I help them get their truck out of the ditch the other three drove it into and stay with them until everything's righted. By the time we're done, the minor injuries from the fight have healed and they offer to share their lunch with me.

"Thank you. I would, but I have to get back. Your efforts are an important part of the community. If you have any problems or wish for a reassignment, come see my office."

"You don't have to tell us," Candace, the strong female, says with a hearty chuckle. "There's no such thing as a pack full of people that can scratch their asses all day, or nothing would ever get done. Someone's gotta do this, and right now it's us. Honestly, I like this assignment better than my last one in laundry. I like being outdoors all day."

I nod in appreciation, thanking each of them again before I head back to the lodge.

Dealing with the disgruntled maintenance workers makes me late getting back in time for my meeting with Timber Hollow Pack's liaison.

"Apologies," I say when I stride into my office. "There was an urgent matter I needed to resolve."

The last thing I need is other packs hearing I don't have things in hand. It won't help my bid for better trade agreements if they think we're in shambles.

The liaison is old enough to be my mother, with her blonde hair pulled into a severe bun. She gives me a judicious once over.

"Thank you for fitting me into your busy day, Alpha Blackburn. Gina of Timber Hollow Pack."

I shake her hand. "I hope your travels were pleasant."

"Quite. The foothills between here and Timber Hollow's forest to the south are beautiful this time of year."

"Let's get right into it," I suggest.

She loses some of her curtness and launches into an overview of this year's gathering. The packs first come together for a welcome feast celebrating our continued harmony before any updates are made to the accords.

As she talks about the formal meeting following the feast, my focus derails. I swear I catch a hint of honeysuckle in bloom and drowsy summer showers spent on the porch through the cracks in the window.

Avery.

My wolf is more interested in following her heavenly scent than sitting through the meeting. Instead of fighting his influence over my instincts again, I hesitate. Her scent acts like a drug that leaves me in a disorienting haze that fills my mind with her, her, *her*.

Everything I shut down floods back in. My imagination is out of control, supplying me with a vivid recreation of the first moments the bond unfurled.

The way she felt pressed against me last night, with her hand splayed on my chest sparks heat in my veins. She fits in my arms so perfectly. Her bright eyes captivatingly locked on me, so soft and lovely. Those full lips parting in awe, inviting me to claim something I used to dream of with her, even after things changed between us.

I struggle to shut down the line of thought, failing to remember why I shouldn't want to kiss her to learn what sounds she makes. Or find out the answer to the burning question I've always wondered—if she tastes as delicious as she smells.

"Alpha Blackburn?"

I stiffen, tuning back in. The liaison peers at me expectantly. I missed the question.

Damn it, this meeting has been on my schedule for weeks. It's important, and I'm sitting here thinking of Avery in every way I shouldn't be. My fist clenches.

Fate changes nothing. I'll never go there with her.

"You've selected the members of your pack you'll be attending the Pack Summit with?" she repeats.

"Yes. We're still appointing volunteers to help Timber Wolf Pack put on the event." As part of the accords, the summit's host bears the brunt of the work with help from each pack to bring us all together. "This list has the Silver Falls Pack members joining me as part of my entourage."

She takes the paper and scans it, copying names down. "And just to confirm for the headcount of your group, you are unmated? I don't see one included here."

"That's correct. I don't have a ma—"

The end of my sentence becomes garbled, my wolf jerking control from me with a howl that rattles the windows. He's pissed at me and the female for discounting his mate. My nails become claws and my arm swings across the desk without my permission, knocking a stack of paperwork to the floor.

The wolf is done with this. He wants to leave, to spend the day at his mate's side. I won't let him take my skin, gritting my teeth until I have him locked away where all my thoughts of Avery should remain—buried in my mind.

I clear my throat, gripping the armrests so hard that my shifted claws dig into the lacquered wood while my expression settles into a blank mask. Rather than apologize or make excuses for my wolf, I plow on with the meeting.

"I'll send a final headcount for the group ahead of the gathering."

"Very well." She quirks her brow. "Please do so with at least three weeks notice so arrangements can be finalized."

I'll be hearing about this outburst from Alistair when she returns to his territory. Great.

"Of course."

She shuffles her notes and stands. "Thank you for your cooperation and accommodation, Alpha Blackburn. We look forward to hosting this year's event and seeing your pack there."

I nod, shaking her hand. "Thanks."

Once she's out of my office, I lean my elbows on the desk and rest my head between my hands. An insistent tug yanks an invisible cord rooted in my chest. Fucking mate bond.

13

———

AVERY

SOMETHING WAKES me with a gasp in the middle of the night. I scramble to sit up, straining my ears.

There it is again, outside my window. Even with better sight, the cloudy night makes it too dark to make out any detail besides the fur of a huge dark shadow. I hope my garden plots haven't attracted bears again.

I slip from the sheets and grab a knife from my satchel hanging on the wall, then creep to the window.

The beast lifts its head, snout raised and ears forward with interest. It's not a bear.

I lower my small knife. It's Caden. He's out there again, this time as his wolf.

Sighing, I brace on the windowsill while he paces outside my room. He rises to his hind legs to sniff at the trim. I squint, tilting my head. He seems more beast than man at the moment.

I'm inclined to believe Caden's not in the driver's seat, so to speak, because there's no way he'd come out here at two in the morning for no reason.

"I don't know what you're doing out there."

He whines, pawing at the ledge. Majestic golden eyes find mine through the smudged panes of glass, begging. Definitely not

Caden, then. I lift a brow and his wolf lowers his head to rest on his paws.

"I'm not letting you in."

He gives a grunt of complaint. I can't believe I'm arguing with a wolf.

I glance at the door, listening to my sisters' even breathing. Sliding my lips together, I give in to curiosity and wrestle with the window to get it halfway open.

Caden's wolf pushes his head through before I've moved back, sniffing at my hands, licking my wrist, then wedging his nose in my armpit with a happy rumble.

"Okay, wait, *wait*," I hiss when he tries to squeeze his massive body through the tiny window.

He nuzzles into my neck when I hesitantly run my fingers through his fur. I'm surprised to find it's thick and soft beneath the outer coat. I scratch behind his ears and a laugh bubbles out of me at the way he melts with a groan.

"I hope you don't remember any of this when you shift back to your usual self." I smile wryly. "I prefer you this way. You're way less of a dick."

I spend far longer than I should petting him. When he finally lets me go back to bed, I hear him pacing outside. I sense it in the bond when he settles on the opposite side of the wall where my bed is.

I cover my chest with a hand, and instead of the constant burning ache, the magic of the bond is warm. Almost comforting.

)))●(((

After three days of enduring kitchen duty, forced mingling with the pack, and Caden's wolf spending every night outside my window, I'm going stir crazy. I want to shift again, but more than that, I need to get out of here.

The kitchen stores don't have anything else I need to fight Lena's cold before it progresses into a full-blown respiratory infection. Yesterday I cornered Alma the first chance I got and buttered her up with the paste I made for her stiff joints. She looked the other way while I took two jars of honey.

I know the town has a fall harvest festival coming up where I could obtain better quality honey from the beekeeper than what the pack imports because it's cheaper. It's too risky to try to get all the way to town with the increased patrols and tightening of Caden's rules since the bonfire—his answer to everything when something threatens order in the pack. Once again, a Morgan is the source of that something.

Going to town might be out, but I do know of some good spots beyond the edges of pack territory that could still have useful plants. The trick will be finding the opening in the patrol schedule now that my usual spot where Caden found me has round the clock supervision from his security team.

Taryn's fiery red hair snares my interest as she stumbles in late under Alma's watchful eye. Her reputation for skirting the rules might be just what I need.

She comes over and busies herself with the bag of flour I'm scooping from until Alma's attention is off us.

"Morning," I say with a hint of amusement. "Did you get lost?"

She frowns into the flour. "Liam's the reason I'm late."

My brows lift. A laugh puffs out of her.

"No, not like that. He shows up to make sure I don't skip out on my assigned rotation, but then he ends up lecturing me like I'm a misbehaved pup." She rolls her eyes. "He drives me crazy."

I hum with a smirk, adding eggs to the bowl to make batter for the pancakes Ace and Emily are cooking on a large griddle. We work quietly for a while until I decide to just ask her outright.

"Hey, uh. I've heard you have a way of evading the enforcers," I whisper.

Taryn's bright blue eyes sparkle and she lights up with a playful smile. "Yeah, why? You want to sneak out?"

I bite my lip, glancing furtively around to make sure no one overhears before nodding. "It's important. My usual route is under constant watch."

"Done."

"I can—wait, done?"

"You can count on me to get you out. I know a spot that's always overlooked no matter how many times they switch up the schedule."

"Thank you." My shoulders sag with relief.

Alma clears her throat, scrutinizing us as she comes over to collect the pancake batter.

"How's the medicine working out? Does it help with stiffness and swelling in your knuckles?" I ask her.

Alma flexes her hand, mouth slanted as close to a smile as she gets. "It does the trick."

Taryn leans in to mutter in my ear when she moves on. "Meet me at the tree with the knot that looks like a face after sunset."

The rest of our morning shift passes fast enough that I'm hurrying back to the cottage to check on Lena before noon while Beatrix is still at her school lessons. Lena should be attending lessons at her age, too. I've been too nervous to let her go. I don't have to worry about Bea holding her own like I would with Lena.

When I leave the dining pavilion, the main lawn is crawling with young shifters doing training exercises for the pack's enforcer team. Tryouts must have started.

One group is blindfolded while Liam barks orders at them to scent where he and the other high-ranking lieutenants are. Another group of males and females are being tested on their agility, shifting back and forth between forms. Caden evaluates them with his arms folded while one of the enforcers from his father's reign marks down times on a clipboard.

I pick up my pace, scolding myself for slowing to observe the stretch of his rolled up flannel sleeves around his magnificent forearms. A spicy hint of sun-baked cedar tickles my nose until I leave the commons.

Once I'm home, I prepare another poultice and smear it on

Lena's chest. She chatters happily about the plot of the book she's reading. It's the same one she's read a hundred times, but I listen with a soft smile.

"The dragon shifter has been cursed to guard the tallest tower, and every year the humans in the provincial town below have to select a maiden to send as a sacrifice to avoid the dragon's wrath. Except this maiden *volunteers* to go because she wants to seek revenge for her older sister being the sacrifice the previous year." She clutches the book and peers over the pages at me. "And guess what happens when she gets to the dragon's tower?"

I curl her silky hair behind her ears. "You've told me before. Sort of spoils the surprise reveal."

"I know, but guess anyway. It's more fun."

I play along. "Does she...slay the dragon and succeed in her revenge?"

Lena gasps for effect. "No! She can't bring herself to do it because the dragon shifter is her True Mate! Their love is written by the Fates. He's been waiting for her for over a thousand years after his rival killed her in a previous life."

"The humans really come up with the wildest ideas about supernatural beings since they learned of us."

"I love it," Lena gushes. "They write it so romantically. It makes me want to go on a grand adventure and fall in love with a forbidden fated mate."

It amazes me that she never complains about her health. When coughing tires her out, I read her book to her until she falls asleep again. Her breathing is still too raspy for my liking.

Sometimes I wish human medicine worked on shifters, but our metabolism flushes it out of our systems too quickly for it to make any difference. Most don't fall ill the way Lena does, other than those who lose their True Mates and grow heartsick.

If only I could control real magic, like Jade's. I've looked for her coven in the mountains to seek out their help with Lena's health, but I haven't seen any signs of them in years.

The extent of my capabilities are basic at best after her guidance. I use simple methods to improve my chances of cultivating soil that isn't perfect, like adding a blessing circle around the border of the garden. Or lengthening the lifespan of my crops by working with the natural magic of the land rather than truly producing magic the way a witch can.

Beatrix bursts through the door, the racket waking Lena. "You weren't going to tell us?"

"Tell you what?" I answer mildly.

"Um, hello? That you're Caden's fated mate?"

"What?" Lena yelps.

My throat closes and my stomach sinks like a stone. "Oh. You heard about that? I'm—I'm not."

"I know." Beatrix softens her tone, coming over to hug my shoulders. "Everyone said something big happened at bonfire night, but they were being vague. You didn't tell us."

I lean into her gratefully and reach for Lena's hand poking from the covers. "Because it's not important."

"But—you're mates?" Lena protests.

I squeeze her hand, not wanting to tarnish her world with the harsh reality that rejecting a mate is possible. "No, buttercup. I have everything I need right here."

The three of us climb into bed with Lena, snuggled together and inseparable.

14

———

AVERY

It's just after dusk when I meet Taryn at the tree with the gnarled formation resembling one of the Farrows elders. This part of the border isn't far from the natural swimming hole I prefer instead of the main one the rest of the pack uses at Silver Falls.

All the times I've slipped away to my favorite secret spot on the mountain, I had no idea I was so close to another way in and out of packlands.

The tree divides a stream flowing around it and is surrounded by a thicket of bushes. Beyond the vegetation, there's a steep drop off to lower ground where the stream becomes a waterfall.

I see now why this point is written off by the security team's perimeter sweeps.

"Ready?" Taryn shows me where to shimmy between the bushes.

I peer over the edge. "How do we get down? I don't see a spring large enough to jump into at the bottom."

"We have to scale it. But don't worry, the root system from the tree goes most of the way down. Or you could go the hard way. I assume you don't want to waste time waiting for a broken bone to heal itself."

"No," I respond dryly. "I'd rather avoid that at all costs."

"Be quick. We've got about ten minutes before a patrol passes nearby."

I let her go first, keeping a close eye on the spots she places her hands and feet. She makes it look easy. My wolf stretches and climbs to her feet when I begin my descent with my satchel swiveled to my back. She'd rather shift and trot the woods herself. I picture snapped stems and plants covered in slobber if I let her have my skin.

There will be time to run later, after I've looked for anything else I can use to help Lena.

"I don't think I've ever been to this part of the mountain." When I reach the bottom I search the surroundings to get my bearings, trying to figure out which way Ashbury is if I were to try this route in the future. "How'd you end up finding this area?"

"By accident when my wolf was running down a rabbit," Taryn says. "I'd gone off on my own after getting separated and we were tracking our way back to packlands. My wolf is a stubborn thing and tried to climb up those roots when she couldn't jump it."

I laugh as she leads me to a trailhead that splits in three directions. I smell humans and guess this is where they hike.

"Did you make it up that way?" I pause a few minutes into the trail to trim sprigs of goldenrod.

"About halfway up before I lost my footing. Landing on a log hurt like a bitch." Taryn rubs her flank. "But I could smell pack— actually, it was mostly Eddie's laundry he rinses in the stream and hangs to dry behind his cabin. You think those are pungent to our noses now? Wait until you catch a whiff of them in your fur."

We both wrinkle our noses and giggle.

"I shifted back and scraped the hell out of my tits and stomach scrambling up," she finishes. "Do not recommend naked hiking. Always go for the wolf."

"Noted." I tilt my head, giving her a sidelong glance. "That's been a new change since I discovered my wolf. That some males smell vile, different from how their scents were for me before, even if it was muted. What's that about?"

"What do you mean?"

I scrunch my face up and crouch to pluck juniper berries from the tip of a shrub branch. "Bad. Unappealing. There was a lot going on that night, ah..." Taryn makes an understanding noise. "When Lorne grabbed me, I almost gagged from how strong and unpleasant his scent became."

She holds open a linen bag for me to brush them into. "What did he smell like compared to usual?"

"I wasn't really analyzing his musk," I say flatly. "Sour? Like milk that's gone bad. I was a bit busy."

"I don't find Lorne's scent appealing in the slightest, but he's never smelled gross to me." She opens and closes her mouth. "I really want to ask what it feels like. Callie keeps reminding me it would be unimaginably rude to make you recount it. But, Fates, I'm so curious, it's killing me."

My mouth twitches. "Honestly, it sucked. It felt like my soul was being ripped from my body and set on fire.

"That's horrible." Taryn grimaces.

"I don't wish the experience of rejection on anyone. Except Lorne, but he's far too much of an asshole for the moon goddess to bless with a True Mate."

She chuckles. "She would never. But no, I don't think all the males smell like rotten milk. A few have overpowering musks, except I don't notice their scents usually."

I purse my lips. "They all smell like it to me now, not just Lorne."

She bites her lip. "Caden, too?"

I close my eyes and shake my head, releasing an uneven breath. "No. He...he smells incredible." I lick my lips, searching for how to describe his dizzying scent whenever it encapsulates me. "He's the kiss of mist on your skin before you jump into the falls, and the smoking logs freshly lit for a bonfire to honor the moon goddess."

Taryn stares at me. "Wow. All the time? Even after...?"

"Yes." My brows furrow and I pick at the strand of twine dangling from my bag.

"Sounds like how True Mates talk about each other and their bond like it's the best thing to ever happen to them. I guess it's how the Fates encourage us to accept it."

I was afraid of that, though the same thought has crossed my mind several times since the bonfire. Hopefully the allure of his scent will fade with time.

We make our way down the meandering trail, stopping every so often so I can wade through patches of wild plants. Taryn observes, then begins pointing out anything she sees asking if it has an herbal use.

"What about those mushrooms?" She indicates the fungus growing on a dead fallen branch.

I grin. "Same ones you saw ten minutes ago. Again, those skull-caps are poisonous and shouldn't be ingested. See the tan umbrella shape of its top? That's how to identify them."

"They kind of look like bread. What happens if I eat it?"

"At first, cramping and puking your guts out. Then kidney and liver failure. Good luck getting our healer to fix it. You'd better hope your accelerated healing flushes it from your system before that happens."

"Okay, why is everything out to kill us?" She hugs herself and shudders.

My gaze softens and my mother's stories come to mind. "I think it's ancient druid magic. The forest's way of protecting itself."

Taryn bows to the dead branch. "You have my utmost respect, elder."

I glance up at the treetops to the stars peeking through. "Let's go for a bit longer, then head back."

The trail winds down another decline and opens to a wide field past the break in the woods.

"Those flowers over there are pretty," she says.

I perk up. "Evening primrose. Perfect, this will be wonderful for Lena. These are great for so many uses, but especially good to treat a severe cough."

I ran low on primrose leaves weeks ago once the chill set in higher up the mountain. They're one plant that doesn't respond well to the concoctions Jade taught me to mix into the soil for longevity even when I try to grow it on my windowsill by the workbench.

"Wait, do you hear that?" She goes still as I harvest, listening. "Something's in a hurry."

She's right. Whatever's racing through the woods is doing it at breakneck speed, kicking up dead leaves, trampling twigs and any other underbrush in the way from the sound of it.

"Deer? No, that's got to be something bigger. Maybe some hikers woke a bear," I suggest when I rise.

I've gathered enough primrose clippings to fill a basket. I should've brought one to carry them back in.

She grins, licking one of her canines. "Or a wolf. In fact, I'd bet on it."

Our laughter cuts off when two males come into view up the slope. The smile drops off my face and my stomach sinks. Instead of hikers, we've been caught far down the mountain by Caden and Liam.

They're running straight for us, not bothering with the zig-zag of the trail. Caden's leading with Liam trailing behind. Caden's flannel is unbuttoned, as if he considered shifting. He doesn't slow until he reaches us, almost colliding with me when I don't budge.

"Shit," Taryn mutters. "Busted."

Caden ignores her and gets in my face, scratching irritably at his exposed chest. It's covered in raw, red marks as if he's been itching it for a while.

"What the hell do you both think you're doing out here?"

I hold my ground, raising my chin. His eyes narrow, suspicion written all over his features. It's not all that different from the last time we were in this position when he caught me before. Except this time his spiced woodsy musk isn't just delicious, it's making my knees weak with the urge to wind my arms around his neck and rub against him. My mouth goes dry.

"I want an explanation, and it better be a damn good one," he says.

"I needed some evening primrose." I hold up my bundle of clippings, waving it in his face. "This variety only grows at a lower elevation."

He releases a rough noise. "And that gives you the right to break the rules whenever it suits you? You aren't the pack's healer and you're outside the border. Without permission."

I press my lips together against the sting of needing to become my own healer. "Oh, come on. I'm only out here foraging for plants that aren't within the border. You can't bend all of nature to your will, too."

Thankfully we didn't go all the way to town. If this is how he reacts to sneaking off packlands, he'd lose his head if he caught us in Ashbury.

He swipes a hand over his mouth. "How did you do it? How did you slip by the patrol team without them catching you?"

"We walked," Taryn replies sardonically.

Liam hasn't taken his attention off her since they spotted us. "It's Taryn's doing." He grips her by the arm with a scowl. "She's always causing trouble and is allergic to any rule. I'll take care of her."

"You wish," she simpers. "You couldn't handle me if you tried. Not even in your dreams."

A muscle jumps in his cheek and he addresses Caden. "I'll take them to the patrol cabin."

"No," Caden growls as he steps in front of me to block me from Liam's view. He stiffens, then blows out a breath. "I'll handle this. You go on ahead."

Liam lifts his brows. "Are you sure?"

"Go," Caden orders with a flash of his lengthening fangs.

Taryn covers a snicker. "Are you sure that's a good call? You could be the dangerous beastie out here."

"Don't question your alpha," Liam snarls as he carts her off.

Once we're left alone, Caden scrubs his pec again. I hope he's breaking out in some sort of uncomfortable allergic reaction to ruin his perfect, sculpted chest.

He scans the trail as if he's looking for any threat of danger. I roll my eyes, then tie my bundle to my bag and start walking back. He catches my arm and whirls me around, intent blue eyes searching my face.

"Where do you think you're going?"

"To spend the night in a holding cell for breaking your suffocating rules, I assume." I jerk out of his grasp with a huff. "I'm not sorry, either. I'll do it again."

He swipes a hand over his face with a grumble. I fold my arms, not sure what's come over me. My wolf's in my corner, though. She's not impressed he ignored us when we walked around the commons today.

"You're not going anywhere without an escort," he says.

"I can handle myself."

"You're a female, alone after nightfall. Out of the question."

I glare at him. "You didn't care before if I was by myself. I've been doing just fine for the last seven years."

His mouth presses into a hard line, accentuating the sharpness of his jaw.

"Shift," I suggest.

His head jerks and his brows furrow. "What? Why?"

"If you won't leave me be, then stalk me in your fur. I prefer your wolf's company to yours. He's far more tolerable to be around."

The corners of his eyes tighten before he tears them from me to glare past my shoulder. "You like my wolf."

I don't think the puzzled mutter is meant for my ears. "It doesn't have to be you at all. Not if I don't want it to be. I'll just wait here for Liam to come back."

At the mention of Liam, he's on me, backing me against the nearest tree. He plants a hand on either side of my head. Something hot and pleasurable tugs low in my gut at his proximity, leaving me breathless even though I'm angry with him.

"Damn it, Avery, there are rules for a reason. You can't just do as you fucking please," he thunders. "No one else but me is around to escort you. Do as I say because I'm your alpha, and you will respect my orders."

I swallow and stare him down. His bare chest brushes against me, heat rolling off him in waves leaving me lightheaded. My pulse thrums for all the wrong reasons.

He's the one who rejected our bond...yet he won't let another male near me, as if I'm *his*.

Caden would have to claim me as his mate if he wanted to make me his.

"Careful, Alpha," I warn with a cold tone to guard against the flutter in my heart. "All your rules are starting to tread a little too close to old pack views you pretend we've moved past."

15

CADEN

THE ACCUSATION IS a slam to my gut. I could never treat pack females like that. I'm not my grandfather's heavy hand when females didn't obey.

Nor am I my uncle or his sons now.

They're the ones that harp about things being better the old way where our females had no rights. The males kept them practically locked up once they were mated, expecting them to roll on their backs and birth pups.

There's no way I'd ever let things go back to that.

My stomach roils at the thought of Avery thinking I could.

Does she believe I want to be this strict on every little matter of pack life?

This approach is the only way I've learned to lead from my father before the injuries he sustained from the challenge with Clark Morgan took their toll on him. The only way I'm able to demand obedient loyalty and trust as the youngest alpha this pack has had.

Her anger stings my nose with the sharp bitterness wafting off her. *Hurt*, my wolf barks, rising to his feet, alert for any sign of danger causing his mate distress. Doesn't he realize it's me that's pissing her off?

She's so close, her body brushing my abdomen.

Mine. Claim.

I shove away from the tree with a grunt, raking my hands through my hair. "No," I push out rigidly. "That's not what I meant."

She sets her jaw. "Why do you care so much about this now?"

It's not because I think she's weak, it's for her protection to make sure no female is vulnerable and unguarded.

And because my wolf is restless at the idea of her out here alone. I don't like it either.

I haven't felt in control, not from the minute I found out she was meant to be my fated. If I don't do something to regain my footing, it could derail my preparations for the summit.

Every night since the bonfire, I've gone to sleep in my own bed. And every morning, I wake up as my wolf sleeping outside Avery's cottage. He's as taken with her as I once was.

I dragged Liam down the mountain because we went for a run to blow off steam after the first day of tryouts. I didn't mean to, but we ended up near Avery's. My wolf took down a boar we both knew was for her. When we went to drop it off at her place, Liam eyed me without saying anything.

But she wasn't home. I could smell her, sweet honey warmed by sunshine and fresh rain, but my wolf insisted it was stale, hours old.

On the way back down the road, I picked up Avery's scent again and felt the bond stretching over the distance between us. The moment I realized how far she'd gotten from packlands, my heart clenched with the worry she was in trouble, like when my mother went missing.

Should I even be able to feel her through the bond? It's broken. It makes no sense for it to act the way a bond does between True Mates that accept the will of the Fates.

I squeeze my nape with a sigh. "I forgot how stubborn you could be."

"You mean before you believed I betrayed you?" At my sharp

look, she shakes her head, rolling her lips between her teeth. "If you're so sure I'm out to stab you in the back, then follow me."

She gives me a fierce glare with her challenge, then abruptly spins on her heel and stomps off without waiting for me. I work my jaw, wondering again why I'm letting her get away with this instead of hauling her ass to warm the benches in the holding cells.

"Well? Are you coming or not?" she calls over her shoulder. "Come see for yourself that I'm not doing anything wrong."

Grudgingly, to my wolf's approval, I follow her. She pauses every so often to gather tree bark or scrape sap into a jar from her satchel.

"What's that for?"

"Plenty of things. This bark can be distilled into an oil for ointments. It can be used for pain relief. To fight infection, depending on the species of tree. Bark is always handy to keep around."

"We're shifters. We rarely need that."

She levels me with an unimpressed stare. "Rarely isn't never, and not all shifters have strength on their side. Like those who are Wolfless. I learned all this to help."

My brows knit, trying to see the forest as she sees it. It's our shelter, a source of food. Yet the weeds she stops to lovingly stroke carry an entirely different meaning to her that isn't obvious to me.

People always whisper she's become a witch holed away on the northern ridge. I've written them off, never smelling spell craft on her, not like the electric, cool tingling scent of the wards woven into our border by witches long ago.

A twinge pulls in my heart because she's different. Still curious and intelligent, but not quite the same person I called a friend. We used to explore together as kids. I've missed out on the exploring she's done on her own.

I'm still thinking about her mouth, though. The fullness of her expressive lips. Kissing them.

"Wait." She smacks her hand into my torso, stalling my thoughts. "There's more over there. We missed it before. Take off your shirt."

My brow quirks. "Why?"

"I didn't bring a basket and I'm not wasting them." She gives me a look that says this should be obvious.

I hold her gaze, shrugging it off and handing it over. She bunches it in her hands, throat convulsing with a swallow. Her eyes dip for a fraction of a second, flickering over my chest and biceps, following the trail of darker hair leading into my pants. The corner of my mouth lifts when her cheeks flush the loveliest shade of pink.

I forgot how pretty she is when she blushes.

A warm tingle spreads through my chest. It gives a gentle tug, encouraging me to get closer to Avery. Same as it has been for days, since the moment this fated connection awoke. My wolf is on board with the urge.

He's fixated on her neck, wanting to glue his nose to it and inhale deeply until he's had his fill, licking, then biting, *claiming* while we mount our mate.

I lick my lips, pointedly not staring at her ass when she bends to harvest more weeds. My wolf yanks at me, grumbling to convince me to watch her present for us. Idiot. Presenting is likely the last thing on her mind.

Those inquisitive murmurings to herself have him all riled up. He wants me to let him out. I swipe a hand over my mouth and squat to examine what she's so interested in.

"What is that? Why do you need it?"

She huffs, showing it to me. "It's a variety of primrose. A wild-flower to most." Her eyes lose the illuminating spark and she tears her gaze away. "It's for Lena. She has a bad cold and this will help her fight it off."

A wrinkle creases my forehead. "A cold? Shifters don't get colds."

The rest of her playfulness evaporates. "Yes we can. And despite what the healer probably claims, they can progress to illnesses that are deadly."

I don't like the weight in her tone, or the implication that there are those not properly taken care of in my pack.

Our healer mostly deals with monitoring pregnancies and setting broken bones after fights or accidents so they don't heal wrong on their own. To my knowledge, no one's ever been in true danger outside of contracting shifter diseases like moon sickness rotting the brain, a lone wolf going feral, or suffering the death of their mate.

"If Lena or anyone else is too sick for the healer, there are other options—"

"Hospitals? Human medicines don't work, and without something stronger like a spell or potion from a witch— "

I growl on instinct, the distrust of witches ingrained in me from birth. She sighs, shaking her head.

"Without the help of magic, or the natural remedies I've learned by experimenting, healing is down to the Fates." She worries her lip. "No matter how much I try to do it all on my own. If the moon goddess made it possible, all I can do is fight an illness with every resource available."

I frown when she holds up the makeshift sling of wildflowers. I should've paid closer attention once I became alpha.

"So." Avery rises and starts off without me. "As you can see, *Alpha*, I'm not doing anything dastardly out here."

Sneaking off isn't any worse than what we got up to growing up together. She's picking flowers to care for her sister, not plotting an uprising.

I scrub the back of my head, catching up to her. "You have my permission to gather as you need. As long as you stay on Silver Mountain. And take a guard with you." My wolf rumbles. I clear my throat. "Liam will make himself available. If I'm not."

Her gaze cuts to me, then darts forward. "No." She halts. "I'll take Taryn with me. Only when I feel like I need an extra hand."

The rumbling increases. "Fine."

I'll be tracking her whenever she goes out. My wolf shuts up.

16

CADEN

WE CONTINUE UP THE TRAIL, my mind wandering. All these years, her family's betrayal has eaten at me, hardening my ability to trust outside of those that prove themselves to me. Loyalty means everything to shifters.

So how can walking beside the girl I swore never to trust again settle the restlessness that's always plagued me once I learned I was named Alpha heir?

For the first time in a long time, I look beneath the blow to my pride at a fear that I keep locked deep within me.

Callie and I were young when our mother disappeared, and because her mating was arranged as a chosen mate, our father didn't suffer the blow the way Clark Morgan did when his True Mate went missing. Losing her was my first taste of having those important to me that I care about ripped away from me, only to go through the hurt again when my father died before his time. It destroyed me to face my father's beta—a second father to me—and his daughter's betrayal because they weren't just pack, they were ingrained in our lives.

I've lived and breathed for the pack and only the pack since that is my duty as Alpha. But maybe it's important for me to look

past what it needs for once, because before everything happened...
Avery was my happiness.

Around her, I always felt just like myself. Not my title or my
duty.

I've felt empty for years without her to fill the void torn from
me when I lost her friendship.

"You don't need to follow me all the way back. We're within
the perimeter now," she points out once we cross into pack
territory.

True. And yet, until I see her home, I have trouble pulling
myself away again. The compulsion takes hold, refusing to be
swayed by any logical reasoning I reach for.

"You have my shirt. And this is my territory. I'm simply
walking it in the same direction as you."

She laughs, a too-short puff of air I want her to make again so I
can capture it and breathe it in with the taste of her lips.

"Sure. If that's what you want to tell yourself, Alpha
Blackburn."

I massage my forehead and temple, remaining her silent
shadow the rest of the way to her cottage. In daylight, it leaves
much to be desired for a proper home. At night, it's so much darker
than the cabins populated by the rest of the pack.

When my father made sure everyone in the pack got electricity, he stopped the power lines at the furthest occupied buildings
because this place wasn't inhabited. I haven't thought about taking
them further or expanding it to the edges of Silver Falls Pack territory. Tomorrow I'll put an extension project on the assignment
schedule.

At her door, she blocks the way with a wary expression that
rankles me. I sidestep her and she growls in warning.

"Aren't you leaving?"

I stare her down. "No. Let me in, then I'll go."

She mutters a curse, motioning to the side of the cabin. "Be
useful, then. Put another log on the fire."

I get two of the best looking pieces of wood from her chop pile.

There isn't enough in it and half the stockpile is little more than kindling. If I don't go on my usual morning run, I'll have time to chop good fresh wood.

Inside, I pull up short. There's a bed shoved into the corner and a rocking chair that's seen better days by the fireplace with Lena bundled in threadbare blankets. Beatrix sits at a table crammed in the corner that seems to double as a counter next to a wood burning stove.

A rough-hewn workbench by the latticed windows takes up the other half of the small room. It's clearly Avery's space, covered in pots and jars of ground powders and pastes. Plants and dried clippings hang from rafters that will need replacing soon to fix the dry rot.

Avery's planted herself in front of her sisters, flashing her teeth at me. Her protectiveness over them against me knocks the wind from me. Her sisters are her own little pack the same way Callie and Liam are mine.

"Caden!" At Avery's throat clearing, Beatrix bends her neck. "I mean Alpha Blackburn. Sir."

"Hello, Beatrix. I brought in some more wood for the fire. Soon you won't have to worry about it," I say.

Avery tenses, her sweet scent sharpening with anxious worry and defiance. "What do you mean?"

I hold my hands out to set her at ease. "I'll be bringing electricity up here."

Her eyes widen. "You will?"

At my nod, she slides her lips together and watches me as she goes to lay out the primrose on her bench. She returns my shirt by tossing it at my head without warning. I catch it before it falls to the floor, then shrug it back on.

Struck by the paleness of Lena's cheeks, I kneel beside her chair, debating how Avery would take it if I scooted her closer to the fire. Lena smiles warmly, welcoming me despite everything I've put her family through.

"I remember you."

Fucking Fates, she was only seven when my father forced them from the Morgan cabin. A child. They all were, even Avery.

The pit of my stomach burns. "You do? You've grown up since I last saw you. It's good to meet you again, Lena."

She pokes a frail hand out from her blankets, fingers cold to the touch. Avery stops plucking leaves, holding a small knife in a white-knuckle grip, the blade pointed at me when I seek her out.

Unlike when we met at the edge of the territory last week, shame washes over me instead of the anger I've clung to for so long.

Lena's smile falters with a hacking cough, and she's unable to catch her breath. I stiffen, unsure how to help. I rub her back until Avery comes over with a fresh leaf and shoos me out of the way.

"Chew on this," she instructs.

The worry lining her face doesn't ease until Lena's breathing evens. She kisses the top of her head, tucking a lock of blonde hair behind her ear.

"She's sick."

Avery serves me a hard look. "I told you."

"How?" I demand under my breath, following her to the workbench.

She blinks when her eyes turn shiny and keeps her voice low. "She's always been prone to illness."

"I remember when she was born. The healer said she was a healthy—"

"She got pneumonia," she whispers harshly. "It happened during our first winter here. I—I almost lost her. I didn't know what I was doing. I had to learn how to make my own medicine."

My stomach clenches and I ball my fists as a distant memory hits me square in the chest. This is my fault.

Not simply because I'm the alpha and it's up to me to make sure my pack is cared for, but because I remember when Avery was poking around for extra handouts. It was under my order that the pack ignored her or turned her away.

Fuck.

My wolf agrees with an angry swish of his tail. His judgment tastes like bile in the back of my throat.

You don't deserve our perfect mate, he rumbles before giving me his back.

I don't. Not after pinning her and her father's betrayal to my family all on her after his death because I was seventeen and blinded by anger.

I'm beginning to question if I was right to make her pay such a heavy price for the last seven years.

No, I'm beyond questioning. I know I was wrong to blame her. To think she was part of her father's challenge. To put her through a punishment she didn't deserve.

This isn't the type of alpha I want to be.

The hatred I've held on to with both fists crumbles to dust and slips through my fingers.

I've been a damned fool. Blind to the truth in front of me this entire time. I need to make it right.

I toss the logs into the fire and stoke it until I have the burning wood rearranged to allow the flames to breathe better. Within minutes, the temperature becomes more comfortable in the tiny cabin, though it's still chillier than it could be. I search the room, not finding any furs to help Lena warm up. There are too many sitting around the lodge in winter I can send over.

Beatrix sprawls in front of the fire with a content hum. "How'd you do that? No matter how much I add , it never gets this warm."

"See how I moved them so one is propped up instead of stacked? The flames can get bigger like that. The trick is not to smother it with the firewood."

"Would you bring me my book, please?" Lena motions to a stack on the floor by the bed. I pick out the top one. "No, the one with the blue cover. Third down. I'm between three books and I'm in the mood for that one."

She beams when I hand it over, scooting lower in the rocker to curl up with it.

Avery concentrates on her task when I prop a shoulder against the wall. She strips every part of the plant, setting aside the leaves in two piles. One she adds to a pot of boiling water on the stovetop. The other she divides onto a tray that goes in the oven, and the rest she chops finely.

Her hands are so nimble. It's impossible not to get lost watching them.

"Are you a witch after all?" I murmur the question without any of the heat I intend at the idea of a shifter learning magic.

She smirks humorlessly. "No. I'm not a witch. I can't do any real magic."

I pick up one of the assortment of jars and sniff the tan powder. The spiced tang is a surprising tickle to my nose.

"That's ground ginger. Put it back. Don't touch anything else, I have it organized."

I return it, eyeing the labels on other tins and phials for herbal roots, seeds, extractions, and salves. Her annoyance with me is palpable, creating a zinging buzz in my chest, yet with her sisters her attitude is completely softened.

She brews tea with the fresh wildflower leaves for Lena, laughing with her when she shows her a passage from her book. Beatrix perches on the arm of the rocker and Avery combs then braids her hair with gentle, nurturing care.

Unbidden, my mind conjures the idea of Avery caring for pups in the same way. My wolf knows she'll be perfect, and I don't know what to do with the unfamiliar longing unfurling within me.

A worn journal pokes out from a lower shelf. I thumb through it, brows rising at years' worth of notes on the mountain's vegetation along with lists of uses, some with question marks that are scratched out. Those have a tiny scrawl in the margin to note ineffectiveness or have *poison* written at the top of the page with several underscores.

It amazes me how much she's learned.

At the back, she's logged pack members she's traded remedies for their ailments or tracking who she's noticed has a problem she could solve and how it would benefit her. This isn't only for her sister, she's seen to a surprising number of females in the pack.

She snatches the journal from me with a gasp. "Why are you still poking around?"

I open my mouth to tell her it's my right as Alpha. The panic flaring in her eyes makes me snap my jaw shut with a shrug. The buzz moving around behind my ribcage gets worse. I massage it and gesture to the table.

"I was interested to see your work. You're helping the pack in your own way. That's a good thing. I'm grateful."

Her cheeks color and she narrows her gaze before going back to ignoring me.

The longer I stay because it feels right to be near her, the more irritated she becomes. I'm a looming presence intruding on her space. She growls at me when I'm blocking her path. There aren't many places to move in the tiny cabin.

After she's tucked her youngest sister into bed, she grabs my wrist and drags me outside. A creaking noise distracts me. I stop to inspect the door.

"Do you want me to send the healer to check on Lena?"

"Don't bother. I've got it covered."

"Are you sure? If I send him, he might be able to help."

"He's a hack."

My frown deepens. The hinges are probably shot and the door's not worth salvaging. I'll need to replace it all to resolve the noise.

"Damn it, would you stop that?" she snaps.

She attempts to push me away from fussing with the door. Even with her improved strength now that she has a wolf, she's barely able to make me budge when I don't want to. She releases a terse sigh when I kneel to examine the ancient, rusted hinges closer.

"It's just—like that, okay? I've tried to fix it," she grits out. "There's nothing to be done."

"You've tried to fix this? On your own?" The question comes out through my teeth and she takes it the wrong way.

"Yes, Caden. When something breaks around here, who are we going to call? The maintenance crew?" She tosses her head with a scoff that rubs my fur the wrong way. "The only one I can rely on for help is myself."

She shakes her head at my sharp look and storms off the porch.

My jaw works and I stretch my head side to side to ease the tension stiffening every muscle in my body. There's no threat to fight. Not a physical one. The growl working its way up my throat is an overreaction caused by this damn bond for leaving my fated mate to fend for herself in such an extreme way.

I was an idiot to think she wouldn't be a worthy Alpha female. A worthy mate. I'm the unworthy one, not her.

My chest constricts with dread. I rejected her. Fuck, is it too late to undo my mistakes? Would she want me if I accept the bond?

I push to my feet with another rumble and make it to her with long strides by the time she reaches the woods. She stumbles and I automatically catch her elbow to keep her steady.

"I'm fine." She yanks free and rubs at her chest.

I feel the urge to do the same because the mad pulsing insisting I drag her body against mine and claim her mouth is driving me to the brink of madness.

"If you came to petition for help, it would be my duty as Alpha to hear you out," I argue, unable to control my volume. "You're still part of this pack."

She halts, shoulders heaving with heavy breaths. Then she turns and meets my eye. The death glare she serves me would be viewed as a direct challenge by anyone, yet my heartbeat races for an entirely different reason.

Avery Morgan is beautiful and entirely too tempting when she's furious.

17

AVERY

"Wʜᴀᴛ ᴅɪᴅ ʏᴏᴜ sᴀʏ?" I'm so enraged, I barely have the capacity to yell.

"That you didn't have to fix creaking doors or broken floor-boards by yourself." Caden raises his hands as I march up to him. "And you don't have to worry about it anymore. You should move out of that death trap. I'll find you somewhere else."

"And go where? To you?"

My voice cracks when I pummel his chest, not even stopping to think about the consequences of attacking my alpha. He allows it and doesn't retaliate. Inside, my wolf rages, too. She's lunging and wild, teeth clacking with each fierce snap of her jaws.

"To tell you the nights were too cold? After your father put us out here because of you when everyone else at that joke of a pack meeting after—afterwards suggested any remaining Morgans be put down or exiled?" I'm breathing hard, everything pouring out of me at once. "Do you expect my thanks for this *mercy* you showed us?"

My body trembles, throat searing. Each thump of my fist against his firm muscles grows weaker.

I hate him.

I hate him so much.

I hate how easily he's shattered my heart twice. It's cracking all over again, the fragile shards ready to burst free.

"You were my friend," I say brokenly. "And you stopped listening to me the minute you thought I'd betrayed you because my father dared to challenge yours. In minutes, you hated me. There was no way to make you see otherwise. Why would I ever beg you for help when you labeled me a traitor to this pack and picked where to cast me away?"

He clenches his jaw and catches my wrists, speaking gruffly as he stares into my eyes repentantly. "I was wrong for that. For too many things. I see it now. I shouldn't have blamed you for your father or made you move up here. There's no excuse I can give to change any of what happened. I'm sorry for—for everything. I'll make it better, I swear it."

I've waited for him to say those words for years. They don't bring the immense relief I imagined they would when I faced the hardest moments of survival. How can I forgive him?

A flutter of yearning pulls at me, gently at first, then more insistent. Part of me wants to believe he's sorry after all this time. Probably the part that was so in love with him back then. Or the part that imagined what being his True Mate would be like.

"I'm sorry," he repeats.

Tears sting my eyes and I try to wrench free. Regret lines his features, his throat bobbing with a heavy swallow. He holds me, tugging me closer until I rest my forehead on his firm chest.

"I know saying sorry won't fix it, and I don't deserve your forgiveness so easily," he says roughly. "But I have to start somewhere. Let me make it better."

The buildup of rage shifts to all the hurt I've kept bottled up, my emotions frayed and overwhelming. A gasp breaks off in a choked sob. The last of my composure snaps and the torrent of frustration and heartache threatens to drown me.

Tears flow in an unstoppable cascade, blurring my vision. Anguished cries scrape my throat.

He holds me through it all, murmuring his apologies against

the top of my head. Years of holding myself together, only falling apart when I'm alone at night so I can be strong for my sisters, unravels in moments. He doesn't let go, his embrace tightening.

I don't know how much time has passed once my tears dry. He's stroking my hair, his other arm and his heady woodsy scent enveloping me. It soothes me until I calm down, blanketing me in a comforting haze that blocks out the weight of the world.

I'm safe now. In his arms, everything is right. I can stay here and he'll take care of me.

My wolf echoes the sentiment. She falls under the thrall more easily, bending her neck as she mewls.

My palms slide up his chest. The vibration of his wolf's inviting rumble feels nice. So does winding my arms around his neck to get closer.

His scent becomes richer, the spiced cedar so intense it's bursting on my tongue and making my stomach dip. I drag my nose along his collar bone, licking his corded neck.

"Avery." He groans it, hiking me closer by a handful of my ass.

I lift a leg, wrapping it around his powerful thigh, pressing on tiptoe to get more of his glorious scent in my lungs. It's not enough.

I want—I want—

Wait. No. This is the bond. The one he didn't want with me.

It's making me need to jump him right now, mate with him to make everything better now that he's apologized and stop being such a colossal alpha asshole.

"Are you okay?" he murmurs.

Not even a little bit. "I think so. Or, I will be. I just need—"

"Yes?" he rasps.

When I push free of his embrace, he releases me willingly, though his handsome features are twisted in torment. I back up and he matches me step for step.

My lips slide together. Turning around is difficult, but once I do some of the strange haze clears. My wolf barks at me, tugging to get me back in our mate's arms. I rub my puffy eyes and pick a random direction to walk.

Yes, shift, my wolf urges, her body wriggling as she lowers her front end playfully. *Shift and chase.*

One glance at Caden over my shoulder and I know that wouldn't be a smart move. Vivid swirls of gold ring his blue irises. We're both feeling the effects of the bond's magic. If I shift now, she'll let his wolf catch her.

An image of him rutting me with my ass up and my head down, hair wound around his fist as he drives into me until my pussy's stretched full with his knot pops into my head to entice me.

My steps falter as hot desire rushes through me. I don't know if it's my wolf's doing or the bond's influence making both of us forget the rejection.

I need to plunge myself in the cooling water at the private spring I like, but I don't want him finding out about it. I change directions and head for the nearest stream instead.

The longer I walk, the more I feel like myself again, and with it comes the world the bond muted.

"Where are you going?" Caden finally asks.

"To clear my head. You can go."

"No," he responds stubbornly. "You do whatever you'd like. I'm staying right where I am."

I toss a warning growl over my shoulder. It only makes him snort and shadow me closer.

"I'm not your mate, remember? You have no right or need to watch over me."

"No, but I'm still your alpha," he counters from right behind me. "It's my duty."

He's so close I feel the warmth of his breath at my ear and the vibration of his chest rumbling in protest.

"Don't placate me. It's bullshit."

I stop and he bumps into me. My throat is too raw when I swallow.

We've entered a clearing full of fireflies. It's far too late in the year for them, yet sometimes there are pockets of nature where I find them gathered, dancing for the sleeping druids. They're beautiful, bobbing and looping through the air, glowing at intervals.

I tip my head back, closing my eyes when his nose brushes my hair and his hands hover at my hips without taking hold of me. I should step away, I need to. He's not my mate.

"Why are you doing this?" It comes out on a hitched breath.

"Doing what? This?" His fingertips skim my sides and his lips drag across my temple. "I can't help it. Your scent right now is so— It's driving me insane. I have to."

I shake my head. "Why won't you stay away? You need to let this mangled bond fully sever."

The fierce growl that tears from him makes my heart clench.

It takes far too much willpower to put distance between us again. I can't handle this.

"Did you only apologize because you feel bad about rejecting me?" I round on him, wounded heart in my throat. "You can't have it both ways, Caden. You threw away fate's gift, and you know what? I reject you right back because—"

Before I give any reasons, he's on me again. He tugs my body against his with a jagged noise, trapping my hands between us.

"No."

It's not clear if he's answering my question or refusing my rejection.

He kneads my waist, piercing eyes flashing gold again as they bore into mine, flickering back and forth. I lick my lips and his focus drops to my mouth. My fingers splay on his chest.

His head dips, my body alight before his ghosted exhale over my throat makes me shiver. My body tingles with awareness of every inch of him pressed against me. He rubs his nose beneath my ear, then traces it down. My fingers curl in his shirt.

He's scenting me. Exploring my neck to map every inch. Leaving his musk all over me, and in turn making sure he smells like me.

Every brush of his stubbled jaw across my sensitive skin elicits tingles of pleasure that race up and down my spine. An ache builds between my thighs that won't be sated by pressing them together.

I want the rigid length of his cock that's pressed into my belly. A tiny noise escapes me and I flush at how needy it is. He chuckles, a deep, delicious rasp against the shell of my ear.

I swallow thickly. "Caden."

His teeth graze my skin, right over the juncture between my neck and shoulder—the spot where a mating bite mark would be if he claimed me.

"Caden," I breathe.

A gasp catches in my throat when his tongue darts out to taste the same spot he scraped with his teeth.

He moves back. This time I'm the one clinging to him in protest. His gaze roves over me with a sensual smile.

"You asked why I won't leave you alone."

I blink, dazed and flushed all over. "Right."

"I'm...having trouble staying away from you," he admits. "My wolf has a mind of his own when it comes to you, but I can't deny that I'm pulled to you, too. I don't know how to stop it. I'm not sure I want it to."

I touch my neck. The spot where he had his fangs teasing my shoulder throbs in time with the aroused pulse in my core.

"You scented me. That's—It's for family clans. Your closest packmates." My stomach feels like the fireflies are dancing inside it. "Lovers."

His eyes darken, burnished gold swirling with blue. He takes my chin and lifts it.

"I'm making sure every male knows to keep their distance from you."

18

AVERY

Caden's admission remains fresh in my head. I've turned it over a hundred times at least between last night and this morning.

I believe it's just the bond making him act like he needs to be around me, maybe even giving him mate-vision so it can entice us to complete the connection. It has to be the reason it no longer so much as twinges to cause me any pain, because it senses a chance to mend what the rejection broke.

Why else would he be compelled to sit outside my window every night in his fur or chop enough wood at dawn to fill my woodshed this morning?

Even if he no longer hates me, I have no idea where that leaves us. His apology in the woods doesn't mean he's changed his mind about us being mates because he didn't kiss me in the clearing, or make any other move to claim me as his mate. Scenting me out of the sense of possessiveness his wolf has towards me doesn't make me his.

Do I want to be his? My pulse staggers.

The kitchen grinds to a halt when I enter for breakfast. I freeze in the doorway, then duck my head and find something to do.

"Back to work. Food doesn't prepare itself," Alma barks after a long pause.

Taryn slings an arm over my shoulder and is completely obvious when she sniffs me. "You smell like—"

"I know." I bite my lip, cracking eggs harder than necessary and fish shells from the bowl.

"After Liam dragged me off last night, I thought you'd be right behind me to be my bunk buddy for yet another night in the holding rooms."

"So did I." I shoot her a wry smile. "Have you considered moving your things into the patrol cabin? You might as well for how often you end up there."

She waves a hand and scoffs. "I think Liam just gets off on seeing me locked up. He has such a power trip whenever he decides I'm doing something I shouldn't be."

"Thanks for helping me even though we got caught."

"Anytime."

I keep myself occupied, volunteering first for every task Alma orders. It backfires when she decides to call on me to send out toast.

"Oh, but—Taryn could do that. I'm watching the bacon," I say.

She shoves the tray of baskets in my hands and nods to the door. "Go on. It was a special request from Alpha Blackburn that you be the only one to serve his food. He'll touch nothing anyone else brings him."

Goosebumps race across my skin and heat floods my face at the look she gives me, like she believes I smell like him because I arched my back and presented for him. For unmated females, it's usually the case.

While none of that's happened between us, despite my bond-induced dreams supplying vivid ideas after last night, him only wanting to touch what I offer sparks excitement in my veins. I squash it before my wolf takes it as a sign to shift and seduce him into hunting with her.

At first, no one pays me any mind. Nina Blackburn's on her way in behind her mate with her baby on her hip. She glances at me and quickly looks away, demurely following him to an open seat two tables away from where Cormac's favored bloodline sits.

The gaping stares and whispers start at the nearest tables I pass, spreading out to the next rows.

It's undeniable who I've been scent marked by. No one has to come near before their nose figures it out.

I could've washed off his mark on me, at least to mute his musk so it wasn't this...overpowering and *fresh*.

Except when I poured water into a bowl and soaked the rag, I couldn't bring myself to wipe it away. My wolf threw a fit that I'd wash off her mate's scent. Admittedly, a small part of me wanted this moment. To see the reactions of the pack members who have shunned me and those who turn their noses up at me in public while sneaking up to my cabin to beg for my help.

Keeping my head held high and my back straight, I march through the hall, not stopping until I'm at the head table.

Caden watches every step, a smile playing at the corners of his mouth and a gleam in his eyes. This is the first time he's acknowledged my existence when I've brought food out to be served. I lift a brow and hold his gaze, dropping off the toast unceremoniously.

"Thank you," he says sincerely.

It's like a switch has flipped in him. His features aren't set in a steely glare, they're softened. Attentive and open.

Liam reaches across to get a piece, freezing when Caden snatches his arm, leveling him with a hard stare.

"Mine," Caden rumbles.

Liam's head jerks. "What? You never care if I eat before you."

Caden grunts, shaking his beta's wrist to get him to drop the toast on his plate. He takes the rest of the basket and dumps it so there's none left for the few other enforcers seated with him. They cover smiles and avert their gazes.

Liam sits back in his chair and folds his arm, studying his friend. "So you're not going to share?"

"Fuck no." Caden shoves half a slice of buttered toast into his mouth.

Hodge, one of the older members of the guard that used to lift me on his shoulders as a kid, chuckles at Liam. "You don't know shit about mates, do you?"

"Here, have this one." I start to set down a second basket, but Caden makes to steal that one for himself, too. My brows jump up. "What's the problem?"

"Mine," he reiterates to me with a playful snap of his teeth that makes my insides swoop with a thrill. "No one else in this pack gets to eat what you bring over. Only me."

I exchange an exasperated look with Liam. He holds up a hand.

"It's okay. Come on, guys. If we want to be fed, looks like we're sitting elsewhere." Liam gets up, motioning to the others.

Hodge pats Caden's shoulder when he rises to follow. Ford and Gabriel head off to find open seats at the table where Emily drops off steaming cranberry scones.

"Satisfied? You're alone at the head table now," I say.

"Very," Caden answers as he licks butter and jam from his thumb, the corners of his eyes crinkling.

Heat blooms in my cheeks at the display. I track his tongue, captivated by his mouth. He eyes me alluringly, giving the impression he knows where my mind's strayed.

Shaking my head, I go back to the kitchen. My wolf is basking in all this. Since he scented me last night, she's on a high, proudly strutting around smelling of her mate in front of the pack. She loves the way it broadcasts that we're *his* to everyone, as it should be.

I bite my lip, stomach tightening pleasantly at the thought. My heart gives several thudding beats. I don't hate the feeling, or the idea as much as I should.

The whispering isn't as bad the second time I go out with eggs and sausages. Surprisingly, there isn't as much hostility either. Maybe that's why he insisted on this, to show the pack he doesn't view me as his enemy anymore. A few people even wave at me and offer tentative smiles. I almost trip, smacked in the gut from how much I've longed to feel like I belonged in the pack instead of existing in its shadow.

Caden thanks me again, then stops me. "Do you want to sit? Have breakfast with me."

I blink. "No. Probably best I don't."

"Why not? Have you eaten yet? Here, try mine."

I back away before my wolf takes him up on the offer to eat off his plate. "I'm fine. Wouldn't want to give anyone the notion you don't mind people slacking off their assigned rotation."

He lets me go with a nod. I retreat to the safety of the kitchen.

The respite only lasts a short while before Taryn finds me.

"Avery," she sing-songs. "Apparently, Alpha Blackburn's appetite isn't satisfied."

She waggles her brows.

"What? He's still here?" I blurt.

She shakes a basket of scones. "He wants more."

"Food," I clarify.

"Of course." She winks. "What else would I mean?"

Sighing, I brave the dining hall to bring him a second helping. This time rather than watch me, he stares down everyone else, giving those that still eye me in distaste a hard glare.

I deliver the food and hurry out of the hall, certain that this will be the end of this bizarre breakfast shift.

Except just as I get ready to leave, Taryn finds me a third time.

"Avery." She can't keep her smile in check and puts another dish in my hands. "The alpha's still hungry. Called for you again."

"Again?" I exclaim in exasperation.

A hot tug pulls in my chest with his will to draw me out. I swallow, fighting how much I want to answer.

Another tug.

Come to me, it whispers enchantingly. I inch towards the dining hall.

Damn it.

I try to give the food back. "You take it."

She smirks, peeking through the window. "I don't think so.

He's watching the door, waiting for you." She nudges me out and smacks my backside. "Good luck. Go get 'em."

This time I circle his table and loom over his chair when I plop the third helping down. "Why do you keep calling me back every five minutes?"

He lifts his amused gaze to me. "I'm hungry."

"Should I stand here and feed you, too?" I mutter.

His enticing hum is laced with intrigue. The deep, smoky noise stirs something pleasant in my core.

"As much as I like that idea, no." His knuckle brushes the inside of my wrist and his lips twitch. "I should get my day started. If Liam pokes his head in here one more time to check on me, he'll drag me out by my tail."

I roll my lips between my teeth, wrestling back the urge to follow him out before he's even left. "Well, I hope you enjoyed this."

"I did." He stands and gives me a drawn out once over, tracing his lower lip with his tongue. "My wolf, too."

"Good," I huff. "Because it won't be happening again."

His mouth curves and he dips his nose, inhaling with the faintest rumble of pleasure that makes my insides melt. Everything in me strains to lean into him, to tilt my head and give him my throat. My cheeks heat at the hooded look he pins me with before he sweeps his gaze at all the packmates in the dining hall.

"I'll see you later."

Caden leaves me standing at the head table with every eye in the room on me. The inside of my wrist tingles with the memory of his touch.

19

CADEN

LIAM NUDGES my boot beneath the desk from his guard position next to my chair. It's the third time he's done that since my office opened for this week's hearing hour.

I tune back in to what Josine Merryweather's come to complain about.

"And I just think it isn't right. Not after all that trouble the Morgans brought for your father when he was such a great man. A capable and noble leader, didn't deserve no challenges to question his right as our alpha."

"Sorry—you're looking for me to...?" My brow quirks.

"Well, do something about it, Alpha Blackburn." She clicks her tongue. "Someone ought to check for sure if that girl wasn't lying about feeling you were True Mates. My daughters both are much worthier matches."

Liam coughs to cover his amusement because it seems all the dams have come out of the woodwork to play matchmaker to find me a mate. He stands at my side, along with others on security detail dotted around my office. The line stretches out the door and down the hall. Possibly out to the covered front porch.

These meetings are open to hear the concerns of the pack. Usually they're an opportunity to bring their disagreements before me, like the elders that bicker over land disputes, applying for a chosen mate ceremony, or requesting a visit with other packs.

Today it's been nothing but this, full of gossip. The first few days following the bonfire, there were only murmurings amongst the pack about what happened. Rejecting your fated mate isn't common, though after the initial shock the pack spread it around that I was right to do it because I needed a strong mate.

Maybe it would've passed if I'd stuck to ignoring Avery. Or at least attempting to while I fought everything in me yearning for her. I'm not fighting the bond anymore. I want to show the pack I accept her, as a Morgan I've forgiven and as my mate.

The whispers returned in full force after this morning when she made her way through the dining hall to the head table. My lips twitch in satisfaction.

Avery smelled *mine*.

Last night in the clearing, and this morning. A message to every male of who she belongs to.

It's the reason I was late getting back to the lodge before we started, lingering far longer than I usually do with a second and third helping just to spend another minute basking in her covered in my scent, sweet delectable honey mixed with my musk all over her.

Josine stares at me expectantly.

"I assure you, it's true that we are fated." I touch my sternum, anchored by the resonation in the bond. "There's no way to fake this."

She blinks in disbelief, growing desperate. "But you rejected her."

I frown, rubbing the ache flaring behind my ribcage. "I did."

"Are you going to accept her, then? It's not right."

"I plan to, yes. Do you have a problem with your alpha accepting my True Mate?"

She squirms at the flat look I level her with, dropping her gaze with a mutter and shaking her head.

"Good." At my glance, Liam herds her out.

"Yes, okay," he says to appease her when she holds him up at the door. "It'll be noted. Next."

Callie's never going to let me hear the end of this. She's been annoyed with me as it is, ever since I made the mistake of spitting in fate's face, as she puts it. I've only seen her at meals in the last week when she deems to join me, and she's spoken maybe three sentences to me in total. She avoids me around the lodge, sticking to her rooms.

I brace myself as another female strides in with her daughter in tow.

"Alpha, I've come to insist you consider my Terra." She pushes her daughter until she's right in front of my desk.

I nod dutifully. "Very well."

Terra squeaks and lowers her gaze. Liam's steadfast composure is close to cracking when the poor girl's made to turn in a circle by her mother and recite some rehearsed babble about her loyalty to the Blackburns. Ford isn't faring as well. He leans heavily on Gabe's shoulder to hide his laughter in his mate's shirt, drawing miffed leers from the older female.

I wave a hand, massaging the dull throb in my temple while they're ushered out and another she-wolf strides in. Each time I inform them I'm not considering any other mate than Avery. The reactions are mixed, ranging from some surprised yet accepting to some who are openly aggressive, trying to make me change my mind with their bias. I berate myself for allowing my wrongly placed hatred to bleed into the pack, wanting to correct their opinion of her.

It continues on for the rest of the hour. Before long, my mind drifts to Avery again.

Holding her in my arms while she fell apart made it clear to me that I wanted to become her strength and take away every ounce of hardship I caused her. Being the cause of her pain wrecked me. It was like being burned alive from the inside out, the bond punishing me for hurting her.

I didn't know what else to do last night other than start with an apology, but it doesn't make me worthy of her forgiveness. Not yet.

It almost killed me not to kiss her. I nearly did when I was scenting her because her pheromones made me wild.

First I need to fix everything I've broken between us, including the bond I refused. I want to deserve her before I claim my mate.

)))●(((

MY WOLF APPRECIATES it when we get under the sun and open sky to oversee the second day of enforcer tryouts. He's grown antsy after being cooped up all morning in the lodge offices listening to criticisms of our mate, only quelled by me refuting every one of them and countering their judgment of Avery.

The nitty gritty of running the pack doesn't hold his attention unless a show of dominance is needed. He's much more interested in running circles around this year's crop of hopefuls for one of the most coveted job assignments in the pack.

Out of all the rules I set, this is the area I'm strictest over. I don't let just anyone join the roster of those who pledge to protect the pack. Everyone is welcome to apply, but only the best make it through.

I squint when I spot Lorne and my uncle watching from the pavilion outside the dining hall. Lorne hasn't shown his face at tryouts after I wouldn't accept him three years ago. He was pissed because he expected his name and our shared bloodline to carry him through, and that's exactly why my gut told me not to let him join.

My cousin was clever enough to wait until my father wasn't Alpha to try out, but also too hotheaded. He's not the type I trust with the security of the pack.

I don't like how any of them treat females, either. Especially the ones mated to them or living within Cormac's compound. His timid mate scuttles around, cowering if any male so much as looks her way. Their daughters and Sylvie's sisters Cormac's farmed off in arranged matings to grow his brood never look happy, but I can barely get near any of them to confirm if they're being mistreated.

Cormac wanted to be Alpha. It's no secret, my father told me as much. He never challenged his brother to claim the pack, and Lorne hasn't outright challenged me. I promised Dad I'd never lose a challenge if Cormac or his sons ever tried to take the pack. I'm ready for the day Lorne finally does so I can put an end to their rank chasing. Until one of them acts, all I can do is keep an eye on them.

It becomes clear why they're there when Cormac's youngest son trots by to join the groups gathered on the commons. Weston isn't as mouthy as Dane or an exact copy of his father like Lorne. Though we all share Blackburn blood, none of them feel like family. Not the way Liam's my brother.

Liam follows my stare. "Want me to mark him down as a fail now? Save us all some time?"

"I'll decide when we've seen how he fares through all the tests," I answer. "Everyone gets a fair shot, those are the rules."

Liam shrugs. "Okay. So make sure he's in Hodge's group?"

Hodge is old school. He's a few years older than my father and grew up with him. He takes no prisoners when it comes to the safety of our territory and gives the hardest tests to pass. Most that end up in his group surrender before the week is out.

I smirk. "Exactly."

"I bet you the stag in our freezer the kid pukes in the first twenty minutes," Ford says when he joins us.

Gabe slaps him in the chest. "Don't bet my food or I'll knock you out. You know I was tracking it all weekend."

Liam snorts. "You heard the man. Don't you show your mate any respect?"

"He gets it..." Ford pauses to smirk.

We all groan, knowing how he'll finish that sentence after how many times he's fired off his favorite quip about giving it to Gabe all night long.

"Go put the hopefuls through hell to see who proves them-selves," I instruct.

)))●(((

IF I THOUGHT my open office time was bad this morning, it's nothing compared to the tang of hostility in the air later at dinner. It sets me on edge when I take my seat. I stare the tables down, satisfied when elders and young males alike back off with their gazes dropped to their plates.

The tense energy dissipates and I relax a bit. Thankfully Avery's not on the rotation tonight. I checked the assignment schedule posted outside the lodge. I need to have her switched off kitchen duty and get her a meeting with the pack healer and his assistant. I consider other ways to rectify the pack's opinion of her by integrating her back into it, like making sure she feels welcome at the next full moon run.

Hodge takes his usual seat. "Good stock this year. Strong wolves, sharp instincts."

"You've got some winners in your group that you haven't killed yet?" The corner of my mouth kicks up and I pass him the gravy.

He chuckles. "My torture sessions haven't come to an end yet. Ask me again in another few days."

I'm relieved he's impressed. One less worry lightening the load on my shoulders if I can put my trust in some new members on the roster to allow older shifters their well-earned break.

Everything's fine through the first half of the meal until a brazen she-wolf approaches the head table in heeled boots. Seline pushes her luck by stepping right up to me like Avery did earlier. She's a few years older than me. I remember her having school lessons with Lorne.

"Alpha, I'm putting myself forward," she announces.

"If you want to be part of the enforcers, the tryout applications go out in the middle of the summer," Liam says.

She flicks a dismissive hand at him. "No, I mean as the ideal candidate to become Alpha female of the pack."

I put my fork down with a clatter. This is why I've never shown any favor to the females, not even to blow off steam.

"No." It's blunt.

She leans on the table, squishing her ample cleavage until she's about to spill out of her low-cut top. "I'm what the females need. I'm ready to challenge any of your mate candidates."

A grumble builds in my throat. "Not interested. Neither is my wolf." I survey the hall, making sure they're all paying attention before I raise my voice. "Avery Morgan is my True Mate."

"She's not a worthy match," someone at the back says before hiding.

My fist thumps the table. "She's more than worthy. She's strong and resourceful. How many of you sought her aid or remedies?" There's a split reaction, some more agreeable and others holding out. "I intend to undo my rejection and claim her."

Hushed chatter breaks out. I wish Avery was here tonight after all. I'm making myself clear to the pack so they back off of her.

I wave Seline off. "There won't be any challenge. Go sit down."

She purses her lips, then strides off with an uppity huff. Liam snorts, pushing the pitcher of beer within reach.

"You believe that? Man's crazy," someone jeers loudly. "Can't be trusted when he doesn't see tits like that right in front of him. Prefers that little witchling to a sexy she-wolf like Seline."

My head snaps up, brows flattening. It's the final straw.

"Who said that? Stand. Now."

Heads swivel to see. My drawn out growl rattles the dishes in front of me when Dane Blackburn rises with a mulish expression. I find Uncle Cormac three seats down and grit my teeth at the smirk dancing on his weathered features.

I click my fingers at Dane, pointing at the open space between the head table and the rest of the hall. His expression falls and he gapes at his older brother.

"If you're brave enough to run your mouth, you face the conse-quences yourself. Come forward *now*." I fold my arms, watching his limbs jerk to obey the power infused in my order. As soon as he's before me, I snarl. "*Shift.*"

Dane yelps as I force his wolf out. A few others are also compelled to change with grunts and surprised curses. Mine fights me for my skin, ready to attack anyone who disparages our mate. His growls thunder from me with his fury. Our mate is amazing. She is our perfect, fate-deigned match.

If I don't control myself, he'll kill my cousin the second I give him the reins.

I keep Dane's wolf pinned beneath an unforgiving stare. He flashes his teeth with an edgy rumble, sensing the imminent danger he's put himself in. Wrong fucking move.

My wolf bursts forward, tearing through my clothes. Then I'm on him with a tackle, knocking him back. He folds his ears and swipes at me. My wolf chuffs, teeth snapping viciously at Dane's flank. He barks, skittering out of reach.

I trot around the circle. Dane isn't a challenge for me to spar with. This is about making a point to the pack that I won't allow anything less than the order I strive for.

And I won't fucking tolerate their disrespect or animosity towards Avery any longer.

He makes another move, hackles raised. The sloppy attack only goads my wolf's thirst for bloodshed. He's faster and three times the size of Dane. He stalks his opponent with a ferocious snarl.

Dane tries to escape, probably wanting to hide under the tables. My teeth close on his back leg, and I yank him back with a vicious jerk. His claws scrabble the floor, a desperate whine flying free.

I bite down harder. Blood floods my mouth, then my teeth crunch through bone. Dane's wolf screams. I release him, licking blood and sticky clumps of fur from my maw.

I allow him to feel his chance at freedom before rushing him to knock him down. Then I break his other leg, wrenching it until a chunk of meat strips off. I shake my snout, spitting the hunk of tendon and flesh to the floor.

Dane drags his injured legs, attempting to stand only to falter and slump to the floor. Panting and whining, he gives in, crawling with his tail tucked and belly pressed to the ground as best as he can get it.

I growl, peeling my lips back until he rolls to his back and exposes his belly. My wolf doesn't want his submission. He still wants to sink his teeth in his neck.

Dane loses his shift, curled up on the floor with a groan and several broken bones. Satisfied I've made an example of him, I take my skin back from the wolf.

"Weston," I call sharply. "Come collect your brother off the floor before he stains the wood."

He bolts over without hesitation. I study him, looking for any disloyalty that would make him a bad choice to approve for the security team. He hauls Dane up and looks to me for my next command.

I search for the nearest enforcer, landing on Tobin at one of the middle tables. "You go with them. Take Dane to the patrol cabin."

Tobin steals another cut of grilled meat for the road and hustles down the aisle between tables.

"Is there anyone else who believes this bullshit rumor that Avery is a witch? No?" I stalk the length of the hall. "Good. Let me assure you, I've investigated the matter myself and can confirm these rumors are unfounded."

"She's a Morgan," says one of the elders loyal to my father.

"She's *pack*." The wolf rides my words as I cast my dominant stare around the room until all I see are bent necks. "My worthy, goddess-blessed mate. You'll all forget your scorn of the Morgan name. And this is the last I want to hear otherwise."

Silence gives way to murmurs of assent. Some are approving, like Candace from maintenance group C and Alisha from the healer's cabin. There's much less opposition tainting the air than there was at the start of dinner. I watch the Blackburn clan table for any other signs of challenge. Their heads are bowed to expose their necks. I'm almost disappointed.

I glance at Liam and without a word from me, he nods in understanding. This is why he's my beta over anyone else. Because if I were to fall, I'd want him leading in my stead.

The door bangs behind me on my way out. I didn't bother pulling on what's left of my shredded clothes, calling the wolf forth before I'm down the steps. My paws land in the grass and I take off into the tree line.

20

CADEN

WHEN I REACH a clearing with a deep pool at the foot of a smaller set of falls cascading from a rocky outcrop, I shift back. The cool water in the natural spring is a welcome balm to ground me when my position becomes too much to bear on my own. I come to this spot whenever I need to clear my head and get away from the burden of being Alpha.

No one knows about it, not even Liam. It's downwind, and anytime he's near enough to know he's around, I go find him first to keep the spring a secret.

The only person I've ever thought of sharing this place with is Avery. When I first stumbled on it, I thought of bringing her here many times.

A rough sigh leaves me after I dunk beneath the surface. I swim around until the last of my adrenaline from fighting Dane burns off, then settle at the pool's edge to unwind. Raking damp hair from my forehead, I peer at the moon cresting behind pine trees.

My thoughts often turn to my father when I'm here. Particularly when I'm questioning if what I'm doing is the right choice.

I wish I still had him here to guide me when I'm at a loss for how to manage the pack. He was a stern man, but he loved us and instilled a strong sense of fairness in me and Callie. My fingers skate over my scars, a memory surfacing of the reprimand he gave me for interfering with the challenge.

He believed no one was above our laws, not even the alpha's family. I respected him above all else, even when I didn't feel ready to take over.

I wonder if he'd be proud of my dedication to this pack if he were still alive. If I'm living up to his expectations.

Not that I wanted to shoulder them in the first place. I didn't want the responsibility of Alpha, with everyone relying on me. Except as the oldest and his only son, I was the heir apparent and raised to succeed him.

The alternative was to let one of my cousins be named heir if I didn't accept. I couldn't fathom my father's legacy sullied by Lorne taking over with Cormac whispering in his ear. They'd run Silver Falls into the ground and undo all the good Dad did for us.

It's why, when it came down to it, I accepted my duty to care for the pack and do everything in my power to continue building a prosperous, comfortable community.

Finding my fated mate never factored into any of my goals for leading them. It takes all my dominance to cultivate everyone's respect as their alpha. When the bond first awoke, my greatest worry beyond my misplaced anger at her was obliterating my efforts to run the pack smoothly.

Navigating how to continue as I have been when any little slight towards my mate makes me fucking feral might prove difficult.

I want them all to see the things my wolf has from the beginning and fought me fiercely over when I denied it. To see what I've realized for myself once I stopped blinding myself to her. How strong and resilient she is, raising her sisters alone and enduring the treatment of the pack, still offering her help to those that needed it. How amazing it is that she tamed the most inhospitable parts of this mountain and bent it to her will to provide where I failed her.

She's more than worthy as a mate—as *my* mate.

Perhaps then I'll feel less inclined to decimate half the pack's numbers for as little as giving her a look I don't like. No matter what, I need to snuff out the idea spreading throughout the community that I'll be choosing anyone else.

The mere thought annoys my wolf. There is no one other than our fated.

He's tempted to track down Avery and reassure himself she's safe despite not being directly involved in tonight's incident. My lips twitch. More like he just wants to rub all over her as much as she'll let him.

My eyelids grow heavy as I imagine her hands stroking my fur. Letting me nuzzle her tits. Pulling her in close to straddle my lap to watch those pretty lips part for me. Those nimble fingers exploring my chest, mapping the bumps and valleys of my abs and following the trail of hair lower before touching my cock.

A rumble climbs my throat and I circle my hand around my erection. I tip my head back with a ragged groan.

Claim. Need to take what's mine.

There's no fighting a scene my imagination has always conjured, long before I knew she was my fate. Golden brown hair I want to tangle my fingers in. An expressive mouth I want to claim for myself. Defiant amber eyes that have always made my heart beat harder, even when I thought she deserved my hate.

Avery's always been in my fantasies. The first female I took notice of. The first one I thought of kissing. The one who haunted my dreams with things I thought I couldn't have in reality.

It shouldn't have blindsided me that she'd turn out to be my mate when deep down this draw to her has always been there. Bonds awake at random, yet the strongest always sense some sort of pull prior to fate revealing its intentions.

A thrumming warmth floods my chest, urging me along now that I'm not resisting this like my life depended on it.

Distant memories surface one after another, brighter and clearer with her gorgeous smile and that laugh—that incredible laugh that never fails to light my heart on fire.

The way I'd reorient myself subconsciously whenever she was around before a tether ever tied me to her.

How I needed her attention on me, whether I realized it or not, because whenever she gave it to another male I didn't like it.

I recognize it now. The signals were always there that she was mine.

Once I've earned her back, I'm claiming my perfect mate. I'll erase the night I rejected her from her mind, overwrite every second until I've proven to her I'll spend the rest of my days worshiping her.

My lips and tongue will know every inch of her body.

My hands will memorize the softness of her skin, the swell of her hips and breasts, the quiver of her thighs when I wrap them around my head to devour her.

My cock will only know her fingers, the heavenly tight heat of her pussy.

Fuck.

I tighten my fist and quicken my pace, imagining what it will be like to knot her. To be locked inside her and feel her stretched around me, her nails scrabbling as she clings to me, beautiful features contorted with a silent cry of ecstasy. Her arousal so thick in the air I can taste it on my tongue. My stomach concaves with desire, a jagged breath tinged with pleasure punching from my lungs.

I want to know what she feels like when she comes on my cock while I'm knotting her. With her legs around me and her hands pinned above her head, with her on top riding me, fucking *fuck*, with her presenting for my eyes only, her head down and ass high in the air just for me.

I want to learn all the ways to make her whimper and her body beg for more when I lick the mating bite I'm going to mark her with.

My teeth sink into my lip, canines close to drawing blood as I picture drawing her hair to the side and seeing my claim on her, grazing it with my fingers, my lips. The way it'll make her blush, and then I'll herd my pretty little mate against the nearest wall and sink to my knees to taste that heady lust making her honeyed scent drive me insane.

A burst of—something pulses in my chest. A reaction to my arousal, I realize. It travels along the delicate threads that survived without fully severing.

Fascinated, I turn more of my attention inward to find the bond, slowing my fist curled around my throbbing shaft to keep my release teetering on the edge. A breath hisses between my teeth at the feel of plucking the strands of magic while I stroke myself, allowing me to feel her while amplifying the pleasure I'm bringing myself.

I grin when there's an answering shudder from her end. She liked that. If I focus, I can direct an astral touch to caress the connection. This time it earns me a shiver in response.

Experimenting, I try giving it a spank. I grip the slippery rocks to keep my balance when an electric jolt rockets through me, then feel an enticing thrill from her, tucked safely away in her cottage. Wicked delight races through me.

I trace my tongue along my lower lip, my shoulder and arm flexing with each glide of my hand over my thick cock while playing with her through the bond, opening myself to allow her to experience everything I'm feeling with my head full of her.

Using projection across the bond, I drag my knuckles over the curve of her tits, circling her nipples before sending my touch in a meandering path down her stomach, dipping between her thighs to pet her clit. The magic thrum pulses with her need, reigniting my hunger for her more intensely when she tugs the connection.

More.

I'll give her everything she needs. I'm relentless, matching the speed I'm jerking my cock with my phantom fingers plunging inside her. When she comes, I feel it, the sensation resonating within me from our link.

"Oh, fuck," I utter.

My balls tighten and I come hard, spilling over my fingers with her name on my lips. I slump back, catching my breath with a puff of laughter. Checking on the bond, I find her languid with tantalizing shivers.

I'm not able to bask in the pride of making her come through the mate bond for long. Liam's scent carries on the breeze. With a content sigh, I hoist myself from the spring and shift back to my fur.

For the first time in years, I feel right. Lighter, a sense of balance within my grasp.

21

AVERY

My name is no longer on the kitchen duty roster. I went yesterday and Alma shooed me right back out the door. Taryn tried to sneak out with me until Alma grabbed her by the collar and put her back to work. When I crossed the commons to find out what was up, I couldn't find my name on any of the assignments, granting me the ability to do as I usually please once more.

It's Caden's doing. Gratitude and something pleasant plucked at my heartstrings until I tamped down on it.

I'm still not sure what to think when it comes to him, or if I can trust that my feelings towards him are truly my own. What if it's only the bond influencing our emotions? Is it the only reason we became friends in the first place, because it was the root of why I liked being around him so much? Without being fated mates, would we have found our way to each other?

I should still hate him, shouldn't I? The feeling of his arms cradling me to his chest and his comforting scent enveloping me like a blanket on a foggy morning makes me think otherwise.

I drape an arm over my eyes in bed, unable to make my mind quiet. I strain my ears, my throbbing pulse calming when I register the steady breaths of Caden's wolf outside. Biting my lip, I roll towards the wall, laying a hand over the crevices where his scent seeps through. I tuck my nose against it, heart skipping a beat when he stirs to sniff where my scent must be bleeding through the tiny cracks to him.

He rumbles inquisitively before flopping down again. I trace the barrier between us, examining the flickers of yearning in the bond to sleep in the arms of my mate. Is it from me or him? I can't tell the source from the way it overlaps on itself, ingrained in the enchanted tethers. There are a few more strands than there were before he followed me in the woods and we almost kissed.

More still after...whatever that was the other night when I was bathing and *felt* his pleasure along the magic threads connecting us.

A shiver races down my spine at the memory of him exploring the bond and using it to touch me. Caressing the curve of my breasts, teasing my neck, and skimming a fluttering path down my stomach to delve between my thighs until he had me shuddering without even being in the room with me. I had no idea fated mates could do such things with the magic...or that I'd come so hard from its stimulation.

A burst of heat spreads throughout my body all over again. My thighs squeeze at the coil of desire, vividly remembering how he made me writhe with his fingers. A soft noise catches in my throat as my core clenches with the need for the real thing, and so much more.

Caden's wolf is still awake. He purrs outside, scratching at the wall.

I swallow, smothering those thoughts, my cheeks burning. Will he remember this when he shifts back in the morning?

My wolf chuffs, sprawling on her back. She thinks my reluctance is silly. This is the way of mates.

An old pang echoes in my heart. My parents were fated, too. It used to make me and the girls giggle when he'd be outside with us until he'd stumble out of nowhere. He'd wink at us and say she was yanking him in for dinnertime.

They were so happy. It destroyed our father when she went missing.

Eventually, I drift to sleep, my endless worries muted by the soothing presence of the wolf on the other side of the wall lulling everything that plagues me to the back of my mind.

In the morning, I get up early to shift with a renewed spark. I'm ready to let my wolf run free again.

Caden hasn't left yet. He's stretching outside my window, the taut muscles in his back and ass flexing in the glow of morning sun. I map the hard planes of his incredible broad physique from his shoulders to his sculpted ass and thighs, struggling to catch my breath.

He angles his head back slightly and I spot the hint of a smirk before I duck from the window. His deep laughter makes my stomach dip.

I wait him out, not leaving until the slack in the bond stretches with the distance between us. The girls are still asleep when I slip out the door. I skip shoes, then pluck at my clothes with a hum. Peeling them off, I tie the leggings and shirt dress together to make a loop my wolf can wear until I figure out a better way to transport my clothes if I don't plan to return to get dressed.

Most people leave out spare clothing draped on a line by their houses or put out a box for sharing. It's not uncommon to see things passed around a few families, often amongst those who have come of age and want to let their wolf out all the time. I don't know if that extends to me yet.

This time it's not as difficult to find the instinct to enact the change, the one I didn't understand at first. It's more natural than my first experience, less like my body is snapping and reforming anew in a state of panic and heartache, more seamlessly transitioning to my fur. My wolf feels more tangible to me now and she helps me through it as I give her control.

I stretch with a yawn, digging my claws into the earth. Caden's scent is even more powerful to my nose now. It's everywhere, all around my cottage, up in the meadow above it, down the road. I waver, my wolf wanting to follow the freshest trail of cedar and oakmoss to find him.

His chuckle when he caught me admiring his body makes the bond dance within me. I want to, but I'll find him later. Right now I want to run and explore to my heart's content.

The first time I shifted, I was too overwhelmed to notice everything. Lifting my nose, I find I'm right about tracking valuable plants to forage. There's a patch of buckthorn fruit growing on bushes I never knew about north from the meadow, and the buttery sweet hints of chanterelle mushrooms calling to me on the breeze. It could expand my little hustle into something greater than I ever dreamed when Jade first gave me direction and helped me find my love of plants.

I paw at the loop I made with my clothes and with some maneuvering with my snout, I'm able to slip it over my head like an oversized collar. A basket, I'll need a basket easy to carry when I go out for plants. And a way to carry my tools, my satchel will get slobbery if I carry it in my mouth.

Ideas spark one after the other, my thoughts coming more fluid and less burdened than they might be in my skin. I chuckle at my lowered inhibitions and it comes out as an energetic yip.

I trot through the woods, learning with my wolf how to do this. All around me nature is alive and it stokes my excitement.

Our lope through the forest takes us past skullcap and puffball mushrooms, a vibrant gooseberry bush, swaths of dandelions in the thick grass beneath evergreens, and beds of purslane. She sprawls on the succulent ground cover weed for a short nap without listening to my attempts to steer her away.

Green. Yuck, she decides after nibbling on the slightly salty leaves.

She catches a much more enjoyable scent—prey. We both perk up at the thought of meat for breakfast, our mouth salivating. We're a big, beastly wolf. Surely it can't be so hard to catch something. This should come naturally for us, we're a predator born to hunt.

My wolf prowls behind overgrown ferns, fixated on the burrow nestled in a hollow at the base of a tree twenty paces away. She doesn't wait long. A gopher with its cheeks stuffed with food comes down from another nearby tree, zigzagging through the underbrush. She's perfectly still, nose barely twitching as the creature comes closer.

Energy vibrates through her limbs and she darts too soon, scaring it out of reach when she pounces. A bark works its way up her throat in her shock she didn't catch it.

She watches her meal scamper off, tail drooping and a put out sigh huffing from her.

I console her disgruntled mood. We still suck at hunting, but we'll figure it out with practice. The first time I tried to eat what the forest provided me, I nearly poisoned myself and look at me now.

She forgets all about it once we're running again, the cool air ruffling our coat and tingeing the air with interesting scents like fresh laundry, baking bread, and the pipes elders smoke on their porches. Someone's being loud, their whining cries filtering through the trees from the direction of Silver Falls. The tang of arousal hangs in the air. Mating. I identify Emily's scent and change directions.

A sleek wolf bounds over a mossy hill with her tongue hanging out from her grinning maw. I freeze.

She stops, tail at attention as she sniffs us snout to snout. Her wet nose tickles our ear when she inspects it, then moves down our neck and front flank. She barks, lowering her chest to the ground. Our tail wags when we recognize her. Taryn. Friend.

We circle each other, jumping and playing. She knocks into me much like she does when we're in our skin and I roll her.

A sharp bark interrupts us. We spring to our feet when another wolf emerges from the trees. He's huge with bright orange eyes that seem familiar. It becomes clear when he pins Taryn's wolf and runs his nose from her chest to beneath her jaw, licking her before he lets her up.

I approach Liam, ears swiveling to gauge his mood. He gives

me a perfunctory sniff and gives my side a headbutt. My wolf bumps him back with her shoulder, putting a paw on his back. He goes still, then takes off, pausing on top of a hill to see if we're following. Taryn shoots off first and I join her, my spirits soaring as the three of us race.

This is what I've missed. Belonging with my pack.

22

CADEN

WHEN THE KID from our carpentry supply delivers the last of the materials I ordered, I load it into the flatbed of my truck with the rest of the things I've gathered that Avery needs and drive up to her cottage. On the way, I pass the crew working on extending the power lines and lift my fingers in a wave from the open window.

Avery's not around, but her sisters are.

Beatrix bursts out the rickety front door while I'm unloading lumber from the truck. The damned thing is first on my list.

If I thought she'd let me, I'd burn this place down. I'm sure it would piss her off when she's put so much effort into making this her space, so I'll fix it up so it stands another century to serve her needs.

"Are you looking for Avery?" Beatrix can't contain a smile. "I heard you're True Mates. Is that why you're coming around now?"

The corner of my mouth lifts. "I'm here for all of you. I'm sorry for making your lives hard for so long. Will you let me make it right?"

She purses her lips to the side in thought, growing quiet. "Is it also true you rejected her? She won't tell me about it no matter how much I pester her. I had to hear it from the others in my lessons, and they say you were a real dick about it."

My head dips. "Yes. I want to make up for that, too."

"Did it hurt?"

A startled huff leaves me. "It does, yes."

"Good."

I rub my chest to ease the twinge at the memory, the bond punishing me for what I did to my mate retroactively. "More for her, I think. If I could go back and change what I've done, I would."

She peers inside a moment, probably checking on Lena. "What are you planning to do about it? Because if you hurt Avery again..." She comes to the edge of the stoop, hands on her hips and a ferocious expression rivaling the females on the enforcer roster. "I won't let it slide."

It strikes me that I'm Alpha and I'm being admonished by a girl who hasn't even come of age yet. She's my mate's family, which makes her one of my own. I need to protect the Morgan girls as much as I need to care for my own blood.

"When we moved here, I didn't really understand why, and Lena was way too young to remember much of anything. It didn't feel right, being so far from the pack. The smells were different and I couldn't hear them." Her gaze hardens. "You know what I do remember? The nights Avery cried after she put us to bed thinking no one could hear her."

The guilty knife lodged in my chest drives a bit deeper. "You have my word that I will never hurt Avery ever again."

I vow it with a hand over my heart that only beats for her.

She gives a satisfied nod after a beat. "If you can make her happy again, then it'll be okay. She deserves to be happy."

My throat thickens. I clear it, squeezing my nape.

"She does. And I will give her anything and everything to ensure it." I gesture to the open bed of the truck. "Starting with a repaired door that doesn't scream on its hinges. If that's alright with you?"

Beatrix perks up, her bubbly energy returning. "You're going to fix the door?"

"I'll fix anything that needs it." I incline my head. "Or, if you'd like, I'll prepare a new cabin for you to move to."

She's right. They shouldn't be so far from the pack. The nearest cabin is close to a mile from here. They need to be around their packmates. Lena and Beatrix should be running around with friends, not cast to the edges of the territory.

"I'd take that option in a heartbeat," she gushes. "But... Avery does like it out here, I think. It's small and kind of shitty, but it's ours. We've made it cozy."

My wolf purrs with pride in our mate. Despite me being the reason for her harsh environment, she's a survivor. He likes that.

"Let's restore the parts that are losing against age, then see if we can convince her there's no need to remain out here," I suggest.

Not when both my wolf and I want her near. In my rooms at the lodge. In my bed. Soft and warm, smelling lush and open in the mornings. Within arm's reach so I can pull her close and sink into her, hear those little sounds she makes when she's needy and hungry for more like the other night in the woods. Fuck, those sounds.

I busy myself with the bag of tools, back turned on Beatrix so she doesn't see the evidence of what thinking of her sister does to me.

"Can I help?" Beatrix wanders over.

"There's a stack of blankets in the front seat and a cooler full of food if you want to take those in."

Her eyes sparkle when she opens the lid on the cooler. "So much meat."

I come around and ruffle her hair, then reach past her for the bag of things I went to Ashbury to get as a gift for Avery. I follow Beatrix inside and greet Lena.

She puts her book in her lap. I'm glad to see some color in her cheeks. I take one of the blankets from Beatrix's stack and drape it around Lena.

"Thank you."

"You're looking better," I say.

She nods. "My cold's almost gone. Avery's remedies are really good to fight off illness."

"Good. If either of you need anything at all, tell me."

"We will," Beatrix says.

I put the gardening tools I got for Avery on her workbench, borrowing a page from her journal to leave a note. My fingers brush the new shears and a smile tugs at my mouth.

Once I survey the cottage to assess the worst areas that need attention, I settle in to work on building a new door. Bit by bit, I'll mend all the things I've broken in Avery's life, from this cottage to every crack I've caused in her heart.

After a while, I split off from Liam and Taryn's wolves to continue exploring. I enjoy running with them, but they turn for Silver Falls, probably wanting a morning swim. Soon I'll get to join them for a pack run.

By the time I shift back, I've made it to the tree line surrounding the commons. The central lawn is bustling with people hanging around the dining hall, coming in and out of a late lunch.

"Good afternoon."

I yank down the shirt dress I'm pulling on and whirl to the cabin tucked into the cover of evergreens. One of the Farrows elders and his granddaughter sit on the porch. I glance around, finding no one else.

"Good afternoon," I stammer.

"There's a nice spread for lunch. Alma hasn't switched with Martine today. Better hurry if you want to get some of her jam donuts she made for dessert," he advises sagely.

"Oh. Thanks, I will." Maybe I'll get some to bring back for Bea and Lena.

He's not the only one to acknowledge me on my way through the commons. A surprising number of people make eye contact, some even smiling at me as if I haven't been a pariah they whispered about for years. My throat goes tight at how nice it is to be acknowledged. Accepted.

There are still a few scathing looks when I enter the dining hall to remind me I haven't tripped through a fae portal to an alternate realm.

I'm scanning for a seat when Callie comes in behind me. She offers a tentative smile.

"Hi, Avery. Are you doing okay?" She twirls her hair around her finger, the same nervous habit she's had since she was a kid.

I return her smile, my heart warming that she's speaking to me. "I am, thanks. You're eating late today."

"I'm avoiding my brother until he takes his head out of his ass. Want to sit with me?"

I chuckle and hike my thumb in the opposite direction. "I was just going to duck into the kitchen to raid the donuts for my sisters. Want some?"

"Yes. That's way better than sitting up there alone."

We loiter by the swinging double doors, grabbing the first opportunity to head to the kitchens. Alma's distracted and I wave at Callie to grab two baskets waiting to go out to tables. Before we're caught, we dash through the side door.

Alma's shout comes behind us. "No eating on the go in my kitchen!"

"I'll bring you a fresh joint salve as payment," I call.

We race by the commissary, not stopping until we reach the wraparound porch of the lodge. Callie's giggles are contagious. We each toast with a donut, humming in unison at the warm sugary dough.

"Are you coming in? I don't think Caden's here if you're avoiding him, too. He went somewhere in his truck and has been out most of the day."

"I'm going to get these back." Her expression falls. "You can come over anytime you want."

"Now?" She bites her lip hopefully.

"Sure."

We fall into step, taking the road to the northern perimeter. She peeks at me occasionally.

"For what it's worth, I never thought you were to blame for anything," she finally says in a rush. "I... I really missed you. And I'm sorry. I was afraid to still talk to you but I wanted to all the time."

My heart wobbles and I wrap her in a side hug. "It's okay. It's not your fault. I missed you, too."

She sniffles, leaning her head on my shoulder, reminding me just how young she was when everything changed for us. It was difficult enough to face my life being turned inside out at sixteen, I can only imagine how confusing it was for her at fourteen. Other than Taryn, I was her only close friend.

"Come on. The girls will be really happy to see you." I take her hand and she holds tight.

When we make it to the cottage, I take pride in giving a tour of the garden, explaining everything planted and how I use it. Her eyes widen with respect by the time we go inside.

"I brought donuts and a surprise visitor," I announce.

Wait.

My head pops up. I try the door again. There's no creak. It swings properly and I realize it's completely different from the crooked one that I've tried to fix hundreds of times.

"Hold on. What happened to the door? And where did you get that fur blanket from?"

Lena doesn't look up from her book right away. She tends to finish a passage before marking her place, then the rest of the world is allowed to exist. Beatrix isn't home. She must've gone out.

"Alpha Blackburn stopped by while you were gone." Lena brightens when Callie waves to her. "Hi! Can we sit outside? He said the porch only needed an hour to dry. I'm feeling much better. No cough, see?"

She breathes deeply a few times without any crackle in her lungs. My lips part and I peer out the window. Sure enough, the crumbling stone's been patched. I missed it on my way in, automatically hopping over the damage while I gave Callie the same instruction.

I'm used to his wolf spending the night outside my window now, accepting what I've gathered from my own wolf that he's not happy unless he's guarding me whether I need it or not. Usually he's gone by morning, unless I catch him like I did before I left today.

I expect irritation to fizzle along my nerves and a need to protect my family, but it doesn't come at the thought of him here.

Mate is protector, my wolf whispers.

I help Lena up. "Wait, is that a new rocking chair?"

"He brought that, too." She smiles at my expression. "He's a lot nicer than you think. He stocked us up with all this food and blankets. Beatrix went with him to get more nails so they can build a new fence for your garden. You should see what he put on your workbench."

I'm at a loss for words, exchanging a glance with Callie. She shrugs.

"Don't look at me. Like I said, I've been avoiding him. He hasn't said a word to me about any of this."

Lena giggles at my flabbergasted reaction to the array of brand new gardening tools at my workspace, including a roll of different sized knives much sharper than the rusted one I use for chopping and a brand new pair of shears.

The note beneath the roll reads: *For whenever I've done something else to deserve it, you can threaten me with your garden shears again. If you need anything else, it's yours. You know where to find me. — C*

I trace his handwriting and my stomach fills with butterflies.

He did all this while I was gone? My lips slide together, a tender smile breaking free.

"He said he's just getting started," Lena says.

I didn't realize I spoke the question aloud. She hugs her book to her chest and beams.

"You haven't smiled like that in a long time. Like you're really happy."

I duck my head, unable to stop. I don't recall the last time I experienced such easy joy. My heartbeat drums insistently as a glow fills me from within.

)))●(((

I DON'T KNOW what to expect two days later when I'm told I'm supposed to go to the healer's cabin. It certainly isn't arguing with the cantankerous male who has been the pack's healer for two and a half generations. He has to be pushing two hundred by now, and could be languishing on the porches smoking pipes and listening to the strum of banjos in the evenings like the rest of the pack elders.

Instead, he's here going blue in the face at my insistence that shifters can be susceptible to illnesses and ailments outside of moon madness.

"This is a ridiculous waste of my time. If you'd just listen instead of yelling over me, you might actually learn something about healing," I say flatly.

"You can't teach me nothin' I don't know about anythin'," he hollers with a stomp of his foot. "I've been minding this pack for longer than you've been born."

"She's right, Eugene," Alisha pleads. "Remember when I had trouble with a skin reaction after my runs and you kept telling me it would get better? It didn't randomly go away. Avery's the one who helped me with a paste to calm down the rash I was getting, and figured out I'm allergic to the ragweed my wolf loves to roll around in."

It's nice that she's taking my side. She's one of my best customers that trades often with me.

"Because people all say she's a witch," he snaps. "Allergies aren't real. Maybe she cursed you with the rash in the first place for lookin' at her wrong. Told you not to meddle with the likes of her, didn't I?"

I'm so used to years of unkind whispers and dirty looks from the pack, his words don't even sting. I rub my temple with a sigh at his incompetence.

Alisha scoffs. "She's not a witch. I've been telling you for years about how all the things she makes from plants helps treat some cases you write off. There are others in the pack that would benefit from us expanding our horizons with her knowledge."

"Hogwash."

"It's not." I toss my hands up. "You only think that because you've never tried anything different. People in this pack need better. I needed better when my sister was sick."

He doesn't like the glare I give him. "I told that pup Caden I didn't want a consult and he didn't listen."

"Alpha Blackburn," I correct sharply, surprising myself. "His age has nothing to do with his rank. He's still your alpha."

He scrunches his face. "This isn't going to work."

"That's too bad, because it's not up to you," Alisha says.

Elder Eugene storms out shouting about not needing extra hands. She stands in the front doorway, waving.

"Go have something to eat before you bother coming back here." She offers me an apologetic smile. "Don't mind him. He's cranky and stubborn and his joints always ache. But we'll get him to come around. I'm really glad to have you here."

A smirk crosses my face. I have several remedies for aching joints, but I'm not sharing them with him. "What did he mean about extra help? Am I being assigned to the healer's cabin?"

I've avoided this place ever since the winter Lena got pneumonia. On one hand, working here could mean improving Lena's health, and give me the opportunity to see who else might need help like she did. On the other, I'd have to deal with him.

"Yes. You have full access to everything here. You can take appointments in the second room, and if you need to bring anything in I've made space for you to store your supplies right through here."

She shows me a spacious pantry closet that's been cleared out.

"Wait. What?"

She doesn't follow my confusion. "Is this not enough room? I wasn't sure how much would be good. When I come up to get the paste you make me, you seem to keep it organized in such a small workspace."

"No, I mean taking appointments?"

"You're one of the healers, so yes."

I stare at her. "I need to go."

Before she gets another word out, I'm rushing from the cabin. Packmates wave as I hurry down roads to the central lawn and head right to the Alpha's lodge. Caden's head is bent over his desk in the middle of a meeting with Liam, Gabe, and some elders who advised his father when I bustle in.

"With the electrical extension project finishing up, we should consider how—Avery."

Everything about him changes the instant he sees me, his commanding tone softening with warmth and something else that fills my stomach with flutters when he says my name like it's the best part of his day.

I falter, realizing I've barged right into his office. Not one enforcer stopped me, either. The implication of why I'd be allowed free rein anywhere in the pack now compared to a short time ago makes me swallow the thick tangle of emotions clogging my throat. My wolf has no such qualms, feeling this is her place.

We might have a mate bond, but we haven't claimed each other to officially become a mated pair. My heart swells and creeps up my throat, my pulse speeding at the possibility.

I shake my head, passing a sheepish look to the elders while Liam chuckles under his breath. "Sorry. I interrupted."

"It's fine." With a wave, Caden dismisses everyone, then circles his desk to lean against it in a casual slouch that puts us at eye level. "What do you need?"

You, the bond sings. My wolf agrees, pressing forward to bask in his reassuring earthy cedarwood musk.

I flatten a hand over my jittery stomach. "I went to see the healer. Did you arrange that?"

"Of course."

My lips rub together. "So I'm essentially co-healer to the pack now?"

His forehead creases. "Is that a problem?"

I flap a hand. "Why?"

"What's wrong? Was Eugene an ass to you? Tell me and I'll sort him out." He catches my fingers and gives them a caress that anchors me. "Is this not what you wish? If you'd like to do something else, by all means do."

"It's a big change. I just—"

Words fail me. My eyes fall shut when he gently pulls me between his legs, then kneads my nape. He brings my hand up, nuzzling the inside of my wrist. Tingles erupt in my belly at the scrape of his stubbled jaw against my skin.

"I thought you'd like it," he murmurs. "If not, I'm sorry. You can do anything you want."

He thought I'd like it. My stomach swoops.

"No, I sort of do," I admit. "It's not something I ever considered for myself. I know plants. I'm not sure that qualifies me for this."

"I think you'd be great at it. I saw your notes," he admits. "You think about ways to help others in the pack."

"I do." I meet his penetrating gaze, breath catching at his sincere belief in me. "I've thought about it a lot. At first because it was a necessity for my survival to understand what was needed."

He tenses, drawing me in until we're chest to chest. His lips brush my wrist. My eyes fall shut and I lean against him tentatively, biting my lip when his other arm winds around me.

"You're focused on the bigger picture as Alpha. There's a lot you don't see," I continue. "Food allotments being shorted, for one. Not just mine, but those who rank lower than others."

He rumbles, grip tightening on my wrist. "Is that why your meat store was so sparse? You were meant to get a fair share like anyone else."

"Things aren't always fair here."

"Then my orders have been disobeyed. No more. We'll make this pack a prosperous, supportive place for everyone. Pack means we're all in this together, part of a big family that we protect," he says. "I want to make life good for all our packmates. The packs will meet soon to honor our accords. At the summit, I'll be submitting a proposal for new trade agreements."

When he became Alpha, I thought he was strictly setting rules to assert his control. I'm starting to wonder if I've had his motives all wrong. Someone who wants to improve his pack's life and create a sense of safety isn't on a power trip.

The other word he used takes root in my mind and my heart. *We.* If he's open to listening to me, we could weed out the hidden injustices that occur in Silver Falls Pack every day.

24

AVERY

CADEN'S back at the cottage again.

Shirtless this time, muscles glistening in the sunlight as he digs near my garden. Not that I'm paying attention.

He's simply in my line of sight through the window by my workbench and he's impossible to miss.

The gleaming tendrils of brown hair curling across his forehead invite me to sift my fingers through. The captivating shape of his mouth when the tip of his tongue sticks out of the side in concentration makes my mouth go dry. The skilled movements of his powerful body lead my mind to imagine him tossing me over his shoulder or chasing me down in the meadow.

Even without the bond influencing me with mate-vision to highlight his tempting features, his draw on my attention is irresistible.

It always has been.

No other male in the pack ever interested me. Only him.

His presence makes my wolf purr and stretch out within me. His scent hangs in the air all around the cottage, finding its way through every crack and crevice to let me know he's there in case I forgot.

I wouldn't. There's no way I could ever be unaware when he's near.

At this point, I've lost count of the number of days in a row he's come here, but there are reminders of him all around.

A blanket I started taking out for him when his wolf returns every night folded over a chair.

Wildflowers he's brought me asking if they're anything I can use dotting the cottage windowsills and my workbench in makeshift vases from spare jars.

The extra water glass on the counter he likes to dump over his head before refilling and downing in long gulps that make me warm while staring at the bobbing of his bared throat, thoughts of licking it and wrapping myself around him tugging at me.

The feelings these visits stir in me leave me lighter and my sisters have taken notice. The hope and trust I buried deep inside me flickers to life, cautiously opening myself back up to him. I've been so focused on surviving day to day, ensuring my family is taken care of, that I didn't think I'd ever find these parts of myself again, let alone because of him when he's the one that shattered them when he broke my heart the first time.

I can't deny that I like it when he comes up here. When I hear him laughing at Beatrix's lively jokes on the porch. When he asks Lena about her book. When he catches my eye and something burning passes between us before he gives me a heart-stopping smile.

I do my best to focus on taking stock of my inventory before I start moving some of it down to the healer's cabin. I told Alisha that I'd ease into being there and she promised to soften Eugene up.

Every few minutes, I find my attention drifting out the window, fingertips brushing my sternum where a soft warmth emanates.

Caden lifts a hoe overhead, treating me to a perfect view when he drives it into the ground with a grunt that's way hotter than it should be. I drink him in, a coil of desire curling in my core the longer I watch. The display teases something primal within me.

He stops, tilts his head as if he's listening for something, then his shoulders shake with a pleased laugh. He shoots me a smirk before returning to his task.

There's no way he knows I was watching, is there? I snap my focus back to inventory. When I least expect it, the sensation of lips brushing all over me makes me drop my pen with a clatter. The phantom mouth begins with kisses to my nape, then progresses in a slow exploration down the column of my throat to the space between my breasts.

I grip the edge of the workbench and bite my lip to contain a whimper. Then it stops, leaving me turned on without relief. I peek at the window, finding him working like he didn't do anything.

The urge to go outside niggles at me. I hold out for a few moments before I venture to the porch under the guise of gathering fresh clippings. He stops working.

"You like your new things?" He nods to my shears, leaning on the hoe.

"I—yes. I do, thank you for them."

"Good." His broad chest puffs with pride.

Something tugs at me. An invisible tether. It's faint at first, then more insistent. My eyes widen as the astral magic jerks me until I stumble off the porch. He's there to catch me with an inviting rumble.

"What was that?" I ask when he steadies me.

"I wanted you closer, so I gave you a tug."

He flashes a grin at me that's full of charming mischief and amusement. A flutter dances in my chest, my heart skipping a beat.

I trace the spot I felt the pull with a soft smile. "How do you keep doing that?"

Curious to know how it works, I search for the bond within myself. It's much stronger now, no longer the tattered mess it was left in by his rejection. The shimmering threads of magic are weaving back together in some places to mend what was broken.

I give them an experimental stroke, startling when it makes him falter. He drops the tool with a groan, throwing out a hand to catch himself on the porch. My stomach dips at his shudder of pleasure.

"Avery," he breathes.

The corners of my mouth lift and I do it again, slower, trying to tease it to give him a taste of what it's like when he does it to me.

"Is that it?"

"Yeah." A huff of laughter slips out with a delicious tinge of roughness to it. "Fuck, that feels so—"

He grabs me with a sexy growl. I gasp, peering into his hooded eyes. They're dark with arousal, his hardness pressing into me. Spiced cedar wrapped with sweet sunshine and rain-soaked earth drowns me. It's the alluring blend of us. Our scents together. I wet my lips, lashes fluttering at how heady it is.

"If you keep doing that, I'm not going to be able to control myself around you," he rasps.

My gaze hones in on his mouth. "You started it."

He buries a grin in my hair. "I did."

Being in his arms brings me so much comfort. I could stay like this all day, pressed against his chiseled body. I'd like to sprawl in a breezy meadow and rest my head on his firm chest to nap after a run together. Feel his large palms petting me all over. Straddle him and sink down his cock until he fills my aching pussy over and over.

Air gusts from my lungs and I shiver. My own control is on the brink of snapping. If I don't move, I might present for him right here in the open. His grip tightens and he inhales with a faint gravelly hum.

It's far more difficult than it should be to pull back, but he releases me without complaint. We untangle and he turns away to adjust himself while I go to my garden to cool the heat blooming in my face.

I spend a few minutes cutting sprigs of plants at random until I feel less like getting on all fours, sticking my ass in the air, and begging for him to knot me.

Caden gives me space, going back to digging. I appreciate how patient and considerate he's been.

I want this. I do, but the intense bouts of need that throw taking anything slow out the window make me hesitate. I'm questioning if I can trust that my feelings are truly my own because of it. Or if he genuinely wants me.

It shouldn't matter this much to me. A fated mate is a shifter's perfect match. My wolf doesn't see the problem either. The complicated history between us doesn't make sense to her. He's our mate and she wants him, end of story.

Deep down I think part of me is still afraid to fully open my heart again so quickly after it's been fractured too many times.

I'm not in heat yet and he doesn't seem in danger of falling into a rut, but I'm worried if I resist for too long the bond will push us together in any way it can to appease the Fates. Hopefully we still have time before it comes to that. I wouldn't want to be lost to the insatiable lust of a mating frenzy our first time.

Once I've calmed down, I lean against the edge of the porch to watch him work. "What are you doing out here?"

"Isn't it obvious? I'm expanding your garden for you."

I laugh, gesturing with the clippings. "The winter months are almost here. I already planted what little will grow."

He frowns, surveying the trenches he's dug. "What do you do if you need something out of season?"

"I dry it and store as much of it as I can."

He strokes his chin with a hum, then leans on the hoe. "Then you'll have a greenhouse so you never have to rely on seasons to grow whatever you want."

My eyes widen and I fight a delighted smile. I've thought about building a greenhouse. The cottage sits over an innate pocket of magic in the earth that connects to a ley line. With a greenhouse, I could really capitalize on my output, maybe try to extract more complex, higher quality oils because I'd have enough plants to work with. I wouldn't have to make the blessing circle Jade showed me around the edge of the garden to keep the dirt healthy and workable during the cold months.

"Aren't there more important things the alpha should be doing rather than building me greenhouses and restoring my cottage? You have a pack to run."

He pins me with his gaze. My stomach dips at the sincerity and affection he doesn't hide as he closes the distance between us and takes my chin. My worries fade whenever he looks at me like that.

"There's nothing more important than this."

Good mate, my wolf interjects. She's all about the attention and devotion he's showing us with.

I lick my lips, breath hitching when his eyes hood and his thumb traces the curve of my mouth. I inch closer, heart beating faster.

"Let me take care of you," he murmurs.

"I've gotten good at taking care of myself," I whisper.

He searches my eyes with remorseful anguish. "I know. You're strong. But let me anyway. You don't have to rely on yourself anymore. You have me."

A lump forms in my throat. I nod shakily, closing my eyes when he rumbles and kisses my forehead. He cups my face, thumb caressing my cheek. His lips skate down, then hover. Tingles erupt in my belly.

He releases a strained sound and brushes his mouth over mine. My heart soars and a sense of rightness echoes within me unlike anything I've ever experienced. He is my mate and he's kissing me.

Before I'm ready, the chaste kiss ends. My body sways towards him and the briefest flash of disappointment zips through me. I was hoping for a different kiss. One that I feel to the depths of my being.

He studies me, rubbing at his chest. "I'll be back soon. I'm going to get what I need to build your greenhouse."

I watch him until his truck disappears, then step onto the porch and lean against the new beams he added to extend the repaired roof.

This place was once my punishment. Then it became my pride when I made it my own. New possibilities spring to mind when I survey the sloping mountainside and dream about what the future might hold. In all of them, he's there at my side.

25

CADEN

"OKAY, that should do it. Fire it up," I tell Ford from the rafters.

He throws the breaker we installed yesterday and Avery's cottage illuminates with the brand new electric we've wired the house with. Satisfaction expands in my chest. This is how it should've been for her and her sisters. Lights and hot water whenever they want it, not dependent on finding kindling for the wood stove or fireplace.

I can't replace the home and its memories I stole from her, only restore this one if she refuses to leave it. If she's ever ready to, I've already made space for her family at the lodge with me and Callie, and saved one of the newly built empty cabins. Whatever she needs, I will give it to her.

I've taken out the rusted stove and antique hand pump sink, replacing them with new appliances. The beds have been updated with fresh mattresses and sturdy frames I constructed. I'm building a table and chairs next, then I'll create another workbench for the greenhouse I finished. There's only so much space to work with. I'm considering an addition because I'd like to give all the girls their own rooms, and give Avery a bigger space for her work.

My wolf is pleased with the improvement to our mate's shelter. Providing for her fills him with pride.

I didn't deserve her three weeks ago. I'm working to be the mate worthy of treasuring her. Wanting her every day hasn't stopped. Not since I realized what I was stupid enough to try throwing away.

Last week when she touched the bond for the first time, I nearly claimed her right there. I'm dying to kiss her for far longer than the too brief peck I stole. Her mouth needs to be savored for hours on end.

It's hell sufficing on kissing any inch of skin I can get away with every time my need for her is too great to bear. Whenever I have her in my arms, I remind myself that it's up to her if she forgives and accepts me or not, no matter how much every fiber of my being craves her.

I jump from the rafters and set my tool bag on the table. "Thanks for helping me finish it. It was overdue. We should've made sure all the cabins were up to date a long time ago."

"Yeah, that's why this was a top priority project." Gabe elbows me with a grin.

I toss him a harassed look. Ford slings an arm over his mate's shoulder.

"You can be honest with us. We get it. There's not much you wouldn't do for your mate."

"This isn't only because—"

Liam bumps my shoulder with his. "Even I know it is. Just like I know that since this is done, you're about to go look for Avery to show her."

"I—" A breath blows out of me. "Yeah, you got me there. She can't be far off. Report if there's anything urgent."

I'm already shedding my clothes to shift so I can track her faster. She left an hour ago to venture into the forest while her sisters spend the weekend with Callie at the lodge. Maybe I can convince her wolf to come out when she's done foraging. I haven't met her yet and I'm eager to know that side of her.

"We've got everything under control," Liam promises. "Go."

When I make no move, he lifts his brow. Ford shakes his head with a snicker, whispering to Gabe. They head out. My wolf eases up, but if my beta doesn't get his ass in gear this is about to get awkward.

"You can't be here without me," I explain when Liam's at a loss. "This is part of my wolf's territory. My mate's home. I don't want any other males around here alone, even you."

"Oh. My bad." He grins. "So everything they say about mate madness tracks? It never bothered you before if I was around the lodge."

I incline my head wryly. "Try me and find out. My wolf doesn't care that you're my best friend and I trust you with my life. Still don't want you stinking up the place."

He raises his hands and bows his head with a laugh, marching out the door. I open some windows to air the place out before leaving.

Once I hang my clothes on a chair, I seamlessly become my wolf by the time I'm off the porch. Her heavenly sweet scent is everywhere. He immediately picks out the freshest trail and trots off. She shifted into her fur. He gets excited, anticipating prowling up to his mate to pounce on her.

Avery's paw prints lead past most of the spots I've guarded her while she forages, but there's no sign of her treading through wild plants or uprooting anything. I slide to a stop on a slab of rock overhanging a small ravine. My ears flick back and forth in search of her, nose lifting to reorient myself. She's definitely this way.

I pick up my pace, loping stride becoming a clipped run as I barrel through underbrush and leap over thick tree roots. There's a stretch in the bond when I focus on it, giving me an indication of the distance she's made it ahead of me. It's a calm hum that doesn't convey any distress.

I'm surprised she's come this far down the mountain. Maybe she's looking for more of the wildflower she found.

The trail's not stopping. It continues beyond the end of the hiking paths on to the road through the foothills. My muscles tense, hackles rising. Something's wrong.

Where the hell did she go? Why would she leave Silver Mountain?

My blood runs cold and I bare my fangs with a snarl. Ashbury. She's going to the human town by herself without telling me or requesting permission to go.

A roar scrapes my wolf's throat. We're both pissed she'd put herself in danger. I push myself hard to get to town, mind racing with the worst possibilities.

My mother went missing from Ashbury. This is why I have a strict rule about not going without me clearing it first and assigning a security group for protection.

Dad wasn't happy, but he didn't look hard for her before deciding she wanted out of their arranged mating. He told me once I was older he assumed she found her True Mate.

But I knew better. It never sat right with me.

This town is dangerous. We shouldn't trust humans. They've been known to exploit supernaturals for their own gain, as have the witches Ashbury's allowed to come and go as they please for years. They're behind her disappearance.

It's the only thing that's made sense to me. Who else would kidnap a shifter but a witch? It would've been easy for them to steal another shifter to control if they crossed paths when she went there alone. The same could be true of others who have gone missing, like Shaylene Morgan.

The blame I've put on my father's beta for his betrayal weakens. Shaylene was his True Mate. His challenge could've been an act of desperation to find her. I have a better understanding of what it's like now. How my heart, my mind, my body are no longer my own. I exist because she exists.

Avery's my mate. I can't let her go. And I won't fucking lose her. Not again.

If anything happens to her—

I cut the thought off with a fierce refusal. No. I won't let anyone important be taken from me again with no way to stop it.

When I find her, she'll know she's mine and I'll always protect her.

I stop to think about shifting back once I reach the outer streets, the foothills giving way to old brick buildings with remnants of aged paint from a bygone era. Ashbury isn't as large or modern as some of the other human towns and cities in the region. It doesn't have any of the lifeless, looming glass buildings of some of the ones I've passed through on my way to other pack territories.

My wolf keeps his nose to the cement and follows the scent of bright sunshine and honeysuckle blowing in the breeze. She's in good spirits. It doesn't take off the edge jangling my nerves.

I bound through the door to a bakery at the top of the high street. Someone screams at my hulking size. There's a fae female in here, masking her presence to blend in with humans. A vampire, too. My wolf shakes his head and ignores them, tracking his mate out a back door.

I cross a street, then double back, slowing as much as he'll let me so we don't jeopardize the peace agreements between the humans and supernaturals by tearing through the town on a feral rampage.

Her scent is all over this place. Some traces are faint, stale with age. Too weak for me to pick up with my own nose when I was here before, but in my fur my senses are sharper.

How fucking long has she been sneaking down here?

I freeze. There. At the end of the block on the opposite side of the main road. She's heading this way, laden with a bag from the bakery.

Avery's okay. She's not harmed. No one's taken her—yet.

I pant heavily, pacing the shadowed alley between the buildings. My muscles twinge every time she waves to a human on her way down the street. She's smiling at them. A growl builds in my chest.

Keep walking, mate.

Come.

Her steps falter. She searches the road with a frown. I debate yanking on the bond again when she doesn't listen to my call and ducks into a bar.

What the fuck?

A car swerves and slams on its brakes when I dart across the road. My snout presses to the tinted window. She's talking to a woman behind the bar, showing her a small vial. A few men have stopped shooting pool, their attention on her.

One grabs a half-empty beer and ambles over to join the conversation. My tail is high and ram-rod straight. He's encroaching on my female. When he puts his hand on her back while she offers him a vial, a ferocious snarl tears from me.

My wolf wants in there. *Now.*

I shift back in a narrow passage beside the bar, about to burst inside and get my female. I freeze halfway to the street. If I crash through the door butt ass naked, the humans will think I'm crazy.

A thrift store has display racks that reach the mouth of the alley. I wrench the first pair of pants I find off the rack. The lime green swishy material doesn't fit over my thighs and I tear it in my attempt to get the shorts on. Gritting my teeth, I force my wolf down and try again, blood simmering. I manage to find a pair of jeans. They sit low on my hips, but it's good enough.

The side door opens behind me and Avery's scent hits me. I whip around, locking eyes with her. She holds my gaze and a terse growl leaves me at the unapologetic, unimpressed set to her mouth.

"Why are you here?"

I'm on her in a second, backing her against the brick wall. Her bakery bag slips to the ground as her hands come up to my chest. I take her wrists and pin them to the wall, bending to run my nose along her jaw.

She releases a strained gasp, then bares her neck for me. I press closer until there's no space left between us, scenting her. She arches into me with another delicious noise I'd enjoy if I wasn't so pissed off.

"I'm here because you are," I push out against her throat in a tense rumble weighted with my wolf. "Tell me what the fuck you're doing here."

She squirms. My grip on her wrists flexes and I trap her gaze. She drops it and I take hold of her jaw to make her look at me. Stubborn defiance shines in her eyes, and, fuck, if I don't love that look on her.

The side door opens again and the pool player comes out.

"You ran off so fast I didn't get your—oh. Hey now. This guy bothering you?"

I move in front of her to block his view. He needs to back the hell away now. I don't even want him looking her way. I need to show this human he can't have her.

"Nope. I'm fine." Avery smacks me. "He's my—man...friend. Husband. That's the word humans use for mates, right?"

The last part is muttered to me. I'm too busy growling at the male with my chest puffed out to answer. She called me hers.

"Caden." She tugs on my waist, keeping her voice hushed. "Stop growling at him. He's not a threat."

My gaze snags hers. I take her face in my hands. Her cheeks are pink, lips parting. *Claim*, my wolf demands.

I dip my face, mouth stopping just before it reaches hers. Her fingers curl, nails scraping my sides. Lashes fluttering, she leans into me.

The last of my control snaps.

My mouth crushes against hers. Powerful. Possessive.

I kiss her the way I wanted to last week—hell, the way I've wanted to for years. Even when I thought I needed to hate her, this mouth has always been mine to claim.

The human says something apologetic. I don't give a fuck what it is.

The only thing I care about is kissing her until she's as wrecked as I am.

Until I've savored every reaction and committed every one of her sounds to memory.

Until I wipe every other man from her mind except for me because I'm her *mate*.

26

AVERY

Kissing Caden is nothing like I used to fantasize about.

It's so much more in every way.

The intensity is all-consuming, burning me up with his onslaught of passion and dominance. The rough tinge of his anger only heightens the experience. His tongue sweeps mine as one of his hands sinks into my hair, tilting my head back to expose my throat and devour me. The kiss deepens, stealing my breath and my sanity.

Even after the human leaves, he doesn't break it.

Liquid heat pours through my veins. I want his mouth everywhere, but if stops kissing me I'm certain I'll die. I feel as if I haven't been breathing until I knew the heaven of my mate's kiss.

He tears his mouth away with a rumble, pinning me beneath his piercing stare. His grip flexes on my jaw. It's not hard enough to hurt despite the anger rolling off him. I feel echoes of it across the bond, taste it like tiny exploding crackles on my tongue, and smell it singeing the air all around us.

"You are *mine*."

My stomach bottoms out at the possessiveness and Alpha power punctuating those words. It washes over me, wreaking havoc on my body. My core clenches with hot need and my nipples harden.

His nose twitches, desire and satisfaction flaring in his hooded gaze. A deep growl rattles from him that makes my pussy ache more. My heart drums harder when he angles his head to trace his nose along my jawline to savor the scent of my arousal.

"None of those men could satisfy you like I will," he rasps. "Only my knot will give you exactly what your body's begging me for because it was made for you."

I shudder with a trembling exhale, rubbing my thighs together. I don't know why he's talking about anyone else. He's the only one I want.

The only one I've never been able to stop thinking about even after he broke my heart. The one I wished for. The one I'll always need.

Caden is my fate.

He nips beneath my ear and brings his lips to it. "But I'm not giving it to you."

A horrifying whine escapes me. I gulp, trying to catch my breath and clear the haze clouding my mind.

"I think humans have laws against nudity and public mating," I stammer.

He rumbles again, his frustration confusing when it overlaps my own in a strong burst across the bond. Warily, I probe the connection, focused on figuring him out. It's a tumultuous mess of magic. Strong-willed discontent. Fear surging up my throat to coat my tongue. A flash of a memory that's gone too quickly for me to comprehend.

When I sensed his presence inside the bar, I wasn't sure what to expect when I came into the alley to explain myself. I didn't think he'd catch me if I was quick. I also never thought he'd track me all the way here to witness me breaking his rules.

He's not happy with me, absolutely. But it's not rooted in any ire towards me. Relief soothes the uncertain tangle reforming in my stomach now that I'm not being swept away by his kiss.

I mourn the loss when he pushes away from the wall to take my hand, then strides for the main street.

"We're going."

He gets two steps before I dig my heels in. He tightens his hold, fiery look boring into me.

"*Now*," he bites out.

The Alpha command presses against my will, but I hold my ground against it. My wolf huffs in the face of his pushiness, licking her paws and ignoring his demands. She'll go when she's good and ready.

Hints of gold flash in his eyes as they flare with something that stirs a fresh bout of warmth in the pit of my belly. His jaw clenches.

"What?"

"We're forgetting my shopping bag. You made me drop it when you mauled me to mark your territory."

He stares me down. I point to the spilled bakery bag. Only two of the pastries the baker loaded it with in exchange for the new samples I brought to pass around fell out.

"Those croissants are Beatrix's favorite. I promised her I was getting them."

"We have that at home."

"Not these ones. Alma's cooking is great, but these are the best."

His jaw works. He scratches his bare pec with a rough sigh, studying me for another beat before retrieving it.

"I got extra for you and Callie."

He grunts, leading me from the alley. He doesn't drop my hand until we reach the foothills, finally relaxing the rigid line of his shoulders as we leave human territory.

"Shift." He pops the button on his jeans. "It'll be faster to run the rest of the way."

I can't help my wandering attention as I unhook the shoulder straps of my coverall dress and shimmy out of the leggings underneath. The weight of his leer is a warm, sensual drag over every inch I reveal. He hisses out a husky gust of air at the sight of me bare and holds my gaze while losing his pants. I bite my lip at his size, a frisson of desire thrumming in my core.

His eyes shut with a ragged groan. "Don't test me more than you already have. Shift."

I tuck my hair behind my ears and use my undershirt to tie the bag clenched in Caden's grip to my satchel. My wolf's gotten better at carrying it without getting it tangled in her limbs. He waits for me to transform first.

The first and last time I shifted in front of him, it was to get away. Things are so different now.

I offer a nervous smile before calling on my fur, then I'm before him as my large roan-colored wolf. She scents him right away and I'm powerless to rein in her excitement. Her tail wags and she rushes him, rising on her hind legs to plop her paws on his chest.

His lips twitch and his fingers sink in her fur to steady her. Tension bleeds from his muscles. She barks and licks his neck. He allows it, lifting his chin to let her do anything she wants. This male smells amazing. He's hers, she knows it.

Strong and willful. A good hunter and protector. Alpha of the pack. Her mate.

"You're beautiful," he rasps. "Magnificent. This is how powerful you've always been."

She melts for him when he rubs her ears affectionately and strokes a large palm down her spine.

"I'll keep you safe," he swears under his breath.

He shifts into his huge black wolf and circles her. She stifles the excitement she overflowed with to give off a sense of aloofness.

You did not claim me.

Caden's wolf huffs, then releases a blustering howl when it doesn't sway her.

He did want her. She is his. It's not his fault. He's been at her side every night since.

He rumbles, nudging her with his snout until finally pouncing on her, nose tucking beneath her jaw. She grumbles and he chuffs, licking her fur. She's content to lay there, pinned beneath him.

I'm fascinated by the way they're able to communicate. They're far less tormented by complicated pasts.

My wolf wriggles free and baits him into chasing her. He stills, head lowering as he prowls for us. A thrill runs through me and her paws dance on the ground in anticipation. He bolts and we're off, weaving a wide zigzag through the trees.

This is exhilarating. I enjoyed running through the forest with Taryn and Liam, but it's not the same as running with Caden.

His wolf is magnificent. A powerful beast that's much faster than he looks for such a muscular build. My wolf has to put real effort into keeping ahead of him.

He catches her with an enthralled purr back where we started. She nips at him and they wrestle, her landing on top. His tongue lolls from the side of his grinning maw as she licks his bared throat as if she was the victor. Until he decides to roll her beneath him once more.

They're both panting. His excitement is hot against my belly. Warmth cascades in my veins.

People say the original shifters did it this way with their mates. They found them once a female went into heat. The male shifted and chased her down to claim her beneath the moonlight, locked together by his knot. Once the swelling went down enough for them to release, they'd shift back and he'd claim her all over again. Shifters used to believe mated pairs weren't truly bound until they joined both ways.

Caden makes an inquisitive grunt, nosing at me with teasing nuzzles like he's flirting. I don't know if he can read where my thoughts are going better as his wolf.

He gets up, waiting for me to follow him. I go for my bag, but he bumps me aside and paws at the strap to maneuver it over his head. We head off at a trot as we begin up Silver Mountain.

I learned the beauty of this forest when I was desperate. It pales in comparison to exploring it as my wolf with her mate at her side. Every fern, every wildflower, every mossy patch—all of it seems much more amazing with my mate's comforting presence to keep me company.

27

AVERY

WHEN WE RETURN to my tiny cabin, his gaze tracks me once we both shift back. It doesn't leave me for a moment, the hot press skating over my body while he grabs a pair of pants he draped over the chair inside. I don't turn my back as we get dressed, enjoying the way it makes his eyes burn.

My sisters aren't here. They've been spending time with Callie and she invited them to stay in the lodge with her this weekend. We have this place to ourselves.

I want to go to him. Wind my arms around his neck. Kiss him until our bodies meld together. Would the ancient kitchen table withstand it if he fucked me on it, or would we go crashing to the floor? My stomach dips and a husky breath rushes past my lips. I can't decide which fantasy appeals more.

Spinning to cool myself off, I spot the new appliances in place of the rusted old hand pump that brought in well water and the wood stove. The old table is gone. Lightbulbs that didn't exist before line the rafters. My heartbeat stutters.

I find a switch and flick it on. The lights illuminate the small space, underlining how tiny the cottage is. I don't care. After years of living by candlelight, it's amazing. I inspect the sink next, grinning at the simple convenience of hot water at my fingertips.

With electricity, I won't have to do everything by hand. I could get better equipment to aid me in grinding dried ingredients and mixing pastes. The greenhouse already planted the idea in my head to try more things. The first batch of oils I made this week are much better than my previous rudimentary trials. With the right tools, I'd be able to make higher quality extractions to infuse with salves and other concoctions.

This cottage could become an herbalist workshop.

"I have running water. And lights." An elated laugh escapes me. "You did all this for us?"

His broad shoulders stiffen and he folds his massive arms with a foreboding expression. "I did. It's why I was coming to look for you so I could show you."

I bite my lip, turning off the tap. "Oh."

"We need to talk about this," he says gruffly. "It's not a day for a trip to Ashbury."

I hold back a sigh, knowing he won't drop it. "Those happen too infrequently."

His head jerks. "For good reason. It's dangerous."

"Uh, no. I wasn't in any danger. There's nothing wrong with town. You just don't trust the humans because you don't like them. But you're wrong." I get the bag from the bakery and offer him a croissant. "The humans there are nice and helpful."

His fist pounds a beam in the wall. It creaks beneath his power. Both of us freeze. I survey the roof, hoping the rafters don't collapse on us after he put so much work into repairing the cottage.

"Shit," he grumbles, hand hovering over the wood. "I'm trying really hard to keep myself in check because I know you're safe now. I still need an explanation. You snuck off the packlands without telling me or anyone else where you were going. Why the fuck were you in town?"

I swallow a feisty remark about stretching my legs, sensing how close he is to blowing up. It's a marked sign of how he's changing if he's asking for a reason instead of the way he would've reacted before catching anyone breaking his rules. Especially me.

"I told you in town. I wanted to visit the bakery."

"My wolf scented you everywhere. You've been there before. Many fucking times."

I'm not hiding the full truth from him. "Yes. You know why? Because when our food allotment was shorted, I needed to find another way to eat. Because when something broke, I needed tools to fix it. I go there to trade with the townspeople. They know me. They helped me when the pack wouldn't."

"They know you?" He stops to reel himself in, breathing heavily. "We have those things here. You didn't have to go. At least without asking me."

"We've been down this path already. You rule the pack with a strict hand. Would you have granted permission and an escort for me if I put in a request to go to town?" I challenge sharply. "You believed I was a traitor to the pack. Your enemy. I had to do whatever it took to survive."

He scrubs his face with both hands, muscles bulging with his wolf. Blowing out a breath, he levels me with a strained expression wavering between impatience and apprehension. He's trying to give me the chance to explain myself. I don't need the bond to see it written across his face.

"Okay. I understand," he pushes out. "I don't like it, but I see why you did it before. But why now? Things are different."

"I was fine," I say in exasperation. "Better than when I thought I was Wolfless."

A tetchy noise tears from him. "That doesn't matter. You went alone. No one to watch your back. What were you thinking?"

"I was trading! I wanted to hand out samples of the new oils I was able to make thanks to the greenhouse you built for me." I sigh, getting the last of the vials from my satchel to show him. "I wanted to see how they went over before I brought the idea to you. Money never did me any good, so I stuck with bartering for what I needed to get by. If the pack sells shifter-made herbal wares, it could bring money in. I could teach others how to forage and make things."

The crease in his forehead deepens and he draws me into his

arms. "When I realized where your scent trail led, I thought I'd lost you. My mother went missing in that town. Witches stole her because she was on her own."

I tense. "I remember she went missing. I never knew it was from town. Are you certain it was witches? You never told me this before."

There could be other covens in the area besides Jade's traveling coven. I know it couldn't be them. They had no quarrel with our pack.

"I've never told anyone my suspicions. It just feels—off. Here." He brings my hand to his chest, clutching it. "I won't lose you the same way."

"You didn't." I search his troubled gaze. "You won't. I'm right here with you. If you promise to be open to less restrictions on going off packlands, I promise to tell you next time I want to go somewhere."

His rumble makes the air thicken around us. I press up to meet his mouth descending to capture mine. His fingers bury in my hair as my arms slip around his shoulders. He switches our positions without breaking the kiss, pinning my back to the wall.

A fist bangs on the door. Caden growls, wrenching his mouth away.

"Alpha," Liam shouts. "It's me."

Caden rakes a hand through his hair, making my knees buckle with the longing his gaze sears me with. "I'm sorry."

"Go. He wouldn't track you down to report if it wasn't important."

He surprises me by calling his beta inside instead, including me in pack matters.

"Report," Caden says.

Liam stands at attention. "Trouble again with another group. This time it's from masonry. Weston came to get me and Hodge when he ran into them shirking duties on his patrol route shadowing Marissa and Tobin."

Caden releases a heavy sigh. "Let's go." He kisses me. "I'll come back after I take care of this."

"I'd like that."

He cups my cheek with a soul-stirring smile, then follows Liam out the door to handle the situation.

)))●(((

AFTER HE LEAVES, I stop by the lodge to drop off pastries for our sisters. It brings a smile to my face to see the three of them together. Callie's plaited Bea and Lena's hair, and they've made a pile of blankets and pillows on Callie's floor where they tell me Lena's been reading her book to them. My heart lifts with joy to see my sisters in such high spirits.

When I'm done, I go to the healer cabin with the rest of my samples. If I'm going to turn my cottage into a shop for my remedies, I have a lot to assess before getting started. Selling to humans won't be a problem. They get excited about anything made by supernaturals. If we could get other packs interested, they might trade with us.

Eugene's out when I arrive. He's made himself scarce since Caden made me a healer, leaving Alisha to handle most of the packmates who come by. She's engrossed in a meeting with a pregnant female in one of the consultation rooms.

I rifle through the storeroom for a basket and create a sign declaring the oil vials free along with the benefits and uses. On my way to the front, Nina enters the cabin with her baby on her hip and Cormac's mate close by her side. Her mate must be back in Cormac's good graces because they've been sitting with his brood's table in the dining hall.

The two of them fuss over the baby until I put the basket on a side table near the door. Sylvie looks past me warily, twisting her fingers. She never speaks much. Not unless Cormac makes her. My stomach sours. If it were up to me, I'd kick anyone rotten like

Cormac, Lorne, and Nina's mate out of the pack for the way they treat females to turn them into husks of themselves.

"Are you here to see Eugene? He's not here."

Nina frowns. "We can return later. I'm sure it's nothing. Trent will be home soon, anyway. He doesn't like it if I'm out when he gets in."

Sylvie shakes her head and feels the baby's forehead. "Too warm. Something's not right." She eyes me again, and something must set her at ease enough to say more to me than she ever has. "I've raised enough pups to know."

"I can check him for you." I gesture to the second room Alisha appointed me.

Nina chews on her lip and nods. They follow me. I clock fading mottled bruises on Sylvie's arms when her sweater cuffs ride up as she passes the baby to me. My jaw clenches.

This can't go on like this. I had no power to change their lives as a pack outcast other than offering larkspur or hemlock as poisonous justice. It's different now. I could take this to Caden. He won't stand for this.

Nina's baby is drowsy and his breathing crackles with mucus. He rubs at his flushed cheeks with a cranky whine. I recognize the symptoms from caring for Lena. I get a basin of cool water and dip a cloth in it, wringing it out before wiping his face. He sighs, turning his big eyes on me.

"Does that feel nice?" I smile when he clutches my hand to keep the cloth on his face.

Sylvie leans over my shoulder. "What's wrong with him?"

"Don't worry. He'll be fine. It's a cold. Take some of the tea tree and peppermint oil from the basket and rub it on his chest to ease his breathing. He probably won't like a cold bath, but you can do cold compresses like this to give him some relief. With rest and fluids, he'll feel better in a few days."

"A cold," Sylvie says, astonished. "He's sick like humans get?"

"Shifters can catch colds, too," I explain. "It's just less common. Usually our innate healing abilities ward it off for us."

"I've never heard of it. I thought he was getting moon sick."

"If you'd like, I have ginger root paste at my place. I can mix in some elderberries, too. Give him that regularly to help keep him strong."

Nina nods. "Thank you."

I catch her wrist. "Just so you know, if Eugene were here, he would've written it off and called your pup weak. He's not."

She slides her lips together, eyes shimmering. "He's not."

Sylvie waves her out, taking two vials from the basket on the way. I follow them through the front door.

"If you need anything else, come to me. Anything," I stress, glancing between them so they understand my meaning. "I'll help you."

Nina drops her gaze to the ground. "Don't talk about that out in the open. You never know who's around to listen."

"Hush, girl," Sylvie mumbles. "Just say thank you and keep your head down."

She nods to me curtly and bustles down the road with Nina. I'll need to talk to Caden about their situation. I don't want females scurrying around in fear.

When I'm finished late in the afternoon, I head home for the night. Caden didn't come to interrupt my work. He must've gotten wrapped up in Alpha duties. Before I reach the split in the road with the trail that leads up to my cabin, five males stop me.

Lorne, Dane, and a handful of the other dimwitted males that hang around them. One leers at me while scratching his ass. Dane and the other two crowd me with smug expressions.

My wolf rumbles in warning, displeased with them encroaching her like this. She rears up, fighting for control. I hold her back with my teeth clenched. If I do as I always have, I'll get out of this.

I sidestep, but Lorne's lackeys shove me.

"Not so fast. We saw you at the healer's with my dam and one of my cousins' mates," Lorne says.

They've been following me that long? They kept their distance enough that I didn't sense them.

He leans into my space. "They were supposed to be home with the other females. Family meeting."

I grit my teeth, giving up ground. It's either back away, or be assaulted by his stench. It's not as strong as it was the night of the full moon run, but it still makes my wolf want to puke.

One of his cousins is at my back. I bump into him. Lorne smirks, blocking me in.

"I don't see how that's my problem," I mutter.

"You're gonna tell us what that little visit was about," he says.

I pretend to think. "How about... No."

His annoying amusement burns away in a flash of wrath. "Are you talking back to me?" He turns the question on his cohorts. "Is this brazen female talking back to her better?"

They chortle and call out suggestions to show me my place. Tension winds down my spine. I should've held my tongue.

Lorne grabs my chin, lip curling. "You've grown bold. You think because the current alpha's your fated that you can get away with disrespecting his bloodline?"

He winds a lock of my hair around his finger, tugging until I'm forced to bare my throat to him. I struggle, flashing my teeth as I scramble to take hold of the bond. It's stretched taut with distance. Caden's far, on the other side of the perimeter. I don't know if he'll sense I'm in trouble, but he still might not make it in time if I yank for him to come to me. I have to deal with this myself.

"Get off me. Caden's bloodline has nothing to do with it. You're being a dick and I don't have to tell you anything. But you know what? When I tell him you were messing with me, he'll be furious."

Dane freezes, shuffling back a step. "Lorne."

Lorne laughs. "Relax. It's fine." He gives my head a shake. "You truly think my cousin gives a shit about you? He rejected you. He doesn't want to claim you. All you're good for is an extra pussy to present for him."

The words sting and turn my stomach, but I know he's wrong. I feel it in the thrum of the mending bond.

"Leave me alone. Now," I snap, kicking out at Dane at my side.

He snorts. "She attacked first."

Lorne grins. "Females should know their place."

He uses his grip on my hair to wrench me to my knees. I go down with a bitten-off cry of pain, my scalp throbbing.

"You like using that mouth so much, you can use it on me." Lorne grabs his belt with a sickening leer. "After we've taught you a lesson."

He lifts his boot to kick me. I roll away before the blow lands, grunting as his toe catches my shoulder instead. The males snicker. They think I'm nothing. They believe I'll lose to them and allow them to rough me up simply because they feel superior to me.

One of them blocks my escape, roughly tossing me before Lorne so I land hard on my knees, scraping my hands to catch myself on the road. Another pulls my hair to make me look up at his arrogant smirk. He backhands me with enough force to snap my head to the side. I gasp for breath, my face on fire.

"This is going to be a long lesson if you don't sit there and take it," he says casually. "How long do you think it'll take her to cry, boys?"

Fuck this.

I've had enough. I'm not a broken shifter who can't defend myself. I'm not waiting for my mate to come to my rescue like I'm helpless. These males have treated me terribly for years, making sure I always knew my place at the bottom of the pack hierarchy. Beneath males like them.

They don't get to hurt me anymore. The rage I've always swallowed down bubbles to the surface, overflowing in an unstoppable flood that demands retribution for myself and all the females shifters like Lorne have wronged.

My wolf bursts from me, shredding my clothes. The transformation startles two of the group back.

"Shit, she's fucking huge," someone balks behind me. "You didn't say her wolf was that big."

I go for him first, herding him back with clacking snaps of my teeth until he's backed against a tree, eyes wide. I prowl a wide circle on the road, then face Lorne in challenge.

Fight me, male. See how strong you are against me. I'll break your bones with my teeth.

He narrows his eyes and rips off his shirt. "You want a fight? You've got one, you stupid bitch. And when I've broken you, I'll make you regret it."

When he shifts, he's smaller than me, covered in wiry gray hair. His eyes are deadly. They're a mark of the danger he poses. I won't underestimate him the way he does with me.

He waits for me to make a move, faking me out until my wolf grows frustrated with his games. She wants him to clash with her head on. When he runs us around in circles, he finally darts in. His charge fails to knock my balance. I headbutt him, then pounce on his back.

He goes down, but he manages to wriggle free, kicking at my feet until I trip over him. I round on him, biting his shoulder as he gets to his feet. He howls, teeth dragging over my ear. I growl at the sting without releasing his fur.

Another wolf barrels into my side. He's slightly bigger, with the same wiry hair. Dane. He pants, attention split between me and his brother. Another of their cousins has shifted, too. The shaggy brown wolf comes at me from behind. One of the males that hasn't transformed throws a rock at my side.

Then all at once, the five of them are on me. My wolf is a formidable beast, but the fight isn't fair.

I swipe at brown fur with my claws and kick at a wiry gray muzzle at my rear flank. Someone's teeth puncture my back when they try to pin me. My wolf isn't going down without giving all of them hell.

She rolls to the side, attacking Dane's leg. He yelps, backing away. Two others are back on me again.

Lorne is within reach. He stayed to the outskirts of the tussle once his friends joined in. If I take him down, the rest will give up.

Rearing up, I throw one of them off. The other keeps on me, biting at my heels as I charge Lorne. He snarls at me, hackles raised.

I leap into a tackle. Someone bites my ankle, but I focus on Lorne. My claws dig into his side and belly. I clamp my jaw around his throat. My teeth sink in, tearing at flesh and fur in warning to demand his submission.

One of them barks and their offensive stops. The one biting my ankle backs away. A furious growl booms from my chest. Blood drips from my snarling maw. They thought they could take me down, but they were wrong.

Lorne's wolf alternates between whining and growling, attempting to swipe at me from the prone position I have him pinned in. He can't beat me like this one on one. My wolf is bigger than his. Stronger.

Yield, I snarl.

He barks, then slumps with a pissed off noise. I keep my teeth bared, allowing him up. He surveys me with his tail rigid and fur ruffled down his spine.

I expect him to attack again with the way he meets my eye without an ounce of remorse. Then he turns tail and runs. The others follow his retreat. Fucking cowards. I bound after them, clacking my teeth at their heels until I chase them off.

Satisfaction and pride dance within me. I'm not coming away unscathed, but I have more than my wits to fight with now. I'm not Wolfless. Nor am I an easy target to pick on. Five males fought me at once and my wolf outlasted them. If any packmate tries me again, I know I'll be able to take them on.

28

AVERY

WHEN I MAKE it back to the cottage, my wolf gives up our fur. The shift back is uncomfortable, my body drained and stiff. I press a hand to my bleeding arm and hobble through the door. At least my sisters aren't here to see me like this.

The worst of the wounds will heal within a day or two. I check myself over and most of it is superficial. I already feel some of the scrapes tingling, but I can make things more bearable to take the edge off. After pulling on a loose cotton shift that ties in the front, I get a bowl of water and a washcloth to clean the deep gash in my arm, setting it on my workbench.

The crash of the door slamming into the wall so hard it almost comes off its hinges startles me. Caden barrels through out of breath, features contorted in confusion and distress, fangs extended, fingers partially shifted into claws.

He stops in his tracks, raking his gaze over me, nostrils flaring. His fists ball and he's at my side in two strides, face set in a feral storm of emotion.

"You're hurt," he says hoarsely.

"It's not that bad. My wolf can handle herself."

"Who did this to you? Who fucking touched you?" His fingertips flutter over my bruised jaw and his wolf becomes more evident in every word. "Tell me *who hurt you.*"

Through the echoes of pain, warmth spreads through me in a rush. I fought my own battle, but to see the way this affects him stokes a fire in me. I wish he could've seen how resilient I was.

"Calm down. It doesn't matter right now."

"Of course it does," he counters fiercely.

I rest a palm on his chest, searching his face. It helps quell him, though he's still a restless force. The bond ripples with probing pulses from him.

"I just want to clean up."

He folds his arms, tracking every movement as I press the damp rag to my arm. At my hiss, he bats my hand away. He takes the cloth and holds my chin, gently lifting it until his piercing gaze captures mine.

"Let me," he says gruffly.

"It's fi—"

"I need to. I—it's hard for me to see you like this. I have to know you're safe."

My heart thumps at the troubled concern and devotion evident in his eyes. My attention drops to his shoulder. The scar is covered by his shirt, but the memory of how my gut wrenched being unable to stop him when he put himself in harm's way by jumping into the fight between our fathers remains permanently etched in my mind. I hated seeing him in danger, and recalling that moment now amplifies it so intensely I struggle to breathe.

He caresses my cheek with his knuckles and takes great care in cleaning the gash. Once he has it bandaged, he checks me over for himself, cataloging the sprained wrist that's already twinging less to the smallest bruise I sustained with grumbles and sharp exhales.

Each injury, no matter how minor, receives a tender, devoted kiss, his burning eyes locking with mine.

Being cared for by him unravels something within me that's been knotted in a tight mess for years.

"My wolf got agitated and I didn't listen because I was still dealing with—*fuck*. I should've been with you."

He scrubs his face, then rests his forehead against mine. I swallow as my heart clenches. It's comforting to know he could feel that something was wrong, even if I was able to manage the problem myself before he reached me. I'm not fighting alone anymore.

"You can't be with me all the time. I'll be okay." I crack a tired half-smile. "You should see the other guys."

A rumbling protest sounds in his chest and he cradles my cheek. "No. You're not okay. What happened?"

"I was on my way back after doing some work. Some males stopped me and got aggressive with me when I wasn't giving them what they wanted. They saw me talking to Sylvie and Nina at the healer's cabin and wanted to know what I said to them. I offered to help Nina get out of her situation and they might've overheard."

"Some?" he presses. "Be more specific. I want names."

I sigh. "Lorne and his friends."

A thundering noise explodes from him, rattling the windows.

I grab Caden's arm, stopping him from storming off. "Where are you going?"

He whirls on me, eyes golden and fangs lengthening, his wolf barely contained. "Where do you think? I'm going to kill whoever touched you."

"You can't."

He snarls, dragging me with him towards the door. I curl my fingers around his bulging muscles and find the threads of the bond to yank him to a stop. He grunts, rubbing his chest.

"You're the alpha. You can't come at them in the same manner they attacked me."

He's still fuming, though he makes no more moves to leave. "This isn't a simple disagreement. I won't stand by and allow anyone to attack you. I got so pissed off about Dane just for making a comment that I made an example of him in the dining hall. They put their hands on you. Do you understand what my wolf is demanding right now for this? I don't want to fight them until they submit, I want to rend them limb from limb."

My wolf is into this and on his side. She'd like to join him, finish chewing those males up and spit them out for thinking they could push us around. They need to bare their throats for us, and if they're lucky she won't tear them out. Our pack will regard us as mates who won't back down when we're challenged. The two of them are making me dizzy.

"I don't want you to. It doesn't do the pack any good if you kill anyone you please. Then you'd be no better than the tyrant alphas of the Original Pack."

His neck stretches in agitation. "I'll destroy them all."

Yes, mate, my wolf gushes, enthralled with him. *He is perfect. He feasts on the blood of our enemies.*

"Caden." I step back so he can see my slowly mending injuries. "I'm fine. This will heal."

The reflective gold glow of his eyes fades back to stormy blue. "I can't let this go without doing something. At least let me call Lorne out in front of the pack for ambushing you. No one will ever dare touch you again."

I grimace, not wanting that much attention on myself. It doesn't matter if things are beginning to revert back to how they were before. I spent so many years at the edges of the pack as an outcast drawing as little notice to myself as possible that it's not an easy transition to make.

"I doubt they'll try anything against me again. They know I won't be as easily pushed around as other females they intimidate. My wolf kicked ass. If it had been a fair fight one on one, I would've beat Lorne."

"You think I won't protect you?" Caden's stormy blue irises flash golden again, then narrow.

"Everyone knows you're the one who re—" I break off at the reminder, then grit my teeth to push the word out. "Rejected me. The pack mostly ignored—"

His fierce growl interrupts the rest of my response. The muscles in his jaw twitch as he works it.

Then he's on me, pushing me back with purposeful strides until my hips hit the edge of the workbench. My pulse spikes as he cages me in and I swallow thickly as he grazes his nose from my temple down to my throat.

"Avery," he rumbles in a fervent tone.

Mate. He didn't use that word, but the reverence matches.

It sends heat racing through me, igniting an irresistible inferno in my core. My breath hitches and my skull thunks against the wall. He lifts a hand to cradle the back of my head, massaging away the fleeting throb.

"I've failed you. I'm *still* failing you when all I want is to make everything right." He continues scenting me, the heady mix of us making it difficult to focus on anything but his proximity. "I won't do that again. I'll protect you. I revoke my rejection and I swear to you I won't rest until I'm worthy of your claim. If you'll have me. I'll be the safe space you can rely on. The guardian of your heart as I always should've been."

My chest squeezes with a stutter that echoes throughout my nerve endings. I waver on the edge of allowing the last of the wall I built around it to crumble for him. Everything in me demands to close the gap between us.

"I'm not helpless. I don't need to be protected," I breathe.

"Whether you want it or not, you have it." His lips brush my skin and I arch into him. "You have me, remember? I'm yours, you stubborn little wolf. I won't let you forget it."

A strangled noise catches when he places a soft kiss beneath my ear. He grasps my waist, fisting the thin material of my shift until the ties strain. My nipples pebble, my entire body aching for more.

Need wells in me. It's similar to the feeling that overcame me when we were in the forest surrounded by fireflies, but I'm more in control of what I want. I grab his hair and pull him into a kiss.

He makes a rough noise and I swallow it with a thrill. He

devours my mouth, pulling me against him with a rumble. His hands grip my thighs, being mindful of my bruises and mending cuts, hooking my knee to lift my leg around his waist. The skirt of the shift hikes up and he fits between my thighs.

I arch with a whimper at the firm ridge of his cock pressing to my center, rocking my hips for more. My body aches to feel him. His mouth parts from mine with a tortured groan.

"I need to taste you," he rasps. "The scent of your arousal drives me insane."

He grasps my jaw and angles my head to lick a stripe up my throat that draws a shudder from me. My nails scrape his back, his shoulders, anywhere within reach to urge him on.

"Caden," I beg.

"I know. Your scent's telling me everything you need."

He kisses a path down my fluttering pulse point to my collar bone and takes the shift in both hands, tearing it down the middle. My desire heightens so fast, I'm lightheaded with it. Cool air kisses my flushed body and my clit throbs.

"Damn it." A husky laugh puffs out of me. "I like this."

"I'll get you a new one. You won't need them in our bed, though. I want you bare for me like this, always. Fuck, you're dripping."

He grazes a knuckle down my slit, smearing my slick wetness. I bite my lip when he brings it to my clit, giving me just enough pressure to tease me. I squirm, trying to grind on his hand. The corner of his mouth kicks up and he steadies my hip, playing with me until I'm panting.

"Is this pretty mess for me? I've barely touched you yet." His sensual hooded gaze snares mine as he licks his finger clean with a groan. "Do you know how incredible you taste? I'll be addicted to you. More than I already am."

He kisses me again, stealing my breath. Fingers finding my clit, matching the slow pace of his mouth on mine. I cling to him as he takes my pleasure higher. Then his hand is gone, spreading my thighs wider as he kisses his way to a nipple, taking it in his mouth.

"Please," I whimper. "So close."

"Not yet. When you come for the first time for me, it'll be on my face. I'm going to drown in your scent and wear its mark for days."

He pays attention to my other nipple, biting it lightly, chuckling at my gasp. My nails rake his shoulders, unsure if I want to drag him back up or need to shove him down to use his mouth where I need him most. I drop a hand to touch myself and he catches my wrist, flashing me a grin.

The bond comes to life with his phantom hands. I cry out as he lowers to his knees, the invisible caresses teasing my breasts, tracing the curve of them, swirling patterns around my nipples. His eyes darken with arousal, illuminated with burnished gold as he admires me.

"Look at me, Avery."

Keeping my eyes open is a struggle when my body sings with pleasure. My lips part at the sight of him, powerful and commanding Alpha staring at me with so much longing, ready to worship me. He looks *mine*.

He gets all rumbly and I'm responding in kind without realizing it, my chest vibrating. Drawing one of my legs over his shoulder, he swipes his tongue over my pussy, a ragged groan tearing from him. My hands search for something to hold on to, sinking into his hair.

"Fuck yes," he praises.

His mouth descends on me, face pressed against me, tongue and lips relentless. Within moments, I'm brought to the edge, faster than when I touch myself, faster than when he teased me across the bond. The sensual coil of heat tightens in my core, hot and cold tingles racing across my skin.

When I'm close, he pauses, hushing my whimper of protest.

"This is where I belong every day. The reason the moon goddess pulled me from the stars to exist at the same time as you," he rasps against my body. "To kneel before you, the only one the alpha bends his neck for to show you I belong to you. And you to me."

I shudder with a strangled gasp, hanging on for dear life. It's too much and not enough at once. I want to grip his hair to hold him in place and grind on his tongue, seeking the edge of the cliff he's keeping me teetering on. My trembling thighs clamp around his head and he rumbles in pleasure, burying his face in my pussy to the point I'm sure he's suffocating, but I don't want him to stop.

I fall apart in an eruption of endless ecstasy, the deep pulses echoing within my core for ages while I cry his name mixed with a litany of pleas.

"That's it," he croons raggedly. "Fuck, you're incredible when you come for me. Your sounds, your taste."

I moan when his fingers shift, nails lengthening into claws. He drags them across my thigh, leaving his mark on me. My heart stutters to a stop.

It's not any mark.

He's writing something on my skin. The slight stinging scrape of his claws heightens my pleasure, keeping the delicious aftershocks going.

We're both panting as he draws the word *mine* into my thigh.

He takes me in, admiring every way he's undone me. When he captures my gaze, he traces the word with his thumb, then lays a kiss over his handiwork as my skin heals.

"What did I say earlier? You're mine, mate. I will chase every last doubt away that you don't belong with me with every breath I draw."

Mate.

The bond thrums with renewed vitality, caressing me from within until I'm shuddering from the intensity. He hushes me, drawing me down to straddle his lap, cradling me in his arms. My eyes prick with tears of relief and elation.

Nothing's ever felt so right as my heart beating in time with his. *My mate.*

29

AVERY

CADEN HELD ME ALL NIGHT, never once letting me stray from his arms. He carried me to my room and took great care in helping me out of the tattered remains of the shift. I marveled at his rugged body when he stripped down to be skin against skin, chasing away the chilly mountain air with our body heat better than the crackling fire.

For once, I didn't have to worry about anything. I could let go and he would catch me. It filled me with a profound sense of serenity.

My lids grew heavy, but I fought sleep in favor of tracing the planes of his chest, meeting his eyes as I brushed the scar mottling his shoulder. He drew me close and kissed me slow and deep for hours until we finally fell asleep.

I could stay like that forever, but for the alpha the world doesn't remain at bay for long. As dawn broke over the meadow, he rumbled in my ear, complaining that Liam was waiting outside for him, and if his beta got any closer his wolf was going to have to fight him. I chuckled and nudged him out of my bed for the sake of their friendship.

He wouldn't leave my side without another kiss that caressed the depths of my soul and the promise to see me later.

Last night fed the inferno he's ignited in me. He wants our bond. He wants me. I'm not fighting it anymore.

Caden has my heart. It belonged to him for years, before the Fates awoke our mate bond. When he broke it the first time, I never thought I'd be able to forgive him for believing I could betray him. The second time when he rejected me, I thought I'd die of heartache.

Yet day by day, piece by shattered piece, he's put my heart back together to reclaim it.

He's fixed up my cottage and helped me realize this place is a part of me I could never let go. It forged the person I am today. He's turned it into a space I'll build into a workshop for my foraging and herbal remedies.

He's restored my place amongst the pack and reversed the negative opinion of my family name. My sisters and I can walk through packlands without fear of being shunned. We're welcomed with the sense of belonging I've felt like a missing piece all the years I spent living as an outcast at the edges of the pack.

There's no one else for me. He is my mate and the only one who makes my heart race whenever he's around.

Caden let me know when he left he has meetings in his office to hear the pack's concerns, as much as he wants to spend every second of the day with me. I can't keep a smile off my face as I go foraging, finding myself stroking ferns and picking elderberries with a bubbling light lifting me up.

When I'm finished, I spend the rest of the day planning for my shop. Taryn stops by with Callie and my sisters to bring me food. Callie elbows me and says Caden sent them to make sure she ate. Warmth expands in my chest while I share my lunch with them.

Caden hasn't returned by the time the sun sets. I take simple joy in flicking on the lights. My head twinges slightly from staring at the notes I've been making all day and some of my joints are still stiff from the fight with Lorne and his idiots yesterday.

I decide to go to the secluded watering hole. It's my little hideaway. The spring joins with the nearest ley line, giving the water an extra boost of vitality whenever I swim there compared to the bustling spot the rest of the pack frequents.

If I soak in the water, I'm certain it'll do the trick along with my speedy healing to rejuvenate me.

A small waterfall cascades from a larger stream over boulders to feed the spring. The clearing is peacefully quiet tonight and the moon reflects off the water. It gives off hints of a flickering glow in the ripples, the natural magic from the land creating beautiful shimmers.

Most shifters probably wouldn't recognize it as magic. I didn't know how much of it was all around me until Jade taught me how to see it.

Stripping down, I sigh in contentment as I enter at the edge of the spring. It's always the perfect temperature year-round. I dive beneath the surface and swim a few laps, enjoying the faint tingle. It's working. I feel wonderful when I stop to relax.

A splash from behind startles me.

Caden's here. He jumped in the water, the buttons of his shirt half undone, only his shoes left behind on the bank of the spring.

"You're here," he says in wonder.

This is my secret spot. How did he find me?

He stares at me as if I've been plucked from his dreams. Moonlight illuminates his sharp jawline shadowed in stubble, his broad shoulders and carved muscles, the thick brown hair falling across his forehead. Reverence flares in the depths of his captivating eyes. The bond thrums with a warm glow, drawing me to him in the same inescapable pull.

"Did you track me here?"

He reaches for me with parted lips. "No. I came to—How are you here?"

"This is my best kept secret." I slip my arms around his neck, biting my lip as my breasts press into the drenched fabric plastered to his hard chest. "I always come here. It's much quieter than Silver Falls."

An astounded huff of laughter leaves him.

"This is *my* secret spot. The place I come to think and unload the burden of being Alpha from my shoulders. The place I can be just Caden again for a minute."

"You've always been just Caden to me." I brush my lips over his between murmuring. "Being named heir apparent never made a difference. It doesn't as Alpha, either. Your only title that matters to me is mate."

He grins, deepening the kiss. I love how much he smiles lately. He's always been handsome, but when he smiles it's breathtaking every time.

"I can't believe we've never met here. I should've scented you if you were here."

"I bet it's the magic." I swirl my fingers in the water, chasing one of the sparkling orbs of light.

"What do you mean?"

"This spring, in fact the whole mountain, touches a ley line deep in the earth. It's natural magic. The original magic of the land, from the time this region was full of druids and the old fae," I explain. "It must hide the scents of anyone who comes in."

"I can scent Liam when he's wandering too close."

"That's because we're downwind. It's not here. I never scented you, either."

He hums, stroking my back. "How do you know it's magic?"

"Look. See the light?" I cup another orb beneath the water, bringing it closer to the surface without breaching it.

"The moonlight?"

"Look closer. Watch it move in my hand. You have to want to see it. Magic is always around you. Not just from the wards at the perimeter."

"Not sure I like the sound of that. I should know everything going on in the pack. How could magic be under my nose the whole time?"

He squints with effort. I giggle. Did I look that obstinate when Jade first met me?

"It existed long before you or I did. Look for the shimmers. Magic is life. Balance. Nature at its purest form."

He studies the water. The breeze shifts, sending a spray of the flowing cascade over us. Droplets bounce into the air from the splash. Each one is full of an ethereal glow, suspended momentarily before submerging in the water.

"There," I whisper.

"I—yeah. I think I see it. That's not a trick of the moonlight?"

"That's magic."

"No wonder witches flocked here when groups broke away from the Original Pack."

"That's not true. We were allies then."

His head jerks. "Before they tried to put shifters under their control."

I sigh. "They're not all bad like we're taught to believe. One helped me. Without her, I would've poisoned myself."

"What?" His grip digs into me to fight an invisible threat.

"Jade. She's part of a traveling coven and came across me when I was so desperate I went out scrounging."

He rumbles unhappily, jerking me close as he listens. I hug his shoulders, resting my head against his chest.

"She was inside the perimeter?"

"She said the wards don't dictate where she goes. I don't know what it means for all witches, but she had no problem getting past them."

"How long was she in the area? What if her coven is behind my mother's disappearance? What if they took your mother, too?"

My gaze locks with his. "Jade's coven isn't like that. She helped me because she saw a desperate, starving girl. She taught me how to see magic and work with its natural occurrence from the land so I could feed my sisters. Why do any of that if she had underlying motives?"

His expression becomes conflicted. "If it wasn't witches, then who could've been behind it? Who would've taken our mothers?"

I shake my head. "I don't know. Have the other packs reported missing packmates? Maybe you should bring it up at the summit."

"We'll do it together."

My heart flutters whenever he says things like that. "Together?"

"I want you to come with me. You should be by my side. It's where you belong."

I kiss him. He cradles the back of my head.

"Your dad would be really proud of the alpha you've become."

"I wish both of our fathers could be here to see us lead our pack," he murmurs. "Yours would be so proud of you, too."

My stomach tightens at the way he calls it our pack. It feels right. I want to be at his side with everything that entails.

"I still regret that I've hurt you," he says gruffly. "That I rejected you and almost lost you. I was such a fool. You've suffered so much when you never should've, and I'll never be able to give you back everything I had a part in taking from you."

My throat closes. "I miss my father, but the challenge was his choice. That isn't your fault."

He nods stiffly. "I overheard one of their arguments at the time about your mom going missing. My dad wasn't listening. He didn't understand what this was like." He lays a palm on my chest where the bond strains for him. "True Mates. He didn't have this with my mom. He wouldn't understand what it's like to be willing to search to the ends of the earth to find your mate."

I cover his hand with my own. "I heard them, too. Dad knew what would happen if he failed against the alpha. I think it's why he told me about the view we should explore. To make sure neither of us had to see them fighting. Neither of us can take blame for it."

"But I can bear it for everything that came after," he mutters.

"You don't have to. I forgive you." My voice thickens with emotion. "It's true I lost everything that day. My place in the pack, my father, our friendship. But you've given me back everything you could and more."

His forehead rests against mine and he releases a ragged exhale, holding me close.

"Fate wasn't wrong, Avery. I was. And I'll spend every day—beyond an eternity if that's what it takes—proving to you that you're *my mate*." He pauses to thread his fingers in my hair, eyes searching, intense and all-consuming. "The only one my heart has ever beat for."

"The only one?" I breathe.

"Avery." His words are gruff and he cradles my face. "This is always what we were meant to be. It's not because of the bond. There's never been anyone for me but you. I chose you before I knew you were my fate. When your laugh became the sound that made me happy. When you'd drag me out to explore the mountain, or the way you'd get this wicked smile that lit me up before daring me to jump the cliff with you only to push me off. Whenever I saw you, I always needed to follow you. Needed to be near you because it made me feel right. I've loved you before I understood what it meant."

Tears well in my eyes and my chest expands with so much happiness that it steals my breath away. When we were friends, I was hopelessly in love with him. I begged the moon goddess to make him my fated mate so we'd never be parted. I never knew he felt the same.

"I'll never let you go again." He traces the junction of my neck and shoulder in passionate captivation. "I want everyone to know you're my mate, my Alpha female, my trusted equal. I want to mark you here with my claim. You are mine as I am forever yours."

I melt against him, seeking a kiss. His lips crash against mine. Our breathing becomes hazy, his hands running over my body fervently.

He pauses to wrestle out of his clothes. I help peel his shirt from his skin and it plops somewhere on the bank when he flings it with a grunt. His pants go next until I feel his body gliding against mine underwater.

He squeezes my ass and lifts me against him. I writhe in his arms, wanting to rub against his firm torso, eager to feel his cock. My breath hitches when he trails kisses down my neck, nibbling at my shoulder. His hand wedges between us, moving between my thighs. He watches me when he finds my clit.

"Yes," I hiss.

The corner of his mouth lifts, gaze burning into me while he touches me. He teases my entrance before sinking the first finger in. My head falls back and my hips rock with the steady pace he sets. He adds a second, working me faster. I squirm, my orgasm just beyond reach.

"More." My hands slip on his wet shoulders and grip his hair.

"Are you begging for my knot, Avery?" He nips my earlobe.

I shudder with a nod. "Yes. *Yes.* I need you."

"Patience, mate. I'll take good care of you. I know exactly what you need."

Water sloshes as he fucks me with deeper thrusts of his fingers. My nails scrape his back and I gasp, locking my legs tighter around his waist to chase my release. It feels so good, but it's not enough. Even as I crest the edge and fall apart with a cry that he swallows. I need more. Need my mate inside me.

He helps me out of the spring, mouth capturing mine with another searing kiss. Then he whips me around and encourages me to my knees, positioning himself behind me.

"Like this." He draws my hair aside, nuzzling my throat with a rough groan. "You smell so damn good."

"Caden." I barely recognize my voice, ragged with over-whelming desire.

I need him. I can't wait another second.

My chest lowers to the ground and I raise my ass in the air with a moan. "Caden. Please."

"Fuck," he chokes. "Come here or I'll explode from the sight of you presenting for me."

He draws me upright against his body, holding my waist. The tip of his cock glides through my slick folds. I push back and he keeps me steady with a hand clasping my throat.

"So needy and wet for me," he rasps at my ear. "And all fucking mine."

"Yes," I whimper.

At last, he gives me the pressure I want. Every inch of his thick length stretches my pussy, leaving me breathless and floating. My body is thrumming and pliant for him.

He doesn't slam into me. He savors it, chest vibrating at my back with a possessive growl. It makes me feel utterly claimed.

When he's worked all the way inside, we both still from the intensity. It's new and exhilarating, the fullness teetering on the edge of too much, yet not enough because my body craves it. Craves my mate. A soft noise catches in my throat.

He stills. "Did I hurt you?"

I shake my head. "No. I—I need more. Don't stop."

He kisses my flushed skin with a strained rumble as I shiver, core clenching. He kneads my hips, cock throbbing before he slowly pulls back and glides back in. The stretch is better the second time.

"Fuck." His nose drags up my throat to bring his lips to my ear. "You feel that, mate? How incredible we feel together?"

Air rushes past my lips, tinged with a desperate moan when he begins to move, each thrust lighting me up. His cock is so big. I feel him so impossibly deep inside it's making my eyes roll back in pleasure.

"I—oh, goddess. I don't know if I can take it. You're so huge," I cry. "It's so good. So—*ah!*"

"Shh." He kisses my shoulder and splays his palm over my abdomen to hold me in place while driving into me. "You can take it, mate. You were made to take me. My cock. My knot. I'll fill you so good with everything you need, sweetheart. That's it, you feel your pussy squeezing me? You want this. My perfect, beautiful mate, soaking my cock with your slick."

I nod frantically with a whimper, clutching his corded forearm as he rubs my clit. My pussy pulses with need and arousal. I'm dripping, wetness coating my thighs the harder he fucks me. His other arm bands around my waist to tease my breast and he kisses the juncture of my neck and shoulder, the sensual glide of his tongue sparking tingles across my skin.

His composure slips, a wild edge taking over. I like it when he thrusts harder and holds me tighter, my own feral side matching his. He's claiming me, but I feel a carnal sense of power equal to the goddess for bringing out this side of him, for making him lose control.

With another savage sound, parts of his beast come through in a partial shift, nails elongating into claws and his strength increasing as he fucks me. A sharp bursting pulse ignites in my core when he grasps my breast, the lightly stinging pressure of his claws on my sensitive skin heightening my pleasure.

"Mine," he growls.

"Yours. I'm yours," I gasp out as it crests.

He senses it, making a sensual noise of encouragement against my neck. "That's it, Avery. Fuck. Come for me."

I'm in freefall when I come, my senses going haywire from wave after wave crashing over me. The ecstasy is endless and the bond feeds it back on me tenfold from both of us. The scent of his arousal grows rich and enticing, our pheromones entangled around us. His cock swells thicker. I crave my mate's knot more than I need my next breath.

Caden's fangs graze my neck. He's going to claim me with his mating bite and I'm ready for it, everything in me screaming for him to mark me. To make me his forever.

30

———

CADEN

AVERY IS MINE. I'm claiming every fucking inch of my mate tonight. She'll bear my mark, body and soul.

Her exposed throat calls to me. I nuzzle into the crook of her neck and shoulder, finding the spot I want her to wear my claim. A quiver of anticipation surges through me, then my mouth clamps down and my teeth pierce her skin. She arches with a heavenly whimper and I drag the burst of her scent into my lungs.

Mine, my wolf howls.

She tastes delectable. I lap at the wound to soothe away the brief pain and help it heal, learning the shape of her new mark with my tongue. I work her clit, thrusting sharper as I kiss the mating bite.

"Oh, it's throbbing, it feels…"

She trails off in a moan, pussy squeezing the life out of my dick while honeysuckle and sweet summer rain burst on my tongue, leaving me dizzy. My hold tightens on her as she falls apart on my cock. I'll never know anything as great as the honor of making my mate come while I'm buried inside her.

She's too good, tight and hot and all fucking mine. I'm close to coming, barely holding off my release. My cock throbs, swelling larger, my balls drawing up.

"Avery," I groan.

I drive into her one last time, panting raggedly as the coil of pleasure snaps, sending me over the edge. I come, my knot filling until it keeps me and the flood of seed deep inside her. Fuck, it feels good, the swell thick and heavy, throbbing against her exquisite tightness made to fit with me and no other.

She gasps, collapsing back against me, trembling with aftershocks of her orgasm. I shudder through my release, licking the bite and holding her. Every slight twitch from her brings me incredible euphoria, my knot extra sensitive.

When I stroke it with my tongue, I feel an answering pulse in my chest where the bond burns strong, anchoring us together. As it should be. As is right.

She feels so perfect locked on my knot. Better than I ever imagined it would feel with my mate, the sense of wholeness profound beyond the heady pleasure.

I caress her clit, grinning when she whimpers, pussy fluttering. She's sensitive. A rumble builds in my chest while I trace where our bodies are joined, shivering with a groan when I feel her stretched on my knot.

"Caden." Her chest rises and falls, arm reaching back for me.

She sounds exquisitely fucked out in bliss. Pride unfurls within me. I grin, knowing I did this to her. That I'm the only one who ever gets to see her like this. The only one who can satisfy her. She's mine and I'll make sure she's taken care of like this every day of our lives.

"I've got you. You're going to come on my knot."

A tiny moan escapes her. Oh, she likes that, and I like the effect the idea has on her.

She arches as I give her more pressure with my fingers, then slide down to make both of us feel how we fit together before returning to rub her clit. I lick the fresh bite mark and she tenses before melting against me with a whimper as her pleasure erupts.

Fuck, she feels good. Her scent is thick all around us, blending with mine, sweet with decadent honey and wildflowers surrounded by my own musk. Her pussy squeezes my swollen cock, making my vision swim in dizzying ecstasy.

"So good for me, mate," I croon.

My wolf sprawls, granting me a sliver of control back. My claws retract and the few patches of skin where I sprouted wiry black fur return to normal.

I keep toying with her body, tracing patterns on her hardened nipples down to her thighs, gathering her slick to smear at the base of my cock. My hips nudge forward in an attempt to sink into her another fraction to feel more of her intoxicating wet heat.

My knot hasn't gone down yet and I already crave her again.

Newly mated pairs are often tangled in each other. I'm insatiable for her. This endless need for my mate hasn't been sated, not in the least. I want to fuck her all over this forest in every way imaginable. I want to make her come with my knot, my cock, my hands and mouth, and drown in the scent of her arousal.

I'm eager for every second I'll spend with her. When she goes into heat, I'll take pleasure in meeting her demands for more until I've surpassed them. She's mine to worship and I'll never allow anything to come between us or be parted from her again.

Her breath hitches when she drops a hand to join with mine. I thread our fingers and bring her hand between her legs.

"Feel us," I rumble.

"So full," she murmurs. "It's so good. I don't want it to end. How long will it be like this?"

"A while, I think. Rest. I have you." I guide her head to lean on me and drop a kiss to her hair.

Avery drifts off. I caress everywhere in my reach, stroking her hair, her sides and thighs, her stomach as the urge to fill my mate with our pups rides me.

Once my knot recedes, I ease out of her and lay her in the grass. She makes a soft, content noise, still drowsy. I hush her with a kiss, moving to pay attention to the mark I've left on her. She shivers at my tongue mapping the healing bite, clinging to me.

My fingers delve between her legs, feeling her swollen pussy dripping with come. I push it back inside with languid thrusts of my fingers as I scent her. The hitch of her breath makes my lips twitch in satisfaction, as does her tight clamp on my fingers when she comes for me again.

I collapse beside her, drawing her into my arms. The entire clearing around the private falls we share smells like us. I smile at the glowing moon and pet her hair.

We doze on and off, replenishing our strength. I wake to something tickling my chest. Cracking an eye, I smirk at my gorgeous mate. Her eyes widen, caught out.

"Sorry if I woke you."

I clasp her nape to pull her into a kiss, murmuring against her mouth. "I want you to wake me all the time. Do you know how many times I've fantasized about you demanding I fuck you?"

Her laughter is a balm to my soul. She swats me, humming when I capture her mouth for another kiss. When it ends, she bites her lip, eyes bouncing between mine.

"Is this real?"

I cup her cheek, brushing my thumb back and forth. "Of course it is."

"I didn't know it was possible to be so happy," she admits. "It's...been a long time."

A jagged noise flies out of me. I circle her in a tight embrace, vowing to make her happy always.

"You'll never feel that way again. I swear."

I brush the edge of her mating mark with my thumb. Nothing will ever keep us apart now that we're mated. She wears my official claim on her.

"Will you go for a run with me? My wolf wants yours."

"So does mine." She lifts a brow, cheeks turning pink. "You don't think they're going to..."

I snort, rolling her beneath me. "My wolf wants his mate, same as me."

She flashes a sly look that tugs heat low in my gut and begins her shift. I join her, our forms becoming our wolves seamlessly.

Her wolf wriggles under mine and he settles down, stretched over her belly.

She licks the underside of his jaw and his tongue lolls from his panting mouth. He pins her to return her affections, lapping her coat until her roan fur gleams in the moonlight. His content howl echoes through the forest and she joins him, their combined calls pleasing him.

His ears flick, listening to his domain. Small prey skitters through the underbrush and crickets chirp over the babbling falls. His mate draws his focus once more as she scents the squirrel nearby. He'll hunt it for her and present her with a meal.

She wants up, budging him with impressive strength. He's on his feet, sniffing her rear flank, licking where the fur is matted to taste her slick. She spins with a bossy yelp, both of them frozen in a standoff. He heeds it, enjoying his mate's shyness mixed with her fearlessness when it comes to putting him in his place.

Then she bows to him with a bark. Challenging him. She runs and he tracks her.

They chase each other in circles, my wolf gaining, then keeping a measured distance to tease her when she aims her playful attacks at him. She puts on a burst of speed to charge him and he barks in delight when she tackles him. They roll in the grass, wrestling with excited growls and yips.

She paws his chest and he clamps his teeth on her throat with a purr, releasing her to inspect the mating mark she bears beneath her fur with his nose. He licks it, chuffing happily.

They both hear a snapping twig, rising to twitch their noses in the air. West of us. Deer.

Avery's wolf bounds off too soon. Mine huffs, trotting after her. Before we reach the bottom of the incline, it's spooked off.

She plops her haunches to the ground with a frustrated whine. I bump her to cheer her up. The instinct is natural. I need to teach her to hunt. She has it in her, I know it.

I lower my head, giving her my neck. Her snout snuffles into it with a little rumble that excites me. *Bite. Mark me*, I encourage, pawing the ground.

She doesn't, only nipping me playfully, but it doesn't bother my wolf. He knows she's his. In her own time, she'll want to give us her mating bite.

We make our way back, heading for the lodge instead of her cottage. I want her in my bed.

When we get there, we shift from our fur. It's quiet, our sisters asleep upstairs. I wrench a curtain from the nearest window to wrap around her so none of the guards stationed around the lodge see her.

"You know they've seen me naked," she points out, amused.

I growl in refusal, taking her hand. "I don't want anyone to see you like this. Only me."

Her giggle echoes down the hall on our way to the stairs. The enforcers we pass keep their eyes down because they know what's good for them.

In my room, I get one of my shirts for her, struck by how much I like this. Having her in my space, my den. The sight of her kneeling on my bed, wearing my clothes. Her smelling like she's mine. The rightness of it all settles in my thudding heart.

My mind runs away with ideas of our future. Her scent infusing my den, my sheets—*our* bed. Waking to her within arms reach and not sleeping well until I have her tucked against me every night. Watching her make it into her nest. Rubbing her back and feeling her belly growing with our pups.

I prowl to her, brushing my knuckles over her jaw. She smiles and I move the neckline of the shirt aside to admire my mating bite.

"Beautiful little wolf," I murmur. "I have you where you've always belonged."

"With you," she echoes in a reverent hush that pierces my heart.

"With me."

31

CADEN

As much as I've wanted to face my cousin from the minute I found Avery injured at the cottage, I wait a few days after he went for her before calling him out in front of the pack before a run. His arrogant swagger when I watch him around the packlands grates on me. My wolf views everything about him as an act of insubordination.

He won't ever touch my mate again.

I'm knocking him down as low as he can get in the pack without me kicking his ass out in exile at the mercy of Wanderer's Canyon or killing him.

No one messes with what's mine.

The commons are festive tonight. The fire is going and the tables are laden with food. Avery and Beatrix are dancing to the fiddle players' tune. I watch, drinking beer with Liam and Gabe.

Taryn and Callie sidle up to me. Taryn tries to goad Liam into giving her his beer. Callie has a poorly hidden smile. She elbows me, nodding to the female I haven't taken my gaze off all evening.

The corner of my mouth lifts. "Are you talking to me again?"

"Well, you're not an idiot with your head so far up your ass you can sniff your own balls anymore. I can't believe you'd be so stupid to reject your own fated mate." She smacks my arm. "What's wrong with you?"

Gabe snorts, covering it with a cough. Liam smirks, whispering to him. He chokes on a sip of beer and Ford jogs over from the other side of the clearing. My heart stirs with understanding, constantly moored to Avery no matter which direction she's in.

I squeeze my nape, pushing off the stab to my gut. "You said it yourself, Cal. I was an idiot."

"Good, I'm glad we cleared that up."

She grins, tugging me to the dancers and Beatrix swaps seamlessly with me, holding my beer. I gladly pull Avery into my arms, basking in her beaming smile. Her joy is everything. I've missed it, a hole carved from my heart of my own making.

"Hi."

I pull her against me, touching my nose to hers. "Hi. Ready for tonight?"

She pretends to mull it over. "That depends. Are you planning on repeating last month's bonfire?" She squints at me. "Reject your mate? Still piss in a circle around her to mark your territory?"

I growl, gathering her in my embrace. "Fuck no. None of that. I'm going to shift with my beautiful, stubborn mate who has my entire heart, and we're going to run with our pack."

Her brilliant smile returns, lighting me up. I kiss her, grinning into it when our nearby packmates cheer. The song ends and I lead her back to our group at the edge of the bonfire, our fingers entwined.

"You're also learning to hunt tonight," I add.

"Am I?" Her brows jump. "I can hunt."

"Tell that to your wolf. She's too eager. Gives herself away with no strategy." My face dips, mouth at her ear. "I'm going to teach you."

She shivers, leaning into me. "I can't read your mind. How are you going to teach me?"

"I can feel what you're thinking," I remind her in a smoky tone.

"Our wolves communicate well. She'll understand by watching my wolf."

"You shouldn't let him teach you," Liam cuts in. "Callie and I are better at guiding the shifters that come of age to navigate it."

I rumble. Avery pats my chest. When she gives him her attention, I wind an arm around her waist.

"I'm teaching her."

She drives her elbow into my abs. "What if I want to hear Liam's advice?"

"His advice is shit."

Liam grins. "Yeah, that's why you made it one of my duties. If you don't like the alpha teaching you, come see me or Callie. You've got other packmates who have your back."

"Like me," Taryn chimes in. "Don't listen to him either. I know the best hunting spots."

Liam sighs. "Doubt it."

"Try me." She sticks her tongue out at him. "But for real, Avery. If you need pointers, let me know."

"Great. Thanks," Avery says.

"Not great," I mutter.

She laughs and presses on tip toe to tuck her nose against the crook of my neck. "Relax. You get to teach me first."

I crush her into my arms, quelling my mild irritation with her scent in my lungs. I have bigger problems to handle tonight than my beta baiting me into jealousy as a joke.

Beatrix hands me my beer and surveys the lively bonfire. "I can't wait to join the runs as my own wolf. I'm going to be so fast, I know it."

Avery chuckles at the sparkle in her sister's eyes and strokes her hair affectionately. "You'll be magnificent."

"And we'll run together." Beatrix hugs Avery, then loops an arm around Lena to pull her in.

Callie joins in from behind Beatrix. "All of us. When you're older, Lena."

"What if I don't have a wolf?" Lena points out.

Avery's eyes shimmer. I put my hand on Lena's back. Her health has seemed better in the last few weeks compared to when I first saw her the night I followed Avery back to the old settler's cabin. She has color in her cheeks and her eyes are bright.

"Then we'll get you a dirt bike or a quad. Something to make it easy for you to get around the mountain."

"I get to drive? You'll teach me?"

Lena lights up and the three sisters laugh. Avery shoots me a grateful look and traces the edge of the claiming mark I left on her.

"Can we paint dragons on it?" Lena claps, bouncing in place.

This pack never should've held so tightly to the old views that being Wolfless is a sign of weakness. I should've put an end to it long ago. Shifters are strong no matter what, and Lena's strength is in the kindhearted peacefulness she exudes.

It's almost time to start. I search the crowd, locking on Lorne holding his own court behind the picnic tables. My lip curls.

"I'm going after Lorne tonight," I tell Avery. "Before the run begins."

She pulls me away from the bonfire, lowering her voice. "Caden, just drop it. If you do this, it'll make things worse. What if he comes after my sisters next?"

"I'd never let that happen," I vow fiercely. "I protect what's mine, and you are mine. That includes your family."

She licks her lips, swaying into me. I want to whisk her out of here, toss her over my shoulder and take her back to the lodge. Spread her on my bed where she belongs, waking me at all hours as hungry as she was for me when I finally claimed her as mine.

I can't believe I once thought I didn't need a mate by my side. I was beyond wrong. My life was nothing without her in it.

"If I do nothing, he gets away with yet another liberty and he's taken far too fucking many. He wants to challenge me for Alpha, but he's a fucking snake about it."

"What do you mean? If he wants to challenge you, he needs to face you. He can't take the pack without beating you first. It's the law."

"He's been undermining me. Swaying people to think he's got better ideas to run the pack. That incident I left you to handle the other day? He's behind it, and it isn't the only one lately. He wants to ensure he's got the pack fractured before he faces me. It's one of the reasons I've made so many rules over the years trying to keep their scheming in check."

"If you know they're behind it, why not exile them?"

"They're being smart about it. I can't exile them without proof they're doing all this to cause a revolt. They know it. I know it. They stick to getting under people's skin to cause minor acts of defiance, just enough to make me feel the pressure of them clawing at my back. None of the people involved in these incidents give up their names. Until they make a move openly, I'd be viewed as too extreme, acting for my own gain instead of the good of the pack. It's written into the accords to prevent alphas from becoming power-hungry like they were in the Original Pack."

"That's ridiculous. If you know they're causing trouble and it's putting the pack at risk, they need to answer for it," she huffs.

"I look forward to the day I can put an end to it." I exhale roughly, caressing her cheek with my knuckles. "But tonight, after I've announced our mating to the pack, he'll know he's gone too far. He fucked up by daring to touch you. I'll strip his rank back to nothing for that."

My wolf paces restlessly, ready to unleash his rage on my cousin.

Liam stands at attention when I nod. He herds the pack into order, gathering them for me. I kiss Avery, then stride to the front of the group. My gaze sweeps over them as they quiet. The majority show deference quickly. I don't like how many take longer to do the same.

"Before tonight's full moon run, there are two important matters to bring before the pack." My booming announcement washes over the commons. "Avery."

I hold my hand to her in invitation. She hesitates before joining me, taking her rightful place and slipping her fingers into my waiting palm. Several murmurs spread through the crowd. She wears my mating bite proudly, eroding any question that she's mine.

"Avery Morgan is my mate. I claim her before you as mine."

Reverence carries in my words. A fervent glow fills me from our bond, her happiness echoing with my own.

The pack breaks out in applause and happy cheers.

Tobin cups his hands around his mouth. "Congratulations, Alpha!"

She laughs airily, leaning into my side when I draw her into my embrace. I drop a kiss on the top of her head.

"Thank you," I say.

Avery returns to stand with her sisters, accepting a hug from Alisha and more well-wishes from Alma. She tucks Lena against her front. Beatrix and Callie are at her side. Taryn on the other. Gabe and Ford position themselves near them, guarding them.

"Liam."

He makes his way through the pack with Hodge and Tobin, the three of them bringing the five culprits before me. The two on the end shift their weight nervously, glancing at Lorne. He's unbothered, amused by my stony expression.

"*Kneel.*"

Two collapse to the floor immediately. Dane goes next, fighting the Alpha command with a grimace. A thundering growl builds in my throat.

"Why have I called you five before me?"

Lorne bares his teeth, fighting my power pinning down his will, demanding his submission. His legs shake. My chest vibrates, anger pricking my patience. His knees give out and he falls to the grass with a miffed grunt.

"Alpha Blackburn asked you a question." Liam clamps Lorne's nape, forcing his head to bow until it's shoved into the grass for his brazen display of disrespect. "Answer him."

"We messed with Avery. She's a traitor," the weakest of the group blurts.

My scowl swings to him. "My mate is no traitor. Watch your fucking tongue."

He cowers, emitting a terrified whine. A pittling sound drums the ground, followed by the stink of piss. He's from one of the smaller family lines. A Dunlop. His family transferred from Crescent Valley Pack seeking better opportunities after they lost everything they had.

"Fighting five against one isn't messing with someone, is it?" I bite out. He doesn't answer. "*Is it?*"

"No, Alpha," he shrieks.

I turn to Avery at the front of the crowd. "Did he hurt you?"

She shakes her head. "He tried to. My wolf took a chunk out of his thigh before he ran off with those two right behind him."

That's my girl. I stroke the bond with praise and she ducks her face to hide a blush.

"She attacked first," one of the ones who keeps looking at Lorne says.

"Unprovoked?" I press harshly.

He opens his mouth. Closes it. Glances at the male beside him for help. The other one shakes his head.

"Take these three to the patrol cabin," I order. "They'll be put on probational work rotation."

Tobin and Hodge cart them off. I study the remaining two Blackburn brothers with distaste. I feel no connection to my cousins whatsoever. My uncle made sure of that when he raised them to be just like him.

"Dane. Didn't you learn from the last lesson I gave you? I'll beat you again if it didn't stick in that thick head of yours."

He nods, then shakes his head.

"Which is it?"

"Yes, Alpha. I knew better."

"And you still thought going after a female—my mate—was a good idea." I glance at Avery, silently asking if he caused her pain. She shakes her head. "Ford. Solitary for two weeks, then assign him to maintenance crew until I think the lesson's really sunk in."

Dane's eyes bug out as he's dragged away. That leaves Lorne. There's no point in dragging this out.

Signaling Liam to stand down, I drop to a knee, wrenching Lorne to me by a punishing grip on his hair.

"Apologize to her," I growl. "Or I'll kill you the way my wolf is begging me to."

He huffs with a smirk. "You expect me to lick your boots, too? It's a disgrace to see you losing yourself over that little traitor."

I bare my teeth and deck him. He goes down hard, catching himself on his palms. He spits blood.

"I expect you to do as your alpha commands." At the mutinous scrunch of his features, I serve him a hard look. "You challenge your alpha, then?"

Lorne's gaze darts to his father watching this unfold from a seat at one of the picnic tables. Fury dances in his eyes. Lorne backs down, shaking his head.

"No, Alpha. I don't," he grits out.

Without a formal challenge, he holds no power to defy me. I'm taking his chances at claiming this pack for himself out of his reach. He loves waving the name of our bloodline around. I'm taking it from him because it's the thing he values the most—his rank.

"You've been dropped from your rank. I revoke your name by birthright. You're not recognized as a Blackburn anymore."

Lorne jerks at the ancient shifter magic passed from Alpha to Alpha infused in my decree, fingers lengthening to claws that dig into the ground. Liam holds him for me.

"You're nothing. You're at the bottom of this pack and your job will reflect it. You're forbidden from full moon runs with the pack beginning immediately. You're to move out of your current quarters and will be assigned a spot in the dormitories with the other unmated males. Your place in this pack will remain on probation until you've proved your loyalty."

My uncle slams his fist on the picnic table with a gnashing growl. I stare him down, hoping he'll lose his composure so I can nail them both at once.

"Would you like to join him in his stripped rank, Uncle?"

He stills, waiting me out for a long stretch. At last, he shakes his head. My jaw works. I nod to Liam, watching him escort Lorne from the commons to pack up his shit in my uncle's compound.

Avery comes back over of her own accord, not needing to wait for my permission or summons. Pride expands in my chest when she lifts her head, my regal Alpha female.

"Anyone who attacks my mate is an attack on me," I declare with an underlying oath of vengeance for anyone who defies me. "Anyone who attacks their packmate is challenging me. This isn't how we do things in Silver Falls Pack."

Assent sounds through the clearing. Avery squeezes my hand.

"Good. Now let's put this behind us and enjoy tonight's run." I wave an arm to the tree line in invitation.

Taryn whoops, the first to peel out of her clothes and go to fur. Callie's right behind her and others join in until the crowd dwindles, packmates taking to the woods as their wolves. Avery returns to her sisters, giving them each a hug.

"Will you two be okay here?"

"Of course. We get to eat as much as we want," Beatrix says.

They aren't the only ones remaining at the bonfire. Some of our oldest shifters barely make the transformation, content to sit around the bonfire and smoke pipes. Some dams have stayed behind to chat while their pups toddle in the grass. Others not of age yet tuck into another plate of meat.

"I'll hang back with the girls," Alma offers. "My knee's acting up. Not feeling a run tonight."

"Thanks. Is it bad? You should've told me. I'll make you some compresses soaked in ginger and willow bark to help. Maybe some arnica, too."

"I'm alright for now. Go let your wolf out. Beatrix, help me prop my leg up by the fire and I'll be good."

"You've got it, Miss Alma."

I draw Avery to the trees. "Ready to run with the pack?"

She smiles and I want to bottle the electric feeling in my heart.

We leave our clothes on a fencepost by the road and let our wolves free. Her stunning red wolf climbs a partially downed tree, taking in the scents and sounds of the forest. Paws thump the ground and yipping barks filter through the trees.

She howls, bounding off to join our pack. I'm right on her heels, marveling at her.

A group of brown and gray wolves link up with us. We explore a hollow in an oak and weave through elderberry thickets. She pounces on the small gray one and one of the other wolves joins the fun. My wolf sits, content standing guard.

Two from the group split off when they scent the groundhog burrow nearby, then we cross paths with a bigger group. I recognize Taryn trotting along with my sister. They run with us.

Avery's wolf releases a series of joyous vocals.

This is how her first shift should've gone. A celebration of camaraderie with packmates.

We reach Silver Falls. Several people have shifted back in favor of swimming or climbing the rocky overhang to plunge into the wide pool. Laughter echoes above the rush of the falls. I wrestle for a bit with Callie's wolf, our sibling bond restored. Then Taryn and Callie drink at the water's edge before flopping to the mossy bank in a dogpile.

Despite the tense start to the evening, everyone looks like they're enjoying themselves, my mate included. I nudge Avery and we go off on our own. Time for a hunting lesson.

I keep my ears pricked, searching for easy prey to get her started on. There's a hawk circling overhead. A couple of wild boars roaming the hillside moving south away from the pack. Fish splashing upstream where a beaver dam interrupts the brook.

When we're far enough from Silver Falls, secluded deep in the wilds of the territory, I crouch low in the cover of ferns, listening. She mirrors me, ears swiveling to me. I rumble until she focuses, then send praise along our bond.

Wait. Listen and wait.

The boars crisscross near our hiding spot. They get her excited, but she remains with her belly to the ground. Good. Progress.

I show her how it's done, tracking a gopher I hear leaving its burrow. I'm completely still, breathing shallowly.

Waiting until the gopher is close enough to be an effortless catch, yet far enough that it doesn't sense the predators stalking it, I make my move, swiftly leaping from the ferns to snatch the gopher before it has time to escape.

I drop the offering at her feet, chest puffed. She tears into it and my wolf purrs. She allows it when he takes a bite for himself, basking in her attention when she licks his jaw. I nudge her back into position for her turn to try.

She scents a prairie dog and dismisses it for the hare that stops to munch on the weeds. Her instincts are sharpening.

I paw at her to signal her when to go. She darts forward in a bolt of red fur, focus locked on the hare. It evades her in a ditch, but she anticipates the opening, jumping to cut it off. It squeals, but it's no use. She's on the creature, teeth snapping its neck as they clamp down.

If I wasn't in my fur, I'd be cheering for her. I race to her, circling her and lifting to my hind legs with a rush of energy. She jerks her prey with a shake of her head.

My wolf is all about providing for his mate. I am, too. But pride fills me to see Avery coming into her own with her wolf. I want to teach her skills to fend for herself because I like seeing her strong.

I'll always fight for her. Protect and treasure her. Never again will she fight on her own, not with me as her mate.

32

AVERY

Hunting is exhilarating. Hunting with my mate? Indescribable.

My wolf is in her element, showing off what she's picking up from Caden's guidance. Every time he watches us with that proud gleam in his golden eyes, she's simpering, enthralled with her mate's attention. She hasn't mastered it by any stretch, but there's definite improvement.

We make an excellent team. He allows me to pick the prey as we lope through the woods and doesn't do much work other than herding our target back to me when it evades me. Some of the smaller critters are fast, intriguing me with the challenge and strategic approach they require. It's not enough to be a hulking red beast of a wolf driven by instinct alone.

While we're drinking from a stream, my ears prick. Grunts and rustling through dead leaves. Boars.

My wolf wants the meat. She goes on the prowl, stalking their trail. Caden's wolf trots after her, hanging back to let her figure it out on her own. Her mate trusts her. Believes in her abilities as a huntress.

The boars prove a new challenge—their intelligence. They

sense her before she's close, skittering off with disgruntled chatter. Annoyance ruffles her fur.

She allows distance to stretch, giving them the idea that they've avoided a predator, waiting until their guard lowers before trying again. This time she climbs to a higher position, balancing on a fallen aspen's trunk wedged between an outcropping of rocks. Sneaking across, she waits until they pass beneath her before making a move.

Her claws swipe one boar's flank, wounding it. They bolt.

Caden cuts off their escape. One goes squealing in the opposite direction from his giant black wolf in a panic. I pounce on it, fangs going for its vitals. Its shrieking cries grow louder, then cut off with a gurgling wail when I tear out its throat.

My wolf stands over the hog, releasing a victorious howl. Our packmates echo it in the distance.

Caden strides over with the other hog in his jaws. He bumps against her side, adding his meat to her catch. *Good job.*

They feast together and she basks while he cleans her coat. The moon is high and she's not ready to give up control anytime soon. She lures him into playing with her, batting him with her paws. He chuffs, rolling to his back, rumbling in contentment when she nuzzles into his exposed throat.

When she wants to run, he races alongside her. The wind sifts through her fur and the ground yields beneath her paws. She stops at the edge of a clearing when a new scent carries on the breeze.

A deer grazes in the meadow. My mouth waters and I succumb to my instincts.

I creep in first, intent on the doe. She has no idea of the danger encroaching on her. I check if Caden's going to herd her like he did for the plump hogs we took down. Golden eyes bore into mine.

Something shifts in his posture. He's no longer hunting our prey.

He's hunting *me.*

My wolf is excited. Unbridled. Shivering in anticipation. She won't let her mate catch her so easily, yet she craves the moment he succeeds.

She forgets all about the deer, taking off in a sprint. The doe startles. Caden's wolf jumps from the high ground. His howl follows through the trees.

It's a promise. A vow of what's to come.

My heartbeat races, veins and limbs warming. I want it. After I make him work for it.

His wolf is powerful and fast. He has no trouble keeping up with mine, hovering at her heels, nipping at them with a series of whuffs that sound like laughter. I manage to evade him when we reach a section of woods I know well from foraging.

A hollow to the left ahead leads me down to an old blackberry bramble that was choked out by vines years ago. My wolf is much bigger than I am, though she manages to squeeze through it and slip down the drop. He can't fit, barking behind me.

I scramble on my belly through the thicket, glad most of the prickly leaves no longer grow. He's still searching, sniffing and padding back and forth above me. I sneak out under the cover of overgrown vines swallowing the dead brambles and double back.

It doesn't take Caden long to figure me out. In no time, his paws pound in pursuit. I run as hard as I can. He still catches up, chasing me relentlessly. He won't stop until he captures me.

My wolf scrambles up a hill. As she crests it, he slams into her.

We go down with a delighted warbling howl, welcoming the weight of his huge beast. She wants to rub her scent all over him. He's hers. He belongs to her and she will claim him. Her want overflows, and her desire is mine.

Caden's wolf purrs, the approval and praise making her melt. His mouth clamps on her neck, over the mating mark I bear, growling possessively. *Mate.*

One moment he's his wolf pinning me to the moss and tufts of grass, the next his warm skin covers me. He hugs me while he scratches my belly, creating a fizzing rush of delight in my core.

"Shift," he murmurs.

My body gives in to his wish, transforming from fur to flushed skin. His muscular thigh wedges between my legs and I writhe against it. He stretches over my back, hard cock nestled against me. I want it, aching to feel him inside me.

His lips coast down my spine, nipping my ass. My breath hitches and my knees scrabble on the ground for purchase, lifting while he spreads me open.

A hazy cry slips out at the first swipe of his tongue over my pussy. His fingers dig into my skin as his chest rattles with a gravelly sound that vibrates against me. I shudder, pressing my cheek to the cool grass with a whimper. He devours me, mouth and tongue bringing me to the brink.

"I'm—I'm going to come," I stammer. "Oh Fates, please."

He sucks on my clit, then works his tongue into me, a ravenous man starved for his favorite meal. My thighs tremble and a tug jerks in my core, unraveling me with an endless ripple of pleasure when I come.

Before I've caught my breath, he flips me over, crawling up my body in a sensual prowl while I'm still floating. My pussy throbs with need and I tangle my legs around him.

He lifts my hips, squeezing my ass as he enters me in a smooth thrust that leaves both of us tensing, our features contorted in bliss. I cling to him, the first to move my hips in a circle.

"Yes," I murmur. "Fuck me."

"I'm not going to fuck you, mate."

He kisses me hard to silence my plea, snapping his hips. I gasp and he swallows it with a rumbling chuckle before bracing above me on his forearm.

"I'm going to own you, body and soul."

My lashes flutter. He pulls back and slams into me, hitting me deep. My back bows. He sets a pace that ignites me. I'm unable to do more than hold on for dear life while he fucks me rough and fast, meeting a wild primal need I didn't know I had until now.

"Don't stop," I beg frantically.

"That's it, mate. Squeeze my cock with your sweet pussy," he praises. "Mark me with your slick so everyone knows I'm yours. You're going to come all over my cock for me, aren't you?"

"Yes!"

"Such a good little mate for your alpha."

He grabs a fistful of my hair, guiding my head back until my neck is bared for him. Demanding my submission. A hot sizzle scorches through me and I fall over the edge with a strangled cry. He licks the hollow of my throat, nipping and kissing his way to the mating mark.

"Mine," he growls against it.

His cock pulses deep within me and he buries his face in the crook of my neck with a groan. "Fuck, I'm coming. I'm going to fill you, knot you until you feel it for days."

"Yes," I breathe.

We both pant, shivering in pleasure when the base of his cock grows. His knot feels amazing. The sensation of it swelling in me, stretching me to the brink, makes me feel drunk. It's more incredible than the first time he knotted me.

It's not painful, my body naturally welcoming him as it's meant to. The pressure against my sensitive nerve endings is endless pleasure, the stimulation so intense every little move steals my breath.

My eyes widen, then close with a gasp of pleasure. Caden's moving inside me, thrusting anew, yet not because his knot is locked in place.

"Are you—?"

His smoky chuckle tickles my ear. "Do you like that? I want to fuck you some more. Can't move, so I have to get creative."

"You're—mm—so good at using this to tease me."

My teeth rake my lip. Focusing is a challenge when he has me unraveling by the second from his astral command over the bond. I search for it within me, caressing the connection.

"Fuck." A breath tears from him. "You drive me insane. I love it."

My laughter breaks off in a moan when he makes it feel like his mouth is on my nipples at the same time while his phantom cock pounds into me. I open my mind to him and let a fantasy unfold where he has me on my knees, fucking my mouth, picturing running my tongue over his knot.

A garbled curse flies out of him and his grip on me spasms. We come together, both of us shaking with it, clinging to each other.

Caden's lips capture mine and I hum into it happily.

33

———

CADEN

THE DAYS PASS QUICKLY, autumn creeping into early winter. The Pack Summit will be here in another couple of weeks.

Avery spends most nights in my bed. Occasionally we end up in hers when she works late until I distract her out of her clothes, enjoying bending her over her workbench.

Waking with her scent in my nose becomes one of my favorite parts of the day. It's drowsy and smooth. It envelops me, luring me to her. I roll on top of her, trailing kisses down the valley between her tits, making my way lower to the crease of her thigh, seeking more of her soft, sleepy arousal.

She giggles, fingers threading in my hair. "Morning."

I hum, rubbing my cheek on her stomach. "You smell incredible." I grind my hips against the mattress, groaning. "Shit, you make me so hard in the mornings."

Her laughter is so sexy. She stretches, then stills.

"Did you hear that?"

I didn't. I'm too busy tracing patterns on her thigh with my tongue, getting closer to tasting her. I want her legs wrapped around my head while I enjoy feasting on her.

She nudges me. "Go check. Someone's coming."

With a ragged sigh, I drag myself from my mate, grabbing the first pair of shorts I find and adjust my dick so it's not so obvious I could carve stone with it. I wait until she's pulled one of my sweaters over her head before opening the door. Callie's in the hall with Beatrix, their expressions matched in mischief. Lena hovers behind them with a book tucked under her arm.

Avery's sisters have been staying here. Beatrix moved her things into the rooms I prepared for them next to Callie's and Lena's migrating all her books.

"Good morning," I say slowly. "Need something?"

Callie puts on an innocent act. "We were just coming to see if you were awake. We're going down to the dining hall for breakfast."

Beatrix snorts, muttering, "And making sure they didn't miss it."

"Bea." Avery nudges me aside, her cheeks pink.

"What? You missed it yesterday," she points out with a giggle.

"And the day before that." Callie feels my forehead. "Are you eating properly? Getting enough to drink? We're starting to worry."

I scrub my face. "Yes. We're—wait, no. Never mind. I'm not discussing this with you."

It's Avery's turn to snort. "Thanks for checking on us and reminding us to come up for air."

"Are you coming with us?" Lena asks.

"Yes. Go on, buttercup. We'll meet you downstairs," Avery says.

Our sisters leave us be. Callie peeks back with a wink before they round the corner. I like having the Alpha's lodge full of life with our family all in one place.

"Did they just call us out?" I muse.

"They're happy we've figured ourselves out." Avery pats my chest. "Let's go to breakfast before the whole pack starts spreading a rumor we're caught up in a mating frenzy and start placing bets on when we have pups."

I catch her waist with an interested rumble, nipping beneath her ear. "I like the sound of that."

She laughs, swatting me. "Caden."

"Mate," I counter warmly.

I let her go for the cost of a languid kiss. We get dressed and join our sisters, walking across the commons together.

Two she-wolves come up to us. I tense at Seline's approach, but Avery is at ease.

"Avery," Emily calls.

She stops for them. Emily and Seline nod to me. I'm relieved when Seline shows none of her previous interest, deferring to Avery respectfully.

"What's up?" Avery prompts.

"We just wanted to say thanks," Seline answers. "For helping us get reassigned for our rotations and understanding why we were interested in doing different work. We start today."

"I can't tell you how glad I am to never look at another frying pan again," Emily says with a laugh. "Thanks for taking us over to meet our crew to make sure no one would give us trouble, too."

"Oh, no problem," Avery assures them. "If you need anything else, let me know, okay?"

Avery takes my hand when she rejoins us, her high spirits infectious. It fills me with pride to see people coming to her as their Alpha female.

She gave me the confirmation I searched for that the females in Cormac's brood are being mistreated. Sylvie shut down when we offered her help, denying any trouble with her mate.

We had better luck intervening to help Nina and her pup get away from Trent when she agreed she was interested in dissolving their arranged mating. We moved her in with Alma for the time being, and Trent's under watch by my lieutenants after kicking up a fuss, threatening to drag his female back to their den by her hair. I dragged him by *his* hair to the commons, then kicked his ass until he submitted and spent the night in a holding cell.

I usher my family to the head table in the dining hall. Hodge makes room for Lena, pouring juice for her. I cast a watchful eye at Cormac's table, making sure he's remaining in line. There have been less frequent incidents since I stripped Lorne's rank. I'm hoping it's the last of it.

More females come up to our table to talk to Avery throughout breakfast. She listens to each of them, offering her advice or promising her help.

"Sorry to interrupt you while you're eating," a young Farrows girl says. "I tried to reach you at the healer's cabin, but you'd left for the day."

"It's okay." Avery sets aside her plate. "What do you need?"

I fill it while they talk, making sure she gets a choice cut of ham before the enforcers at the table pick at the steaming platter.

"I'm worried about my dam," the girl explains. "She works in carpentry and says her arm is bothering her. She swears it'll heal if she leaves it alone, but her appetite's not right."

"Your cabin's on the lower loop, right? Okay, I'll come by tomorrow to see her."

The girl's smile breaks free in relief. "That's great. Thank you."

"You're a natural at this," I praise once she returns to a table at the back.

Avery blushes. "What do you mean?"

"You've taken your place as Alpha female. You care for the females. You give them all a voice and make sure none are overlooked. Liam and Hodge told me you organized a class on identifying poisonous plants."

Her eyes widen. "Oh. Well, I wasn't thinking of it that way, but yes. I want to help when people come to me. And teach them what I know so they can help themselves."

"You've done more than that." I cover her hand with mine. "Helping Nina get away from Trent. The job rotations overhaul. Keeping an eye on the food allotments to ensure they're fair."

She's smiling now, pleased and shy. "I wanted to help her before, but I didn't have the power to change anything. Not until now. The rest isn't a big deal. Some females like Emily and Seline didn't like that they always ended up assigned to laundry or kitchens and told me they were interested in being trained to do electrical work with the maintenance crews."

I add another helping of sausage to her plate. "They feel safe coming to you. They put their trust in you. I'm glad to see it."

Together we're working to make our pack a strong, happy community. I thought I had to do it all on my own, but now I see. Leading a pack isn't a duty for an alpha to bear on their own. I needed her at my side, to anchor me, to make me better. It doesn't matter what lies ahead for Silver Falls Pack, we'll face it together and overcome anything.

The change in my attitude hasn't gone unnoticed amongst the pack. I asked Liam while we were on patrol why the requests stacked on my desk have doubled. He laughed so loud it startled birds from their perches in the trees. According to him, the word is that I've mellowed out now that I'm with my fated mate.

)))●(((

AFTER BREAKFAST, Avery goes up to her cottage. She's getting it ready to convert into a workshop. I'm not able to stay away from her for long. I get through my morning duties as quickly as possible, then head up to bring her the tart berry turnovers she's always liked and the gift I've been crafting in secret.

New paths are being carved by the teams I commissioned for the project, expanding the roads for the upper packlands to be easier to navigate. It takes me half the time to reach her place.

I find her inside, stocking the shelves I've expanded along the other walls with tins of salve. The bed's been moved into her room to make space for a storage bench and a larger counter to replace the table.

"What are you doing all the way up here, Alpha Blackburn?" she teases.

Warmth flows through me. I hold up the pastry. "I thought you'd like some of these. Alma made a batch today and I told her to set aside some for you."

"Thank you."

She takes some with the same gusto she's always had when it comes to these when we were growing up. I enjoy watching her tiny shiver of bliss when she pops the bite in her mouth with a hum.

"I have something else for you. A surprise I've been working on whenever I have a minute."

She lights up. "What is it?"

I tilt my head to the door. "Come see. I left it outside."

She follows me. I cover her eyes before we round the corner. Her laughter is airy and her fingertips graze my forearms.

"Watch your step," I say.

"Hard to do when you're blindfolding me," she says airily.

"I've got you. Ready?"

"Yes."

I drop my hands. The wooden sign rests against the house. The plants were the hardest part to carve in the design. I used a primrose as the main motif. It always makes me think of her whenever I spotted it growing wild in the last couple of months.

"Caden."

Her voice thickens with emotion and she covers her mouth with her hands. I slide an arm around her waist.

"You like it? I wasn't sure if you wanted to make it yourself, but when I asked Lena and Bea, they thought it was a good idea."

"I love it. It's perfect." She burrows into my side for a tight hug. "Thank you."

I kiss the top of her head. "I'll hang it for you."

"Then I'll be officially open for business."

While I get to work, she takes clippings from her garden and fills a basket with herbs. I head in once the sign is hung above the porch declaring the cottage her apothecary and herbal shop. She's on a stool to reach the rafters with a length of twine between her teeth and a bundle of rosemary sprigs, hanging it with her collection of drying plants.

"Ready to go home?"

She hops down with a smirk and returns to her workbench, giving a sassy sway of her hips that snags my attention. I step into her while she works, kissing her temple.

"Thinking about getting me into bed already?"

"I always want you in my bed. But more than my bed, the lodge is your home. You know that, right?"

She fusses with the bundle of sage she's preparing to hang for drying, head bowing. My nose twitches with the change in her scent. It sharpens with bitterness, putting me on edge. She's nervous, but why?

"What's wrong? Have I said something to upset you?"

"No. It's not that I don't want to be at the lodge. It's—you'll think it's silly."

I rumble, hugging her tightly to take away her worries. "No I won't. Whatever it is, tell me, mate. You can tell me anything."

She spins, eyes shimmering. "Of course I want to be with you. And providing the best for my sisters is always a priority for me. They've really enjoyed spending time with Callie and being more integrated in the pack. They come up here way less than I do now, and they've pretty much moved into the lodge." She sighs, rubbing her forehead. "Part of me is reluctant to move out of the cottage. Like I'm losing it if I leave."

My heart twists. My wolf grows agitated and panicked, scratching at the veil between us. He senses she's distressed and wants to protect her. I pull her close.

"You were in survival mode for years. This is your cave. The safe space you carved out for yourself. You won't lose it. I'd never take this from you."

She huffs, snuggling against my chest. "I know. See? This is why it's silly. I know you aren't. You're helping me convert it into my shop."

My lips brush her head. "You don't have to move into the lodge if you're not ready. Or if you'd rather, I... There's a cabin I've held —it's near the commons off the main road. You'd have everything... I mean, until—if—you wanted..."

She quiets me when I struggle to finish the alternative suggestion. "No. I want to be wherever you are. Forever."

I blow out a relieved breath, the tightness in my chest unraveling. "Thank fuck."

"When you said that, I think it finally helped me realize what I need." Her smile is equally soothed. She surveys the room. "Can we do it today?"

"Right now. Give me twenty minutes. Start packing."

I kiss her, then I'm out the door, shifting to my fur the minute I've shed my clothes to race for reinforcements.

When I return in my truck, I have Callie and Liam riding with me to help move everything.

"Avery!" Callie bounds up the steps. "Caden says you're finally moving down to the lodge officially!"

Liam comes around the truck while I drop the tailgate. "You're going all domesticated on me."

I grin. "I'm a mated man. Trust me, if you ever find yours, you'll see how blindly you're walking around until they smack you right in the chest."

I illustrate it by thumping his sternum. He grunts, shaking his head with a smirk.

"Nah, I'm good. That True Mate shit's not for me."

"You say that now."

Avery comes out with a basket overflowing with clothes and pushes it into my arms. My world reorients as it always does when she's near.

"It's not much," she says. "Just the essentials. Callie's packing the rest of Lena's books she left here."

I drop the basket on the bed. "Not just the essentials. This isn't a weekend away. Bring it all. Come on."

"I don't have a lot," Avery says as I usher her back inside.

"We're taking everything," I insist. "And whatever you don't have, I'm getting for you."

"I find it best not to argue with him when he's like this," Callie says. "He's stubborn."

"Oh, I know it," Avery responds fondly.

It doesn't take more than an hour to get everything loaded in the truck. Callie chats Avery's ear off on the ride back to the lodge, planning a girls' weekend with her sisters. Liam takes off once we get her stuff inside. Callie spots Taryn across the commons and skips over to join her friend. Beatrix is at lessons and Lena's reading at Alma's while she naps the afternoon away.

It leaves me alone in my den with my mate.

"We can put all this away later. Want a drink?"

"Sure."

I take her hand and bring her to the lounge. The room where I like to relax is decorated with cushy leather furniture and dark accents. I get us two glasses and pour us each a finger of whiskey.

Avery strolls around the room. She's been here before when her dad was the pack beta.

She moves a pillow from a couch to an armchair by the fireplace, then rearranges the stack of quilts in the basket beside it, flinging two from the pile. When she's finished, she emits a little grumble and goes back to drag the armchair to the opposite side of the fireplace.

I rub my chest, my wolf growing excited. My mate is nesting. Viewing the lodge as her den, making it just how she likes it.

"Those blankets need to go. They don't smell right. And this." She points at the couch. "This needs to move. It's all wrong."

"Tell me where you want it."

She peeks at me. "You don't mind?"

"Nope. I'll spend all night moving anything you want. It's your home, mate. If you're not happy with it, then I'm not either."

Her lips twitch with a hint of a smile. "Okay. Can you pull it this way, please?"

"Like this?" I hoist it by the leather armrest and adjust it.

She bites her lip, tilting her head. She shakes it, moving around to study the room from a different angle.

"No, it needs to be more towards the window. Can you—?"

I nudge the furniture, watching for her cue. She relaxes, relief smoothing her pretty features.

"Yes. That's better."

My wolf purrs. It fulfills him to please her. I'm right there with him.

We move room to room until we make it to my—our—bedroom. This one she has the least to change after spending so many nights here. I didn't realize it before, but she's been making this space her own bit by bit.

THE PACK SUMMIT comes after the first decent snowfall on Silver Mountain.

I spend the week before we leave checking and double checking my proposal, dragging Liam along the perimeter line daily, issuing new patrol routes for scouts, and taking the entire enforcer roster through drills to ensure the pack's safety while I'm away.

There's no sending a pack representative in my stead, an alpha must be present. I'm worried about leaving the packlands when things have been strained amongst my people. Lorne's bullshit has been simple enough to thwart when it was only him and my uncle disapproving of my rules, but now he's created fractures that could easily snap.

They've been quiet after I stripped his rank, but my gut tells me things aren't over with the trouble they've caused.

Avery reassures me when she wanders into my office late in the evening and settles in my lap that everything will be fine—the pack under Hodge's watch while we're gone and the summit we're traveling to.

Each Alpha is allowed three enforcers to accompany their group. Liam and two of our older lieutenants from my father's time, Angus and Benedict, are with us. We also bring a small handful of appointed volunteers from each pack to manage the welcome feast. Taryn landed herself a spot on that list weeks ago with another one of her stunts. It makes Callie happier compared to her usual boredom being dragged to these gatherings.

The journey isn't far for us, roughly half a day's run from Silver Mountain. Other packs venture from the edges of the region to meet in the central location deep in the forest. Rather than drive until the roads end, we shift, able to cover more ground faster. Our clothes are divided amongst us in packs we sling over our wolves' backs. When we're close, we give up our fur.

We arrive at the summit's neutral grounds, snow giving way to a magically preserved oasis untouched by cold seasons as we pass through towering archways with greenery wrapped around the columns. It's sacred land that belongs to no pack.

Stone structures and temple ruins blend seamlessly with the ethereal forest. Vegetation grows freely over the buildings, and the pavilions and gazebos open to the nature surrounding them with many windows, or no roofs in some places to welcome the stars.

Avery halts, taking it in with a gasp. "This is beautiful." She touches the leaves of a drooping vine crisscrossing between the trees overhead. "Is this heaven? I feel like I've walked into paradise."

My gaze softens at her wonder. "It's enchanted."

"Wait until you see the guest quarters," Callie says. "You'll love them."

"Are they luxurious?" Taryn gets a dreamy look on her face. "I hope the beds are big."

Liam prods her back. "You'll be with the other volunteers sleeping in the common chamber."

Taryn hangs her head with a groan. "That's boring."

"Should've thought of that before you were caught stealing extra food from the kitchen stores in the middle of the night."

"I was hungry!"

They glare at each other. Liam folds his arms, uncompromising.

"Sneak out later. We can bunk together," Callie whispers to her.

"I heard that," Liam grumbles.

Avery laughs. "You two bicker worse than pups fighting over the same toy."

"Tell me about it," I mutter.

We follow the winding path to the main hall. Its flagstone veranda sprawls from the large arched entrance. Twin fountains with wolves spouting water from their howling mouths decorate either side.

As hosts for the event this time around, Timber Hollow Pack's alpha and his family greet the traveling parties as we arrive. Alistair Ryan stands tall and proud, his beard peppered with gray. Regina, his mate, and their oldest son, Atlas, join him.

"Caden. Welcome," Alistair says jovially.

"Alpha Ryan. It's good to see you." We clasp forearms in greeting.

"When you sent word of your changed status and that you'd be arriving with your mate, it surprised us." He chuckles. "I recall you once denouncing the need to ever take one during your training time in Timber Hollow Pack."

I slide the hand resting at Avery's lower back around her waist, pulling her against me, possessiveness and pride expanding within me. My wolf puffs his chest out.

"I was an idiot," I say plainly.

Avery chokes, clearing her throat. She flashes me a sardonic look that tugs on my heart. My eyelids grow heavy at the hint of her scent, warm and sweet with her tender affection.

"This is Avery Blackburn."

The bond throbs, surprise and delighted pleasure rushing from her end. It's the first time I've introduced her with my name. From the moment I marked her with my claim, she became mine in every way.

She leans into me with a pretty shade of pink coloring her cheeks. "It's nice to meet you."

"Likewise. Never doubt that the Fates rest. They are always at work to guide us," Alistair advises.

"Whether we want them to or not," she adds in an amused tone.

"Especially then," Regina says. "I didn't want anything to do with this one. The Fates had other plans for us."

"And I thank them every day." Alistair chuckles heartily. "Can you believe it? The arranged mating my father planned turned into a fated match. We hope the same will be true for Atlas when the time comes for his arranged mating with the prestigious bloodline we've selected."

Atlas pulls a face that makes Callie snicker with Taryn. He shoots them a charming grin. I edge in front of my sister and her best friend with a raised brow. His flirtatious smile drops.

Alistair's attention moves past us and his cheerful demeanor hardens. "Alpha Bell. Welcome, Crescent Valley Pack."

Rooke Bell and his traveling group make their way to the veranda. Unlike Alistair, he's meticulously groomed, dressed in a sharp suit while the rest of us are in casual clothes.

"Alpha Ryan." He nods to me. "Alpha Blackburn."

Rooke passes. Alistair doesn't take his eyes off him until he's inside.

"He's rumored to be meeting with Moonlight Lake's pack frequently," he mutters to me.

My brows shoot up. The packs may be unified in peace, but it's not common to continuously conduct business one on one outside of the summit gatherings without the other packs' knowledge. It's also no secret that things are strained between Alistair and Rooke's packs.

"Is it true?"

He shrugs. "I haven't been able to confirm it myself. Watch him. You never know what he's up to. Whatever it is, I'm sure he's angling to make his pack stronger."

"Alistair," Regina chides. "Pack business later. Today is for celebrating together."

"Right." He invites us in with a wave of his arm. "Don't let us keep you from settling in. We'll see you for tonight's feast."

)))●(((

LATER IN THE EVENING, we prepare for the feast. The first night of the summit begins with a formal banquet and dancing. I've always kept to the edges and left early, finding the ball trivial. Oddly, I'm looking forward to tonight's festivities and showing my mate off.

Avery's seated on a tufted stool before the mirror when I finish dressing in a suit. I freeze, drinking her in. Callie told me she had Avery's gown for the welcome feast covered. In my wildest dreams, I couldn't have imagined this vision.

Her caramel toned hair cascades down her back in soft waves. The dark blue dress brings out her amber eyes, making them bright and rich. It's slinky and fucking sexy, the bodice hugging her, flaring out in a skirt that resembles starlight.

My mating mark declaring my claim of her is on display for all to see. Everyone will know she's mine. A possessive noise reverberates in my chest.

"Can you get the back of this? Callie left to finish getting ready in her room," she says while she's distracted by her jewelry.

"Maybe," I choke out.

"Maybe? What do you mean, maybe?" She finishes putting her earring in, catching my eye in the mirror. Her lips part as she admires me. "You look handsome."

"I promise, I don't look anywhere near as good as you. I think I'd rather get you out of it than help you put it on." My gaze rakes over her hungrily. "I can't decide if I want to peel it off inch by inch or tear it to shreds with my claws."

She gasps, clutching the bodice covered in delicate crescent moons. "Don't you dare ruin it."

The lush tinge of pink in her cheeks suggests she rather likes the second idea. I give her a slow, predatory grin.

"Caden," she warns.

I tease her, emitting a gravelly rumble. Reaching for the bond, I trace my knuckles along our connection. Her eyes darken with desire. She blinks it away with a husky exhale.

"You can't. We'll be late to the welcome feast. We should use tonight as an opportunity to feel out whether the other alphas will be open to your trade proposal."

Licking my lips, I rein my desire in. "Okay. But later? You're all mine."

Her gaze flares with heat in the reflection. She draws her hair aside and I move behind her, watching her reaction in the mirror while I trace my claiming mark at the crook of her neck.

My fingertips skim her spine. She shivers, peering over her shoulder. I place a kiss at her nape before securing the clasp for the delicate neck strap. She rises with my help.

"Wow," I breathe.

She tucks her hair, giving me a spin. "Yeah? I've never worn anything this fancy before."

Fucking Fates. The low-cut backless design and high slit that runs to the top of her thigh will do me in tonight. My wolf is single-minded in his interest to follow the part in her gown to the crease of her thigh to inhale her enticing scent.

"Yeah," I rasp. "You're stunning."

"I'm not the only one who looks good." She steps into me, resting a hand on my chest and tucking her nose into the open collar of my shirt. "I like the suit."

My wolf rides me, fighting for my skin. He wants to rub all over her. I hold him back with a strained laugh.

"We need to go. Otherwise, I won't be responsible for losing control."

She takes my offered hand. Angus and Benedict fall into step a few paces behind us.

Hundreds of candles line the paths until we reach the staircase descending to the main hall we entered through earlier. The back has a terrace leading to gardens through the drape of willow vines. Warm light and music spill from the open doors, inviting us in.

A banquet table laden with food lines the far wall of the long room. The ceiling is open to the twinkling night sky, the moon casting a bright glow. Many are already here, dancing and drinking. The volunteer packmates from each group serve wine in goblets.

Callie comes in, escorted by Liam. Avery hugs her.

"You look amazing!"

Callie beams. "Thank you."

Several shifters' attentions snag on Avery as we make our way across the room. My wolf grumbles in warning at anyone looking at her for too long.

Thank the Fates my claiming bite is a beacon to all of them. She is *mine*. If they try anything, I'll end their existence.

Alistair's chuckle sounds behind us. "I remember what it was like during the summit when the mating bond with Regina was fresh. I nearly broke the accords at least four times, going mad with jealousy." He claps my shoulder with immense strength. "You'll get through it."

"It was closer to six," Regina corrects with a wry smile. "And you still haven't forgiven Rooke Bell for bringing me a drink."

He grumbles. "He did it on purpose to cause an incident."

"Thank the moon goddess I had the good sense to pass it off to someone else before your temper got the best of you," she says.

I scan the room with a fresh sense of dread. No one will dare try any bullshit like that to take Avery from me. My wolf paws the ground, stalking back and forth right up on the veil. I guide her to our seats and open my mouth.

She holds up a hand before I speak. "No, I won't be accepting anything from anyone. But you can get me a glass of wine."

My tongue traces my lip as it curves at her assertive tone. "Yes, mate. As you wish."

I pour her drink as the others take their seats, then hold her gaze as she takes a sip, admiring the bob of her throat. A pleased throaty noise leaves me. She tilts her head and it highlights her mating mark. I touch it, not giving a damn if we're being too open when I tease her across the bond.

She stifles a faint moan and hisses, "Caden."

"Yes, my heart?"

She purses her lips at the mischief lacing my voice. Narrowing her gaze slyly, she sips her drink. It's my turn to cover for myself, grabbing blindly at the back of her chair to fight the tantalizing sensation of her nails skating down my chest and stroking my abs lower, lower, *fuck*.

"Sit down," she says.

I collapse into my seat at her side, brushing my knee with hers under the table. "When I get you alone..."

She hums, cheeks flushing. I snag her wrist and bring her hand up to kiss.

Callie sighs from her spot diagonally across the table. "I should be grossed out because you're my brother, but it's sweet to see you two together. I hope I find my True Mate someday."

Avery's blush deepens. "I'm certain you will."

I frown, not wanting to think of the males she could be fated to. "But not for a long time."

Callie clicks her tongue. "I'm only a few years younger than you. At some point you have to stop treating me like a baby."

"Not happening."

The banquet begins with a toast to our continued harmonious unity. Once dinner is underway, Alistair leans across the table to talk to me.

"I hear you're making your first bid this year."

"I am. It's a proposal to update trading with Silver Falls Pack." His brows rise in interest. "As it stands, we share resources in spring and summer."

"We hope to foster a strong, fruitful relationship between our packs year-round," Avery says.

The corners of his eyes crinkle. I fight not to tense under his scrutiny of us. Shit. Have I misstepped? I watched and waited to make my proposal until after I felt out how the other packs would respond so I wouldn't come on too strong.

"What's that smile for?"

"It shows great initiative. And dedication to your pack. I'm proud to see it since I feel like I had a hand in preparing you to become an alpha," he answers.

Avery puts a hand on my back. I relax.

"It's good to be a young alpha." At the chorus of bawdy laughter from the others near us, Alistair inclines his head. "Not for that reason. He's not stuck in most of the old ways like the rest of us."

"A young mind has young ideas," Alpha Bell muses a few seats away.

"Which isn't a bad thing," Alpha Shepherd from Twin Rivers Pack says further down the table.

"I certainly have my full strength," I offer with a smirk.

Alistair's laughter booms. "That you do. But don't think I couldn't match it just because I'm old enough to be your father."

"It's been a while, but if you're looking to be my sparring partner again, I'll take you on," I joke.

He raises a glass in toast. I clink my goblet against his.

Partway through dinner, Taryn makes her way down the table to refresh drinks. She stops to talk to Callie and Kyra Bell, the three of them giggling. Atlas slips from his seat by his father and joins them, standing close to Taryn. She's amused by whatever he says. He gives her a lopsided tilt of his mouth, not being too subtle about his interest in her.

She empties the pitcher into Kyra's cup and rolls her eyes at Callie, trudging back towards the kitchens. He follows her after a beat, stopping her by the door. She sets the pitcher down on a pedestal and he leans into her space, hand propped against the wall by her head. They're too far to hear what he's murmuring.

Liam watches the entire exchange with a set jaw. The moment Atlas cages her, he moves from his guard position with the other betas to intervene. Atlas looks between them with confusion, backing off with his hands raised.

Taryn huffs, spinning on her heel to enter the kitchens. Liam shakes his head, staring after her for a beat before he returns.

"What was that all about?" I ask when he passes me.

"Nothing. Don't worry about it," Liam mutters.

I smirk, arm draping over the back of Avery's chair. Dinner begins to wind down as we finish our meals. I'm only paying half my attention to the conversation with the alphas, more focused on using the bond to trace Avery's mating mark. She squirms while she chats with Regina, touching it, finding I'm not actually touching her.

I keep doing it when groups break away from the table, guiding her around the room with her hand tucked in the crook of my arm. A male we talk to from Moonlight Lake Pack eyes her mark with a glimpse of envy.

I draw her closer into my side, kneading her shoulder so my fingertips brush over the bite mark. Her breath hitches. I keep my hand resting on her shoulder, thumb caressing her nape. The bond lights up with her enjoyment. The male tears his attention from her mark at my rumble, clearing his throat in apology.

A satisfied grin twists my mouth. The best way to keep any of them from coveting Avery is to rub it in their faces that she's mine.

The banquet takes on a new purpose for me now that I've found a way to enjoy the festivities. I go out of my way to talk to as many in attendance as I can, relishing introducing my mate and her coy reaction each time.

AVERY

THE FEAST IS unlike anything I've ever experienced. I've only been to parties on packlands, never something as extravagant and enchanting as the Pack Summit. It's wonderful to see the leaders and their delegations from each pack come together in support of each other.

I have a good feeling about tomorrow's accords. Everyone seems interested in the youngest alpha in the room and what he brings to the table.

Caden whisks me around all evening. A permanent blush heats my cheeks because he's showing me off, proudly introducing me to anyone we meet as his mate.

The way he says it makes my stomach dip and sends a shiver down my spine where his hand rests at my lower back. *My mate.* It's warm and smoky like a sip of whiskey.

In the brief times we're parted throughout the celebration, his gaze is on me. His phantom touch, too. It caresses me when I least expect it, teasing my exposed back and dipping between the high slit in my gown to trace up my inner thigh.

When I nearly moan in the middle of talking to Alpha Ryan's mate about my interests in foraging and cultivating my herb garden, I slip outside for air. We've been teasing each other with the bond all night.

Caden tracks me down moments after I leave the festivities, catching up to me in a courtyard that opens to gardens lit with hundreds of lights. Music from the feast filters through the over-grown ivy creeping up the stone archways and the ruins of an old tower.

"There you are. I think this counts as you conceding victory to me," he says.

I respond by plucking our magic connection like a spank. He jolts, balancing on the wall with a bitten off groan. My brows lift in smug satisfaction.

"Are you sure about that? I'm not giving up," I taunt.

He closes the distance between us, grasping my waist to yank me into him, playfully growling, "I'll make you."

I bite my lip around a smile. He chuckles, dipping his head to scent me. I'm pliant for him, giving him my throat. His smile brushes my skin as he rubs his jaw against me. He takes my hands, lifting one to rest on his shoulder, guiding me to the soft music.

"What are you doing?" I giggle when he twirls me, then draws me in again, tucking me close.

"Dancing with you."

"You like to dance?"

He leans close like he's divulging a secret, amusement and tenderness lacing his tone. "I like doing anything with you. From watching you inspect every leaf you pick to dancing with you beneath the moon and stars."

My chest swells with affection. Our slow dancing comes to a stop and I step into him.

"I love you," I murmur.

His gaze softens, roving my face. "My heart. My mate. I love you with all that I am."

He crooks his fingers, lifting my chin for a kiss. I melt against him. It's full of passion and love, a kiss that touches me to the depths of my being, brushing the bond with his devotion to me.

When we part, we remain close, his hot breath ghosting across my lips.

I meet his fathomless blue eyes. "Do we need to go back in there?"

"Not if you don't want to."

"Good."

Taking his hand, I drag him in the direction of our quarters. He chuckles at my urgency, riling me up by locking an arm around my waist, drawing me back against his chest.

"Where are you going in such a hurry, mate?"

He clasps my throat in a loose hold, then guides my head back, kissing me until I'm swaying with dizziness. I tear away with a gasp.

"I want you."

He nuzzles my neck, kissing his mating mark. "You have me. Always."

I close my eyes, enjoying the tingles racing across my skin. Our fingers lace together over my stomach. I sigh contentedly, tethered by his embrace.

"Will you come with me?"

"There's nowhere in this realm or any other I wouldn't go with you."

With one last kiss to my shoulder, he sweeps me into his arms, carrying me to our room. I laugh, tucking my nose against his throat, lashes fluttering in bliss as I drag in lungfuls of his spiced musk.

"I'm capable of walking," I tease.

He rumbles with a smirk. "I like my way better."

In our guest quarters, he sets me on my feet, circling me with a heady, gravelly vibration in his chest. My wolf responds. My fingertips slide beneath the lapels of his jacket, pushing it off. He touches his lips to my temple, undoing my dress.

I step out of it, backing away in nothing but lace panties. He matches me step for step, gaze hooded, stalking my retreat until my back hits the wall. Grasping my thighs, he lifts me, guiding my legs around his waist while I unbutton his shirt to get to his chest, splaying my hands over his firm pecs and chiseled abdomen.

We collide in a searing kiss. Our hands are all over each other. Mine in his hair, his skimming my sides and kneading my breast. He grinds his hardness right where I want him until I fall apart with a shuddering gasp.

He's still wearing too many clothes. I tug at them without breaking the kiss. We manage to get his shirt half off while he kicks off his shoes.

His hands partially shift and he uses his claws to tear my panties off. My fingers slip on his pants and a desperate exhale blows out of me. He bats my hands aside and gets them open, then lines up without bothering to take them off.

My head tips back when he sinks in. He tucks my hair and kisses beneath my ear.

"Is that what you needed? Your mate's cock filling your pussy?"

I nod, unable to form words. He flashes me a handsome lopsided smile, resting his forehead against mine. It's so divine when he moves.

"You feel so good," he says reverently. "So perfect for me."

Everything feels more intense than usual. I'm not sure if it's the magic surrounding us in this sacred landmark, but I'm ready to come again, my core taut with quivering pleasure every time his cock glides inside.

When he stops moving, I nearly claw him. He hushes me with a kiss, keeping me supported while stripping off his pants. Then there's nothing left between us. He adjusts his grip on me, pinning me to the wall to fuck me.

Yes. This is what I needed.

I writhe against him, pleading for harder, faster, more. He meets my demands.

Fucking Fates, his scent. It's incredible. Mooring me, bursting on my tongue. He's a warm crackling fire and the most refreshing drink of spring water. He's the forest all around me.

He's home—my home.

My chest vibrates with a rough noise. I bury my face in the crook of his neck.

Instinct takes over. The faint rumble grows into a possessive growl that rolls on continuously as I scent him, dragging in rich cedarwood and feeling the misty kiss of the falls on my skin. My fangs descend and my nails shift into claws, pricking his skin in my urge to get closer.

Caden releases a husky laugh tinged with desire. "Fuck, that's hot. You're getting so loud, mate. You'll let every pack here know you're claiming me."

Claim. Yes. That's what I want. I need him. He's mine. My mate. I want to mark him.

"Caden," I plead.

"I know. Come here." He holds me close with ease in his strong arms, backing us from the wall while he's inside me. "I'm not going anywhere. I'm yours, mate. Always yours."

"Yes."

Need unlike any I've ever known surges through me. I need to claim him. *Now.*

I kiss him hard, cutting his lip with my sharp canines. He doesn't care, grinning into it, guiding us to the bed.

"Mine," he rasps against my mouth. "My stunning mate. I want to watch you ride me."

My core throbs with desire. I sit up, giving an experimental rotation of my hips. My teeth rake my lip at the way his cock hits me deeper and the delicious friction on my clit. He kneads my hips and thighs, pinning me with a heavy-lidded smoky gaze, his wolf purring in approval when I find my rhythm.

"Does it feel good?" He skims a palm up my inner thigh, finding my clit.

I nod with a whimper. He strokes the bond at the same pace he's rubbing my clit until I throw my head back, mouth open with a silent cry of ecstasy. My hips circle, riding out my release, lit up by how deep he's buried in me.

I collapse against his chest and he takes control, thrusting into me at a new angle that tears another gasp from me. I'm going to come again, the pressure builds in a crescendo, his cock hitting me at the perfect spot.

My mouth clamps over his sinewy shoulder to muffle my scream. The urge returns with a force, the bond expanding around my heart in a warm glow.

Mine, mine, mine, it chants. My wolf agrees.

"Mark me as yours," he commands.

There's a mark already there. My wolf freaks out. We are fated. He is hers. He cannot belong to another.

He doesn't. They're his scars from trying to protect his father from mine. My heart clenches. I kiss the faint ragged lines left by claw marks.

Caden shudders, arms locking around me to hold me tighter. We fought the Fates' design and still found our way back to each other. Our past can't haunt us anymore. We only have our future together, bound and mated.

My bite covers the old scars, teeth piercing his skin. He groans, cradling the back of my head, uttering encouragement. His cock jerks, buried inside me.

I lick the mark, empowered by the way it makes him twitch with pleasure. His fingers sink into my hair.

"Mine," I hiss against the healing wound.

His grip flexes on me and his hips jolt with a sharp thrust. Biting out a curse, he yanks me into a kiss. I swallow his groan as he comes.

The bond thrums between us with a burst of magic, the electric sparks intoxicating and wonderful. Then it settles. I feel him more deeply, not just sensing his emotions through the bond but feel more anchored to him, as if we're interwoven in the fabric of our beings.

We are one. Whole. Complete.

36

———

CADEN

In the morning, we gather with the other alphas at an oblong table with high-backed chairs. For years since the packs broke away from the Original Pack and formed their own territories, pack heads have come here to set the terms of the alliance between us all. Arched stone windows draped in creeping ivy overlook the lush gardens, giving the sense we're outside, one with nature. It's what I like best about the summit grounds.

I guide Avery to our seats next to Alistair and Regina Ryan with my hand at the small of her back. Liam stands behind us, matching the other betas taking their support position with their alphas. Some others are joined by their mates, some, like Rooke Bell of Crescent Valley Pack, only attend with their beta and a handful of advisors.

"This is a lot more formal than I always pictured in my head," Avery whispers.

I lean into her, admitting, "I was intimidated as hell when I first came, and once I was Alpha."

Things begin with Alistair's beta reading out the accords as they currently stand, outlining the alliance and peaceful relations between all the packs present. The representative Timber Hollow

Pack sent to meet with me stands at a podium with him, shuffling through paperwork.

"Alphas, to start, do you have any heirs to name since we last met?" Alistair prompts, residing over the meeting as this summit's appointed host.

I remember the one my father brought me to when he officially named me heir apparent. Despite being raised as heir, I didn't want the responsibility. I was afraid I couldn't fill the role. I know I'm capable of it now.

"Twin River Pack has named Oliver Bailey," Alpha Shepherd announces.

He waves his nephew forward to a round of applause. The lanky kid turns beet red, shuffling back to the alcove. The other packs continue around the circle. Northwest Boulder Pack declares Tanner Marshall's first pup his heir. Then Wispy Plains Pack names a pack member outside of Alpha Goodwin's bloodline.

Alpha Bell shakes his head when it's his turn. My brow creases. Rooke's daughter is around Atlas' age, and Alistair already named his son to take his place as the head of Timber Hollow Pack during my second summit as Alpha.

"Not your daughter?" I prompt.

He wrinkles his nose. "A female for a pack alpha? Not a chance. I won't be naming Kyra as my heir."

His statement sparks some murmurs around the table. Avery shifts in her seat, her scent turning bitter and sharp. I rub her back to soothe her disapproval.

Alistair signals his beta to move on. He outlines the Alpha heir program where heirs travel pack to pack for a few months at a time. Each pack provides a helping hand in training future heirs, allowing them to see how each pack manages its people to guide them to becoming a well-rounded alpha.

"Atlas Ryan, heir apparent to Timber Hollow Pack, you'll spend time with each pack as part of your preparation to become a future alpha," Alistair says. "You'll learn from the pack alphas before you. After the summit, you'll return with your first host, Alpha Blackburn, to Silver Mountain."

Atlas steps up to the head of the table and bows his head. His father shoots me a wink. It's my turn to return the favor guiding his son.

I didn't think I was ready to train anyone else how to be a fair and decent alpha because since I took over for my father it felt like I was treading water beneath the thundering pressure of Silver Falls, fighting to stay afloat. It wasn't until Avery opened my eyes to how tightly I was gripping the reins that I wanted to do better. Being a good alpha isn't about being perfect, it's about dedicating myself to giving my pack the best I can.

I'm looking forward to keeping Atlas on his toes the same way his father did with me.

The next few topics are dealt with quickly. Some packs have brought lists of those who would like to apply for a transfer to move to a new territory.

When trade terms come up, I lift a hand. "Silver Falls Pack would like to submit a proposal for sharing resources."

Timber Hollow Pack's representative passes out a copy of what I'm asking for from others for the winter months and the lumber, stone, and other materials I'm offering in exchange.

"We also have an addition." I invite Avery to speak with a nod.

"I brought samples of what we'd like to offer to your packs in addition to the mountain's resources. Please enjoy them," Avery says. "Liam? Would you?"

"Of course." He accepts the basket from her and circles the table to offer the selection of vials, jars, and bundles of dried herbs in sachets.

"What use do these have?" The beta from Moonlight Lake Pack stops the alpha and picks up a sachet, sniffing dubiously. "Looks like witchcraft to me. What is Silver Falls Pack playing at?"

Several distrustful rumbles sound around the table, including the loudest from my wolf at the accusation of our mate. I shoot to my feet, stance broadening.

"My mate is no witch. Take that back immediately, or face me in a challenge." I bare my teeth, canines growing.

Avery grasps my hand with a soft smile, encouraging me to sit. "It's fine. There's no need to fight to defend my honor. Allow me to explain."

I drag her chair closer with a terse sigh, scowling at the beta and anyone else who looks at her in a way that irks my wolf. He paces, emitting tetchy noises that reverberate in my chest like a motor. The only thing that calms me down is her touch when she rubs her thumb across my knuckles and glances at me with an expression that broadcasts *get it together*.

"Don't be so close-minded. Use your senses. You can't smell magic, can you?" She's fearless in the face of their allegation, exuding confident satisfaction when a handful of them shake their heads. "These are herbal remedies made from wild plants that I forage and what is grown in my garden."

She demonstrates by taking the salve Regina Ryan picked and smoothing it on her wrist. When her skin doesn't melt off, their wariness fades.

"They help your elders manage pain and stiffness as they age. Aid our healing abilities to make things more comfortable."

"Like human medicine?"

"Hardly," she scoffs, then backtracks. "Well, in the modern sense. Their chemicals are useless on most supernaturals. There are other uses to calm the mind or offer relief from fatigue."

Interest and curiosity buzzes around the room. Smugness twists my lips. They should be interested. My mate is incredible.

The alphas deliberate my proposal amongst their factions of advisors and mates. My stomach clenches until I sense a soothing stroke along the bond from Avery to set me at ease.

"Crescent Valley Pack agrees to the trade terms with Silver Falls Pack," Alpha Bell declares. "It's only right that we help each other out."

"Timber Hollow Pack agrees as well," Alistair says. "I'm intrigued."

"You would be," Rooke snarks. "You love to welcome humans to your packlands. I wouldn't be surprised if you welcomed witches to your doorstep, too."

"Not witchcraft," Avery reminds him. "Just the gifts that nature provides to those who know their uses."

A few others chime in with their agreements, Cove Coast and Twin River Packs. More than I expected when I submitted my first proposal to the accords. It worked. We're more successful than I hoped. I hiss out a relieved breath without drawing attention to myself.

Avery laces her fingers with mine. Her smile is everything, lighting me up with her proudness. I've questioned if I'm on the right path, or if I'm only Alpha out of a sense of duty to keep my cousin from grabbing power. My chest buzzes with a sense of rightness. I'm meant to be Alpha. I take pride in Silver Falls Pack and I want to be their alpha.

"What's next to discuss?" Alpha Marshall prompts. "Or have we finished?"

"Before we bring the accords to a close, there's one last thing," Alpha Shepherd says solemnly. "I'm afraid Twin River Pack needs to report a disturbing number of our pack going missing. My enforcers have looked into the complaints from families of them not coming home. We've found nothing concrete yet, and I bring it before you here to warn you to be on guard of the same happening in your territories."

I exchange a look with Avery, a knot of tension forming in my gut. If other packs have had the same mysterious disappearances, it could mean we aren't alone in the way we lost our mothers. This could mean it's possible to find answers we never got.

"Missing?" I press. "We also wanted to bring this before you all for unexplained cases involving two females in Silver Falls Pack."

Alistair's brow furrows. "Your mother? Dempsey told me she found her True Mate and left him."

"He assumed that was the case, but Avery's mother also went missing. It's what drove her father to act so brashly when he refused to listen to Clark's concerns for his mate. Neither of them ever knew for sure what happened."

"We think they could be connected," Avery says. "Tell us more about these disappearances."

"They go off and vanish without a trace when someone goes out in their fur to look for them," Alpha Shepherd explains.

"Are they not rogues splitting off for Wanderer's Canyon?" Alpha Bell suggests skeptically. "I won't indulge in undue alarm. This sounds like they went moon mad and ventured off."

"It's not that," Avery says. "There were no signs of restlessness or my mother's wolf going feral from moon madness."

"But this was years ago," Alpha Bell points out.

"That doesn't mean it's not related," she says.

"She's right. We had a strange disappearance about two years ago that could align with the larger picture being painted now," Alpha Goodwin says with a frown. "But it wasn't a shifter alone, it was a mated pair. Their pups were orphaned. We thought..."

He trails off with a grimace, his implication hanging in the air that they went to their deaths together. Avery finds my hand and I give it a squeeze.

"I checked Twin River Pack's records," Alpha Shepherd says. "There's been at least four disappearances in the last fifteen years. They're spread out enough to not cause alarm, but in the last two years it's increased enough that it's become noticeable."

"We shouldn't write these off as shifters going rogue or feral," I propose. "What if they're being taken?"

"I agree." Alistair strokes his beard. "We should all remain vigilant and send word of anything out of the ordinary."

"Very well," Rooke concedes.

Murmurs of assent go around the table. The knot in my stomach loosens with the packs' agreement to work together.

Alistair stands. "Any other matters to address?" When no one puts anything else forth, he claps his hands. "Right then. With that, this meeting of the packs is adjourned. The accords will be updated and copies delivered to your territories."

Everyone rises, chatter filling the room. Alistair keeps an eye on Rooke Bell as he leaves first with Moonlight Lake's alpha, their heads bent together.

"I never imagined what happened to our mothers could be tied to something affecting all the packs in the region," Avery says in an undertone while people filter out.

"It never crossed my mind, either. Or my father's." I tuck her hair behind her ear. "Even if our mothers aren't still out there somewhere, I feel better knowing we could find out what happened to them one day."

She nods. "Me too. And we could all stop the same from happening to others in our pack and in others."

"We'll keep an eye out for everyone."

"Do you need me for anything?" Liam checks.

"No. Go enjoy yourself." I squeeze his shoulder. "You've earned the downtime."

"You're sure? Should I check on Callie?"

I wave him off. "She's probably keeping Taryn company. I'm sure she's fine."

"Taryn told me something," Avery says with a wry twitch of her lips.

Liam narrows his eyes. "What's that?"

"That you can't spell the word fun."

He grumbles, gaze flicking to me when I stifle a snort. "Hilarious. Fine, see you both later. If you need me, let me know."

Alistair stops us on our way out to the gardens. "You've changed."

My head jerks. "I have? How?"

"You've mellowed out. You're not as on edge as I've known you to be in the past," he commends. "I'm glad to see it."

Heat prickles the tips of my ears and my nape. I clear my throat.

"I'd say it's largely in part to finding my mate," I reply gruffly. "She balances me."

"Ah, as any good partner should," Alistair says.

He clasps my arm and catches up to Atlas. We stroll through the vibrant gardens while everyone else disperses. With the accords coming to a close, I relax, able to appreciate the beauty of the grounds. Maybe because my mate looks resplendent against every backdrop here.

"He's right," Avery says.

"About what?"

"How you've changed." She studies me, a smile playing in the corners of her mouth. "Definitely for the better. You've lost that whole constant scowl you had going on."

I gather her in my arms, heart swelling with warmth. "Because I have you." I walk until her back hits a pillar swathed in moss and vines, kissing her. "And you make me want to smile all the damned time. Unless someone's wronged you, then they'll face my wrath."

She laughs, cupping my jaw. My wolf purrs. He loves the sound of her delight.

"You can't go around fighting everyone who looks at me in a way you don't like," she says in fond exasperation. "You'll get a reputation for being mate-crazed."

"I can and I will. Reputation be damned because I'm already there." I kiss the inside of her wrist, then sweep her off her feet, striding through the gardens at a brisk pace with her nestled in my arms.

"Where are we going?" She rests her head against my shoulder with a radiant smile.

"There's time before the closing feast. I'm going to show you how crazy I am for you, mate."

37

AVERY

Caden's spirits are high on the journey home from the summit. He's bolstered by our successful trade proposal with the other nearest packs, and opening up to the idea of selling to humans to bring in more money for the pack. On our walk through the foothills at the base of Silver Mountain, he's animated and I'm charmed by it, unable to keep a smile off my face.

"You said Ashbury hosts a market. We could start there. Word will spread amongst the humans that our pack is selling handmade goods from our apothecary," he suggests.

"Oh, so now you're on board with me going to town?"

"With me there to protect you," he concedes. "I'll never leave you alone."

"Are they like this all the time?" Atlas mutters to Callie. "I thought Caden Blackburn was supposed to be this badass. He's the youngest alpha, but he just seems like a lovesick fool."

Liam snorts. "Get used to it, pup." His amusement drops, growing serious. "And watch your tone, or I'll whoop your ass."

Caden flashes me a sly look, stealing a kiss before he makes a move. He catches Alistair's son and heir off guard, sweeping his legs from under him. Atlas overbalances, landing on the ground. Taryn cracks up.

"Lesson one," he says with a smirk. "Always be ready. Especially when everyone else thinks you're too distracted to act."

"Right."

Caden offers him a hand up and slaps him on the shoulder. "You'll learn."

We're getting close to our territory, starting up the mountain. I drag in a lungful of crisp air, smiling. Eagerness to be home stirs within me.

Then a ripple disrupts the air, zipping across my tongue with a crackle. Magic. We halt and a coil of unease forms in my stomach. Something's wrong. My wolf is alert, teeth bared.

The bushes rustle. Caden tenses, throwing an arm out in front of me. Liam takes point beside him, blocking Taryn and Callie.

They relax somewhat when Hodge, Ford, and a few others from our pack come out of hiding. Alisha helps Alma over a large stone and checks behind them. My stomach drops at Alma's healing bruises. They're all worse for wear, Ford favoring his left arm, Hodge's forehead sporting the remnants of a healing gash, and the others with torn clothes.

My heart rises into my throat. Our packmates have been attacked and hurt.

"Alpha," Hodge says gravely.

"What's going on? Why are you outside the perimeter?" Caden demands.

Before they answer, more people emerge from the trees, shimmers of magic unveiling their presences. They're witches, some dressed in eccentric swaths of fabric decorated with baubles. A few dress like humans, but their scents and the electric aura of magic they aren't masking give them away to a shifter's heightened senses.

Caden growls, his wolf riding him. "What the fuck is going on?"

I put a hand on his arm when I recognize the witch leading the small group, standing between her and my mate. "Jade. You're back."

She looks the same as the day I met her, regal and mysterious, her age just as indiscernible. "Yes. My coven's returned to these woods."

"Caden, this is Jade. She's the witch I told you about. The one that saved my life."

He eyes her warily, nudging me behind him. I grip the back of his sweater.

"Calm down. She's good," I insist. "Jade, this is my mate, Caden."

"I know who you are. We're here to help," Jade confirms. "I wish we'd returned to your region under different circumstances, though I'm glad to see fate's worked out for you, little wolf girl."

"What? You knew my future?"

"I'm not a seer by any stretch," she explains. "But the Fates are all around us if we open ourselves to listening. I had a good feeling about you when I came across you trying to poison yourself."

"I wasn't—it doesn't matter. Hodge, what's happened? Why are all of you injured?" I leave Caden's side to check them over.

"It's not as bad as it looks," Ford says.

Hodge's expression shutters. "We failed you, Alpha. I'm sorry."

Caden's jaw works, his shoulders a rigid line. "Tell me."

"It's Lorne and Cormac. They've taken the pack," Ford says. "Lorne's named himself Alpha."

Caden roars, slamming his fist into a tree. It splinters, the cracking trunk sending a shocking echo through the woods. I cover my mouth in horror. This can't be real. Caden worried there was a risk in leaving, but I didn't think anything like this could happen.

"Those fucking conniving bastards," he snarls. "I'll kill them all for this."

"Anyone who they've gathered favor with helped them. They ambushed us on patrol the night after you left and captured a lot of the enforcers that didn't bend their necks like Weston and Abbott." Ford looks like he might be sick. "Gabe. They've also got Tobin, Marissa, and the others being held."

"We managed to escape the territory in the chaos and Jade helped keep us hidden to scout out what's going on inside.

Everyone who didn't make it out's been rounded up in Cormac's compound," Hodge says gruffly. "I'm sorry we couldn't stop them."

"It's okay." Caden grips his shoulder, features set in resolution. "We're going to fix this. I'll take the pack back. They've broken shifter law. They can't take a pack by force without challenging me."

"My sisters?" I choke, struggling not to panic. "Are they okay?"

Hodge nods, morose. "They have them. I'm sorry I wasn't able to get to the girls in time to protect them."

"What about our way in? We need to free our enforcers first before we go for their throats," Liam says.

"We've been watching. They've got a few patrols, but most are avoidable," Ford says. "It's the compound that'll be a bitch to infiltrate without anyone noticing."

Caden and Liam exchange a glance, able to understand each other without words.

"You guard Avery, Callie, and Taryn. Ford and Hodge, you're with me."

"With my life," Liam swears. "We'll go to my cabin."

I grab Caden's arm. "You expect me to sit tight in a hideout? Hell no. I want to go with you. My sisters are in there."

His chest reverberates with a rough noise and he takes me by the shoulders. "Yes, damn it. I can't fight knowing you're in danger. I need you safe. I'm going to end this."

"I can help," I protest.

"You'll help by staying put with Liam." He lays a hand over my heart. "I need you to do this for me. I promise everything will be alright."

My throat tightens. His eyes bore into mine, bouncing back and forth. I don't like it, my wolf just as pissed, pressed close against the veil. She's ready to tear through the territory on a rampage for harming her pack, her family.

I give a jerky nod. He presses his forehead to mine, then captures my mouth in a blistering, heart-stirring kiss that ends too soon.

"Caden," I rasp.

He studies my face, cupping my cheek. I bite my lip.

"Don't you dare lose. Not to Lorne or Cormac."

The corner of his mouth lifts, his expression turning savage and driven. "Never. No one could take me from you, mate. I'll wipe their existence from this earth for touching everything that's mine. My family. My pack."

His fierceness sends a shiver down my spine. I hug him before he goes to fight the corruption infecting our pack.

"Be careful. I love you."

He crushes me to him. "I love you, too. I'll finish this quickly."

"We'll join you." Two of Jade's coven members step forward. "We've sensed magic inside your packlands."

"Dark forces are at work," Jade says. "It's the same forbidden black magic we've been tracing for years. Whoever's casting it needs to face the council. That's why we've come."

"What about me?" Atlas asks.

Caden jabs a finger at him. "You stay out here. The last thing I need is another pack's heir getting underfoot."

"What? No! I'm your ally. Let me fight with you."

Caden's jaw works. "I don't have time for this. Alma."

Alisha supports her as she makes her way over and grabs Atlas' ear. He yelps in complaint.

"Behave, pup. You've got a lot to learn about the way of things," she says.

I watch Caden lead his men through the trees until they're out of my sight. Then I turn to the bond to feel the distance stretch between us. Swallowing thickly, I follow Liam the opposite way to sneak through the perimeter to his cabin at the opposite end of the territory. Jade comes with us.

No one's around. It's eerie to see the packlands so empty and lifeless.

"Here." Jade hands me a velvet bag from her belt once we make it to Liam's cabin. "These are spelled for protection. Place them at the back door to ward off those that wish us ill intent. I'll get the front."

I'm grateful for something to do to distract me from my worries about my sisters. Inaction is making me restless, spurred on by my wolf. She hasn't stopped pacing. Her agitation tightens my muscles until my skin feels stretched uncomfortably tight. She's not happy to be sitting out when she's ready to fight anyone who dares threaten her pack.

We're strong, she seethes. *We should fight.*

Part of me agrees. I promised Caden, but I don't want him fighting on his own, either.

Blowing out a breath, I step out back on Liam's deck to set Jade's protective barrier. A twig snaps to my left and a figure hobbles out, tripping against me when she tries to take the steps to the deck two at a time. I stiffen, then relax when she makes it to me without setting off Jade's spell.

"Avery?"

Sylvie clings to me desperately. I help her up.

"Oh, I'm so glad you're here. Saw you from where I was hiding. I—I ran. I couldn't stand it no more. Cormac, he, he—" She breaks off with a gasping sob. "He's so cruel. I'm sorry. So sorry. I should've listened. You said you'd help me."

My gaze narrows at the way her fear smells. It's making my wolf gag, shaking her head to dispel it. It's off, overpoweringly foul and bitter, but there's something else, a sour note underneath the stink of terror. She's lying to me.

"Sylvie," I snap. "Where are my sisters? Do you know?"

"I do, I do." She pulls at my clothes, encouraging me to move. "I can take you to them. Come with me now. I'll show you."

She's insistent. Too insistent. I want to rescue my sisters and get them to safety, but there's no way I can do it on my own.

"They sent you to lure me into a trap."

The cold accusation makes her flinch. Real tears well in her eyes. She doesn't bother denying it.

"I'm sorry," she whispers. "I have to do whatever they tell me to. If I don't obey, Cormac hurts me."

"It doesn't matter. Come with me." I drag her inside, grip firm around her frail wrist. "They know we're here. They sent her as bait to trap me."

Liam unfolds his arms with a growl, hauling Sylvie off her feet by the collar of her jacket. She wails, kicking her legs.

"Stop," I order. "She's not important right now. I'm going to get my sisters."

He grits his teeth, setting her down. "No. Caden gave me an order to stay put and keep you safe."

"And I'm telling you I'm not staying put and waiting for him to handle this." I bare my teeth. "I'm Alpha female. Either you're with me or you're not."

"I'm with you," Callie says.

"Me too," Taryn chimes in.

Liam sighs, outnumbered by three willful females. "Fine. Only because I know if I refuse you're going to do something anyway. If we're doing this, let's be smart about it."

"Tell me where my sisters really are," I growl. "Are they with everyone else?"

Sylvie cowers. I signal Liam with a glance. His violent rumble makes her balk and bare her neck.

"They're not," she stammers. "I bring their food. They're being guarded in a basement. It's a cabin near the back of the compound. There's a hatch to it from the outside."

My stomach clenches. If Caden's taking Lorne on, he won't know where they are. I have to get them out of there.

"You're not going run back to give us away," I say. "I'd rather keep you here."

"No, no. I'll help. A distraction—You need a distraction, yes? I'll bring some food for the guards," Sylvie promises.

"I'll help keep you properly motivated," Jade interjects. "Just in case."

She whispers an incantation, fingers tracing a sigil in the air I'm only able to make out faintly. Sylvie sways against Liam, eyes going glassy and unfocused for a moment.

Liam grunts. "What the hell did you do to her?"

"She'll seem like she's sleepwalking until I release her," Jade explains. "She won't cause any problems."

I give her a grateful nod. Sylvie blinks, her demeanor serene. "Let's go."

We leave Liam's cabin, sneaking through the packlands. We avoid the few scouts we encounter by following Liam's direction to stay downwind. I spot larkspur growing on a hillside, gathering as much of it as I can.

"We can take out whoever's guarding the basement with this. If we slip it into the food Sylvie gives them, it'll be easier to over-power them."

"What does it do?" Callie leans in to sniff it.

"Careful. We have to ingest it for it to have an effect on us, but larkspur is toxic. When they eat it, they'll lose control of their motor functions."

Jade gives me an approving once over. "You've learned well."

Sylvie takes us around the outer stone wall Cormac built around his compound years ago. She shows us a part covered by a blanket of ivy overgrowth where there are footholds. Liam climbs up first, checking if the coast is clear before hoisting us up one by one.

"Take us to the basement," I order.

Sylvie leads the way. The cabin she stops at isn't much bigger than my cottage, the wooden logs suffering from dry rot. I send Sylvie for food while we hide out of sight. The guards watching the basement hatch are playing cards. One groans, complaining that his partner is cheating.

"Can you cast the same spell on the guards?" Liam asks Jade.

"I need to be able to touch their aura to cast it. They're too far away," she says. "I'll do it when we're closer."

When Sylvie returns with two bowls of stew, I break up the

larkspur flowers and grind the rest of the plant with two rocks, mixing all of it into their food.

"Lunchtime already?" The lankier guard pats his stomach as Sylvie approaches. "I could eat."

"Stew again," the other says with a sigh. "Don't you know how to cook anything else?"

Sylvie shakes her head. "Stew is what Cormac likes."

They exchange a look at her dreamy tone, shrugging. My heart doesn't stop thudding until they've taken a few bites of food.

"Is yours, like, really spicy?" asks the lanky one.

The other one shrugs. "Kinda. My throat burns. I like it, though."

I hold my breath. The poison's taking effect. It doesn't take long for one to start coughing and gagging. They both pass out, slumping off their chairs. Sylvie stands off to the side peacefully.

"Now," Liam urges.

We rush to the basement hatch. Callie picks up the padlock while Jade casts a spell on the guards.

"Check one of them for a key," she says.

"On it." Taryn pats them down, deftly finding it looped around one of the guards' necks on a length of twine. "Here."

"How long will that keep them out?" Liam toes the closest guard.

"Long enough with Avery's poison. As long as I need with my spell," Jade answers.

Relief spirals through me when Callie gets the door unlocked. I race down the steps into the dank, dark basement. The girls are huddled on a cot shoved into a corner.

"Avery!" Lena covers her mouth to keep her voice down. "You came for us."

My sisters rush me. I catch them both in a tight hug.

"Of course I came for you. I'd never leave you behind. Did they hurt you?"

"No," Beatrix answers. "They just tried to scare us."

"Dane said really mean things." Lena whimpers into my neck. "Like how he wanted to make us his personal maids."

A growl flies out of me. I'll cut off his tongue.

"Let's get out of here." I take my sisters' hands and hurry to the steps up to the hatch.

Liam curses under his breath and yanks us behind him. Male voices come closer. We peek around the corner. Dane ambles around with Trent.

"Hey. No sleeping on your watch. And why's this door open, you idiots?" Dane and Trent nudge the unconscious guards. "Oh, fuck. I think he's dead. What the hell?"

"Shit," I hiss.

"Shh." Liam edges back, shooting Jade a questioning look. She shakes her head and he exhales heavily. "I'll attack. You all run."

"By yourself?" I bite out. "Dane, sure. But Trent's huge."

He levels me with a firm look. "He's also an idiot and he swings wide. Trust me, I know how to handle them. Your job is to get yourself to safety, okay?"

"Got it. Girls, stay close and be ready to run. Lena, if it hurts to breathe you have to keep going. Promise me, buttercup."

"I'll carry her," Beatrix says. "We look out for each other, right?"

I squeeze her hand. As Liam watches for an opening, I whisper to Jade.

"If this goes wrong, I need you to make sure they're safe." She nods. "Thank you."

Liam moves the second both their backs are turned, bolting up the steps and knocking their heads together. Dane and Trent stagger with shouts of anger as he shifts, biting Dane's leg.

The rest of us make our escape while Liam fights the guards. Taryn and Callie take off, watchful for others that might hear us. I'm right behind them with Jade and my sisters.

"Go get them!" Dane barks.

I push the girls in front of me. A determined grunt sounds behind me. Arms lock around my waist.

"I'll make you pay for stealing my mate!" Trent yells.

"No!" I fall under his weight bearing down on me.

"Avery!" Lena slides to a stop.

"Go," I yell. "Get out of here!"

Jade, Callie, and Taryn don't stop. Lena fights them, struggling to breathe.

"No! Stop! We can't leave without Avery! Avery!"

Her screams crack my heart open. Beatrix picks her up, casting a terrified glance back. Tears sting my eyes. It doesn't matter what happens to me. They'll be safe.

Pain pricks my neck. I struggle against Trent picking me up with a ferocious growl, shifting to my fur. My clothes tear and he buckles under the weight of my massive wolf. He drops a needle when I sink my teeth into his arm and wrench, breaking bone.

Fuck. He injected me with something.

It's fast working. My head spins, vision blurring. I stagger, losing my shift. My knees hit the ground hard.

I try to call out for Liam, panicking as Dane knocks him out when he shifts back. I'm going to be sick. My wolf rages, barreling against the veil to come back out. I can't feel her, going numb all over.

Everything mutes. My senses. My strength. My wolf.

And the bond. My heart lurches because I can't feel Caden. Can he still feel me? The world dims to blackness.

38

——

CADEN

RAGE SIMMERS IN MY BLOOD, but this is no time to lose my head. I need to fight for my pack. Root out my cousin and uncle for good and stop their absurd bid for power. They've waited all this time believing they can be brazen now. That they're strong enough to steal my rank and my pack from me.

They haven't won. Not by a fucking long shot.

My wolf is restless and ready to take my skin the moment I give him control. He'll bring every shifter on this mountain to their knees and have their submission to him as the rightful Alpha.

"Where are the enforcers being kept?" I demand as we swiftly make our way across the perimeter.

"Patrol cabin," Hodge answers. "They rotate the guards every few hours."

"We should be catching them near the end of a watch," Ford says.

"Let's be quick, then," I decide. "We'll free Gabe and the others to have more numbers on our side if the next guard change comes when we're breaking them out."

The packlands are eerily still and deserted except for the pair of scouts we come across when we cut through the lower ridge line from the south to get up to the commons. I signal Hodge and he shifts, sneaking up on them from behind.

They're not trained for the security team. That much is obvious from their lack of awareness that wouldn't fly for one of my enforcers entrusted with the safety of the pack. One's a Merryweather from maintenance group C that caused the fuss several weeks ago. The other's one of the younger Hooper brothers who's flunked out of enforcer tryouts three times.

When Hodge attacks, neither of them sense him coming. Hooper's head cracks on the ground, knocking him out. Merryweather tries to run, scrambling away. He trips on a divot in the path and Hodge tramples him.

He screams. "I surrender! Oh, gods, I surrender! Please don't kill me!"

This is the best my cousin could do? It's a fucking insult.

"Knock him out," I direct.

One of the witches with us steps out to the path, bending over Merryweather. He startles at her entering his periphery, squirming with renewed distress. She whispers something to him, then he relaxes, going still.

"He's subdued," she calls.

The witch casts the same spell on Hooper and Ford drags them into the woods, hiding them in a hollow under a jutting rock. We continue on, not encountering anyone else before we finally reach the patrol cabin. Kip's hanging out front, leaning next to the door with a bored expression.

We stay downwind, creeping into the cabin's back entrance. The annex is empty. Someone's talking on the other side of the door. I scent Weston and Abbott with a frown. One of the witches casts a spell over us.

"They won't sense our approach," she explains. "We'll appear like ripples in the air at the corners of their eyes until you touch them. There aren't any witches here, either. Only shifters."

I nod in thanks, delegating to my lieutenants. "Get our people out of the holding cells. The rest of us will take care of the ones on watch."

I'm the first one through the door. Weston glances up from one of the logbooks, brows furrowing. He shakes his head and bends over the desk again. Abbott paces lazily at the other end of the cabin. I wave Ford out.

He scans the holding cells and goes to the second one where Gabe is. Gabe jolts, stifling his surprise. He peers at Weston with a disgusted glare, then puts a hand on the bars. Ford squeezes it. Gabe's eyes fall shut, a wobbly smile stretching his mouth.

Weston jumps up. "We've been through this, Gabe. Go sit down. You're not tricking me again. Nothing you say will get you out of there unless you're ready to come to our side."

"You're an idiot," Gabe mutters.

Abbott laughs, coming this way. "We're not the ones behind bars."

Tobin grabs the back of his shirt when he passes his cell, yanking him in. "Won't be that way for long. When Caden finds out what you did, you're all dead meat."

"Caden's a weak fucking pussy who isn't fit to call himself Alpha. A real Alpha—"

I cut off his words, grabbing him by the throat. The spell hiding me from them sloughs off like water trickling down my back.

"What were you saying?" I seethe.

"Oh shit," Abbott chokes. "A-Alpha."

I slam him against the bars with a snarl. He grunts and swings his fists at me. I block one and catch the other in a punishing grip, flinging him aside like a rag doll.

"Weston has the keys," Gabe shouts.

Ford whirls on Weston. He takes a fighting stance, attention on me. His bravery crumbles at the sound of Ford vaulting over the desk to get to him. When Ford shoves him against the wall, he drops the keys on the floor. Ford punches Weston and retrieves the keys.

Weston covers his nose and shuffles into a corner once Ford

goes to let Gabe out. Abbott gets up and jumps on my back. He thumps my head and winds an arm around my neck to choke me out. I grunt, driving him into a column repeatedly until he lets go. He staggers to the side, then comes at me again.

"Get him, Alpha!" Tobin cheers.

The commotion draws Kip in from outside and two more guards from the security team from upstairs. Jordan flies down the steps with a curse, Lyle on his heels.

They pass by Hodge, still hidden by the spell. He snags Lyle by the scruff of his collar, dragging him backwards. Lyle compensates, throwing his weight to jerk Hodge to the floor with him. Hodge doesn't let him get away, wrestling him.

Gabe emerges from the cell, blocking Kip's charge. Ford tosses the keys to one of the witches and joins the fight.

The other witch shoots magic at Jordan. He dodges, clothes shredding as he lets his wolf out. Jordan leaps at her and attacks her shoulder, biting down. She screams, wrenching his fur in her grip to get him off. His bites are brutal and relentless. Fuck, I need to get over there.

I shove Abbott against the wall with all my might. He hits it hard and collapses with a groan as he loses consciousness, taking the chair he reaches for with him. I'm too late to help the witch. Her hands loosen, falling away. Her blood coats Jordan's snout and the floor.

Weston pushes away from the corner with a yell. To my surprise, he doesn't join the fight to attack my loyal guards. He goes for Jordan's wolf, shifting as he tackles him.

His wolf's a scrapper, smaller than his older brothers, but a cutthroat fighter. Jordan's a fast wolf, yet in a confined space like the cabin, he can't outwit Weston when he clamps his teeth on his back leg, rending it with a hard toss of his head. The bone fractures and Jordan's wolf screams in agony. Weston wastes no time breaking the other one, then goes for his throat.

"Stop," I command.

Weston freezes. I push him aside and drag Jordan by his scruff into an open cell. The remaining witch closes it.

Ford and Gabe have Kip beat. Hodge is up. He hoists Lyle off his feet, glowering.

"Enough," he barks.

Kip struggles, but Gabe doesn't let up, twisting his arm to the breaking point behind his back.

"It's over. Give it up," Gabe bites out. "You lost."

Ford holds the cell door open while his mate shoves Kip inside. He slams it behind him with a scowl, surveying Kip and Lyle's cells.

"Get comfy. We'll be back to deal with you assholes later." Ford points at Kip with a deadly glare. "Your days are numbered. You never should've touched my mate."

"Ford, I'm fine," Gabe mutters.

Ford releases a rough noise, pulling Gabe into his arms and tucking his nose into the crook of his neck. Gabe clutches him, murmuring to his mate.

Weston's wolf crawls on his belly to my feet, whining. His tail is tucked between his legs and he covers his snout, muscles twitching continuously with how hard his wolf shakes. At my booming growl, he shifts back, remaining crouched and bowing his head. The others watch in silence.

"I'm sorry," he pleads.

"You turned against your brother," I say.

"He's not Alpha. You are." He bends his neck, shoulders quaking as hard as his voice. "I'm sorry. I failed you. I should've been stronger. I—I was afraid. I didn't know what to do."

I grit my teeth. "Did you join the security team so you could feed them information?"

"I—" He gulps, forcing out the words shamefully. "Yes. They made me. I didn't tell them everything—only the patrol schedules and the route map."

He cuts off as my wolf makes himself known, my hands beginning to shift. "You betrayed the pack. Betrayed your alpha. I should kill you for that."

Weston presses his face to the floor with a fearful noise. "I know. It's what I deserve."

I work my jaw, staring him down. He's no threat to me. He might've been swayed down the wrong path by pressure from his family, but he doesn't smell like trouble or lies. When it came down to it, he did the right thing.

"Who do you pledge loyalty to?"

"You," he answers immediately.

"Not your brother? Your father?"

"No, Alpha Blackburn," he declares. "They're traitors. I give my life to serve you."

My gaze narrows. "You have one shot to prove I can trust you. Understand?"

He nods quickly, uttering a relieved cry. "Yes. I won't let you down. We have to get to the compound. Lorne's waiting for you there. He knows you're coming back today."

My lip curls. The smug bastard expects me to go to him? I want to rip his spine out by his tail.

"Get up. Help Tobin unlock the other cells and meet us there."

We check the entire patrol cabin. There aren't any other guards under Lorne's command here. The witches ward the entrances and windows to keep out anyone who would help the traitors we captured escape.

"You three come with me," I tell Hodge, Ford, and Gabe. "Tobin and Marissa, meet up with the group that made it off the packlands. Keep an eye out for any runners. Let's go."

I vault off the front steps of the patrol cabin, relinquishing control to my wolf. The transformation ripples through me before my paws touch the grass. His senses sharpen, listening for any signs of enemies. None are near, the stench of a threat wafting on the breeze from the opposite direction.

My lieutenants follow my lead, shifting to their wolves right behind me. My chest reverberates with a dominant rumble and they paw the ground, licking their jowls.

We take off for the Blackburn compound to the western slope of the mountain. It looms from the trees as they open to the wall he built around the territory he claimed for himself. I growl at the affront, not stopping my charge. I crash against the barrier to knock the outer wall down with a forceful blow of my shoulder. The stone gives. It's no contest for the Alpha power flowing in my veins, giving my massive wolf immense strength.

The courtyard is empty. No guards. No one inspecting the unsubtle entrance.

Offense roils my stomach and ruffles my wolf's fur as we careen through the compound. No one stops our group from busting through the doors to Cormac's massive lodge set at the edge of a cliff face.

Power driven by my fury radiates from me with every bounding step. I shift back mid-leap, landing in a crouch at the center of the great room.

Lorne sits in a regal chair with my uncle at his side on the raised platform backlit by windows overlooking the valley like he's won. Like he's the Silver Falls Pack alpha.

I'm pissed as fuck, furious growls tingeing every panting breath. Outrage rockets through me at the sight of females cowering behind the males who all wear self-important expressions. At how many of my pack has accepted Lorne's takeover. At my beta in Dane's headlock near the front of the crowd to my left.

My heart stops. An unconscious female is sprawled at Lorne's feet.

Avery.

Something's wrong with the bond. I can't sense her.

I'll fucking kill him for this. He's harmed my mate and my pack. My wolf surges forward to take my skin again, ready to destroy everyone in the damned room to get to our mate.

My outraged roar rattles the glass and sends half the room to their knees cowering. Those that manage to remain standing look to my cousin.

Lorne gives me a vicious grin.

"Cousin." He rises, spreading his arms. "I've been waiting for your return. I challenge you for the title of Alpha."

39

CADEN

"Good, because I'm going to kill you." My wolf is evident in every word. "Come down here and face me."

Lorne doesn't move right away. The disrespect and disregard for my authority rakes over my patience, stirring the need for retribution and my impending rampage until I'm strung tight like a bow ready to snap.

He doesn't realize how much danger he's in. My wolf won't be satisfied until he spills blood.

At last, Lorne rises, coming off his false throne with measured steps that make my skin prick with the urge to punch him repeatedly and squeeze his throat until the light goes from his eyes. I force out a breath to remain in place. He'll come to me.

I'm not giving up a fucking inch for this sniveling cocky little shit that thinks he's beaten me without earning my rank from me.

He keeps his distance, faking me out a few times. I don't fall for it.

When he's within range, I attack, going for the opening with a brutal punch that snaps his jaw to the side. He bites back a groan. I rear back and throw another. He blocks poorly, but manages to slip away and dance around me, bouncing on his toes in a fighter's stance.

"Have to be faster than that," he goads.

Lorne wants to draw this out. My lip curls at his insolence. I'm going to smash his face into the ground and paint the damned walls and floor with his blood.

My gaze cuts to Avery for a brief second. She's not waking up. I don't like how little she's moving. How I can't sense her properly. Even though I can't feel the bond, I reach for it anyway, using it to urge her to open her eyes and escape to safety. It doesn't work.

I block Lorne's sloppy left hook, stepping inside his guard to jab him in the stomach. He keels over with a grunt, then slashes at my stomach. His claws slice my torso. I back out of reach with a scowl.

The cut isn't deep enough to slow me down. It tingles, the skin knitting back together until it stops bleeding and only angry pink lines remain. My gaze narrows, attention darting to check on Avery. She hasn't moved.

For a harrowing second, I fear her heart's stopped, grabbing hold of the bond blindly. The shroud ebbs away, the connection pulsing warm and steady in my grasp. I blow out a breath, swinging my focus back to Lorne.

I'm done. This ends now so I can get to her.

"Stop running," I grit through my teeth when he evades my advances.

"I'm not, you're just too slow." He smirks, wiggling his fingers. "Your instincts aren't as sharp as you think. It's why you're a lousy alpha. You're too blind to wield the power the way it's meant to be. To rule absolutely."

I don't bother responding, swinging my fist just to shut him the hell up. I don't give a shit about what he's saying. He sounds like he wants to run my pack like the alphas of the Original Pack. He doesn't care about the people in it, all he wants is power and to be on top.

He shoves me back, sneering when it does little to upset my center of balance. Mistake. I grab him by the throat, squeezing. His eyes bulge and he knees me in the groin. I stumble back, clenching my jaw as pain burns through me.

Lorne's nerve boosts again once he's out of immediate danger. "I've waited so long for this day," he taunts. "Once I'm finished taking this pack that should've always been mine by birthright, I'll be taking your mate, too."

I see fucking red, roaring. He'll never have her. My wolf charges, bursting from me with immense power. He's done waiting.

Lorne doesn't shift immediately. His mask of confidence cracks, his smile and the corners of his eyes tight. He knows he's no match for me. I'll end him here and now.

Fight me, my wolf howls.

He glances at my uncle, earning a glare. I toss my head. There's no interference in a fight for rank. He issued the challenge and he needs to see it through. There's no tapping in a second.

I prowl the floor, inching closer to Lorne each time I circle him. His throat bobs, eyes skittering about the room.

Shift. My wolf's snarl carries Alpha power.

It forces Lorne's wolf out. He buckles under the change, falling to his paws as he transforms. His tail tucks and he shuffles back when I stalk up to him, baring my teeth.

He lunges for me, too desperate and wild with cowardice. It's stinking up the room, his scent unable to trick my wolf's nose. I take him down with a precise tackle, scratching his belly when he rolls. He whines, kicking at me with his back feet. It throws me off, but not for long.

I twist, landing on my paws. He's rolling to get up. I charge him before he's on his feet, pouncing once more to keep him pinned. He goes down harder this time, clawing the floorboards for purchase. It's no use. My wolf outranks him on every level, including size.

The challenge is over. He's lost.

It's time to finish this. My snarling maw opens to sink my teeth into his throat in victory, fangs dripping with saliva.

Before I can, a weight slams into me from behind with a fero-cious growl. I roll, whipping to face the one who would dare break shifter law to interrupt an Alpha challenge.

It's his father. My uncle. I should've known Lorne would fight dirty. He never stood a chance of winning any other way.

Cormac's wolf joins Lorne's, both of them attacking at once.

40

AVERY

Something warm and familiar brushes me from within. I cling to it, following it from the dark abyss my mind is trapped in. The bond. *Caden.* I cling tighter to our connection, waking to the bond screaming.

I take in my surroundings, squinting at the crowd groggily as my healing fights to flush whatever I was injected with from my body. They're in a circle around the edges of the room. They're not looking at me, they're watching a fight.

Ice drives into my chest. Caden's here, circling his cousin. It's a rank challenge.

Lorne's gloating about taking the pack and me. My stomach convulses. I struggle to move my body.

I gasp, shivering as magic washes over me. Jade's voice whispers through my head, her words too soft to make out. She's here somewhere. I hope she got my sisters away before coming back for me.

I'm able to move, my senses coming back with a pop of my ears. Sluggishness leaves my body. The room grows loud with shouting and thick with too many scents at once. I clutch my head, curling on my side.

Caden's worry flows inside me. I stroke it, tucking it close to my heart. The jangling bond smooths out, strands resonating.

When I turn my attention back to the fight, Caden's wolf is a beautiful sight to behold, sinewy muscles rippling beneath his thick black fur with every step. He roars with command, forcing Lorne to shift with undeniable Alpha power.

Lorne's efforts falter against Caden's massive wolf. He's outmatched, failing to gain an advantage in the fight. When Caden pins him, jaws going for Lorne's neck, relief floods me. It's over.

A wolf flies over my head, heading straight for the challenge circle.

No. Horror and wrath fill me at the sight of Cormac's wolf attacking Caden's unguarded back. Caden doesn't see it coming, unable to escape the underhanded blow to keep him from winning.

This isn't happening. I just got my pack back. They won't take it from me again.

No one will take Caden from me.

Chaos breaks out all around me simultaneously. Those on Lorne's side shift, clashing with Caden's lieutenants.

Liam breaks free of Dane and melts into his fur.

He's a blur of furious motion. Before Dane has a chance to become his wolf, Liam's is on him, deadly and vengeful. Liam's wolf snaps Dane's neck with a fearsome clench of his jaws around his throat. Dane's body jerks, then collapses with a hard thud against the floor.

My wolf rises to my call. Our sights are set on Cormac, blood singing with the promise of violence for touching our mate.

I leap from the platform, my wolf landing on Cormac's back. He snarls, swiveling his head and bucking to unseat me. I sink my teeth into his fur, growling and shaking my jaw. A piece of his pelt tears off. He howls, rolling me to the ground.

He leaves Caden for Lorne to deal with on his own, turning his cruel gaze on me. His wolf isn't as big as mine, but he's built. Wiry gray fur shot through with silvery white covers him, tufting from his ears. One's missing a chunk and his eye is clouded with permanent damage from a fight in the past.

He sinks low, then bolts for me faster than I expect for an older wolf. I sidestep him, my wolf vigilant, her gaze sharpening. He doesn't put his weight on his front right arm where she bit his shoulder.

I charge, head butting that side. He goes for my tail, grabbing it between his teeth to drag me. *Fuck*, that hurts. I kick his snout until he releases me.

I swing around, ready for his next attack, but he's not going for me. He leaps at Caden's side. Caden growls, dropping to roll out of the way. I go for Lorne, knocking him off balance when he isn't paying attention.

He flashes his teeth at me. I draw him away, switching opponents with my mate.

At last, I face Lorne one on one. This time he doesn't have an unfair advantage.

He pins his ears, growling with bluster. My wolf thinks he's a joke. She doesn't want to play games, springing into the air with devastating speed and strength. He tries to avoid it, but I land on his side, taking him down. We skid across the floor.

I close my teeth around his throat, pinning him. He's not going anywhere. I won't kill him, only hold him for Caden.

He releases a violent bark. Calling for help won't help him. He's lost. I put pressure on his neck to silence his plea.

My jaw stiffens against my will. I couldn't bite down fully if I wanted to. My limbs don't obey, not working when my wolf struggles to move. She doesn't like it. She feels trapped, jerking hard to free herself. A jolt of fire licks up my spine and she shrieks.

Magic burns in my veins.

I writhe, unable to fight it off. What the fuck is this? What's happening and who's causing it? My gaze darts around but all I see are shifters, unable to find the witch casting the spell.

It's terrible. Pinning down my will, bending me to its

command. Urging me to submit. No, no, no. I refuse to succumb, panting heavily. It gags me, twisting my mind.

Lorne knocks me over with much more force than before. I fly back, slumping motionless. The magic stops abruptly and something explodes overhead. My wolf shakes her head, scraping her snout with her arm at the intense taste of magic crackling on her tongue.

Someone screams. I can't focus on it, returning my attention to fighting Lorne.

He tackles me when I stagger to my feet. I go down again, the wind knocked from me. Shit, how did he get that powerful?

Lorne stands over me, a murderous gleam of victory in his eyes.

I snap at him with my teeth, not giving up. He plants a paw in my chest, crushing me to the floor. I yelp in pain, clawing at him. It's useless. I'm not able to get enough leverage to do more damage than feeble scratches. He tosses his head with a whuff, grinning with his maw like he's laughing at me.

Fuck him.

I plant my hind paws in his stomach and kick with all my might, my wolf growling brutally. He doesn't budge. Shit.

Changing tactics, I scratch his face, managing to catch his eye with my claws before he rears back with a bellow. He peels his lips from his teeth. My heart thuds.

A barbaric noise to our left distracts him before he attacks. Caden and Cormac are locked in a remorseless battle. Both of them are bleeding from bite marks and angry slashes on their flanks and sides. Cormac adds another to Caden's chest, dragging his claws with a ferocious swipe.

Caden turns the tables, jumping on his uncle's back, sending him to the ground. His jaws squeeze the scruff of his neck. Cormac wrestles to free himself, seizing when Caden jerks his head.

The snap of Cormac's bones breaking resounds over the cacophony of fighting. His wolf's eyes bulge, then fade to a dull gray as he falls with a resounding crash, lifeless. Lorne releases an enraged howl and goes for my throat, intent on taking me away from my mate.

Caden locks his deadly gaze on Lorne and charges.

His wolf tackles Lorne with a feral roar, getting him off me. I roll to my feet as they crash beside me, the floorboards splintering beneath Lorne from Caden's force.

There's no hesitation in him when his jaw clamps down. He's merciless, tearing out Lorne's throat with a wrenching bite. Blood pools beneath Lorne, matting his fur. He gurgles in agony and panic, limbs flailing as he struggles to breathe.

Caden growls thunderously as he bites down again, spitting mangled pieces of tendon and furry flesh aside, ripping Lorne to shreds. He's unrelenting even when Lorne stops fighting for his life, eventually going still. He's not satisfied until the head severs with a terrible crack of bone.

I have no sympathy for Lorne. He got what he fucking deserved. So did his father. Neither of them will ever harm my mate or my pack again. I bump into Caden's side, resting my snout over his back.

Standing over Lorne's dead wolf, Caden howls in victory.

41

CADEN

Avery's wolf licks Lorne and Cormac's blood from my jaw, nosing at my wounds with faint whines. I headbutt her gently, reassuring her we're okay. I'll always protect her and our pack. Together we stopped the coup attempting to claim it from us.

My wolf stands proud over his fallen challenger.

The chaos ended the minute I finished Lorne. Any denouncers left alive who followed him fall to their knees before Liam and my other most trusted lieutenants, abiding the law of challenges. They'll all be dealt with in time. I won't have anyone slipping through the cracks to stir unrest amongst the pack again.

Victory is mine. By our laws forbidding interference in rank challenges, it was mine the minute Cormac attacked me.

We shift back. I pull Avery into my arms, pressing my lips to my mating mark. The setting sun casts long beams of light through the windows, illuminating her from behind when I rake my gaze over her, checking for injuries.

"I'm fine. Nothing as bad as this." She brushes my chest where the deep gashes from claws are slowly closing.

"I'll heal. As long as you're okay. That's all that matters to me." My brow creases. "How did Lorne get you?"

Her gaze falls. "I freed my sisters. I'm sorry, but there was no way I could leave them. Sylvie came to lure me into a trap." She swallows, clinging to me. "She was waiting for us. They sent her and she followed us to Liam's cabin. We got my sisters out, but before we could get away Dane and Trent captured Liam, then me. They injected me with something and it blocked off the bond."

My forehead rests against hers, my throat thick. "I thought I'd lost you when I saw you lying there."

"You didn't," she promises. "Never."

A rumble builds in my chest and I kiss her. She cups my jaw, mouth opening for me.

"We did it," she murmurs.

"We did. And I'll never allow anything like this to happen again."

"We," she corrects. "I don't care what shifter law dictates. If anyone else tries to challenge you, I'm fighting by your side to stop them."

I nod with an amused huff at my mate's fierceness. "Together. Always."

Someone passes us clothes. I dress her first, tugging an oversized sweater over her head to cover her. Then I jam my legs into a pair of pants and survey the room.

Liam and Hodge direct the guards to round up the rest of the traitorous Blackburns who survived the fight. Tobin restrains a spitting-mad Eugene, dragging him outside. I spot Ford kissing the hell out of Gabe and checking his mate over for injuries once more.

After a few minutes, Liam makes his way to us with a chagrined frown. He's worse for wear, favoring his right leg, a gash oozing from his forehead, and a tooth missing from the numbers he fought to keep at bay from backing up Lorne and Cormac.

"A few ran before you finished Lorne off. We'll send out scout teams to track them down."

"Good," I say. "They don't get to choose their own exile. They'll all face me for this."

Liam bends his neck, his tone somber. "I failed you, Alpha. I couldn't protect Avery. They captured us."

I exchange a look with my mate, kissing her forehead before dragging my beta close for a one-armed hug.

"All that matters is that you fought with everything you had. I'm glad both of you are safe."

He relaxes. "I'll take care of everything and report to you when we're done."

I nod in gratitude. "Be careful. Don't let your guards down until we've got them all."

Jade and the witch who helped me liberate the patrol cabin come up to us, dragging a dark haired girl between them. Her arms are bound by a spell and she gives them a scathing look.

"Thank you for your help," Avery says.

"I'm sorry about your friend," I offer.

"Our sister knew the dangers," Jade says somberly. "This is the one we've been after. She tried to intervene by casting a spell to control you."

"Yeah, it sucked." Avery shudders. "I never want to feel that kind of magic invading my mind again."

I rumble, tucking her against my side. She lays a soothing hand on my chest.

"I was able to trace her magical signature to her hiding spot in the loft upstairs and stop the spell before she finished," Jade explains.

I tower over the witch Lorne snuck in. "Why did you help Lorne? What did he promise you?"

She jerks against her enchanted bonds, sneering, "I'll tell you nothing."

"We'll get her to talk," Jade assures. "We'll take her to the high council of witches for questioning. They'll pass judgment for her actions to upset the balance."

"We should deal with her here. She infiltrated my territory," I say firmly.

"No," the witch hisses.

She opens her mouth and whatever she's about to say sticks in her throat. Her eyes grow wide and she starts convulsing. Black lines spread from her mouth, running down her throat. They stink of nasty magic, like rotten eggs burning over coals.

"What the hell?" Avery yelps.

She reaches out as if she wants to help. I snatch her back, edging her behind me with a growl.

The witch tries to claw at her chest with her bound hands, swinging a terrified gaze between all of us. Tears well in her eyes as they bulge larger, her strangled choking cutting off. She crashes at our feet, bile that smells like the same foul magic dripping from her mouth.

"She's dead," Avery whispers.

"Fucking Fates," Jade mutters.

She kneels to examine the witch, shaking her head. Her coven sister casts a light yellow orb spell that roves over the body.

"A curse," she confirms.

Jade sighs. "It was probably a pact amongst her coven to prevent anyone from finding out their secrets. The council won't like this. We'll need to leave as soon as possible to inform them."

"Go. We can handle ourselves here," I say. "When you know more, send word."

"We will," Jade agrees. "This won't be the last we see of each other, Alpha Blackburn."

"I hope it's not so long next time. And under way better circumstances." Avery hugs Jade when she rises.

Jade gives her a smile. I draw Avery away, rubbing her arm. Callie and Taryn appear in the doorway with Lena and Beatrix tucked under their arms. Avery gets choked up, towing me by her tight grip on my hand. They rush to us.

"You're safe!" Beatrix reaches Avery first. "Don't ever do that to me again."

"Never," Avery swears.

They hug and Lena joins them, wedging herself between the pair. Taryn throws her arms around the three of them and Callie collides against me. I grunt, embracing her tightly.

"I'm glad you're okay," she mumbles.

"Nothing's taking me down," I promise.

"Whoa, Lorne's headless," Taryn says.

"I should've torn him limb from limb," I mutter.

"If I had my wolf, I would've done the same," Beatrix growls. "Then I would've peed on him."

Avery releases a watery laugh, resting her cheek on Lena's head. I chuckle, reaching over to rustle Beatrix's hair.

Taryn searches the room, spotting Liam. She slips away from us to talk to him. I'm certain she admits she's glad he's okay. He stares at her, dumbfounded for a long beat before he pulls her into a hug. He catches me watching them with a raised brow, ducking his head.

The bond pulses, strong and warm, filling my chest. I meet Avery's eye over her sisters' heads and draw them all into my arms with Callie.

Avery is mine. My pack. My heart.

42

AVERY

In the following days, Caden and his inner circle of loyal enforcers question everyone they've captured who were involved to find out how long Lorne and Cormac have been planning this. Turns out, they've been feeding their horrible ideals on how males are better than females to certain males in the pack for years, but it wasn't until Caden took over the pack after his father's death that they saw their chance to draw loyalty from the alpha.

They failed. Only a handful of the ones left alive cling to the delusion they deserve to live as Lorne promised.

For everyone else, loyalty and rank are held in the highest regard amongst shifters. The pack recognizes shifter law and knows Caden is the rightful Alpha, not Lorne. Taking control of a pack by force, claiming the rank of Alpha without earning the title, and interfering in a rank challenge all condemned Lorne's disgraceful actions in their eyes.

Caden questions if we could've avoided this when we're tucked in bed or swimming at our secret spring. If he should've exiled Lorne or killed him when he attacked me. I believe even if he had, Cormac, or perhaps someone else swayed by the desire for power, would've acted eventually. The only way to root this out from our pack is to eradicate anyone like them meticulously until the blight is gone.

I sit in on some of the sessions when Caden insists he wants my input in passing judgment for the traitors. Weston kneels before Caden in a narrow room of the lodge lined with windows, submitting to him with his neck bared. His boyish features are twisted with guilt and misery.

"I recognize Alpha Blackburn as the true Alpha of Silver Falls Pack. I repent for going against you," he pledges solemnly.

Caden considers him for several moments. Liam stands guard at his side and I lean against the wall by Hodge. Caden shoots me an inquisitive look, seeking my thoughts. His jaw is clenched, yet the hardness in his eyes falters. I shake my head, believing in Weston's will to repent. He nods in agreement.

"You'll be watched closely until I say otherwise," Caden decides. "As I said before, you need to prove yourself to me. The second you step out of line, that's it. No more chances."

Weston's breath rushes out. "Of course. I'll do anything you ask without complaint."

"For starters, you'll be moving into the dormitories. We're tearing down Cormac's compound and rebuilding there. You report to Liam, Gabe, Ford, or Hodge three times a day. If you don't, you're out."

Weston nods. "Thank you."

Caden motions to Liam and his beta sees Weston out. "Who's next? Kip?"

"Bring him in," Ford growls. "I volunteer to be the one to drive him from the packlands after you exile him. No promises he makes it to Wanderer's Canyon."

Gabe snorts. "Be more obvious, I beg you."

Ford's attitude changes with a sly grin, his voice lowering. "You know I like it when you beg."

"No one's next," I say.

Caden's gaze darts to me with a spark of interest, the corner of his mouth curling. "Why's that, mate?"

I grasp his wrist, tugging him from his seat to lead him to the adjoining door to his office. "We've been at this all morning. It's time for a break."

His hum is pleased until he spots the jar of salve I pull from a pocket of my satchel to put on his wounds. I bat my eyelashes innocently at his grouchy frown.

"Were you hoping the invitation for a break was code for something else?"

"You know I was," he mutters, pulling me against him. "Make my day a million times better. Let me lay you out on my desk so I can eat your pussy before I fuck you on it."

I bite my lip, desire tingling in my core. "You had me this morning. Twice."

"I'll never have my fill of you, sweet mate."

His gravelly tone makes me want to climb on his lap and ride him for the rest of the afternoon. I shiver, pushing his chest. He leans against his desk, a smirk stretching his mouth when I unbutton his shirt.

"That's more like it." He kneads my waist, drawing me between his spread legs. "I love it when you can't wait to get your hands on me."

I duck, hiding a smile. "I want to check how you're healing and apply this."

He sighs, nuzzling my jaw with kisses. "It's barely a scratch now. You have nothing to worry about."

My wolf gives a bossy warning growl. His grin is wide against my skin. He listens to her, admiring me with a hooded gaze while I skim my fingertips over the fading lines marring his chest and shoulder. I smooth the salve I made with calendula and yarrow to every lingering wound.

One cut bisects his old scars and my mating mark. I kiss the spot, then take extra care rubbing it with salve.

He catches my wrist, bringing my palm to his mouth for a kiss. "Avery."

My breath catches at the thick desire lacing his tone. I want him as much as every part of me always does, always will, because he's mine.

"Later," I say with an airy laugh. "I'm going to visit the healer's cabin to see how Alisha's doing as the new pack healer."

He lavishes the crook of my neck with attention, his stubble scraping my mating mark deliciously. "My Alpha female always sees to her pack's comfort and happiness. She has no time for her mate."

"I always have time for you." My arms loop around his neck and I meet him in a tender kiss. "Try not to be too strict in your judgments for the ones that went along with things out of fear, like Sylvie, or we'll have a population problem on our hands by the time you're through with them all."

"I can think of a few ways to turn our numbers around if it comes to that," he muses against my lips.

"I think I like the sound of that," I murmur. "We have time for everything. Our future is ours. Our whole lives are ahead of us."

"Every moment with you is one I'll cherish." He rumbles, splaying his fingers on my stomach. "I look forward to all of it. Especially the day your belly is filled with our pups."

Joy expands in me. I kiss him passionately, picturing every happy moment that lies ahead for us to experience together. I want all of it with him. We'll make up for the time we lost by devoting every day to loving each other.

"Me too," I say.

He holds me closer, stroking my hair. Our hearts beat as one.

"You're mine. You make me happier than I ever dreamed."

He kisses my forehead. "I found my way back to you and I'll never let you go. I'll always take care of you, Avery. You're mine to protect. Mine to love."

Mine. My wolf's delight is entwined with my own. I'm right where I belong, in my fated mate's arms.

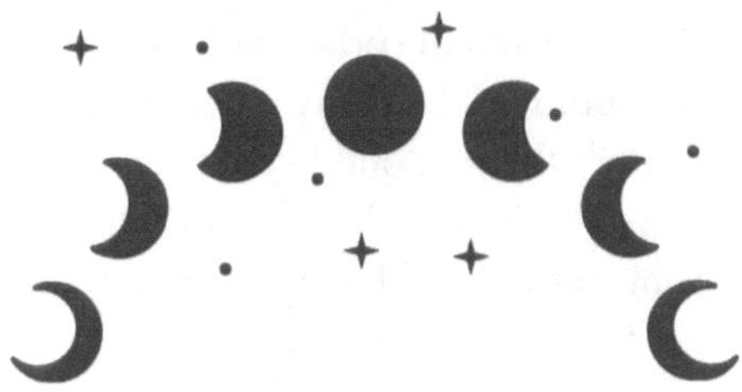

EPILOGUE
CADEN

Four Months Later

WINTER IS ENDING and the first signs of spring are making themselves known. Things have calmed down, the pack enjoying peaceful times once more.

My uncle's compound has been torn down. Every pack member questioned whether they were happy or not. Those that sided with Lorne and still showed any sign of discontent were given the option to leave because Lorne's promise to them of living in the old ways will never fly as long as I'm Alpha. Most bent their necks, respecting my authority once more. The enforcers keep a careful eye on them.

My days are spent seeing to the needs of my pack. It no longer feels like a burden. Instead, it brings me pride to see how much stronger it's become.

Avery's herbal remedies have taken off, not only increasing our trade between packs, but the demand has soared amongst humans wanting to get their hands on supernatural-made goods. I haven't gone as far as Timber Hollow Pack does, inviting humans into my territory, but it's nice not feeling the need to rely as heavily on traded resources between packs thanks to her success. We've yet to hear word from Jade or from the other packs about Lorne's witch or any missing wolves, but we'll be ready when we do.

As long as Avery's the first one I see when I wake and the last before I fall asleep, I'm happy. More than happy, I feel like I've become who I'm meant to be. The alpha my father saw in me. It's all because I have her as my mate, my guiding light that gives me the strength to accomplish anything and the anchor that keeps me grounded.

Without Avery, I'd be incomplete.

Evenings are my favorite lately. The two of us usually end up sitting on the porch swing I installed at the lodge watching over the commons. Kids run around the clearing and people strum banjos. Pipe smoke tinges the air along with chatter and laughter.

Sometimes Lena joins us to read her book outside, bundled in a heap of blankets until Avery stops fussing over her. Then Beatrix or Callie will come out, and Taryn inevitably makes her way over at some point. They fill us in on pack gossip until Liam joins us when he finishes his nightly patrol and squints at Taryn to figure out if she's causing trouble.

Then I'll thread my fingers with Avery's and invite her on a run. I love running with her. So does my wolf.

I can't wait until tonight. My wolf is restless and she's the only one who can settle him. I need little push from him, taking any excuse to track down my mate. I head for the cottage she's turned into her apothecary, nodding to anyone I pass on the road. They don't comment on me hauling ass, everyone aware of the direction I'm going.

The cottage has transformed from all those months ago when my wolf dragged me to her doorstep, claiming her whether I realized how much I needed her or not. The greenhouse is full of lush foliage, her propagations filling the steamed windows. I've built new additions to expand the shop, giving her more space to grow.

My heart swells when I spot her through the lattice windowpanes, a breathtaking smile illuminating her face as she chats with two elder females. She brushes the loose strand of hair that's escaped her braid aside, probably explaining something about the uses and benefits of ginger root or butterfly weed. Warmth rushes through me, building in my chest with a pulsing glow.

Avery looks out the window, our gazes colliding. The corners of her eyes crinkle as her smile grows wider.

I rub my chest, giving her a lopsided grin. *Mine.*

My wolf strains to get me moving, tail wagging and paws dancing in excited taps. He doesn't have to pull hard. I vault up the steps, taking them two at a time, bursting through the door. Avery levels me with an exasperated, affectionate look.

"Alpha," she greets. "Welcome in. Is there anything in particular you're looking for?"

"Very particular."

She blushes, browsing the shelf Beatrix helped me build to display the ready-made items. "Is that so?"

"Yes. It's the only cure for what ails me. Do you have it in?" I hold my hand at her height level. "Gorgeous. Amber eyes and golden brown hair. Smart mouth. A bit of a stubborn streak if you piss her off. Smells like the summer sunshine after a fresh rainstorm. I'm afraid I'll need your entire stock. Nothing less will do."

She covers her mouth to hide her smile. "Is that right? Sounds serious. Maybe I should examine you to see if there's anything else to give you relief."

I waggle my brows, catching her in my embrace when she comes near. "I can think of a few things. A kiss, for one."

She obliges, lifting her chin, eyes sparkling. I seize her mouth in a deep kiss, my world realigning. She melts against me, lips parting with a faint sigh that embodies exactly how I feel, the bond resonating between us.

"That does make me feel a little better," I rasp.

"Does it?" Avery teases.

The customers titter amongst themselves, not hiding that they're watching.

"How charming. I'm glad to see the alpha so taken with his mate," one observes.

Her friend nods with a fond smile. "Reminds me of when my Fergus and I were that young." She drops her payment on the counter. "I must go find him. Right now, in fact. I'm off. See you next week, Avery."

The elder female hustles out, leaving her companion behind stifling laughter. She waves to Avery with a sly look and makes her way out.

"Enjoy your afternoon," she calls.

"Oh, I intend to," I murmur to my mate. "Want to go for a run first?"

She hums, pretending to consider. "Tempting."

"And after my wolf chases yours down, I'm going to lay claim to you." My lips drag along her jaw, teeth scraping the edge of my mating bite.

A moan sticks in her throat. "Let me—" Her breath hitches as I draw her shirt aside for better access and dart my tongue out to trace the mark. "I'll finish up quickly. Then we can go."

I allow her to slip free, adjusting my erection without taking my eyes off her. She flits around her workspace, tapping ground powders into their pots and sweeping dried leaves from her bench. I tease her with a quick tug on the bond, grinning unapologetically when she almost drops a bundle of sage. She lifts a brow and gets me back, as she always does, using the bond to trace an invisible touch down my chest to tease my cock.

"Fuck," I hiss. "You're getting much better at that."

She hums in amused satisfaction. "Have you seen Taryn?"

"No. Why?"

"She said she'd stop by. She's thinking about joining me here as my apprentice."

The corner of my mouth lifts. "Liam's probably chasing after her tail for getting into mischief again."

It makes me wonder if there's something more there. Maybe the Fates are at work in the same way I was drawn to Avery before I knew she was my heart's destiny.

"Okay." Avery steals my attention back. "I'm ready for our run. And to kick your ass hunting."

I smirk. "We'll see about that. Your wolf's improved, but she's still not a seasoned hunter like mine. He likes taking down things for her."

"And she likes showing off," she sasses.

The curve of my mouth stretches into a grin. "He likes that, too."

I offer my hand and she slides hers into it. Outside the cottage, I strip her, burning for every inch of skin I reveal. She helps me out of my clothes, pushing her hands beneath my t-shirt, palms gliding over my muscles as she takes it off.

We leave our things draped over the railing, gazing at each other without needing words for the love and need flowing within us. Our mate bond glows with it.

My knuckles graze her cheek. I dip my head, hovering my lips over hers.

"Run for me, little wolf. Run so I can always catch you and remind you that you're mine, mate."

Her lashes flutter. I trace the curve of her mouth with my thumb. She kisses it, then meets my gaze with a challenge flaring in her eyes. She dashes for the woods. I admire her, ignoring my wolf's impatience to take her in with a hungry focus.

She is mine. And I'm going to get her.

Her shift is beautiful, her wolf bursting free from one step to the next, roan coat gleaming when the sun hits her.

Mate, my wolf howls in my head.

I give him control, bolting after her in hot pursuit, paws pounding the ground. She's fast. I could push harder and close the distance swiftly. Instead, I draw it out, hunting her beautiful wolf all across our territory. She doesn't make it easy on me, outsmarting me by doubling back on her scent trail and hiding in the spots she likes to forage.

We encounter other packmates out for a run in their fur, joining them for a while before our game is back on. By the time I catch her, we end up at our secret spring. Rays of warm sunlight cast our spot in an ethereal glow, sparkling off the cascading falls.

My wolf pounces on hers near the bank and she concedes with a warbling cry. She swats him with her paws when he rolls her to her back and straddles her in triumph.

Avery shifts back with laughter bubbling out of her, arms going around my neck as best as she can reach. My wolf wags his tail, flopping down on her with a happy rumble, licking her throat to enjoy more of her delectable scent.

I force him out, taking my skin back, his tongue becoming my lips, kissing and licking a path across her collar bone, moving lower, intent on spending a long time lapping between her thighs until she's wrung out from coming before I bury myself inside her. She arches, sinking her fingers in my hair.

"Caden," she whimpers.

"I've got you. Now and always."

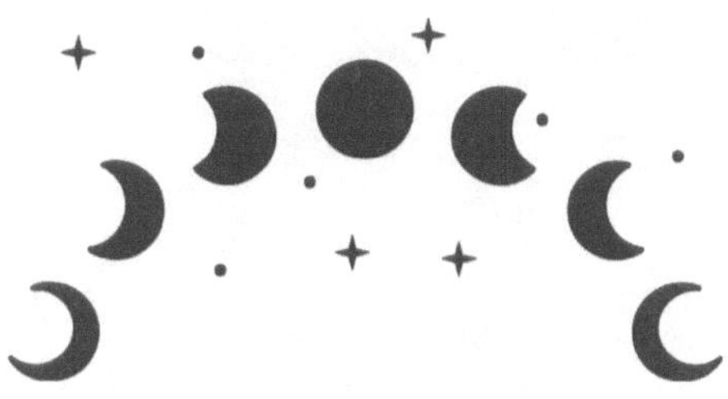

BONUS CONTENT

If you can't get enough of Caden and Avery, enjoy a free bonus scene! Additional bonus content is available on my website. Visit the address below or scan the QR code to collect all available bonus content.

BONUS CONTENT:
www.veronicaeden.myflodesk.com/lunalarkbonus

ABOUT LUNA LARK
WILDLY MAGICAL ROMANCE

Luna Lark is a pen name for USA Today and Amazon Top 30 bestselling author, Veronica Eden, sweeping you away with wildly magical romances. Find your escape in her fantasy and paranormal worlds to indulge in spicy love stories brimming with alpha heroes, strong heroines, and swoony HEAs.

Email: lunalarkauthor@gmail.com
Website: http://lunalarkbooks.com

ALSO BY LUNA LARK

Rejecting Fates

Alpha's Burden

Standalones

Hell Gate